TRIANGLE

TRIANGLE

A NOVEL BY

MARGARET FALCON

iUniverse, Inc.
Bloomington

Triangle

iUniverse books may be ordered through booksellers or by contacting:

iUniverse
1663 Liberty Drive
Bloomington, IN 47403
www.iuniverse.com
1-800-Authors (1-800-288-4677)

ISBN: 978-1-4620-3149-8 (sc)
ISBN: 978-1-4620-3150-4 (ebk)

Printed in the United States of America

iUniverse rev. date: 07/26/2011

To God for everything.

Special thanks to Dr. Joseph Webb for his friendship and guidance.

Prologue

AT A HIGH SCHOOL, A boy stood by a fence and watched a cheerleader at practice. She was the most beautiful creature he'd ever seen! Her skin was like porcelain, her body petite. Pale blue eyes were framed by exquisitely long lashes. Her blonde hair appeared to be made of silk, and he wondered what it would feel like, wrapped around his hands.

Even though they shared some classes, and saw each another in the hallways, she didn't know he existed. She always had her arm wrapped around some jock.

It wasn't that he was unattractive. In truth, he was relatively handsome. Maybe he was a little skinny, and not so much the athletic type, but he was blessed with lovely light brown skin, black wavy hair, and eyes of blue.

Day after day, he pined for this girl, and day after day, his heart was broken, as he was yet to be acknowledged by her.

One day, he overheard her talking with some friends.

"Karen, where are you going to college?"

"Mountain View State," she'd replied.

Later when posed with the same question, he answered, "Mountain View State" as well.

Now as he stood by the fence, he brought his camera to his eyes and focused, waiting for the right time. It came when she leapt into the air, pom poms held high, hair flowing. The camera snapped, freezing the moment. It captured this, along with her beautiful smile.

He took the film and had the picture developed, then enlarged. He hung it in his bedroom, beside a weight machine, and began working on his plan.

When they entered college in the fall, she would be his . . . .

TRIANGLE

CHAPTER ONE

I T WAS THE EARLY WEEKS into the fall/winter semester. The antiquated college lay nestled in the heart of the North Carolina mountains. Though it was the first of October, the sun beat down on the red earth, casting a comforting warmth on all who were outside. Trees, spreading their majestic arms towards the heavens, acted as shields against the sun. The sun, refusing to be defeated, slipped its rays through the branches and poured diamonds of light on the green grass below. The overall scenery was like one lifelike oil painting, with violet and blue mountains lining a cloudless sky.

Beneath the mountains and the tall trees, students walked in countless directions. Many hurried to afternoon classes, while others strolled, fatigued, to their dorms. Still, others ran like children, throwing Frisbees and enjoying the warm afternoon. Here and there, lovers stood quietly under the trees or sat on concrete benches, whispering words of affection or softly kissing.

In the midst of all this mayhem, two students, a boy and a girl were arguing.

"Why won't you go out with me tonight, Karen?" the boy pleaded, his vibrant blue eyes clouding with disappointment.

"Do we really have to have this conversation?" Karen asked. Her mind was a mixture of plausible excuses.

"Yes, we do," Kevin insisted. "We've had this planned for days."

"I have to study for a biology test," Karen replied firmly. "I forgot about it, and if I don't study, I'll flunk for sure!"

Kevin was not going to give up so easily. "How could you have forgotten about a test in your favorite subject?" he persisted.

Karen rolled her eyes. "Good grief, Kevin! I'm human! I forget things like everyone else, so don't be so hard on me!"

She noticed the hurt look in his eyes, and immediately she was sorry for having spoken so harshly. Putting a hand on his shoulder, Karen looked him in the eyes. This time she spoke with a kinder voice.

"Look, Kevin, I really want to go out with you. You don't realize how stupid I feel about forgetting the test. We'll go out this weekend—I *promise*! I'll make all of this up to you, and we'll have a great time!"

As Kevin stared into her soft, pale blue eyes, the iceberg that was in his heart began to melt. He shifted his feet, feeling guilty for the way he had argued with her. He loved her, and if she was forgetful, he should understand. How many times had he forgotten something? Kevin knew he couldn't even begin to count the times, but that was not his main concern at the moment. He felt like a jerk, and all he wanted to do was to make things right.

Very gently, he took her petite, delicate hand in his own muscular brown hand. Looking at her, he smiled warmly.

"I'm sorry about the way I acted," he said softly. "It's just that I had really looked forward to going out with you tonight."

Karen nodded understandingly. "It's OK."

"You study tonight, but I want you to know that you're going out with me this weekend, no matter what."

Karen smiled. "No matter what," she repeated.

With that settled, Kevin leaned forward and kissed her softly on the lips. Reluctantly, he watched her walk away, until she was absorbed into the mass of students on the sidewalk. How he hated to see her leave! It was always so lonely for him when he was not with Karen. It wasn't that he couldn't get other dates; he just didn't want anyone else. He only had eyes for Karen, and in those eyes, she could do no wrong.

Many a girl on campus would have jumped at the chance to date Kevin, and many a girl stared at him in longing. He never noticed the glances or the subtle hints, for he was a boy in love. Karen was the perfect girl for him; everyone else was second rate. In fact, she had always been perfect, but it was only recently that he had been able to win the girl of his dreams.

He had wanted Karen all through high school, but she had never acknowledged his existence. She had, without a doubt, been the most popular person at Cleveland River High; Kevin had probably been the least. He was so skinny and shy back then! He winced now at the thought of it! Yes, Kevin remembered the days of being the last one chosen for the basketball team. Those were the times he had feigned sickness in order to be excused from those humiliating games.

Whether it was shyness, or the inability to play well, Kevin had grown away from sports. He preferred listening to music or taking pictures. He wasn't effeminate. He was definitely destined to be a ladies' man. Though Karen didn't know him at the time, many of the other girls did. He was a skinny, yet very good-looking Italian boy, with wavy, jet black hair, and eyes of the most intense blue. Kevin wasn't very tall. He was of average height, and the girls he had dated found that to be a sexy attribute.

Truly capable of winning hearts, he had only won the hearts of girls he wasn't interested in. They had all been pretty, but it was Karen who he had wanted. He was absolutely obsessed with her. Many an hour had been spent staring at her, and he had even spent more time daydreaming about her. Kevin would hide behind trees, gates, and bleachers just to watch her at cheerleading practice.

Karen was so pretty! She had a cute figure, petite, but blessed in the areas that all girls want to be blessed in. Her face was like that of a porcelain doll, with pouting lips, dainty nose, and sparkling blue eyes, almost the same color as Kevin's. Looking into those eyes was like looking into a sky that promised no rain.

What they had in common with their eyes, they had equally uncommon with their skin. Hers was creamy white; his smooth and brown.

How he loved the way that skin felt, so warm and so soft, the way her eyes flashed when she was angry, and the way her mouth pouted when she didn't get her way! She was so special—like a goddess to him!

Snapping out of his hypnotic state, Kevin glanced around. The sun was low in the sky, and students were crowding towards the cafeteria for supper. He breathed in deeply, and went to join them.

*   *   *

Back in one of the dorms, a girl stood staring out of a window. Her tanned body was clad in a loose blouse and satin panties, while her jeans lay rumpled on the bed. Turning from the window, she reached up and put her hand in front of the air-conditioning vent for what seemed like the hundredth time. Frowning at the weak flow of air, she wondered to herself if the college was rationing electricity.

She glanced around the room, noting the not so subtle differences between her and her roommate. Her bed was covered in a second hand slate blue bedspread; her roommate's in a high priced floral print coverlet. Both beds had an assortment of stuffed animals on them, yet the animals seemed to look better on the fancier bed.

The dressers, though made identical, were also noticeably different. Her dresser had a few sparse objects on them, including a photo of her aunt, some toiletries, and a few makeup items. Her roommate's dresser was deluged with novelty items, makeup, cologne, and of course, all those annoying photos of herself and her boyfriend. At least the boyfriend was something pleasing to look at.

Going back to the window, she pulled the shade down. The late afternoon sun always beamed on that side of the dorm, making it hotter than usual. Small beads of sweat had formed on her forehead, and she softly brushed them away with her hand.

She was a beautiful girl, with soft, brown skin all over her body. Hers was a natural beauty, healthy and strong, but completely feminine. Beautiful without makeup, she was stunning with it.

Her straight, dark brown hair fell to the top of her shoulders, and framed her face with bangs. Her caramel eyes were wide and sensual, surrounded by thick, black lashes. She had a small, straight nose, and full lips that could expand into the most welcoming smile. Hers was the kind of smile that could make the most awkward person feel secure.

Though she had a pleasing personality, she was a bit of a loner. Her name was Tina, and she'd known a hard, sad life.

At twelve years of age, her parents had left her with an aunt. They had gone away for the weekend—a second honeymoon, and they'd never returned. The day that Tina's aunt had gotten off of the phone, no words were needed. Tina knew that she would never see her parents alive again. They had been the victims of another driver who had fallen asleep at the wheel, and who had hit them head on.

Time had healed most of the wounds for the young girl, but an aura of pain refused to leave. It had implanted itself in her heart, returning when she least expected it.

Going on with life had been the only answer, and Tina had done it with zest and vigor. She had taken on a part-time job as soon as she had been old enough. Juggling school and work was difficult, but it had kept her mind occupied and her heart happy.

Though her aunt was kind to her, and the weather exquisite, Tina had dreamed of the day when she could leave Florida. She'd wanted to go to college, to run from home and all her painful memories. Finally the day had come when she had told her aunt 'good-bye'. She'd climbed on the bus that would lead her to her dreams, and she hadn't looked back.

Now she turned from the window, walked to the closet and took out her bathrobe. It would be nice to take a shower, and wash away the humidity induced sweat. Fortunately each room was equipped with its own shower. It was expensive to live in such a dorm, but it sure beat walking down a hallway in one of the other overcrowded dorms, just to take a shower.

She was headed towards the bathroom, when the door to the room flew open. Karen came rushing in, throwing books and papers haphazardly on her bed. When she saw the bathrobe in Tina's hand, she began pleading.

"Tina, I really, *really* need to take a shower! I've got somewhere to go, and I kind of got delayed! Please let me go first!"

Tina grinned. "Another date with Kevin?" she asked.

Karen looked down and studied a spot on her shoes. She glanced back up at Tina and answered meekly, "No, I'm seeing someone else tonight." She waited for some kind of response, then added, "Please don't tell anyone."

Tina nodded. They had been through this before. "You mean don't tell *Kevin*," she said disapprovingly.

Karen rolled her eyes and answered sarcastically, "That's right, 'Miss Guilt Trip', don't tell Kevin."

She glared at Tina, who only shrugged her shoulders, then she turned up her nose and pranced into the bathroom.

As soon as Tina heard the water running, she fell back onto her bed. She wondered how Karen could give up Kevin for an occasional jerk. Of course, Karen didn't see them as jerks, but Tina was still baffled. How could Karen take someone like Kevin for granted? He treated her like a queen, and Tina longed for a fraction of his attention. If only Kevin treated *her* that way! She wondered what it would be like to be Kevin's girl. Closing her eyes, Tina began imagining being Kevin's girlfriend. She daydreamed about touching him, kissing his sensuous lips, and making love to him. Yes, being Kevin's girl would be nice—so nice!

* * *

Karen silently made her way through the dark woods that surrounded the campus. Almost everyone at college knew that she and Kevin were going together, so she always had to be careful. Shuddering from the chilly night air, Karen hugged herself to keep warm. She regretted only wearing a thin, long-sleeved blouse, but at least her jeans were keeping her legs warm.

Walking alone through the woods at night was very frightening for her. Noises all around her startled her, making her jump. She thought of turning back when her eyes caught the familiar glow of Clyde's lantern. As she came into the clearing, their eyes met. He had an impatient look on his face as if to say, "It's about time you got here!"

Karen studied him. His tall, muscular body was leaning against a tree, and he shook blonde bangs out of his eyes. Clyde had a mischievous appearance about him—blonde, unruly hair, blue eyes, and an awkward smile. He, too, was used to having his own way, so he and Karen were no strangers to argument. He held out his arms, and Karen slid into them, then they embraced.

"I'm getting too jittery for this," Karen confessed. "These woods give me the creeps!"

Clyde smirked boldly. "Hey, Baby," he said, "it's not the woods you need to be afraid of; it's the wolves in it!" He growled and pulled her closer.

Karen laughed and punched him in the arm. "You jerk, I was serious!"

Loosening his grip on her, he purred, "So was I!"

She smiled, then they began kissing. This was the third time that they had met like this, and Karen was beginning to really like him. The biggest problem was that they were both childish and spoiled, their dispositions frequently colliding. Tonight, however, was special, and their kisses became more and more passionate.

Soon they were lying on the cool ground, fumbling with each others' clothes. Caught up in the moment as she was, Karen gasped when Clyde put his hand on her breast.

"I don't think I'm ready for this," she said, pushing his hand away.

Clyde ignored her. When he leaned in for a kiss, Karen relaxed a little, and kissed him back. However, when she felt him undo the first button on her blouse, she tensed up, again.

"It'll be alright," Clyde purred into her ear.

Karen tried to push Kevin's face from her mind. The more Clyde touched her, the more difficult it was. As his mouth trailed a path from her neck to her open shirt, she started to change her mind.

"What's wrong?" Clyde asked, pulling her shirt away.

"Nothing," Karen lied. She didn't say anything else. She did look away once, as he got undressed in front of her. It would be alright. It was just sex, right?

She repeated the mantra in her mind, as he removed the rest of her clothes, then lowered himself on top of her. Kevin's face came back to her with each thrust, until she had to finally close her eyes, and let Clyde finish.

When his body finally shuddered, and he collapsed beside of her, Karen sat bolt upright. The stunned, hypnotic euphoria that she'd experienced earlier was wearing off, and reality was setting in. Waves of guilt hit her conscience like ocean waves crashing into boulders.

Immediately Clyde noticed her change in attitude, so he put his arm around her. "What's wrong?" he asked.

Karen stared at him blankly. "Nothing—nothing's wrong," she lied. "I've got to go now—nothing's wrong."

In a few quick movements, she gathered up her clothes, dressed, and ran out of the woods without looking back.

Clyde watched her, shaking his head. When she was gone, he stood up and got dressed, too. She was a decent lay, beautiful, but kind of peculiar.

*　　*　　*

Tina was asleep when Karen returned. Shaking Tina gently, Karen tried to awaken her.

Tina blinked her eyes. When she saw that it was Karen who was shaking her, she closed her eyes and snuggled deeper into the covers.

Karen frowned and shook her again. "Did Kevin call?" she asked.

Tina rubbed her face, then answered sleepily, "No."

Grabbing Tina's arm, Karen asked desperately, "Did he stop by?"

By now, Tina was awake. She glared at Karen, answering bluntly, "He didn't call! He didn't stop by!"

Karen breathed a sigh of relief, and went to sit on her bed.

"What's going on?" Tina demanded.

Biting her lower lip, Karen answered faintly, "I slept with Clyde tonight."

Tina sat straight up in bed, her eyes wide with shock. "Is this the first time you've slept with someone behind Kevin's back?" she asked.

"Of course it is!" Karen snapped. "I'm not a slut!" She glanced at the floor, then lowered her voice, "I mean, I wasn't one before now."

Tina ignored Karen's comment. "Just tell Kevin that you want to date other people," she suggested. "You're not married to him, you know."

Karen shook her head. "I don't want to date other people," she said honestly. "I'll just never do something like this again."

Tina lay back down, nestling her head against her pillow. "You shouldn't do it again," she agreed, "not unless you tell Kevin. That way he can date other people, too."

"Thanks heaps," Karen responded.

Tina excused the sarcasm and blew Karen a kiss. "Goodnight, Karen."

Pulling her shoes off, Karen glanced at her friend and smiled. "'Night, Tina."

CHAPTER TWO

THE FOLLOWING AFTERNOON, KEVIN STOOD near the building where Karen had her biology class. Since students left when they were finished with their tests, he knew she would be out shortly. She was usually one of the first people out.

After standing there awhile, Kevin saw some people leaving. He recognized one of the students, so he threw up his hand.

"How're you doing?" the other boy hollered, returning the gesture.

"I'm doing fine!" Kevin shouted. "How was the test?"

The other student appeared confused, then he cried out, "There was no test today—thank God!"

Kevin watched as the fellow sauntered off to his next class. His face was troubled, and his stomach felt weak. All he could do was to run from the building before Karen came out.

When Karen left her class, she glanced about. It was almost a ritual to meet with Kevin after class, and she strained her eyes searching for him. By now, quite a few classes had let out, so she tried to find Kevin in the sea of faces that passed by her. After waiting for what seemed like an eternity, she gave up and retreated to her dorm.

That night, she bumped into Kevin in the cafeteria.

"Where were you this afternoon?" she asked him.

"I had some studying to do," he lied.

Though she doubted his words, Karen didn't pursue the subject. She felt it would be in her best interest to discuss something else.

"What are we going to do this weekend?" she inquired.

Kevin thought for a moment, then he suggested, "Do you want to go to a movie?"

After turning up her nose, Karen asked, "Why don't we go dancing?"

Though she knew he hated the nightclubs and the wild crowds, Karen felt sure that she could get Kevin accustomed to them. Maybe he'd eventually grow to like them.

At Karen's suggestion, Kevin's face fell and he winced.

"You know I can't dance, and that I hate to get up in front of people!"

Karen put on her most convincing pout and purred, "Kevin, you're majoring in drama. You get up in front of a lot of people when you act in those plays. What's the difference?"

His face still held a disgusted expression, so she tried another approach.

"I'll teach you what I know," she offered. "I know you can dance if you'll just try! If you take me dancing on Friday night, we can go to a movie on Saturday night!"

"I work at the grocery store on Saturday," he answered solemnly.

Taking him gently by the arm, Karen said, "That's no problem, Honey. We can go to the movie on Sunday night; just *please* take me dancing Friday!"

Kevin knew that he was losing the battle, so he gave up. He managed a smile and told her, "We'll go, but if I don't like it, we'll leave."

"Oh thank you, Kevin!" Karen squealed. She threw her arms about his neck, squeezing him tightly. "I promise, you'll love it!"

Kevin hugged her back, but deep in his heart, he wished Friday would never come.

*   *   *

Friday arrived with the speed of a lightning bolt. Spirits were high as students eagerly anticipated the excitement of the weekend. For a couple of days, books and lessons would be forgotten. There were places to go and people to meet—the options were countless!

Back in his dorm, Kevin felt no excitement. If he felt anything, it was resentment. For the first time, he thought of Karen as being selfish. She *never* wanted to do what he liked! How could she feel comfortable tonight, when she knew he was going to hate every moment?

He was putting the finishing touches on his hair, when his roommate, Alan, came out of the bathroom. Unknown to Kevin, a frown had plastered itself to his face, and Alan began to laugh.

"Whose funeral are you going to, tonight?" he questioned jovially.

"No one's," Kevin responded disgusted, "I'm going to a club."

"With Karen?"

Kevin nodded, which made Alan laugh all the harder.

"Man," he said, "you're the only guy in the world I know who could act like this! You've got a terrific looking chick, who's going out with you tonight! What do you do? You pout like a baby because you've got to go to a nightclub! Man, I could go to a garbage dump with Karen and have a good time! If nothing else, I'd spend the evening just looking at her!"

Kevin smiled. He couldn't help but to smile at Alan. The guy was rare! He was ordinary and unpopular, but he had no cares or worries. Alan just took life as it came.

A plump fellow, he had a remarkable sense of humor. When rejected for a date, he'd throw his nose up in the air, declaring, "I'm sorry—I overestimated you. I thought you were the type who could handle nine inches!"

Plopping down on his bed with a bag of chips, Alan opened his latest girlie magazine. After flipping the pages to the centerfold, he asked, "Why don't you want to go dancing?"

"I don't know;" Kevin answered, running the comb through his hair once more, "maybe I just march to the beat of a different drummer."

He adjusted the collar on his shirt, then turned around to face Alan.

"How do I look?"

Alan pulled his eyes away from the centerfold and studied Kevin.

"Like crap!"

With eyes wide, Kevin glanced again in the mirror.

"Kevin, I was only kidding!" Alan said, laughing. "You could put anybody to shame!"

Whirling about, Kevin lowered his eyebrows. "Let's not get carried away, OK?"

Alan chuckled, then spoke in a serious tone, "You look fine—now go knock them out!"

Kevin tried to appear confident. "I hope," he whispered.

*   *   *

The club that was popular with most of the college students was about four blocks from the campus. Since the night was clear and comfortable, Karen and Kevin decided to walk. They strolled arm in arm, pausing now and then to window shop.

Kevin took advantage of the opportunity, and as they approached the nightclub, he stopped at almost every store and stared into the windows. Karen, growing impatient, began tugging at his arm.

"Kevin, please!" she begged.

He began walking, only to halt at the next store and glare inside.

"Kevin!"

Dragging his feet, he prayed silently that the nightclub would be closed.

They strolled for half a block, when he suddenly stopped again.

"Wow!" he cried, pressing his face to the glass.

Karen peeped into the window, also. Inside was an impressive display of weapons. Guns, knives, and swords hung threateningly from the case behind the window.

"What I wouldn't give to have those!" Kevin exclaimed.

Karen gaped at Kevin, surprised. She couldn't imagine her gentle Kevin being interested in such weapons.

"Let's go," she suggested. "Those things give me the creeps!"

Reluctantly, Kevin pulled himself away from the window. As they left, though, he couldn't help but to glance back.

When they finally reached the nightclub, Kevin grudgingly shoved his money under the window. He entered the club with the enthusiasm of an animal headed for the slaughterhouse. Once inside, Kevin knew he hated the place. It was packed with so many people! He couldn't imagine where they'd all come from! The rank odor of cigarette smoke filled the air, burning his nose and stinging his eyes. Then there was the noise! He'd have to shout if he had to say anything to Karen! The bass that was thumping from the speakers seemed to have rooted itself into his chest. It pounded and pounded until he was sure his heart would burst from the pressure!

Weaving through the mass of sweaty bodies, he and Karen made their way to the bar. Kevin was surprised at the number of people that he recognized. They shouted and waved as they passed. Kevin returned their greetings, feigning a smile.

Upon reaching the bar, Karen ordered a glass of wine. She turned to Kevin with questioning eyes, and he ordered a beer. As Kevin watched the bartender pop the cap off the beer, he grimaced. He hated beer, but he hated wine even more. If he planned to have a good time, though, he'd have to drink a lot!

Karen and Kevin took their drinks, then Kevin paid the bartender. He studied the amber liquid in the bottle, and gingerly took a sip. Curling up his nose, he took another swallow.

Laughing, Karen held out her glass. "Try this," she said.

Kevin shook his head. "No thanks," he answered, "this is bad enough!"

They were just about to leave the bar, when they heard a familiar voice.

"I'll have a glass of rose', please."

They turned around to see Tina standing at the bar. She picked up her glass of wine, and as she was turning to leave, she noticed Karen and Kevin. Immediately, her eyes lit up, and she smiled.

"Karen!" she cried. "How're you doing?"

"Fine!" Karen shouted above the music.

Tina looked at Kevin. "How're you doing?"

"Fine," he mumbled.

Tina glanced back at Karen. "He doesn't like it here, does he?"

"How could you tell?" Karen responded jokingly. She nudged Kevin gently in the side, and winked at him.

Irritated, Kevin grinned slightly, while he toyed with his beer.

"Who are you with?" Karen asked.

Tina smiled. "I'm by myself," she announced. "That way I get to dance with everybody. That is—everybody who's not taken!"

She stared at Kevin and laughed.

He didn't laugh back.

Tina swallowed, wishing the uncomfortable moment would end.

"Let's look for a table!" she finally suggested.

Karen nodded, so the three of them weaved through the crowd. All the tables were taken, except for a round one on the upper level. Tina sat down before anyone else claimed it, and Karen followed suit. Kevin took his time before joining them.

Sipping on their drinks, they watched people on the lighted dance floor. A rainbow of colors blinked to the beat of the music, and reflected on the bodies below. The cigarette smoke rose above the dancers' heads. It whirled around in mesmerizing lines, rising higher and higher. Sweat glistened from the dancers. It mixed with a hundred different colognes, creating a bittersweet aroma.

Karen wanted to dance. She stole a glance at Kevin, impatiently waiting for him to finish his beer. After what seemed like an eternity, he swallowed the last of the bubbly liquid.

"Come on, Kevin," she cried. "Let's dance!"

"I've got to go to the bathroom first," he answered.

Karen pouted in a teasing manner. "Excuses, excuses!"

"Sorry."

"Oh, well," she said, "I'll let you go, but hurry up!"

"I don't have an accelerator on it!" he returned playfully.

They all laughed, and Kevin got up and walked away.

He hadn't been gone long, when a boy strolled up to Tina's side of the table. He was tall, with blonde hair, and he was so built! Even with clothes on, anyone could tell that he did a lot of weight lifting!

"Would you like to dance?" he asked Tina in a husky voice.

Tina's eyes grew large as the gazed at the living, breathing hunk before her.

"Sure," she said, the word falling from her lips.

As she stood, she winked at Karen. This was definitely a good one!

They left the table, walking hand in hand towards the dance floor.

Karen watched them, smiling to herself. Now she was alone with her glass. It had just enough wine in the bottom of it to wet her tongue, so she reached for it.

Without warning, someone grabbed her hand. Gasping, Karen turned to face the person. Her expression changed from surprise to fear as her eyes met Clyde's. He was swaying above her, and she could tell that he was very drunk.

"Hey, Baby," he muttered.

Before she could answer, he leaned down and planted a kiss on her lips. Karen jerked her hand away, and wiped at the spot that he had kissed.

"You stupid jerk!" she sputtered. "Kevin's here! He'll be back any minute now!"

Clyde just stood there staring at her and smiling.

"Get out of here!" she shouted.

Grinning evilly, Clyde purred, "Don't tell me that you've forgotten about the other night."

Through her fury, embarrassment found its way into Karen's emotions. She blushed deeply, then lowered her head.

"Please leave," she begged.

He shook his head. "No way," he announced. "You'll have to dance with me first."

Jerking her head up, Karen stared at Clyde incredulously.

"Are you crazy?" she cried. "Kevin's going to be here any minute!"

16

"So," Clyde replied sarcastically, "he can have the next dance."

He jerked Karen up, and pulled on her arm so roughly, that she cried out in pain. Cursing and screaming, she was practically dragged to the dance floor.

Kevin came back to an empty table. He'd had trouble finding it, because he had been looking for Karen and Tina. Shrugging, he sat down. They must have gone to the restroom, also.

Since he was there alone, he had nothing to do but to watch others. He scanned the place, studying the different people. Most of them were drunk, and he just laughed to himself. People actually liked coming here! He couldn't figure them out!

A slow song began to play, and his eyes were diverted to the dance floor. Couples were pressed together, their bodies slowly swaying to the music. All of the couples, that is, except for one, seemed to be enjoying the moment. Kevin stared at one of the fellows struggling to keep his girl on the dance floor. She broke away from him for a brief moment, and Kevin's heart stopped. It was Karen! Some guy had hold of her, and she was trying to get away!

He hit the table so hard with his fist, that people nearby glared at him. Ignoring them, he cursed, his eyes never leaving the dance floor. Kevin fought his way through the crowd, pushing people whenever they wouldn't budge. With each step, he grew angrier and angrier. By the time he reached the dance floor, he was blinded with fury. His only objective was to help Karen. Stepping up to the guy, he jerked him away from Karen so fast, that he ripped Clyde's shirt.

"What the—?" Clyde sputtered, as he examined his torn shirt.

By now, people had stopped dancing, and were watching Kevin and Clyde. Tina came running up, also, leaving her fellow behind.

Kevin took a punch at Clyde and missed. Tina watched in horror as Clyde's fist tightened up for a return blow.

"Noooo!" she screamed.

It was too late! Clyde's fist came crashing into Kevin's face, sending him reeling backwards onto the dance floor. Karen shrieked and ran to Kevin. People gasped, and a bouncer was called, but no one else helped.

Clyde wasn't finished with him. He walked over to where Kevin lay in a heap, with Karen kneeling beside of him. Rudely, he pushed Karen aside, then stooped to jerk Kevin back up.

Feeling a tap on his shoulder, Clyde glanced up. This time, it was Tina who punched him, and he fell unceremoniously to the floor.

Completely forgetting about Kevin, Clyde got up. Blood flowed easily from his bottom lip, and he wiped at it roughly with the sleeve of his shirt. He was cursing a blue streak as he headed for Tina. Eyes wide, she stood her ground, waiting for the inevitable blow. She stared in fear as Clyde raised his arm.

Suddenly the guy who had asked her to dance was standing between Clyde and Tina. He towered over Clyde and glared down at him.

"I wouldn't do that if I were you!" he growled.

Awestruck, Clyde lowered his arm. The bouncer came running up, jerking Clyde off of the dance floor. As he was being led away, Clyde looked back at Tina and screamed, "You're going to get it, you whore!"

He caught Karen's eye and added, "You too!"

Karen kneeled down on the floor and held Kevin in her arms. She was crying and wiping his bloody nose with a napkin.

"Can we go now?" he asked weakly.

"Yes, Honey, we're going to leave now," she said choking back a sob.

Some of the people helped Karen get Kevin to a standing position. One boy offered them a ride back to the campus, then ran ahead of them to get his car.

As they left the dance floor, they passed by Tina. She stood there, looking very unsure of herself.

Kevin stared at Tina blankly, as Karen held the napkin to his nose. She was too busy to notice Tina. They left her standing there, wondering if she'd hurt Kevin's pride by helping him.

CHAPTER THREE

T HAT FOLLOWING MONDAY, AFTER HER morning classes, Tina walked alone to her dorm. She still felt apprehensive about Clyde's threat Friday night. Would she really 'get it'? What would he really do to her if he had the chance? Tina felt sure that Clyde wouldn't kill her, but she was unsure of anything else. He could do her great harm if he wanted to, and she shivered at the thought.

Tina stared at the open, semi-vacant campus. Most of the students were in the lunchroom now. Her own appetite seemed to have disappeared since breakfast. It was then that she'd managed to eat some toast and scrambled eggs with juice, but it wasn't the food that bothered her.

What had really shattered her nerves was the dirty look Clyde had given her when she'd gone to put her tray up. It was a look of pure evil and hatred for her, and she couldn't make herself forget it. Now on her way to the dorm, Tina kept hoping that she could avoid him. She approached two dorms connected by a breezeway, and she went between them. Though they were two buildings, they were considered one dorm. The building to the right was very old, having been there since the college opened. Its scarlet bricks were cracked in places and covered with moss. Its windows were ancient in appearance, surrounded by dingy white paint that peeled and curled away from the building.

On the left, the newer structure stood proud in its modern decor. It was built to accommodate students as the college grew, and everything about it spelled 'm-o-n-e-y'. No paint would peel from this facility! It had smooth vinyl siding, surrounding crisp, tinted windows. Its bricks matched those of the older buildings, except for the cracks and the moss.

Under the breezeway, it was cool and dark, but on each end, the sun stretched its long rays. It tried to grasp the darkness and bring warmth.

Tina sucked in lungfulls of the sweet, cool air. The building seemed to hug her, protecting her from the outside world. She imagined the new building as a mother, the old one, a grandmother. Though it was a little dark there, she felt safe for the first time that day. She could finally relax.

Suddenly she heard a noise from behind, and she whirled around. Someone moved on the far end of the breezeway.

"Who's there?" Tina called out.

There was no answer, but she could definitely make out a shadow.

In her bravest voice, she called out again, "Who's there?"

Again there was silence, but this time the shadow moved, then a horrible thought came to Tina. It might be Clyde!

Without looking back, she started running. She came to a door, and jerked it open. Glancing back, Tina saw that someone was following her! She dashed into the unfamiliar dorm to hide and to get help should she need it. Running up several flights of stairs, she finally stopped to ease her pounding heart. No one seemed to be around, so she just stood there listening.

She'd hardly rested, when she heard the door open downstairs. She could hear footsteps as someone entered the building. They hesitated at the stairs, contemplating, as tears welled up in Tina's eyes. She was praying that they would go in another direction, when she heard them ascending. Nearer and nearer they came, until she felt her heart would burst.

Not being able to stand it any longer, Tina raced in the opposite direction and scurried downstairs. She had to get out of the building! Each step brought her closer and closer to safety, until she'd reached the last stair. There was one corner to go around, and she barreled around it blindly.

Without warning, arms grabbed Tina, and she let out a bloodcurdling scream. The arms let go of her, and she stared into Kevin's face, embarrassed.

In his transparent blue eyes, Tina saw sadness and confusion.

"Why were you running away from me?" he questioned softly.

Tina regained her breathing, calming down in his steady gaze.

"I thought you were someone else! Anyway, why didn't you say anything?"

Kevin shrugged his shoulders, "I don't know," he answered. "I was so confused with you running from me, I guess."

"Yeah, well I thought you were Clyde—the monster from the club!"

Kevin grinned. "I don't think he'll bother you, especially if you keep hanging around giants!"

Tina thought for a moment, then her face lit up.

"You mean that guy at the club?"

Kevin nodded.

"I don't even know his last name! We just danced that night! I might have gotten to know him better, but you know how the evening turned out!"

Again he nodded, and together they walked back outside. It wasn't until they were away from the breezeway that Tina thought something was strange. She stopped dead in her tracks, and stared at Kevin questioningly.

"Why were you following me?" she demanded.

This time it was Kevin who blushed. "I wanted to thank you for what you did the other night—for taking up for me. I don't know any girls who are that brave; Karen's certainly not."

Tina gazed at him, then her deep brown eyes became cloudy.

"Karen's just different from me—that's all," she said softly. "That's why you care for her the way you do."

An uncomfortable silence followed, and Tina couldn't stand it any longer. "I've got to go back to my dorm," she said.

She turned to leave, then remembered something. "By the way," she stated, "you're welcome."

With that, she smiled and ran in the direction of her dorm.

As Kevin watched her leave, he wondered about her. She was such a nice girl. He just couldn't understand why someone who had such a beautiful smile had such sad eyes, also.

Upon reaching her room, Tina dug into her jean's pocket for her key. She had one hand on the doorknob while she searched for the elusive key. Accidentally, she pushed on the door, and it opened with ease.

"Leave it to Karen," she muttered.

Tina stepped into the dimly lit room. The sunshine had yet to make its appearance on that side of the building, so she turned on the light.

When the light came on, she spun around. It was then that her heart stopped. There was Clyde on her bed, grinning evilly! Tina made a beeline for the door. In one swift motion, though, Clyde was upon her. He jerked her around with an almost inhuman strength, kindled with hatred and anger. They stared at each other; his eyes filled with mockery, hers with fear.

His hands gripped her arms tighter and tighter, until she winced in pain.

"You're not so brave now, are you?" he taunted.

"Go to hell!" Tina hissed through clenched teeth.

That only infuriated Clyde. He leaned down and kissed Tina. It was a hard, abusive kiss, filling him with a sick passion.

Suddenly he screamed and drew back. She had bitten him! His hands dropped from her arms as he examined his swelling, bleeding lip.

Tina quickly wiped his blood from her own lip, and once again ran for the door. Clyde caught her by her shirt and whirled her about. This time he punched her hard in the face. The blow caused her to crash into a dresser, and she cried out in pain. Bottles and whatnots tumbled all about, breaking into hundreds of unrecognizable pieces.

Tina whimpered at the hopelessness of the situation and at her own pain. Leaning over the dresser, she tried to regain her strength. It was then that the broken vase caught her eye, and she snatched it off the dresser.

Holding it threateningly in front of her, she stared at Clyde like someone gone mad.

"Get out!" she screamed.

His answer to that was a swift kick in her abdomen. As he watched, Tina's back hit a wall, and the piece of vase flew from her hand.

Blood was trickling from her nose and her lips, and he glared at her, unfeeling. As he stood there, bold and undefeated, Tina sank into a heap on the floor.

She was about to faint when Clyde strolled over. He straddled her, not caring that all of his weight was upon her, almost crushing her. Putting his hands on her shirt, he began to tear it off of her.

The first seam had barely come undone, when he heard a click from behind. Slowly turning his head, he suddenly stiffened, for out of the corner of his eye, he saw a gun. It was pointed right at his head, and Clyde remained where he was, frozen.

"Back off!" Kevin ordered. His hand was rigid, his face firm.

Clyde obeyed promptly, holding his hands up, and moving away from Tina.

When Kevin felt that Clyde was far enough away from Tina, he ordered, "Drop your pants!"

"What?" Clyde cried, bewildered.

Kevin's finger toyed with the trigger. "I'm not going to repeat it!" he growled.

Clyde jerked his pants off, and threw them into Kevin's outstretched hand.

"Now take off the rest," Kevin said.

"You're crazy!" Clyde shouted, his face turning a brilliant shade of red.

Kevin glanced at Tina, lying battered on the floor. Her blood had flowed into the carpet, and her body was still.

"No," Kevin replied sternly, "you're the one who's crazy. Now do as I say before I blow off your private parts!"

When Clyde had everything off, except for his socks, Kevin ordered, "That's enough!"

Clyde stood there, embarrassed. He was unprepared for Kevin's next move, which was to open the door wide and shove him out of the room.

Clyde stumbled and fell onto the cold linoleum floor. He looked up just in time to see his clothes being thrown in his face.

Female voices were drifting up the steps, as Clyde rushed to get dressed.

After Kevin had slammed the door, he stood there for a moment, listening. Sure enough, the girls were getting back from lunch. Whistles and cries began to fill the hallway, as the girls watched a peep show, starring Clyde.

Tina moaned, and Kevin rushed over to help her up. Wincing in pain, she leaned against him as he led her to her bed. He pushed the stuffed animals off and pulled the covers back. With as much gentleness as Kevin knew how to use, he situated Tina on the bed. When he was sure that she was comfortable, he laid the gun down and went into the bathroom.

When Kevin returned, he held a wet washcloth in his hand. Sitting on the bed, he began to softly wipe the blood from Tina's face. Some places were still bleeding, so he held the cloth firmly in those places.

Tina's hand reached up and brushed Kevin's hand away from her face. "Why did you come back?" she asked, her voice cracking.

Kevin momentarily stared at the ceiling while he toyed with the cloth.

"When we finished talking, I saw Clyde sneaking into your dorm," he explained, his eyes meeting hers. "I figured he was up to no good."

Kevin took a good, hard look at Tina's bruised face. "Unfortunately I was right. I would have gotten here sooner, but I had to get that," he said motioning to the gun.

"Where in the world did you get a gun?" Tina asked.

Kevin smiled. "I got it from my room, but it's not even real! It's just a prop from a play that I've been working on!"

Tina's eyes grew large, and she began laughing.

"Ouch!" she cried, hugging her sore ribs.

Kevin reached out to feel if anything was broken. Gingerly he touched Tina, and even in her pain, her body grew warm at his touch. Unable to stand it any longer, she took his hand, and gently moved it away.

"I don't think anything's broken," she whispered.

He was about to protest when the door to the room flew open, and a confused Karen surveyed the room. Her glance began at the mess by the dressers, then ended at Kevin and her beat up roommate.

"What happened?" she asked, her voice shaking.

"That animal from the nightclub—the one who had harassed you—he came here and attacked Tina!" Kevin cried.

Karen began to feel faint. Dropping her books on her bed, she went and sat down beside Kevin. She was unaware of her mouth, still open in shock, as she stared at Tina.

Kevin handed Karen the bloody cloth. He stood up and went to the door. His eyes were different; they were wild with anger.

"This has got to stop!" he declared through clenched teeth. "That creep can't go on terrorizing women all of the time! He'd never think twice about raping someone, so there's no telling what else he would do!"

Karen and Tina watched Kevin in fear. Neither of them had ever seen him so angry. He was almost like a stranger to them now.

"I've got to take care of this!" he said. "That jerk has brutalized his last victim!"

Kevin bolted out the door and raced down the hallway.

"Kevin!" Karen cried. She ran to the door and scanned the hallway. It was too late; Kevin was gone!

Her hands trembling, she went to the bathroom and rinsed out the bloody washcloth. Her eyes were blurred with tears, and she stared in a trance at the red trail going down the drain. It was a brilliant red at first, turning to pink, then finally clear.

It wasn't until Tina called her name, that Karen snapped back to reality. She wiped her eyes with the back of her hand, then wrung out the washcloth.

When Karen came out of the bathroom, Tina was looking at her with questioning eyes.

"I wanted to get all of the blood out," Karen lied.

She again sat on the bed and finished wiping Tina's face. Her eyes were filled with worry, and she had to ask the inevitable question, "Did you tell Kevin?"

Tina put her hand on Karen's and pulled the washcloth away. She stared at Karen as if to say, "You just don't care, do you?"

Putting her finger on her cut lip, Tina wiped some blood off. She marked 'no' on her white sheet, lay back, then closed her eyes.

Karen's eyes grew large. She suddenly became ashamed of herself. Here she was worried about everything except her roommate, who'd taken a beating because of her. She hadn't even asked Tina if she was all right!

Getting off the bed, Karen went to the door. She fixed the handle so it would lock behind her. Her eyes were on the floor.

"I'm so sorry," she said in the tiniest whisper, then she left.

CHAPTER FOUR

O N THE EDGE OF THE campus, a tall, sleazy young man leaned against a tree, waiting. He wasn't a student, so it made him uncomfortable to be in that particular area. He held no job, yet his wallet was never empty. His method of survival was in dealing. He called it "sales". Almost anything that could be bought or sold passed through his greasy hands: drugs, stereos, jewelry, or guns. It didn't matter to him as long as he got his money. He always swore that his merchandise wasn't stolen, but people knew better. Most of the time they didn't even care.

Today's request had been for a handgun. A friend of a friend and so on, had passed the word on to him. It made him very happy to be selling a gun today, for he always got double his money on a gun purchase. Personally, he would have carried a knife until he was of the legal age to buy such a weapon. He wasn't there to question, though; he was just there to make a few bucks.

Shifting around uneasily, he scanned the grounds for any sign of police officers. It was the only drawback to his kind of living, for he feared the law and the way it jeopardized his freedom.

A noise startled him. He whirled around to see what it was. A student nonchalantly approached him, so he waited to see what would happen.

The "customer" said nothing, but instead handed the dealer an envelope stuffed with money. As the man counted it, he chuckled to himself.

"Trouble on campus?" he asked.

There was no answer.

"Scared you're gonna get attacked?" he questioned sarcastically.

Again there was no reply. The student extended a gloved hand in impatient anticipation of the gun.

"Here," the dealer said, as he handed over the weapon, "don't do anything I wouldn't do."

The student practically snatched the gun and ran off as the man watched. He shook his head, then proceeded to leave.

"They get stranger every time," he mumbled to himself.

* * *

Two people stole across the campus that evening. Quietly and quickly, they headed for the pool area, taking advantage of the full moon for their light.

Upon reaching the pool area, Clyde and his date, LeAnna checked the place for any signs of life. The security guards who patrolled the campus would have them expelled for what they were about to do.

"See anything?" Clyde asked.

"It's clear," LeAnna answered. "Let's get in before anybody shows up!"

Digging in his gym bag, Clyde produced a shiny gold-plated key. It would open the gate that led to the swimming pool. As he turned the key in the padlock, Clyde smiled smugly. "You've got to know the right people," he said proudly.

"You mean, you've got to suck up to the jocks," LeAnna corrected. "Just how many keys have those guys duplicated?"

"Who cares?" Clyde responded. "As long as I get to borrow one when I need it, they can have all the keys floating around that they want!"

He started to go into the pool area, when LeAnna grabbed his arm. "How do you know we'll be alone tonight?" she asked nervously.

"We'll be alone," Clyde assured her. "The word's been spread that I've got the pool tonight."

"How do you know they'll listen?" she asked.

"They won't bother us!" he snapped over his shoulder.

Once more, LeAnna glanced around, then she quickly went inside and followed Clyde to the pool. There were glass doors that surrounded the pool itself. Clyde easily opened them with the same key, and they went inside.

Clyde had spoken the truth about other people being aware of his rendezvous. He had spread the word mainly for privacy, but he'd also bragged about it exceedingly. Just letting others know that he'd be skinny dipping with the beautiful, auburn-haired LeAnna fed his male ego. All of the guys that he knew would kill for the chance to date her. They'd be so jealous tomorrow when he would brag about having had sex with her!

News of Clyde's escapade had reached other ears, too. As Clyde and LeAnna stripped off their clothes, someone stood in the shadows, waiting.

LeAnna's clothes dropped to the cement floor, as she stood there gazing at Clyde who was already in the pool. Drops of water beaded and rolled off of his pale, muscular skin, as the moonlight shone through the Plexiglas ceiling, bringing out the gold in his hair.

Clyde swam over to the pool's steps, and helped LeAnna get into the water. When her body was next to his, they began to kiss.

When their passion became too intense, LeAnna pulled away. She dove under the water and swam to the far end of the pool. Coming up for air, she saw that Clyde remained at the shallow end of the pool, and she laughed.

"Come to me," he said, arms outstretched.

"Come and get me," she challenged him.

Clyde couldn't stand it any longer. LeAnna's long hair was draped tightly about her shoulders. It stopped just over the curve of her breasts. Water glistened on her face and rolled off her sensual lips.

He swam to her, gathering her naked body into his steel arms. Every inch of her was inevitable pleasure, and he knew that at any moment, she would be his.

Each kiss was followed by another one more passionate than the first. They kissed and treaded water until they felt that their lungs would burst.

"Let's go back to the shallow end," LeAnna finally suggested, gasping.

Clyde nodded; he was growing tired, too.

Together they swam back to the shallow end, and Clyde took her once again into his arms.

"Where were we?" he asked playfully.

LeAnna planted her most sensuous kiss on Clyde's mouth. It was deep and demanding, taking him by surprise.

We definitely hadn't gotten *that* far yet!" he exclaimed as she released his quivering lips.

As he stood there absorbed by her beauty, he wanted her more and more. They began to kiss again, and to touch each another so intimately, that he knew it was about time to take her completely.

Suddenly LeAnna pulled away and looked about frantically. Shocked and infuriated, Clyde glared at her.

"I heard something!" she whispered fearfully.

Clyde listened, but he heard nothing.

"There's nothing out there," he said assuredly, pulling her close to himself again.

She jerked away from Clyde, her eyes wide. "I wasn't hearing things!" she hissed.

Clyde tried to put the thought of sex out of his mind. Holding her again, he strained his ears to hear.

Just when he was about to mock her for her fear, he heard it, too. It was the faintest sound, kind of muffled, like someone walking ever so softly.

Clyde tensed up, and LeAnna sensed his growing apprehension. Her fingers dug deeper and deeper into his flesh, but he didn't feel the pain.

"It might be a security guard," he whispered. "Just be quiet, and maybe he'll leave."

The darkness which at first had seemed so romantic, was now like an enemy. Clyde strained his eyes so much that they began to burn, making it even harder to see. He blinked a couple of times, then stared into the darkness again. The sound was coming from a hallway adjacent to the pool, and now it drew nearer.

"Get down!" Clyde whispered frantically.

LeAnna obeyed, and together they crouched as far down into the water as they could. The chlorine water was just under their nostrils, burning. They breathed cautiously.

As they huddled together, a cloud passed over the moon, cutting off what little light they'd had. Something splashed into the water right beside of them, causing them to jump back, afraid.

"What was that?" LeAnna whispered nervously. Tears were in her eyes, making Clyde's own frightened face a blur.

He felt all around for whatever it was that had fallen into the pool. When at last his hand touched something, he jerked his arm away.

"What is it?" LeAnna cried.

"I don't know—it startled me. I thought it was a snake."

At the mention of the word "snake", LeAnna bolted for the pool stairs. She'd just have to risk getting kicked out of college!

Clyde jerked her back. "Are you crazy?" he hissed.

Now LeAnna was crying, and Clyde feared being discovered.

"It's not a snake," he promised her, putting his arm around her.

With his free hand, he felt once again in the water. His hand brushed up against something, and this time he grabbed it. At that moment, the clouds left the moon.

"What is it?" LeAnna asked, sounding like a broken record.

Clyde held one end of a drop cord. Part of the cord had been stripped away, leaving wires exposed.

"This doesn't make any sense," he mumbled.

As he held the cord, contemplating it, he heard another sound. This time the steps were not muffled; they were very distinct.

Clyde summoned the courage to glance over the side of the pool. Still holding the cord in his hand, he watched with horror as a dark figure stepped out of the shadows. The other end of the cord trailed to the figure in black, whose head and face was covered with a shabby piece of black cloth. The cloth was held in place with a crude rope tied about the neck of the stranger. Unfeeling eyes peered out of holes that were cut into the cloth.

Recovering slightly from shock, Clyde remembered that he still held the other end of the cord. Just as he was about to let go, the person in black plunged the plug into an electrical socket.

Electrical currents pulsated through Clyde's and LeAnna's bodies. Their screams filled the pool area, echoing off the walls. Undaunted, the figure in black stood by watching the two bodies shaking in their deadly water traps.

One scream after another filled the air along with the odor of burning flesh. Finally the last scream came and slowly faded into nothingness. The stranger watched as the two burnt bodies sank below the water's surface. Satisfied, the person unplugged the cord, then disappeared back into the shadows.

CHAPTER FIVE

T HE SUN SHONE BRIGHT THE following morning, blazing against a pale blue sky. Birds chirped happily in the massive trees, decorated with the rich colors of fall. A certain peacefulness filled the air. It was like a calm before a storm—serenity that would end as more students woke up to start another day.

On the sidewalk, a heavy, middle-aged woman waddled rapidly towards the pool area. Once pretty and athletic, she now moved with difficulty. Her mouse brown hair, cut short, was speckled with strands of gray. Smoking and shouting orders over the years had robbed her of her melodic voice. Now she looked and sounded like an army drill sergeant.

Her job was that of a physical education instructor. Since hers was the first swimming class of the day, it was her responsibility to open the pool area.

Students were already gathered outside the gate, waiting for her. With her clipboard in one hand, and her keys in the other, she brushed past the crowd and unlocked a door. Students rushed in like water from a broken dam, as they listened for the familiar order.

"Hit the showers before you get into the pool!" the teacher shouted like clockwork. She watched out of the corner of her eye, students going to the shower areas. They were all so young and strong!

"Wait until you see what time does to you!" she thought regretfully.

The double glass doors leading to the pool were locked, so the teacher unlocked them and propped them open. Even as she did so, a sense of foreboding began to envelop her. Something was amiss, yet she was frightened to find out what it was.

Scolding herself for being so childish, she began to scan the area. It was at that moment her eyes fell upon the drop cord. The plug lay just underneath the socket, while the rest of the cord slithered in the direction of the pool.

A fear that she had never known suddenly gripped her heart. The pool was a few yards away, hiding the end of the cord. Try as she might, the instructor couldn't get her feet to move. The fear that was choking her told her that something else was in the pool.

"I've got to be strong," she thought to herself over and over. Her mind was prepared for shock, but her body wouldn't allow her to budge from her safe spot at the glass doors.

Voices filled the hallways again, growing louder and louder as the students returned from their showers. This was a rambunctious crowd, somewhat immature. The boys pinched and teased their scantily clad female classmates, making them squeal.

"Don't run," the teacher thought. It was the second most spoken command, usually shouted with steel lungs. Now the words remained glued to the back of her mouth, refusing to even fall from her lips.

One particularly rowdy couple came darting past the instructor. The boy pinched his girlfriend in her rear, causing her to lunge forward. As she did, her foot hit a puddle of water, and she slid. She fell forward, almost going into the pool headfirst. She landed with a thud right by the edge of the pool, then she began screaming uncontrollably. As others rushed to help her, they began screaming, also. Some of the students clung to each other, speechless with fear, as they stared at the blackened, lifeless bodies of Clyde and LeAnna. They bobbed about with unseeing eyes, their faces still wearing expressions of deep shock.

The teacher remained at the glass doors, unable to move or to speak. She barely noticed the fellow who bumped into her on his way to call the police. All she could do was stare. Finally a single tear rolled down her round cheek.

The police cars and an ambulance were already at the scene as Karen was walking to her aerobics class. The class was in a gym adjacent to the pool. Tina walked with her. She just didn't want to be alone at the moment. Every move that she made was met with excruciating pain. Even the sun seemed to penetrate her sunglasses, searing her tender eyes.

Karen glanced over at Tina and noticed a limp. "You want to go back to the room?" she asked.

Tina shook her head. "No. I'll be missing classes today as it is. Anyway I can use the fresh air."

Karen frowned as she studied her friend. The sunglasses and the heavy makeup hid most of the cuts and bruises, but not all of them. Even if they did hide it, there was no disguising the limp.

"Why don't you call the police?" she asked.

"Maybe he'll leave us alone now," Tina answered halfheartedly.

"Yeah, well what if he doesn't; he might kill you next time. He might kill me, too!"

Tina looked at Karen. She was wearing an electric blue leotard that made her great figure appear even better. Her makeup was flawless, and her long wavy blonde hair was drawn back into a flowing ponytail. It seemed as if Karen had taken hours to get ready, but Tina knew that she had not. A sting of jealousy quickly passed through her.

"Well?" Karen asked, bringing Tina to the present.

"Well, what?" Tina repeated thickly.

"What if he comes back for us?" Karen cried.

"I don't want to talk about it," Tina answered sternly.

Karen was taken aback by Tina's rudeness, and was about to comment, when she noticed the police cars and the ambulance by the gym. Scores of students were clustered around the building, blocking her view. She squinted her eyes against the brilliant sunlight, trying to make out what was going on, but it was no use; there were just too many people.

She ran down the small slope that led to the gym, barely noticing Tina limping painfully behind her. Tina almost lost her balance, and she moaned out loud. When Karen heard her, she backed up, taking her by the arm and leading her to the crowd.

They tried to see over the wall of people, but it was impossible. Finally Karen tapped a male student on the shoulder, and he turned around.

"What happened in there?" she asked urgently.

He shrugged his shoulders. "I'm not sure. Somebody must have drowned."

Karen let out an exasperated sigh. She tightened her grip on Tina and began pushing her way through the crowd. People were crying and holding one another, while others stood speechless.

Once again Karen tapped a student on the shoulder. "What happened in there?" she asked.

A girl turned around, tears rolling down her face.

"A girl from my math class and this guy are dead," she answered, her voice quivering.

"Who is it?" Karen questioned desperately.

"LeAnna Richard and Clyde Walker."

Karen's eyes grew large as her hand flew to her mouth. Tina felt faint and nauseated. She started to sway, but Karen helped her regain her balance.

Just then, the EMTs rolled two bodies to the ambulance. The obvious lumps in the bags, two people who had been alive the day before. Several police officers followed them solemnly. When they got near the students, one of them stopped.

"Two students are dead," he announced. "Some of you already know who they are. I'm not allowed to give out that information, though, until the families have been notified. I'm going to ask you to please stay around if you know anything; otherwise, you need to go on to your other classes, or to your dorms. Officers may be in touch with you later, depending on what we find out. Now please go—we've got work to do, and there's nothing left for you to see!"

Slowly the students began to leave as the police officers began putting up the terrible yellow tape around the pool area. Karen and Tina walked back to their dorm in stunned silence. Even the bright sunlight couldn't seep through the thick gloom each of them was feeling.

Suddenly a horrible thought hit Karen. She grabbed Tina by the arms, her eyes filled with fear.

"Oh, Tina!" she cried. "What if it was Kevin?"

Tina stared at her, not understanding.

"What are you talking about?" she asked.

"Don't you know?" Karen practically shouted, then she lowered her voice. "Kevin said that he'd see to it that Clyde would never hurt us again!"

Tina's eyes grew large as the impact of what Karen was suggesting hit her. "We need to find Kevin!" she cried.

Together they traveled as fast as they could to Kevin's dorm. Karen ran; Tina half-ran, half-limped. By the time they reached the dorm, both girls were out of breath.

Karen had a key to Kevin's room, but in her hysteria, she forgot about it. Instead, she beat frantically on the door.

"Kevin!" she cried.

"Come in!" Kevin hollered from some spot in the room.

Karen started to yell at him to open the door, when she remembered her key. She tried with some difficulty to get it in the lock, and finally succeeded on the third try.

As they entered the room, Kevin greeted them from over his shoulder. His back was turned to them as he dug in his dresser drawer.

"I can't find the mate to this stupid sock," he grumbled, oblivious to their anxiety.

Karen and Tina watched as he searched the dresser drawers, cursing under his breath. When that didn't yield the elusive sock, he fell on his knees to look under the bed. Karen couldn't stand it any longer.

"Clyde is dead!" she blurted out.

Kevin, holding one sock in his left hand, and fishing for the mate with his other hand, froze on the spot. His head jerked around as he turned to face Karen, his eyes filled with shock.

"Clyde is dead?" he repeated.

Karen nodded, and Kevin ceased his search. He got up slowly, then sat on the bed. His blue eyes were filled with concern. When he looked back up at Karen and Tina, his face held a look of astonishment.

"What happened?" he asked softly.

Karen related the story as she had heard it, then without thinking, she blurted out, "Did you do it?"

"Did I do what?" Kevin asked. He hoped she wasn't asking what he thought she was asking.

Karen rolled her eyes, then wailed, "Did you kill Clyde?"

With that, his eyes filled with anger, and his jaw became firm. He stood up quickly, stomping over to Karen and Tina so fast, that they feared he would strike them. Instead he got right in front of them, and shoved his finger in their faces.

"I'm getting ready for class! You come here beating on my door just to accuse me of killing a guy I hardly know! What's the *matter* with you two?"

"Kevin!" Karen began.

"Shut up!" he shouted, causing her to burst into tears. Tina instinctively put her arm around Karen.

"As for you," he said, glaring at Tina, who could not meet his eyes at the moment, "how could you think I'd do something like that?"

Tina had no answer, so Kevin just shook his head. "I know I couldn't stand the creep, but I'm no killer!"

With that, he snatched an odd color sock out of his drawer, grabbed his shoes and books, then dashed out of the room. Karen ran after him crying, "Honey, I didn't mean it—I just had to be sure! *Baby*, stop!"

Tina stood alone in Kevin's room and listened as Karen's voice trailed off. Suddenly, a sharp pang went to her head, and she put her hands there as if to ward it off. It continued hurting, though, so she locked Kevin's door, and began walking to her dorm.

When she finally reached her dorm, she went straight to the bathroom. There she took something to stop the throbbing pain. She peeled off her jeans, then reached under her T-shirt for her bra. Comfortable at last, she crawled under the covers of her bed, and gently laid her head on her pillow. The pain medicine started taking effect, and she fell asleep.

In her dream, Tina was standing on the shallow end of the pool. She was wearing a one piece white bathing suit, and her hair fell softly about her shoulders. Slowly she descended the three steps into the pool.

With a deep inhale, she surface dove into the water. Halfway across the pool, she came up for air. The ladder on the deep end of the pool was not far away, but as she swam, it seemed to move away from her. She began to grow tired, and her arms ached. She gasped for air, while the sound of her heart pounding echoed in her head.

Just when it seemed that she would give up and drown, the ladder came within her grasp. She reached her wearied arm out for one of the rungs. Suddenly the blackened body of Clyde emerged from the water. His eyes were rolled back in his head, and his face wore a horrible expression.

Tina began screaming, her hand trying desperately to reach the ladder. Clyde's hand came out of the water, and it grabbed her wrist. She screamed hysterically, and fought violently, but could not free herself. Clyde's dead body began to gradually submerge, taking the terror-stricken Tina with him into the black water—

Just then, Tina woke up, and let out a long, loud scream. She was still screaming, when Karen burst into the room. As soon as she noticed Karen, Tina stopped screaming. She then began crying uncontrollably, as if she would never stop. Karen sat on the bed and took Tina into her arms, gently rocking her like a baby.

"It's OK," she said. "It was only a bad dream."

Tina was speechless while her body shook with sobs. Her eyes were wide with fear as she scanned the room, trying to push the horrible nightmare out of her mind. Finally she gave up, and passed out in Karen's arms.

CHAPTER SIX

F OR A WHILE, THINGS AT the college were in complete chaos. Aside from the drop cord, the police were unable to gather any other physical evidence from the pool site. The cord had nothing but dirt and smudged fingerprints from years of use. No one was even sure where it had come from.

Students were questioned, including Kevin, but that also failed to yield any information. It seemed that before his tragic death, Clyde had gotten into several fights with other students, also. His reputation became more and more unfavorable with each questioning. The police were unable to connect anyone in particular with the hideous crime.

In the administration building, things were in an uproar. The president of the college paced the floor of the conference room, sometimes pleading, sometimes shouting. A spokesperson was selected to keep the press at a distance, and another person was ordered to hire more security guards. In addition, the locks on the pool were to be changed. The meeting ended solemnly, with the president leaving for his office to take yet another Valium.

Students were also uneasy, for the place where they had previously felt safe had now been violated. Each knew that there was a killer loose, and most students took extra precautions, such as double checking locked doors, and walking with others. At night, few students were outside the dorms. Everyone felt vulnerable.

Time went by, and with time, people felt more secure. The memories of the victims faded, as students tried to go on with life as usual. There was still a faint apprehension in the air, but all in all, things were getting back to normal.

Karen seemed to have a harder time dealing with Clyde's death. She begged Tina to go everywhere with her, for she seemed terrified to be alone. It was as if she didn't trust Kevin. At first, Kevin was annoyed at Tina's constant presence. He didn't understand why she had to follow them all of the time, not knowing it was Karen who had put Tina up to it in the first place. Against his will, though, he began to grow fond of her. She was like a breath of fresh air, always laughing and smiling. When he said something funny, she would really laugh, sometimes throwing her head back. Her hair would fall back, revealing a face that Kevin found more and more beautiful.

The three of them took long walks. Even when they didn't talk, there seemed to be music going on in Tina's head. She would softly sway, as if listening to a melody that only she could hear. Then the melody would apparently stop. She would then begin a conversation, or just stare quietly at the scenery, keeping pace with Karen and Kevin.

Though Tina enjoyed the sudden attention, she knew that she was being used. Karen seemed to fear Kevin. It was as if she could not accept his denial of having nothing to do with Clyde's death.

As for Tina, she could not believe in a million years that Kevin would ever be capable of such violence. Sure, he was a likely candidate. Sure, there was a killer loose, but not Kevin. He was just too special. She knew that he sometimes resented her being there, but she couldn't help but to like being around Karen and Kevin. It was hard at times, though, for she had a tremendous crush on him. It had to just be a crush! She couldn't possibly be in *love* with the boyfriend of her best friend! That would just be too weird! Besides, how could she do that to Karen? Karen was her constant companion, except for those few occasions that Tina was left behind. They saw the best and the worst of each other!

Tina tried to ignore her feelings for Kevin, but more and more she found that she was comparing herself to Karen. If *she* dated Kevin, she would treat him so good! There would never be any reason to look at another fellow! She wouldn't cheat on him the way that Karen had, nor would she take him for granted the way Karen did! Tina yearned for a fraction of the attention that he poured on Karen! Just by a glance, he could make her feel special. By just a different glance, he could also make her feel so stupid! There was so much power behind those eyes of his!

She often stared in the mirror wondering what Kevin didn't see in her. Karen would come up behind her, though, and then she would remember. Karen was *so* beautiful! She was like a serpent, holding Kevin in a trance. Try as she might, Tina would never stand a chance of releasing him from that spell. Even if she could, dedication to Karen would prevent her from trying. She would just have to be satisfied with the few times that Kevin did take notice of her. For her, some attention was better than none.

She found a temporary escape for her sexual frustration and guilt. It came in the form of a place called "The Fitness Center". The "Center" was nothing more than a large room with a lot of workout machines and weights. It was a haven for those who liked to get away from the college crowd, for it was seldom packed. Most of the students used the gym at the college, but Tina found it to be too popular. She was glad to spend a little money in order to avoid the aggravation.

It became a habit of hers to work out every day after her classes. Sometimes she would go back to the college to run around the outdoor track. She began to look and feel better, but most importantly, she was able to keep her mind off of Kevin.

One afternoon as she was leaving the "Center", she encountered Karen and Kevin. Embarrassed by her T-shirt, sweatpants, and messed up hair, she told them "Hi", and kept walking. As usual, Karen called out to her.

"Tina, where're you going?"

Tina, who was now at the corner of an intersection, pointed in the direction of the football field. "I'm going to run a couple of laps around the track!" she called out.

Karen turned up her nose. "We're going to the Burger Shak; come with us!"

Tina glanced at the traffic light. It was safe to cross, but her feet hesitated. She looked back at Karen, who was smiling and motioning for her to come.

"Come on, Tina!"

Tina ran back to Karen and Kevin. "I feel so dirty—you'd better go on without me!"

Karen looked past Tina's shoulder and pointed to "The Fitness Center".

"Does that place have restrooms?" she asked.

Tina laughed. "Of course it does," she replied.

Karen turned to Kevin. "Wait here," she said.

Kevin nodded, then sat down on a bench while the two girls went in "The Fitness Center" to get Tina freshened up.

Tina observed Karen as they made their way to the restrooms. She glanced about the place, confused. Finally she stopped at one machine and studied it. Her long, slender fingers slid down the cold metal of the machine. She cocked her head, trying to figure the thing out.

"What's this for?" she asked.

Tina tried to keep from laughing. "It's an AB machine. It's kind of like doing sit-ups, only easier."

Karen raised her eyebrows, obviously impressed.

"I could use that," she commented.

Tina's gaze went to Karen's slim waistline. "Yeah, you *really* need that, don't you?"

Both girls burst out laughing, then continued towards the restrooms. Tina noticed the guys noticing Karen, and for a moment she was jealous. Who could blame them for looking, though? Karen's hair flowed freely over her elbow length burgundy sweater. Her body filled out in perfect detail the pants that matched, and on her feet were low heeled patent pumps in raven black. Not one detail was left undone, and it made Tina feel self-conscious of her own appearance. She felt inferior to Karen, and was glad to reach the haven of the restroom.

Once inside, Tina noticed that she didn't look as bad as she had previously thought. Her eyes had a sparkle, and her cheeks were flushed from her workout. Still, in her opinion, she was incompatible to the gorgeous blonde next to her.

"Look at me," Karen said, interrupting her thoughts.

Tina obeyed, then Karen wiped her face off with a damp paper towel. She reached into her purse and pulled out different makeup items. Tina closed her eyes as Karen carefully applied the makeup to her face. The strokes mesmerized her, and she was almost disappointed when Karen said, "There, I'm finished."

Tina opened her eyes. Karen was smiling proudly. She took Tina by the shoulders, and turned her about to face the mirror. Tina was stunned! It was more makeup than she usually wore, but she looked beautiful!

"Karen!" she exclaimed. "This looks wonderful!"

Karen smiled. "It's amazing what a little makeup will do! I don't know how I could live without it!"

Tina started to argue about Karen's "need" for makeup, but before she opened her mouth, Karen was already saying, "Hold still while I brush your hair."

When she was done, Karen stepped back, admiring her "creation".

"That looks good now," she stated.

They went back outside and joined Kevin. He tried not to show his surprise at Tina's appearance. She was beautiful, yet something in him wanted to yell at her for wearing that makeup. Did she want to look like every other girl on campus? How many of *them* could show their faces without makeup and still look as good as Tina? She had a gift of natural beauty, so why would she allow herself to hide it?

Deep inside, though, he would not admit to himself the real reason for his frustration. When Tina and Karen had returned, something inside of him had been moved. For the first time, he saw the brown-eyed friend of Karen's as a woman. It made him feel betrayed. Tina was just a *friend*. She wasn't supposed to make him think of her as being sexual, was she?

"Well, how did I do?" Karen asked, interrupting his thoughts.

Kevin barely glanced in Tina's direction. "It's all right," he mumbled.

Tina's heart sank. He hadn't even noticed! She was just plain old Tina, the tag-along of Karen's! With a sigh, she followed them into the cafe'.

Once inside, a wrinkled old waitress showed them to a booth in the center of the restaurant. It was a place frequented by the college students, and known for its succulent hamburgers and delicious fries. The atmosphere of the place left something to be desired. It had plain pale yellow walls with few pictures. The floors were a dingy shade of beige, and the booths were covered in red vinyl. Most of the employees there were retired men and women, who didn't care about being gracious. Sure they could be cordial, but they did not for one moment put up with any junk.

They had barely been seated, when another student entered the place. The waitress began to seat him, also, but when he noticed Tina, he motioned towards their table. Strolling over, he stopped over to where they were sitting, and looked directly at Tina. She raised her eyes from her menu and stared at him blankly. Laughing, he broke the silence.

"Hi, Tina! How're you doing? Remember me from English class?"

Tina gazed into his emerald eyes. How could she forget him? Every girl in that class made over him! They were not to blame, though, for he was so handsome! He was a tall fellow with a medium build. His jet black hair was cut short, parting a bit on the side. A chiseled nose hovered over lusciously full lips. His smile was charming, revealing pearl white teeth, and prominent cheekbones. The clothes he wore appeared to be very expensive, making him seem as one who had just stepped out of a fashion magazine.

"Sure I remember you," she finally said. "How's it going?"

"Fine—it's going fine," he answered, then motioned to the empty spot beside of Tina. "Do you mind if I sit down?"

Tina glanced across the table at Karen and Kevin, who had been watching the event with much interest. Karen winked in approval, and Kevin smiled.

Blushing slightly, she answered, "No. I don't mind; sit down."

The young man exhaled in relief as if he may have been turned down. Sliding into the booth, he extended his hand, introducing himself to Karen and Kevin.

"I'm Brad Porter," he announced.

Kevin shook his hand and replied, "I'm Kevin Russo, and this is Karen Mitchell."

Brad took Karen's hand also. He seemed unaffected by her beauty, which automatically pleased Tina.

With the introductions over, he turned to Tina. "What can I buy you today?" he asked.

"I'll take a cheeseburger basket and a large soft drink," she responded.

When the waitress returned, Brad gave his and Tina's orders. After a couple of minutes, Karen and Kevin gave theirs. They always had a hard time choosing, but ended up getting the same thing every time.

After the waitress left, Tina looked across the table at Karen and Kevin. They were exchanging glances as though this was her first date. They seemed so happy for her, but she wanted to scream at them. She wished they would quit treating her like a child, and suddenly she wished that Brad would leave. She felt as though her private dream world was being invaded. Her heart had an invisible door on it—one that had been locked since her parents' deaths. The only person who had the "key" to enter it was Kevin, but he was not interested in unlocking that part of her.

Sighing, she managed a smile and turned to Brad. They began talking, and soon Karen and Kevin joined in the conversation. The main topic of discussion was the big Christmas party to be held in the college's reception hall. The place was a huge room lined with old paintings and antique furnishings. It was an elegant setting for any occasion, especially the annual Christmas party.

Each year, the college spent thousands of dollars on the event. There were numerous trays of hor'd'orves, a huge "wedding type" cake with a sparkling fountain, and bowls of punch that always managed to get "spiked". There was always at least a twelve foot Christmas tree, elaborately decorated with handmade ornaments and shiny balls, perfuming the area with the sweet, spicy scent of evergreen.

During the meal, Brad kept hinting around in a feeble attempt to find out if Tina had a date or not. She didn't have a date, but she never came out and actually said so. Finally he glanced at his watch.

"Oh no! I've got to get out of here; I lost track of the time! My biology lab's in five minutes!"

He looked at Tina, "Want to race me to the building?" he offered.

Tina laughed. "How can I run? I've eaten so much, that I'll probably have trouble walking!"

Brad stood up and grinned. "OK, you win; there's no race today. I'll see you again, though—*soon!*

He went to the register and paid, then went out the door running to his class.

Karen beamed at Tina. "He's after you, Tina! I just know it! You got lucky—he's good-looking!"

Tina grinned tightly. "I don't know," she mumbled.

Karen made a face at Tina, looking at her as if she came from another planet.

"Come on, Tina! Don't you know a pass when you see one? That guy really likes you!"

"I think she's right," Kevin added.

Tina glared at them, then exploded, "So what if he's good-looking? So what if he likes me? He's not the best thing in the world!"

She got up and ran out of the restaurant, leaving Karen and Kevin sitting there, stunned.

"What's wrong with her?" Karen asked in amazement.

Kevin smiled smugly. "She's scared out of her wits!"

He looked at Karen and she burst out laughing. "You mean she's got "butterflies"?"

"Exactly," he commented, as they got up and paid, then walked out hand in hand.

*   *   *

After Tina had run out of the restaurant, she bypassed the football field and headed for the library. The college library was a monstrous building supported with gigantic white columns. It was surrounded by weeping willow trees, making it look more like a plantation, than a library. Tina entered the three-story structure, and took the stairs to the bottom floor. As her foot left the last step, she glanced behind her to make sure that she had not been followed. All of a sudden, she felt a jolt as she bumped into another girl. Tina gasped, and looked up to see a well dressed couple. The students stared at her blankly while she blushed, remembering her own casual appearance. Immediately she apologized, then ran to the other end of the room, disappearing behind some bookshelves. The two students merely shook their heads and walked away.

Tina grasped the corner of a bookshelf, watching as the couple left. She looked around to make sure she was alone. She was. Breathing easier, she made her way to the shelf that held the books she needed. Her fingers made delicate movements as they floated over the assorted titles. Finally she stopped. Her hand rested on a thick red book. She glanced around again to make sure she was still alone. Pulling the book from the shelf, she clutched it to her breast, and walked slowly between the bookshelves, scanning the room for a secluded table. She found one nestled in a corner of the room, far away from curious eyes.

Settling in the chair, she propped the book up on the table and gingerly turned the pages. It was an illustrated book about sex, written in detail. Tina read with much interest, occasionally looking over her shoulder. So what if she was a virgin? No one else had to know! She knew about sex; as least she thought she knew enough. She just wanted to be sure she was ready if the appropriate time ever arrived. Perhaps there were things she was unaware of! It would be embarrassing to be caught looking like a novice, so she read until her eyes hurt. Finally she closed the book, satisfied. She placed it back on the shelf as carefully as she had removed it, then quietly left the library.

CHAPTER SEVEN

MANY OF THE STUDENTS WHO attended college relied on some form of financial aid to pay for their tuition. The college offered part-time jobs to those who were interested in using that as a method of payment. There were so many areas of the facility that needed the extra help, that no one had difficulty in finding a place to work. All one had to do was fill out the necessary forms, then perform ten to fifteen hours of work each week at the assigned job.

Tina's job was in the cafeteria during the lunch hours. Five days a week, she spent two hours in the serving line, the other hour in the kitchen. Day after day, she scooped up spoonfuls of casseroles, or handed out chicken. At first the food looked good, but in time she began to see it as disgusting and greasy. She developed a craving for pizza, but she was always too busy to order one. As a result, she ended up eating some of the casserole that she'd been staring at for so long.

As if that were not bad enough, she had to help wash dishes for another hour. She would get in front of the sink and close her eyes, wishing for the mess to disappear. Of course it would not, so she would simply sigh, then start loading up the machine that sterilized the dinnerware. By the time she finally finished, her hands were chapped, and she was sticky with sweat from the hot steam that emitted from the dishwasher.

Her "uniform" was comical. It was a polyester white smock, with matching white pants. Of all colors, they had to wear *white*! No stain could be covered or removed completely in a white outfit, yet that was what they were required to wear. There was another problem—her hair! She had to either tie it back in a ponytail or wear a hairnet. Tina opted for the ponytail. The older women who worked there full-time had no qualms about the unflattering things, but Tina flatly refused to wear them. If she had to humiliate herself by donning polyester clothes, she would not make things worse by sporting a hairnet.

Not a day went by that she was not teased about her uniform or her job. Some cocky guy would always say things like, "Hey, Tina, you've got yesterday's lunch on your tit!" or "Tina, if you'd wear a sexier outfit, it'd make this crap easier to digest!"

Each time she'd just shake her head, then slam a spoonful of food on the fellow's plate, making a bit of a mess. The "wise guy" would look down at the jumbled food as if to say, "What'd you do *that* for?" When his eyes met Tina's again, she'd smile sweetly and purr, "I'm so sorry!", then she'd motion to the end of the line as if to reply, "Get out of here!"

One day after she had finished washing dishes, she went to help one of the cooks wrap up some leftover food. The woman she stayed to help was a black woman named Inez. She was a tall, slightly hefty lady, who on the surface appeared harsh and impatient. Many students were intimidated by her, but not Tina. She knew that Inez's sharp tone was a bluff, used to keep her children in line when she was younger, but now used to deal with rowdy college students. Tina saw through her outer appearance, and found her to be a very kind woman. She enjoyed the few occasions when things weren't hectic, and they could talk.

When they were finished wrapping the food, they loaded it onto a cart, then Inez went to put it in the cooler. She left her prized work possession, an eight inch butcher knife, on the counter. Tina felt mischievous, so she picked up the knife, sneaking up on the woman as she unloaded the cart.

"Inez, I'm gonna slice you in two!" she teased, holding the knife up threateningly.

The older woman turned around, her eyes wide. She gasped and put her hand to her breast, causing Tina to burst out laughing.

"Child," she scolded, "put that thing up! Knives are for cutting, not for playing!"

Tina lowered the knife. "I'm sorry, Inez. I didn't mean to scare you that bad—I guess I'm just a little restless."

Inez put her arm around Tina. "What you need is a good man, Child. Surely there's one on this campus!"

Tina left to take the knife back. Inez watched her go, but didn't hear Tina reply, "There is one, but he's taken."

*　　*　　*

Kevin had a part-time job also, but it was not at the college. He worked at a grocery store close to his house. He'd worked there while he was in high school, and he'd kept the job when he started college. He liked the extra money, plus he wanted to pay back some, if not all of the money his father had spent to send him to college. It was not mandatory that Kevin do so; it was just something that he *wanted* to do.

Another thing he wanted was to live on campus. Though he and his family got along well, Kevin liked the freedom of living away from home. He was close enough that visiting was not a problem. He took Karen there frequently, especially for Sunday dinners. Everyone in his family seemed as taken with her as he was, and it was easy to see why.

His method of transportation was a compact two-door car. His savings from his job at the grocery store had helped him to buy it. It was nothing fancy, just a simple blue used car. Nonetheless, Kevin was proud of it, and after two years, it still served him well. He often remembered the excitement of driving it for the first time. It held many memories for him, especially those that began when he started dating Karen.

The grocery store was a nice place to work. Kevin knew everyone who worked there, and he knew most of the people who shopped there, also. The manager was good to work for. He made Kevin's schedule so as not to interfere with his classes, plus he gave him a lot of weekend evenings off. Every time Kevin would thank him for a Saturday night off, the manager would smile and say, "Take it; you deserve it. You work and study all week. You need time to nurture your love life!"

Karen, unlike Kevin and Tina, did not work. She chose instead to reap the rewards of her parents' and Kevin's labors. Her education as well as her red sports car were from her parents; her amusement and her many off campus dinners were from Kevin. Unfortunately, she could not be completely satisfied, for she craved fun and excitement, like the dry earth thirsts for rain. With an almost savage hunger, she absorbed those moments that she and Kevin went out. Together they ate meals by candlelight, then hand in hand, they would stroll to the local theatre to see a movie. Unless it was very cold or raining, they chose to walk. There was something about the cool mountain air that made them feel as though they were suspended in their youths. The future would be temporarily ignored as they held hands, thinking that things would never change. The problems of others were illusions, for to them the world revolved around them, making nothing else matter.

Karen's and Kevin's outings, though fun, cost money, and eventually there would be that evening where Karen was at her dorm, bored, while Kevin worked. She would pace the room like a caged lioness, trying to decide what to do. She felt that she had to always be doing something fun, and it drove her crazy to be cooped up with nothing to do.

Tina would watch Karen on those nights, wishing that her friend would stop fidgeting. All the nervous movements got on her nerves when she was trying to study. It seemed as though every time she had a test to study for, that was the night that Karen was stuck without a date.

"Come on, Karen," she would finally say, "sit down and help me study for our history test. I bet you don't even know half the answers."

Karen would stop what she was doing, staring at Tina as though she had suggested something dreadful, such as plucking her eyebrows.

"Well, do you know the answers?" Tina would question.

Karen would plop on her bed and jerk open her textbook, aggravated.

"Ah ha!" Tina would cry. "You *don't* know them! That's what happens when you date almost every night!"

Defeated, Karen would pick up her notes, then she and Tina would take turns testing each other. Tina would always know most of the answers, which made Karen envy her a little. The envy soon ended though, for she knew that Tina led what Karen considered to be a boring life. Sure she made good grades, but Karen knew that her friend was lonely for a boyfriend. She could tell by the sadness in Tina's eyes that she needed someone. It made her feel sorry for Tina, but at the same time she was frustrated with the girl. If Tina was so lonely, then why didn't she go out more? She seemed to avoid the guys who paid her attention, as if she had some invisible emotional barrier about her. Whenever they asked her out, Karen noticed that Tina almost always had some excuse for not accepting.

The only fellow who had seemed to make any progress was Brad. He was hard to avoid, Karen guessed, for he was so handsome and insistent. He had taken Tina out a couple of times, and they were going out again this weekend. Though he and Tina dated other people as well, Karen felt that if Tina would forget about those others, Brad would date her steadily.

Unknown to Karen, Tina *did* like Brad. That was part of the problem; she only *liked* him. She felt no sexual feelings, nor love for this tall, beautiful young man. Sometimes she thought that something must be wrong with her. She knew that many other girls wanted to go out with Brad, yet she had the nerve to take him for granted. He was as sweet, sexy, and charming as she could ever expect a man to be, but the electricity was just not there. Whenever Kevin looked at her, she grew so hot that she felt feverish. Whenever Brad looked at her, she felt as though she was with a good friend. She knew that he wanted more, and that she would not be able to give it. Secretly she planned in her mind how to let him down gently. Nothing seemed kind enough, so she figured that she would have to just do it slowly.

*   *   *

Brad picked Tina up the following Friday night. For dinner, he took her to a local steakhouse. Brad chatted excitedly about everything from the events of the past week to the movie they were about to go see.

"I hope you like drive-in movies, because that's where it's playing," he said.

"Aren't we going to get cold at a drive-in this time of year?" Tina asked nervously. She wasn't worried so much about the weather as she was about being alone with Brad.

"We won't get cold," Brad assured her. "If I have to, I'll let the car run, and turn the heater on. If that doesn't work, we still have each another for body heat!"

Tina flushed, then looked back down at her plate. Was tonight the night something would happen between her and Brad? She wasn't ready for that, at least not with him. Perhaps if she could get Kevin off her mind, she'd enjoy being with Brad more. It wasn't fair to him. She knew that she needed to move in one direction or another—to either break it off, or let him know that she only liked him as a friend. That way, if Brad wanted more, he'd have a chance to remain her friend or to find another girl who felt more for him.

They left the restaurant, then drove to the movie. On the way, they were mostly quiet, listening to the radio. Tina watched the lights of the small city pass by her. She wondered what Karen and Kevin were doing, wishing for a moment that she was with them.

They finally arrived at the drive-in. Brad winked at Tina as he paid the woman at the window. For a fleeting moment, a chill ran through her body, but she dismissed it as the night air.

"Are you going to park near those other cars?" Tina questioned nervously.

"No, it's too crowded. I'll park closer to the back where we can have more privacy. Besides, we'll be closer to the snacks!"

When Brad finally stopped the car, he turned to Tina.

"Do you want something to eat?" he asked.

"After all that we ate just a moment ago?" Tina responded.

Brad smiled. "Come on, Tina. There's always room for popcorn!"

"Alright, I'll take some, but only if a candy bar is included in the deal!"

"What about all that food we just ate?" Brad teased.

"I can't help it," Tina confessed. "After I eat something as salty as popcorn, it makes me crave chocolate."

"Oh well, I guess I started this," he said holding his hands up in mock surrender. "OK, I'll get you a candy bar, too. You sure can eat a lot, but it doesn't show," he added, glancing at her waist.

Tina was thankful for the darkness, because it hid her scarlet face. She watched as Brad got out of the car and walked to the concession stand. Other people were coming and going, also, their bodies silhouetted against the building. Tina stared as some poor guy, arms full of snacks, dropped a box of candy. She giggled as she watched him struggle, trying to retrieve his lost "treasure". Finally another person came by and helped him.

When she grew tired of looking at people, she fumbled with the radio dial. She found a song that she really enjoyed, then she leaned her head back against the car seat. She closed her eyes, enjoying the smooth, sensual sounds that caressed her ears. She was almost on the verge of drifting off to sleep, when the car door opened. Brad got in, smiling like a tiger from a hunt, as he handed Tina her snacks.

The movie was a horror flick about a werewolf terrorizing a small, helpless village. Tina cringed every time the werewolf killed another villager. Brad watched her, wondering if he'd made a mistake by bringing her to see that kind of movie. He leaned over and whispered in her ear, "Do you want to leave?"

Tina's eyes grew large, for she realized that he had been watching her, and she became embarrassed.

"No," she assured him, "this is fine; I like suspense."

Suddenly a scream was heard as the werewolf killed yet another victim. Tina and Brad looked at the screen, then turned to each other.

"It's the graphic effects that kind of make me sick," she admitted.

Brad smiled warmly, then put his arm around her.

In another car at the same drive-in, Karen sat fuming. She had gone out with some guy named Dennis. Dennis, she was finding out, was a big jerk. He was already tipsy when he met her in the college parking lot. On the way to the drive-in, he drank some more. Now he was just plain drunk. Karen glared at him. Had she thought that he was *cute*? She figured that she must have had mental fatigue after a grueling biology exam, because at the time, he seemed to look nice. Now he stared at her, eyes bloodshot, and curly red hair out of place.

"Kisth me," he slurred. His breath made Karen wince. He smelled like stale beer.

"Just get on your side of the car!" Karen hissed at him.

Dennis just smiled and tried to touch her. His hands became like those of an octopus, because they were all over Karen's body faster than she could push them away.

Having enough of him, Karen reared back and slapped him hard in the face. She opened her door and got out of the car. Dennis was furious. His eyes were almost closed as he tried to speak. No words came out, though, for he began vomiting.

Karen stared at him from her safe spot outside. She curled her lip up. "You're disgusting and pathetic!" With that, she slammed the door in his face, then began walking to the concession in hopes of finding another ride back to campus.

Back in Brad's car, Tina was having her own struggle. She knew the time would come when Brad would make a pass at her. They had been dating on and off in the past month, and he was human. Tina knew the time would arrive, and now it was here. He had been stroking the back of her neck with his hand, slowly but firmly massaging her stiff muscles until she became relaxed. When he felt that she was no longer afraid, he took her chin in his hand, and tilted her face up. Very gently, he kissed her lips. Tina almost shivered when he kissed her. His lips were so soft—like velvet! His kiss was not like those high school kisses that she'd received—wet, inexperienced kisses. His was one that spoke of gentleness and seriousness. When their lips parted, Tina stared at him, stunned. It was dark, but she could feel his breath on her face. She feared what might happen, what the next kiss might lead to. Panic began to creep up her body. Brad leaned over to kiss her again when she noticed a familiar figure walking towards the concession stand. Though it was obscure, Tina recognized the profile, the confident strut. The lights from the concession began to reflect the golden mane on the figure.

Tina let Brad's lips meet hers again. She tried to forget Karen—tried to ignore the questions that were forming in her mind about why her friend was at the drive-in and with whom.

Against her will, she found herself kissing Brad back. He began to moan, his hand moving up her jacket. The moment the zipper had caught the first notch, an image flashed in her mind. It was the face of the one who she cared for, but who did not love her back. Tina became alarmed. She thought if she made love to Brad, then her chance for Kevin would be lost forever. She'd never try to split her friends up, but if he ever left Karen, he'd think she had a steady guy. Her thoughts scrambled unreasonably, and her virgin body panicked. She grabbed Brad's hand, and he looked at her, shocked. His eyes questioned her, and she almost wanted to cry.

"Brad," she simply said, "I can't."

He looked stunned, then embarrassed. "I'm sorry, Tina. I wasn't trying to scare you."

Tina held back her tears. He was still the same considerate person as always.

"Please don't hate me," she whispered.

He nodded, sitting there silently.

"I need some time to think," Tina explained. "I saw Karen at the concession stand. I want to ride home with her."

She got out of his car, slowly, feeling like a child. Before she closed his door, she leaned back in and said, "It's not you; it's me."

Brad stared in disbelief as she walked away. He was too hurt to stay and finish watching the movie, so he started his car and left.

Tina didn't find Karen at the concession stand, so she went around the corner to the restrooms. Inside, she found Karen, brushing her hair in front of the mirror.

Karen's eyes registered surprise and happiness upon seeing Tina. "I didn't know you and Brad were coming *here*!" she exclaimed. "I'm lucky—now I have a way back to our place!"

Tina's face fell. "I don't have a way to the dorm," she confessed. "I just walked out on my ride."

Karen's eyebrows came together. "What happened?" she asked.

The tears of fear and embarrassment, held for so long, now fell. "Oh, Karen," she wailed, "I've made such a fool of myself tonight!"

Karen smiled sympathetically, then put her arm around Tina.

"It'll be OK," she promised. "The first time is frightening."

"How did you know what I was talking about?" Tina questioned, wiping the tears off her face with the back of her hand.

"I've been there, friend," Karen said. "I put sex off for so long with my first boyfriend! I kept telling him that I had my period. He finally figured out that my "period" was lasting two weeks at a time! I was just scared—that's all."

Tina managed a smile, then asked, "How far is it to the dorm?"

Karen speculated. "About half a mile. You want to walk?"

Tina laughed despite herself. "We don't have much choice, do we?"

Karen grinned and shook her head. She put her arm around Tina's shoulder, and hugged her, her blonde head resting momentarily on her shoulder. She eventually let go, then together they walked out into the darkness.

*   *   *

The following Monday, Tina saw Brad. She was behind the serving line in the cafeteria when she saw him coming up behind the other students. Well, what did she expect? He had to eat, so they were bound to face each other again.

When he finally stood before her, her eyes were downcast, and the blood was slowly rising to her cheeks.

"We need to talk," he said in a whisper.

Tina stared into his serious eyes, then nodded.

"Meet me back here at four o' clock," she told him.

"OK, now let me have some of that," he said pointing to an interesting looking casserole.

"*That* is beef," Tina told him. "Nobody's figured it out yet."

He grinned as she scooped up a generous portion into his plate, then he slowly made his way down the aisle behind the other hungry students.

Tina quickly blinked away tears, managed a smile, and said to the next person who was pointing, "Yeah, that's chicken. Yes, it looks kind of dry. How about the beef?"

At the end of a long table at the far end of the cafeteria, Karen and Kevin were eating lunch. Karen was quietly picking at her food, while she was listening to Kevin talk almost nonstop. He swallowed another large amount of food, and continued his conversation.

"So you see, Cindi was just standing there checking out these customers—she's been working there five years. Anyway, I was bagging groceries for her, when her boyfriend came in. He was raging mad! He stood in front of her, and asked her if she'd been seeing someone else. She denied it, then he shoved this picture in front of her eyes—I didn't see it until he left. Well, she turned red in the face, and he cussed her out, grabbed her hand, and jerked the ring off of her finger. He yelled that the wedding was off, then he stormed out of the place!"

"What'd Cindi do?" Karen asked.

Kevin frowned. "She just burst into tears, and ran to the back of the store. She left her customers standing there. Another cashier had to take care of them. Anyway, I found the picture; it was laying on the floor. I guess her boyfriend must have dropped it in his hurry to get out. I looked at it, and it was her and some guy at a party. She was half-dressed, sitting on his lap, while he had his hands on her breasts. They looked pretty drunk. They probably didn't remember anyone taking a picture!"

"I wonder how her boyfriend got that picture?" Karen pondered.

Kevin shrugged, then put another bite of food into his mouth.

"Who knows?" he mumbled. "That relationship is over, anyway; Cindi blew it."

"Oh, Kevin," Karen grumbled. "You sound just like a gossip magazine. Who says that they won't work things out?"

Kevin looked up from his plate, stunned. When he spoke, he had authority in his voice, and fire in his eyes.

"How do I know? One word can sum it up—pride. That's the one thing a fellow has, that once it's been crushed, it's almost impossible to mend. A woman can talk hateful to her man. She can spend all his money, and treat him like dirt. He'll put up with it most of the time, because he loves her. If she cheats on him, though, that's a totally different story. When she does that, she's saying that her man's not good enough for her—that's she's not satisfied. I believe the same would hold true for a woman, if her man cheated on her."

Karen chose her words carefully, "So what you're saying is that when someone is caught fooling around with someone else, it's over?"

Kevin nodded solemnly, then answered, "Yes."

*   *   *

At five minutes before four, Brad entered the cafeteria. He glanced at the long rows of empty tables and chairs. It was so much different now! The only sign of life was the sound of dishes, clinking against one other in the kitchen. Brad walked over to the double doors that led to the kitchen, but the small windows on the swinging doors revealed nothing. He turned around, then went to a table by one of the lunchroom windows. He sat on the table, and stared outside. The late October sun shone on the deep green grass. In the background, the last leaves on the trees beckoned him. They seemed to call out, "Look at us! Enjoy us while you can! We'll soon be gone, and the ugly nakedness of the trees will be before you!"

He took in a deep breath, sucking in the air slowly. As he exhaled, he turned his head, and saw Tina standing there. A beam of sunlight came through the window, gleaming on her. Her hair, free of the ponytail holder, brushed softly against her moist face. Her make-up was slightly faded, but it only made her brown eyes stand out more. They focused on Brad, and he was momentarily lost. Not being able to stare any longer, she turned her head to look out of the window, breaking the spell.

"Here," Brad said, as he got off the table, and pulled out a chair for her, "sit down."

Tina quietly sat down, watching as he took a seat beside of her. She opened her mouth to speak, but he put his finger to her lips.

"Shhh," he whispered.

She smiled, and sat back to hear what he had to say.

"Look," he began, "I don't force myself on anybody. I never have, but how can you tell when someone's ready for sex, unless you try? I guess I should have asked you, but it's hard for me to talk sometimes. I guess what I'm trying to say is that I don't rush things. If you're not ready, that's OK. I just didn't want to look like a jerk to you. That's why I had to come here and set things straight. If it was someone else, it wouldn't matter as much, but you're special to me. Did any of that make sense? I'd hate to sound like an idiot!"

"Oh, Brad," Tina answered. "You don't sound like an idiot! You're very considerate, and I really appreciate it! I don't know what my problem is; maybe I'm just scared. Let's just forget the other night, and keep things like they were. I know that you date different people. I do too, but you're my favorite."

"All it would take for me to stop seeing others is one word from you," Brad said. He was now holding both of her hands in his, trying to fight his desire to kiss her.

"I know that, Brad."

He got up, carefully releasing her hands. "I'll give you some time. If you need me, you know where to reach me. Is the Christmas dance still on, though?"

"Oh, yes," Tina exclaimed. "I promised you that two weeks ago!"

"Well, then, it's settled," Brad said. He turned and walked out of the cafeteria. Outwardly he was bold and sure of himself, but inside, small pangs of rejection stung him. His pride kept him from breaking their date to the Christmas dance. Maybe she would come around by then, and accept him more. Tina was like fire and ice. She could physically be there with him, but her mind and her heart always seemed to be somewhere else. To reach her heart was like struggling through a blizzard. He just hoped that he would not freeze before he arrived there.

CHAPTER EIGHT

IT WAS HALLOWEEN. TREES REACHED up with naked branches towards a sky filled with clouds. Every once in a while, the sun would break through, attempting to warm the frigid air, but would not succeed. The atmosphere was cold, with a chilling wind that whipped through clothes. Only those who wore very heavy coats were protected, but then their faces caught the onslaught of the chill.

The days were short now, proving that summer was definitely over. The nights, however, were often alive with a brilliant display of stars. They twinkled merrily to an ever dwindling audience. Tonight they would be hidden by the clouds, but they would return, shining as bright as ever.

In the dorms, Halloween decorations were plastered all over doors and walls. Everything was decorated in the traditional orange and black. Streamers also hung from the ceiling, with paper ghosts dangling.

A Halloween party had been planned. It was to be held in one of the houses on the campus. It was a place mainly used for orientations or receptions. The home had originally belonged to the founder of the college. Through the years, it had seen many faculty families come and go. Now it was almost empty, except for a few basic pieces of furniture and folding chairs.

That evening, Tina watched Karen as she got dressed for the party.

"Tina, help me with my ears," Karen said. She was standing in front of the dresser mirror, a small pout forming on her vanilla complexion.

Tina stopped what she was doing, then stood behind Karen to help her put on her cat ears. She looked so sexy in her costume, that Tina couldn't help being jealous. A black leotard hugged the curvaceous body. Though it was not low cut, the tightness of it pressed against Karen's firm breasts, pushing them up slightly. Her necklace slithered down to a sensual cleavage. Black silk stockings caressed her legs, accentuating the high-heeled black pumps. The only thing that looked odd was the long furry tail attached to the back of her leotard.

Tina heard a giggle, then looked up, embarrassed. Karen had been watching her!

"I'm sorry for staring," Tina said quickly. "It's just that your costume is so nice—you look amazing."

"I like your costume, too," Karen admitted.

Tina managed to say 'thanks', but deep inside, she was beginning to feel very childish in her ballerina costume. In the beginning, it had seemed the perfect thing to wear. The leotard was a pale pink with matching stockings. The tutu was ankle length, decorated with pink and clear sequins. It stopped just inches above satiny pink slippers. Her hair was worn up in a ball, with soft brown strands gracefully falling on each side of her face. Now Tina thought that she looked so stupid.

"I should have worn something sexier," she grumbled.

"You look sexy in that," Karen said.

"Yeah, right," Tina mumbled.

"You do, so quit complaining," Karen ordered. "Anyway, I'm sure Brad will like it!"

"Yeah, maybe he will," Tina said hopefully. For one fleeting moment, she felt pretty, but then she glanced at Karen again. She was no match for the vision of perfection standing before her. Sighing, she sat on the bed, waiting for Brad.

*   *   *

Tina was still waiting when Karen left with Kevin. Getting up off the bed, she strolled over to the dresser where Karen had just stood moments ago. Makeup was scattered all over, and Tina picked up one of the lipsticks. It was a dark, creamy raspberry color that Karen wore frequently. Tina carefully applied it to her own lips, then she closed her eyes. She imagined Kevin kissing her with that lipstick on herself. The daydream was beautiful, but when the kiss ended, it was Karen's face that she saw, instead of Kevin's. Tina snapped back to reality, guilt overcoming her. Roughly, she wiped away the lipstick with a tissue. It, like Kevin, belonged to Karen. She had no right to touch it.

There was a knock at the door, and when Tina opened it, Brad stood there, smiling.

"Come in," Tina said. "I've got to get my coat."

"Before you do, let me know how this looks," Brad said, taking off his jacket.

Tina looked at Brad, stunned. He was dressed like a pirate, with scarlet pants, black belt, and black boots. On his chest he wore nothing but a black leather vest. She'd never seen him like that before, with so little on. It frightened, yet excited her at the same time. His chest, sporting a small amount of raven hair, teased her from beneath the leather. Around his forehead, he wore a red bandanna, with his hair tousled playfully about it.

Tina was still standing there when Brad spoke.

"Well, say something. Do you like it?"

Tina snapped back to reality. "Oh, yes, I do—you look good in that!"

Brad laughed in relief. "Well, let's go; I'm ready to party!"

As Tina got her coat out of the closet, he called out, "I'm glad you called me. I think this party is a great idea!"

Tina joined him. "I just felt so weird about the last time we went out—"

Brad put his finger to her lips. "Let's not talk about that."

Tina nodded, then they left the dorm. Along the way, they passed all kinds of creatures and monsters. A lot of the girls seemed to be going as cats, also.

"You'd look good in one of those costumes," Brad said, when they'd passed the fifth cat.

Tina looked down at her dress. "You don't like what I'm wearing, do you?"

"Oh, yes, I do. You're so pretty, that if you were in a cat costume, you'd put all those other girls to shame."

Tina blushed, but she doubted that she could put others to shame, especially Karen. She was about to comment, when someone growled and jumped out of the bushes. Tina screamed, and Brad raised his fist up. The prankster was one of Brad's friends, dressed like a werewolf. He took off his mask, laughing. "I scared the crap out of you!" he cried.

"Yeah, but I was about to *beat* the crap out of you," Brad retorted.

The "werewolf's" eyes grew large. He looked at the moon and howled.

"I gotta go, friend and ballerina. There are more people to scare!" He put his mask back on, then turned on his heels to find more unsuspecting students.

Tina held her hand to her breast. "Let's keep away from the bushes."

Brad nodded, and they walked away from the bushes, and closer to the lights. Luckily there were no more werewolf "attacks".

When they arrived at the house, they could hear music blaring. People who had already gotten drunk were outside hanging onto the staircase railings. Outside, a monster was chasing two girls dressed as witches. The girls screamed with delight, as others standing nearby, laughed.

Some couples were already leaving for their cars or dorms, so they could get laid. Tina imagined that there would be a lot of that going on tonight. She wondered where Karen and Kevin would end up, but then pushed the thought out of her mind.

Once inside, Tina looked around the room for her two friends. She and Brad weaved in and out of the crowd, but still could not find them. Finally they just resorted to going to the refreshment table. Among cookies, cake, chips, cheese, and meat, stood an enormous bowl of punch. Naturally it was spiked. Tina winced as she took a sip, and Brad laughed at her.

"Powerful, isn't it?" he asked.

"I think they left the punch out," Tina agreed.

Brad laughed again. He put his arm around Tina. "Let's dance," he suggested.

Tina finished the rest of her drink, enjoying the warm sensation that was beginning to envelop her. She went with Brad to a spot in the living room, and they began to dance. People were dancing in just about every room, their bodies bringing forth a pleasant warmth to the place. There were a few lights on, but they were very dim. Most of the light came from candles which were placed randomly all over the house. Here and there, jack-o-lanterns grinned at them with fiery eyes and crooked mouths.

They had been dancing for some time, when Brad suggested they go back for another drink. Tina followed him to the refreshment table. She was not one to drink much, but when Brad offered her another drink, she accepted. The second drink did not seem as powerful as the first, for her mouth was growing numb.

As she tilted her glass up for a second swallow, she spotted them. They were dancing in a corner, Kevin the vampire, and Karen the black cat. Tina stared with growing jealousy as Kevin tipped Karen back a little to bite her neck. As he pulled her back up, she laughed with the confidence of the most beautiful person in the world. Tina clenched her teeth, seething inside. The alcohol made her feel bolder. Brad watched with wide eyes as she quickly gulped down the rest of her drink. He followed Tina's eyes, then spotted Karen and Kevin, also.

"There are your friends! I figured they'd decided not to come. Let's go talk to them!"

Tina nodded. She really didn't feel like seeing them now, but the alcohol helped her to be more confident. She took Brad by the hand, and held her head up.

In the corner, Karen was getting another bite on her neck. She laughed with delight, her eyes closed and her mouth opened sensually. When she opened her eyes, she saw Brad and Tina standing there. Embarrassed, she blushed, then tapped Kevin on the shoulder. He stopped biting, blushing as well. Karen straightened her cat ears, smiling.

"Hi Tina! Hi Brad!"

They exchanged greetings, then Karen grabbed Tina's hand. "Let's go to the bathroom," she said.

Tina had no chance to answer, for Karen was leading her to the bathroom. They went in, and Karen laughed. "What took you so long?" she asked.

"I had to wait on Brad," Tina answered. "Besides, I didn't see you getting laid in the corner until just now."

Karen put on a look of mock innocence. "Me get laid *here*? No way—but when we get out of here, he's mine!"

Tina cringed inwardly, mad with jealously at the thought of Karen making love to Kevin. She managed a phony grin, though, and commented, "So you're finally dedicated; that's good."

Once again Karen looked at Tina. "No, I'm not exactly dedicated. As a matter of fact, I'm pretty booked up next week."

Tina let out an exasperated sigh. "Karen, why don't you just give it up? You know if Kevin finds out, it'll be over!" She was surprised at her own boldness.

Karen checked herself in the mirror, then turned around and smiled at Tina.

"He won't find out, now will he?" she questioned. She kissed Tina on the cheek, and went out the bathroom door, swaying to the music.

Tina leaned on the vanity, staring at herself in the mirror. She was just as guilty as Karen. She knew what Karen did, yet she kept her mouth shut. How could she tell Kevin, though? It would break his heart! The situation was hopeless. She put her head down, shaking it slowly, then turned around to leave the room.

When she found Brad, the music had a slow tempo. They found a comfortable spot, and began dancing. As they did, Brad held her close, his arms firm about her, making her feel secure. Through her leotard, she could feel the warmth of his chest. She relaxed, laying her head against his shoulder, inhaling the familiar scent of his cologne. It filled her lungs pleasantly, returning to be inhaled again. When her lips accidentally brushed against his neck, she licked them. They felt moist and tasted salty. Tina felt Brad's hold on her get a little tighter, pressing her closer to him. All of a sudden, she became aware of his whole body. His thighs pressed firmly against her, causing her to feel a hardness she'd never felt before. It sent burning sensations to her most sensitive areas, and tingles up and down her spine. With gentle strokes, he ran his fingers up and down her bare back, until she felt overcome with desire. On impulse, she tilted her head up, kissing him passionately. The kiss took him by surprise, and he returned it with a great hunger. It was as if he had weathered the storm of the past few weeks, and had finally reached his destination.

When the song ended, he was so afraid of breaking the spell, that he took her by the hand, leading her to the front door. Their coats were lost in a huge pile of other coats. As Brad searched for them, Tina went back to the table, and had yet other drink.

They went to Brad's dorm. It was so empty and silent, that they walked softly to preserve the peacefulness. He opened the door to his room, and led her inside. After he had locked the door, he turned to her. Holding her face in his hands, he stared at her passionately. She closed her eyes as he kissed her again. When the kiss ended, she opened her eyes, looking at him nervously.

"I'm afraid," she whispered.

He leaned over and turned on a small lamp, then shut off the overhead light. "There's nothing to be afraid of," he assured her.

Tina let him kiss her again, but when he put his hands on her shoulders, she grew stiff. "Brad, I've never—."

He kissed her on the neck. "I know," he said. "It's OK; I've got what we need. There's nothing to worry about. Just go along with your feelings."

He stood back, holding her by the shoulders, "I won't hurt you," he promised.

Tina nodded, and closed her eyes. Brad kissed her emotionally as he undressed her. When her breasts were revealed, Tina grew stiff again, so he turned off the small light. She relaxed again while he peeled off the rest of her clothes. She let him lay her in his bed, and waited as he got undressed. When he was naked, also, he gently laid on top of her, embracing her. They began kissing again, and he touched her in places no one had ever touched before. The different feelings confused and excited her. She was afraid to touch him, but she finally got the courage to do so. He was warm, yet strong and firm.

Suddenly a vision of Kevin's face flashed before her, making her realize that she wished it was him there, instead of Brad. As Brad entered her, she tried to push the vision out of her mind. Brad moved gently, careful not to hurt her. When he was completely inside, they moved together slowly and quietly. Kevin's face had disappeared for the time being, and they kissed passionately, moving in unison, until their points of desire had been reached.

Afterwards, they lay there together, Brad stroking her hair.

"Are you OK?" he asked.

"Yes," Tina said, but she wasn't sure. She got up and began dressing.

"Let me walk you to your dorm," Brad said. He sat up to get dressed, but Tina shook her head.

"No," she said, "I can manage. I'll be OK."

"Are you sure?" he questioned. "It's so late."

"Brad, I'll be alright, really."

He sat there, afraid to argue with her. She was like an untamed animal. He'd finally gotten her close to him, and he feared that if he was too aggressive, she'd run. If that happened, he knew he'd never have her again. With great difficulty, he sat there while she finished getting dressed. When she had her coat on, she came to him.

"Goodnight," she whispered, as she kissed him once more.

"Goodnight, Tina," he responded, hiding the longing in his voice.

He watched as she left his room, then he lay down to try and sleep. He had an odd feeling, though, that tonight was the first and the last time Tina would ever make love to him.

*　　*　　*

Tina ran all the way to her dorm. To her relief, Karen wasn't back yet. She stripped off her clothes, then got into the shower. She washed and washed, but something didn't feel right. For some reason, guilt covered her. It seemed as though she had given herself to the wrong person, though at the time it had seemed right. Should she have waited for Kevin? That was so stupid, though; he'd never want her! She wept quietly as the water ran over her body. Confusion, along with too much alcohol, overwhelmed her, making her feel nauseous.

As she got out of the shower to dry herself, she heard Karen come in. Not wanting to look like an idiot, she tried to gain some composure. She looked at herself in the mirror, polishing her smile. It didn't fool her, but perhaps Karen would fall for it.

When she stepped out of the bathroom, she found Karen laying face down on her bed.

"Karen?" Tina called out, concerned.

"Please just let me die," Karen begged.

"What's wrong?" Tina cried.

"The room's spinning, Tina. Make it stop!"

Tina laughed. "We'd both better get some sleep. I think that's the only thing that's going to help us at this point!"

Karen started wailing, "I *can't* sleep!"

"Why?" Tina asked.

"Because I gotta pee!"

Tina grinned, then helped Karen to the bathroom. Afterwards, she helped her friend get ready for bed. As soon as Karen's head hit the pillow, she was asleep.

Tina went to lay in her own bed. The room was spinning for her, also, and she feared she would vomit. Even when she closed her eyes, she still felt as though she was moving in circles. Finally precious sleep came to her, and the spinning stopped.

They slept late the next morning, but woke up with tremendous headaches. Karen offered to run to the cafeteria and get some coffee and doughnuts. On her way out, she found an envelope by the door with Tina's name on it. Curious, she handed it to Tina, watching as she opened it. Inside was the red bandanna that Brad had worn the night before. Tina smiled, putting it to her face. It still bore his scent, and she closed her eyes in reminiscence.

Karen frowned. "Why the heck would he want to give you *that*?"

Tina gently held the cloth, smiling. "Who knows?"

"Wait a minute!" Karen cried. "You're not saying what I think you're saying, are you?"

"I didn't say anything!" Tina teased.

"You didn't have to," Karen pointed out. "Did you really do it?"

Tina blushed scarlet, and nodded.

"Well, I can't believe it! How do you feel?"

"I don't know, really," Tina confessed. "I mean, he was wonderful, but it wasn't the magic I'd hoped for."

Karen rolled her eyes. "That sounds typical, coming from you. Well congratulations, friend. When I come back with the coffee, you can tell me all the details!"

*   *   *

In the days that followed, Tina began to distance herself from Brad. She didn't know why, exactly, except for the fact that a serious relationship with him frightened her. It made her feel bad, but she didn't know how to put her feelings into words. Instead, she had to bear with the disappointment in his eyes whenever they saw each other. Then there were the endless questions from Brad. Did she feel that they had gone too fast? Was she OK? Did she feel like going out again? The list seemed to go on and on until it made her head spin. She just needed some time to get her head together, but she couldn't seem to get the courage to tell him.

One day the phone rang, and Karen answered it.

"No, Brad, Tina's not here," she lied, following her roommate's orders. "Yes, I'll tell her that you called."

She hung up the phone, then turned to Tina, who was sitting on the bed, studying.

"Do you mind telling me what's going on?" she asked, exasperated.

Tina shrugged. "I don't know exactly what it is," she answered. "It's been two weeks since that party, and he's calling me all the time! If I see him, he asks me so many questions! I'm not used to that, especially with someone I don't really love."

Karen's eyes grew large.

"I thought that you two made it," Karen said.

"We did," Tina replied. "I thought that I cared for him, but now I don't know. Maybe I did it because I was drunk—I just don't know! I'm so confused!"

"Tell Brad how you feel," Karen cried. "Don't go around playing with his feelings!"

Tina jumped off of the bed and stood directly in front of Karen. In her eyes was a look of pure hatred.

"How dare you judge me!" she snapped. "You play with Kevin's feelings all the time, yet you stand here and condemn me!" Her hands were clenched into tight fists, and there was a snarl on her face. "You're sick!" she shouted, then she started for the door.

"Well, you're stupid!" Karen shouted after her. As the door slammed, she added, "You're giving up a good thing!"

CHAPTER NINE

KEVIN BAGGED WHAT SEEMED TO be his thousandth bag of groceries. He looked up at the clock on the wall with great impatience. The minutes seemed to drag by sometimes, especially today. It was Saturday, and since he didn't have classes, he worked eight hours at the store. Tonight he would go out with Karen. Tomorrow he would study most of the day. Monday would come all too soon, with his hectic class schedule back in full swing.

He put the last item in an older woman's shopping cart, smiling as though he genuinely enjoyed his job. Charmed, she returned the smile, and walked out of the store as Kevin followed her, pushing the cart. He started a conversation in which she happily joined.

Back in the store, two girls stood where the older woman had been just moments before. Kevin hadn't even noticed them, but the cashier had. They looked like trouble, and she immediately formed a dislike for them.

One was a tall, slim girl with a boyish figure. She had long, lean arms and legs, small breasts, and just the tiniest bit of a rear. Her hair was cut very short, and was parted on the side. It was very light brown, silky hair, which lifted gently with each breeze that passed through it. Her features were beautiful. She had alabaster skin set off with large brown eyes. Her lips were perfectly round and full, her nose short and pointed. She could have easily been a model, for she had that look about her: the confidence, the body, and the aura. For whatever reason, though, she was not. Perhaps she had yet to be "discovered".

The girl standing beside her was shorter and heavier, though not fat. She was very firm, and somewhat muscular. One could tell that she was into bodybuilding, though not at a professional level. Her hair was raven black, tumbling down her back in numerous curls. Emerald eyes stared from below thick, black eyebrows. She was a pretty girl, with a bad attitude, who mainly kept company with the taller girl.

The lofty girl, Hope, glanced in the direction that Kevin had taken with the older woman. "I wouldn't mind going out with that, Allison."

Allison grinned mischievously, nodding in approval, but the cashier interrupted their thoughts.

"That boy's taken," she said. "He dates this gorgeous blonde at the college."

Hope turned up her nose and handed the girl her money. "Honey," she replied sarcastically, "that's *never* stopped me before!"

The check-out girl practically snatched the money, then almost slammed the change back in Hope's hand. She glared at them as they walked out of the store, laughing with annoying confidence.

*   *   *

As the situation usually goes with friends, Karen and Tina were on speaking terms within a couple of days. On a particular afternoon that November, Karen, Kevin, and Tina were walking across the campus after lunch. Karen looked up, then motioned discreetly to Kevin and Tina.

"Do you see those two girls over there by the library?" she asked. "They sure are staring. Do either of you know them?"

Kevin squinted his eyes. He shook his head.

"They don't look familiar to me."

"That shorter girl looks like one I've seen at 'The Center'," Tina commented. "As a matter of fact, I'm sure that's her. She's *weird*! All she does is work out and give everyone dirty looks!"

"Maybe she wants to beat you up," Karen joked.

Tina rolled her eyes, then laughed. "I'd like to see her try!"

Up by the library, Hope watched with jealous eyes as Kevin and the girls walked out of sight.

"I want him," she said, more to herself, than to Allison.

Allison snickered. "You don't stand a chance in hell! That girlfriend of his has him right where she wants him!"

Hope's face lit with anger, and she slapped Allison with the back of her hand.

"Look," she hissed, "I've helped you before when you wanted somebody! You'll help me now!"

Allison resisted the temptation to rub her sore arm, and grinned instead.

"Sure, Hope," she promised. "I'll help you."

*   *   *

Two days before Thanksgiving break, Karen walked into the room to find Tina crying quietly. Concern overcame her, as she rushed to the bed and sat down beside of her friend.

"What's wrong?" she asked softly, putting a protective arm around her roommate.

"Today I saw Brad," she sobbed. "He was with this other girl! I knew that I was pushing him away, but I didn't think it would bother me when he gave up. I just saw him, and something happened inside of me! I was so mad and hurt—she was so *pretty*, too!"

Karen nodded in understanding. "Sometimes things aren't special until we lose them," she explained. "He was a good person, but you weren't really happy. There are so many guys here! This is college—the perfect place to meet guys! I know it doesn't mean much now, but you'll find another one—maybe one that makes you *really* happy."

Tina dabbed at her eyes with a crumpled pink tissue. She nodded in agreement, then went to the bathroom to refresh herself. When she came out, Karen was packing things into a small suitcase. Karen was silently debating between a pink nightgown and a white pajama set. Indecision clouded her face, until finally she shoved both items into her bag. Glancing up at Tina, she smiled.

"What are you doing for Thanksgiving?" she asked.

Tina shifted on her feet uneasily. She put her head down in mild embarrassment.

"I'm staying here," she answered. "Since I'll be flying to Florida for Christmas to see my aunt, I can't afford to leave now."

Karen's face lit up with excitement.

"Come spend Thanksgiving with me at my parents' house!" she cried.

Tina shook her head.

"Oh, Karen, thanks a lot, but I can't! That's a time for the family to be together! I'd feel so bad if I intruded!"

"You *are* family—as of now," Karen said. "Now pack your suitcase. You won't need much; it's only a 30 minute drive, and we'll only be gone for a few days. I'm not about to let you stay here and eat that crap in the cafeteria on a holiday!"

Tina opened her mouth to protest.

"Now!" Karen ordered her.

In happy defeat, Tina started packing.

*　　*　　*

Back at Kevin's dorm, all the fellows were getting ready for their holiday. Some were packing; others were already leaving. The happy sounds of good-byes and good wishes echoed throughout the whole dorm. Pranksters had decorated the dorm in various ways, including a life size cardboard cutout of a turkey holding a beer.

Kevin was almost finished packing. His house was closer to the college than Karen's, so he wasn't in much of a hurry. He looked over at his roommate Alan. Alan was sitting on his unmade bed, finishing a bag of peanut butter cookies. Kevin shook his head.

"Alan, if you were a turkey, you'd be the first one they'd shoot! The way you eat, it's a wonder you can walk!"

Alan had a mouthful of cookies, and as he spoke, crumbs fell out of his mouth and onto his bed.

"If I had somebody like Karen to impress, I'd still eat a lot. Food's important—like good sex!"

Kevin laughed.

"When was the last time you had good sex?" he asked.

Alan straightened up proudly.

"I had excellent sex last week with Amy Parker," he answered.

"Amy Parker?" Kevin echoed. "Who's that?"

"This girl from my Grammar and Comp 1 class. She likes me a lot—I think."

"So does everybody else," Kevin admitted. "I was just kidding about you being a turkey. Nobody would shoot you."

"What do you mean nobody would shoot me?" Alan asked in alarm.

Kevin shut the lid on his suitcase.

"Give me a break, man," he said, laughing.

Alan laughed also, then went back to eating his cookies as Kevin left the room.

*   *   *

Tina and Karen talked so much during the ride, that before they knew it, they were pulling up in the circular driveway. Tina stared in wide eyed wonder at the house Karen had grown up in. It was so beautiful! The massive two-story English Tudor home loomed above them. It was surrounded by clusters of gigantic blue spruces and bare oak trees. In the yard, a gazebo beckoned invitingly, and nearby a large wooden swing awaited some company.

"This is so beautiful!" Tina finally managed to say.

"It is," Karen agreed. As she sat back in her car, she stared at the house. It wasn't until now that she realized just how much she'd missed it. Eagerly, she opened the door, and Tina did the same. Karen opened the trunk, while Tina still gazed at the lovely house.

"I can't imagine living in something so beautiful," she confessed.

Karen smiled. "It's all I've known; I've lived here all my life."

"I hope I don't get lost in there," Tina joked.

"If you do," Karen said, "just yell very loudly. Somebody will find you!"

Tina laughed, as they walked up the stone walkway to the front door. Karen put down her suitcase, and fumbled for the key.

"Aren't your parents home?" Tina asked.

Karen shook her head.

"Not yet," she answered. "They'll be home from work in a few hours."

Karen opened the door, and the two of them went in. The inside was even more amazing than the outside. The hallway had a marble floor, with tall houseplants lining either side. There were rooms to the sides of them, and as far as Tina could see, there were even more rooms stretching on almost endlessly. Oil paintings, enhanced by the light of a chandelier, decorated the hallway. Tina stood there open mouthed, wishing she could drop her things, and just go exploring.

Before she could share her thoughts with Karen, an older woman came racing towards them, her arms outstretched.

"Karen, darling," she cried, "I didn't hear you come in!"

Tina watched as the woman embraced Karen, her arms around the girl, as if she'd never let go. Tina stifled a giggle as she took in the scene. The woman was wearing a plain gray shirt dress with an apron. In one hand she held a feather duster, which was all but hitting Karen in the face. Her hair was brown, with plenty of gray, and she had the most pleasant face. It was round, with high cheekbones, which held the lightest trace of pink. Her hazel eyes sparkled, as she beamed while holding Karen.

When she finally let go, Karen laughed and motioned to Tina.

"Tina," she said, "this is Emily. She's been our housekeeper for as long as I can remember. She got me out of a lot of trouble when I was small!"

"Emily, this is Tina, my roommate and my best friend from college."

Emily smiled brightly, then hugged Tina as if she'd known her for years, also.

"It's wonderful to meet you, Darling!" she cried. "You look so sweet! I'm glad my Karen's made a good friend in college; I was very worried about her being away from home! Her friends from high school went off in so many different directions, that I was afraid she'd be lonely!"

"Emily, I've got Kevin, too, remember?" Karen teased.

"Of course, dear," Emily admitted, "but it's important to have a good girlfriend, as well."

Karen kissed the housekeeper on the cheek. "We're going to go upstairs, and get unpacked now. I'll talk to you more in a while, OK?"

"Oh, how silly of me," the woman answered. "Yes, go upstairs; your room's ready for you."

Karen and Tina smiled at each other as Emily followed them to the bottom of the stairs.

"If there's anything you girls need, let me know!" she called out after them.

Karen answered with a wave of her hand.

"She's unusual," Tina commented, as they went up.

"That's Emily for you," Karen agreed. "She's one of a kind."

When they reached Karen's room, Tina gasped. The place was a rectangular array of peach, accentuated by bright floral draperies. In the center of the room lay a queen-sized canopy bed, covered with a matching floral bedspread and overstuffed pillows. A large white teddy bear grinned at them from his place between the pillows.

White dressers, on which various keepsakes rested, complimented the bed. There were also pictures on the dressers, mostly of Karen and Kevin. Tina glanced at those, but her eyes rested on one with a little girl in a frilly dress. Tina knew who the blonde haired child was without asking, and she smiled at the innocent girl in the small frame.

"You were always beautiful," she whispered in amazement.

"What?" Karen called from across the room. She'd already started unpacking, and was unaware of what Tina had said.

"Nothing—just talking to myself," Tina answered.

Her attention was diverted from the picture to a bay window at the side of the room. It was large, maybe five feet long, and had a place to sit for gazing outside. Tina strolled over to the window and looked out.

Karen joined her friend, then glanced outside, also. She could remember many hours sitting by that same window, reading a book, or just staring at the beautiful yard below.

"It's breathtaking, Karen!" Tina commented.

Karen nodded in agreement. She pointed to the swing that they'd seen earlier.

"Let's go out there," Tina begged.

A childish twinkle lit up Karen's eyes.

"OK," she replied.

They ran down the stairs like two frenzied teenagers, laughing, trying to see who would reach the bottom of the stairs first. Tina got there before Karen, and was about to make a beeline for the front door, when Karen grabbed her by the arm.

"Come here first," she said.

Karen led Tina to the kitchen, where she poured each of them a tall glass of milk. Then she went to the familiar cookie jar—the blue ceramic teddy bear. Its color was faded, and one of the ears was chipped.

Karen pulled the top off, and retrieved a handful of chocolate chip cookies.

"These are my favorite," she explained. "I told Mom to be sure they would be here before I was! I can be really grouchy if I don't have my chocolate chip cookies on hand!"

Tina laughed. "I'll be sure to stock up on some when we get back to the dorm!" she promised.

"Won't do any good," Karen said, inhaling the delicious scent of fresh baked cookies. "Nothing's as good as homemade."

"Well, I'll just have to borrow Inez's oven, and bake my own!"

"You do that, Tina, and I'll be the perfect roommate!" Karen joked.

They strolled outside into the cool, late autumn air. Everything was quiet, except for an occasional whistling of the wind through the trees.

"It's so peaceful here," Tina said, as they reached the swing and sat down. They finished their cookies in happy silence, enjoying the laid back atmosphere away from college. As they were finishing the last of their milk, Karen asked the question that had been on her mind for so long.

"What happened to your parents, Tina?"

Tina's usually bright eyes clouded, and she was silent for a moment, trying to summon the words that were still so hard to speak.

Karen noticed the change in Tina, and was immediately sorry for prying.

"I'm sorry, Tina. I shouldn't have asked that; it's none of my business."

Tina blinked away tears, then gathered herself together. She managed a smile, despite the pain.

"It's OK," she answered. "I'm just not used to talking about it. You see, they died when I was very young, about twelve years old. They had gone away for the weekend—just the two of them. It was supposed to be like a second honeymoon. On the way back, they were hit by a truck driver who'd fallen asleep at the wheel."

A single tear rolled down her cheek. Even now, years later, it still hurt so much!

"The highway patrol said that they died instantly."

Karen sat there in an uncomfortable silence.

"I'm sorry," she said.

Tina smiled, then wiped her face with the back of her hand.

"Let's talk about something else," she suggested.

Karen looked up thoughtfully. "What do you want to talk about?"

Tina grinned. "What about you and Kevin? How did the two of you get together?"

"Well," Karen began, he'd had a crush on me since high school—we went to the same school together. Anyhow, I never realized it, because I never even noticed him! He'd been following me around *everywhere,* and I never even knew!

Later, after we'd dated a few times, he showed me this huge picture that he'd taken of me and had enlarged. I mean it was poster size! I was a cheerleader, and he'd snapped my picture right in the middle of a jump. It was really good! I was so flattered—

Anyway, back to what you asked—right after we started college, before you and I really started being good friends, he sent me this bouquet of roses. Remember seeing them on my dresser?"

Tina nodded.

Karen continued. "When I opened the envelope to see who they were from, there was nothing in there except a ticket to the first college play of the season. I felt really weird, but I had to go see. I was dying of curiosity!

Well, while I was watching the play, I kept thinking I recognized the lead character. Come to find out it was Kevin! I vaguely remembered him from high school, because like I said, I'd never noticed him. Suddenly it came to me, just fuzzy visions of him, mind you. He'd changed so much since then; he was so good-looking!

After the play, he walked right up to me, in front of everyone, and gave me another rose! I was shocked! Before I could gain any composure, he invited me out to dinner that same night. I went, and as they say, 'the rest is history.'"

"Why didn't you notice him in high school?" Tina asked, unable to comprehend *anyone* not noticing Kevin!

Karen scowled. "I was dating this jerk named Ted Harmon. I thought he was so right—the football star, good-looking, rich, and so on! Now that I look back, I was stupid, because he treated me like he owned me! He thought he was the best thing in the world; I guess all I did was feed his overstuffed ego!

Well, because he was so good in football, he got this scholarship to another college—one I didn't care to attend. He expected me to go there, too, but I told him I'd already picked out a college. He got this real macho attitude and said, 'Baby, if you don't come with me, it's over! I can't do without sex just because you're being a stubborn little rich girl!'

"What'd you do?" Tina asked.

"I jerked his class ring off my finger and threw it at him. Then I told him to eat his jock strap and drop dead!"

"That's so gross!" Tina cried.

"I know," Karen answered proudly.

Before they could say anything else, Karen saw her parents' car pull up in the driveway.

"They're home!" she cried. "Come on—you've got to meet them!"

She took Tina by the arm once more, and led her to the house for the introductions. Tina should have felt out of place; she usually did in unusual surroundings. For some strange reason, this time, she did not. Happily, she walked up to the house to meet the parents of her best friend. It was turning out to be a good holiday, after all.

CHAPTER TEN

THE NEXT DAY WAS A busy one. Karen's mom, Karen, and Tina worked in the kitchen, preparing Thanksgiving dinner. Emily had been given the day off to spend the holiday with her family. As Tina glanced around the kitchen, she was amazed at the amount of food before her. There seemed to be enough there to feed a tremendous crowd, but it was just going to be the four of them. They'd be eating leftovers for days! Tina imagined Karen's family still sighing at Christmas over the turkey that just wouldn't go away. She stifled a giggle, then glanced over at Karen, who was working diligently on a sweet potato casserole. Karen paused for a moment, then dipped her finger into the soft orange mix. She brought her finger to her mouth and delicately sucked the food off.

"Ummm," she said, "that's so good!"

Karen's mother slapped her hand playfully.

"You're not going to have any appetite left, if you start tasting everything now!" she scolded.

"I can't help it," Karen protested. "It smells so yummy!"

Tina laughed at Karen, who still had a speck of sweet potato on her lip. She wiped it off for her, then looked at Karen's mother. She was sprinkling cinnamon over an apple pie, and when she saw Tina looking, she smiled warmly. Tina noticed that Karen's features were mirrored in her mother's face. They both had the same ice blue eyes, and the same shade of blonde hair. The mother's hair was shorter, though, ending at the curve of her neck. It was styled in soft curls, with straight bangs framing her forehead. Her complexion, like Karen's, was flawless. Tina imagined that she'd never smoked and seldom sunbathed, for the only wrinkles she saw were a few laugh lines around her lips. Her age was hard to guess, and Tina wondered if she and Karen were ever mistaken for sisters, for she still looked very young. Her figure, like Karen's, was petite, and she was dressed fashionably, even now. Karen, on the other hand, had opted for a white sweat shirt and jeans.

Tina, not recognizing her own beauty, tried to push her jealousy aside. She had on light make-up, and her face was rosy with all the laughter she and Karen had shared on this break from college. She was also dressed in a sweatshirt and jeans. It felt good to just forget about studying for once.

A mischievous mood hit her, and she went over to a vegetable casserole that was next to Karen. Playfully, she snatched a carrot out of the dish.

"Hey, stop that!" Karen cried.

Tina giggled and tried to grab another one, but Karen popped her hand.

Karen's mother looked over at the two of them, shaking her head. There was a twinkle in her eyes, though, and the hint of a smile on her lips.

"Little snitch!" Tina whispered.

Karen replied by sticking out her tongue, like she did when she was a child. For a moment she wondered if this is what it would have been like to have had a sister. She was glad to have Tina as a friend, and thought that if she'd had a sister, she'd have wanted her to be like Tina.

Just then, Karen's father strolled into the kitchen. He went to his wife, locking his arms about her waist, and sniffing the numerous delightful scents.

"When will this be ready?" he asked. "I'm starving!"

"Give it about another forty-five minutes," she answered. "While you're waiting, put that dish in the lower oven," she said, motioning to a container. "After that, make a gallon of tea, but don't overdo the sugar."

"Geez, I should've stayed in front of the TV," he teased.

"You'll get to go back soon enough," his wife replied. "For now, get to work, before I hit your rear with this spatula!"

Tina blushed at the way Karen's parents flirted with each other. Hers used to do things like that, and for the first time since she'd arrived, a small pain entered her heart. She tried to concentrate on her task, but visions of her parents overtook her. She remembered their Thanksgiving dinners together; how she waited with a watering mouth for her mother to get dinner ready. Then how she'd always end up eating too much, but relax contentedly for the rest of the lazy day.

A hand rested on her shoulder, causing her to jump just a little. She glanced up, embarrassed, at Karen's father. He had his other hand on Karen's shoulder.

"Looks wonderful, girls," he commented.

Karen and Tina smiled. He kissed Karen on the head. When he walked away, Tina watched him. He was a tall man with a small frame. His hair was honey-colored, and parted on one side. Tina had noticed earlier that his eyes were hazel, and his eyebrows thin for a man. Like his wife, he sported a look of sophistication, dressing relatively nice, even though he was off work. He was a handsome man, with a hint of a tan leftover from the summer.

Finally all the food was cooked, the table set, and the meal eaten. Satisfied people sat around the table wondering how they could have eaten so much, but thankful for having so much to eat.

After a while, Karen forced herself up and began picking up dishes. Tina got up to do the same, but Karen's mother held her hands out.

"You girls take a break," she said. "These can wait awhile. I'll put the leftover food up, and stack the dishes in the dishwasher."

She glanced over at her husband.

"I'm sure there'll be more dirty dishes by this evening," she added.

Karen's father heard her comment, but was too full to retaliate. Deep inside, though, he knew she was telling the truth.

"Thanks, Mom," Karen said. "I think I'll take Tina for a drive around, and maybe stop over at Kevin's house."

"OK," she answered. "I'll see you girls later."

Karen rushed upstairs to get her shoes, and Tina followed to freshen up. They washed up, reapplied make-up, brushed hair, checked their clothes, and brushed hair again. Finally they were convinced that they were suitable enough to face the world.

"Let's go," Karen said, as she grabbed her keys and her purse. Together they thundered down the stairs, and waltzed through the front door.

Karen drove Tina all over her town, pointing out spots of interest and answering Tina's questions. Tina adored the place. It was small, but there were so many beautiful homes, and lots of things to see! Tina appreciated the way each home had its own large lot of land, instead of being stacked on top of one another. There were homes of every shape and size, but none of them seemed to look like the one before it.

They passed through the inner city, with its side-by-side shops. Each boasted its goods with tastefully decorated window displays. In the center of the town was a small park, complete with park benches and old-fashioned light posts.

"Most of these stores are family owned," Karen told her.

"It's so beautiful here!" Tina observed.

"I'm going to drive by Kevin's house, if you don't mind," Karen said.

"I don't mind at all," Tina answered.

They drove out of the city limits. The snow-capped mountains rose up in the distance, showing off their beautiful blues and grays in the late afternoon sun. Tina gazed at them in awe. She thought she could never get enough of seeing them. Florida was beautiful, but this was even more so. She was learning to love the mountains more and more.

Karen turned right when she reached Kevin's neighborhood. The houses in this particular area were smaller, but spaced apart by about a half acre each. Tina immediately recognized Kevin's car parked under a tree at one of the homes. Karen pulled into the driveway of a one story red brick home. It had an open porch at the front, and a bird bath in the yard. The lawn was decorated with pine trees and bare dogwoods.

Kevin came outside before Karen stopped her car. He smiled ear to ear, while Karen rolled down her car window. As soon as it was down, he put his head inside the car. He kissed her tenderly on the lips, while Tina tried to pretend she didn't see.

After he had kissed Karen, he bid Tina hello.

"Come on in," he invited. "We're just cleaning up from dinner."

Karen and Tina got out of the car, and Kevin closed the car door behind Karen.

"We would have been cleaning up, too, but Mom gave us the afternoon off," Karen explained.

Kevin laughed. "Well, since you're bored, I'll let you two help me!"

"Trust me," Tina said, "we're not bored at all!"

Kevin held the front door open for the girls. They entered an adorable home with simple furnishings, and handmade country decor. Tina immediately felt welcome. The place had a simple, yet comforting feel about it.

"You two can sit at the table; I'll be finished soon," he said.

They all went to the kitchen, where Kevin introduced Tina to his parents. He picked up a towel, but his mother stopped him.

"You've helped me enough for the day, Darling, besides, I'm almost finished."

He kissed his mother on the cheek.

"Thanks, Mom."

She smiled, and went back to work.

Kevin led the girls through the house. He took them to a room at the end of a hall. Tina knew immediately it was his room. On one of the walls, a poster sized picture of Karen loomed over them. It was beautiful! His room was simple. It had brown carpet, and dark blue curtains with a matching bedspread. There was a desk on one side of the bed, and a nightstand on the other side. Under the picture of Karen, there was a set of weight equipment. Kevin picked up a set of barbells, and held them towards Tina.

"Here you go," he joked. "You don't need to skip working out just because you're on Thanksgiving break!"

Tina shook her head, and tried to ignore the muscles that flexed as he held out the barbell.

"I think that's way beyond what I'm used to lifting; I'll pass on it!"

Kevin laughed, and put the weights back down. He pulled out the desk chair for Tina, then sat on the bed with Karen.

They spent the afternoon just talking and laughing. Kevin got out a photo album and motioned for Tina to join them on the bed. She felt the blood go to her cheeks, but if they noticed it, they didn't say anything. As she sat next to Karen, a sudden rush hit her. She was actually on Kevin's bed! She fought thoughts of him lying in that bed bare-chested with his dark hair tousled. She fought even harder trying not to imagine herself there beside of him, with her cheek against his chest, listening to his heart beating.

Karen nudged her, shattering the fantasy, and Tina focused on the photos. One album contained pictures of Kevin and Karen. Another had nothing but pictures of Karen. Tina flushed when they got to the last page, because right in the center was one picture. It was of Karen and Tina. She felt warm all over to think that he put it in there, and maybe even looked at it at times. She was surprised that she looked good in it, but that was not strange, because of her doubts about herself.

When suppertime came, they went to the kitchen and fixed turkey sandwiches with milk to drink. They sat in the living room watching TV, balancing the sandwiches on paper plates, and the glasses between their legs.

Finally it grew late in the evening. They told Kevin good-bye. Tina sat in the car and watched Karen telling Kevin good-bye one more time at the front door. She looked sad, but Tina could understand why. Inside, she hated having to leave, also. Karen eventually made it to the car, and they drove off.

Kevin stood at the door, waving until they were out of sight.

*   *   *

As it usually happens, time passes quickly when people are having a good time. Thanksgiving break was no exception. Soon everyone was back at college, and things got back to normal.

One night while Kevin was at work, Hope came into the store, alone. She'd only come into the store for one reason, which wasn't to shop. Not wanting to appear ridiculous, however, she selected a few mundane items, then went to stand in the check-out line.

She hoped silently that Kevin would come to the lane in which she was standing. It would be better. That way he would have to face her; he would have to say something. There was a moment of disappointment when he left the store with another customer, but he returned shortly. Miraculously he came to her lane and without even glancing at her, began to bag her items.

"Hi!" she said, managing her most seductive smile.

Kevin looked at her. He might as well have been looking at a wet dog by the bland expression on his face when his eyes met hers. Casually he returned the greeting.

"You've got your mind on something, haven't you?" Hope asked, trying her best to sound concerned.

"No," Kevin retorted, "I just didn't recognize you without your permanent attachment."

Hope forced a smile. Deep inside, though, she wanted to slap his face.

"You must mean Allison," she said sweetly.

"If that's her name, that's who I mean," he replied, maintaining that same sarcastic tone that was infuriating Hope.

He finished bagging her things, then walked reluctantly with her to her car. He placed the things in the trunk, but when he turned to leave, she was standing in his path.

"You know," she said, "I'm looking for a 'permanent attachment', but I don't need Allison for that. She's a good friend, but I need more than that. I need someone I can have a relationship with—a physical relationship. I want it to be you, Kevin."

Kevin stared at her, shocked.

"In that case," he said, "you're looking in the wrong place. I suggest you try a nightclub, or better yet, a cold shower. Grocery stores aren't good places to find someone to lay."

Hope's eyes grew wide at the brutal rejection. She opened her mouth to say something, but he was back in the store before she could think of anything. Furious, she got in the car, slammed the door, and drove away in a rage, leaving tire marks behind.

*   *   *

Back at the dorm, Tina and Karen were studying. Tina sat at her desk, chewing on her pen. It was a habit that she'd had for a long time whenever she was really concentrating. Karen was at her desk, also, reading a textbook that was increasingly boring with each passing minute. Occasionally, she would look at the clock, then impatiently roll her eyes.

Suddenly the phone rang. Tina jumped, and the pen bounced off her desk, landing with a quiet "tink" on the floor. Karen dove for the phone, and picked up the receiver.

"Hello? Oh, hi there!! No—nothing. Just studying. I'm about to slip into a coma, though!!"

There was a pause as the other person spoke. Tina watched as a smile spread across her friend's face.

"Sure, I'd love to get out for a while. These walls are closing in on me!!

There was yet another pause, and Tina felt the blood rush to her temples, until she felt her pulse pounding away. She picked up the pen in hopes of blocking Karen out of her mind.

"OK, I'll meet you by your dorm in ten minutes."

Karen hung up the phone, then ran to the bathroom to freshen up.

Tina glanced at the clock. Unless Kevin had gotten off of work early, it was someone else. Anger grew like cancer within her. She tried to kill the evil feeling within her with kind thoughts, but it didn't work. The anger triumphed.

Karen came prancing out of the bathroom.

"I'm going out for a while," she announced.

Tina looked back down at her textbook and nodded.

Karen stood there waiting for Tina to make some kind of eye contact. When she didn't, Karen rolled her eyes, impatiently.

"Keep quiet about this, OK?" she asked.

Tina slammed her pen down so hard on the desk, that Karen jumped a little. She wasn't prepared for that kind of reaction.

"Just what do you want me to say if Kevin calls, comes by, or sends smoke signals?" she snapped.

Karen stood there, shocked.

"Just say that I went to get a snack with this friend from math class," she answered coldly. "Is that so hard for you to do?"

"No," Tina grumbled, "I don't suppose it is."

*   *   *

Much to Tina's surprise, there was a knock on the door about an hour later. She got up and opened it. She about fainted when she saw Kevin standing there. He smiled, and entered the room. Tina's heart fluttered at the thought of them being alone there, at the warmth of his body as he brushed past her. Then she remembered why he was there. Fear began to grip her.

"Is Karen here?" he asked.

"No!" she almost shouted, then in a calmer voice repeated, "No."

Kevin glanced around the room.

"Well, do you know where she is?"

Tina shook her head, a little too rapidly, then got control of herself.

"What I mean," she said, "is that I know that Karen went out for a snack with a friend from math class."

Kevin nodded.

"I don't know where they went, though," she added, feeling like a traitor.

"When did Karen leave?" he asked.

Tina looked up at the clock.

"She left about an hour ago," she answered, a little more calmly now that she was telling the truth.

Kevin turned to leave.

"Just tell her I stopped by after work," he said. "If she has time, tell her to call me. If not, I'll see her tomorrow."

Tina stood there in a stupor. "OK," she said, lamely.

When he'd closed the door, she collapsed against it. Her heartbeat was finally slowing down, and her breathing returning to normal. She smelled something pleasant, and she closed her eyes while she breathed it in. It was Kevin's smell—a soft aroma left by the cologne he'd been wearing. It was a wonderful smell!

She pried herself away from the door, then fell to her bed. She lay there thinking how good he'd looked for someone who had just gotten off work. His hair had been a little tousled, his blue eyes sleepy and sensuous. She felt sleepy, too—so very sleepy.

She was awakened a while later by Karen coming in. She rolled over, and realized that she'd fallen asleep in her clothes. As she got up to change into her nightgown, she almost fell backwards. Karen caught her by the arm.

"You stood up too fast," she said quietly.

Tina nodded as she went to the dresser for her gown.

"Kevin came by," she said casually.

Karen panicked.

"What did he say?" she cried.

Tina sat on the bed, slipping her clothes off, then the gown on.

"What'd he say?" she asked, again.

"He wanted you to call him if you were able to," Tina said. "If not, he said he'd see you tomorrow."

"Great," Karen said happily, "everything went smoothly!"

Tina lay back in her bed, shutting Karen out of her mind. She fell back asleep soon after her head hit the pillow.

*   *   *

In her room, Hope stood fuming at the window. Allison came out of the bathroom with a robe on her body and a towel on her head.

"You're still pouting?" Allison asked.

"What does it look like?!" Hope snapped.

"Well," Allison pointed out, "it serves you right. "How the heck did you expect him to fall for you the way you acted? You came off looking like a whore!"

Hope glared at her friend.

"You're supposed to help me—not make me feel like an idiot!"

Allison threw the towel on the bed and picked up her hair dryer.

"I know, Hope. I wasn't with you, though. You need to take a more subtle approach. This guy is apparently in love. You've got to attract him in a way other than sexual. He won't pay any attention to you, unless you pretend to be his friend. By acting the way you did tonight, you've put him on the defensive. First get him to trust you, then the rest will happen naturally."

Hope ran her fingers through her hair.

"I suppose you're right," she agreed reluctantly. "I just hate this waiting—it's driving me crazy!"

"Get out and date other people. Stop wasting all of your time on a guy who's already taken," Allison suggested. "When he falls for you, just ditch the other guys if you want to."

Hope nodded, then she began getting her things together for her shower. Allison was right. She would date other guys, but she was determined to win Kevin's affections. She would have to be a friend. Though it would be hard, he would like her better that way.

She got in the shower, vigorously shampooing her hair. All the time she kept thinking, "If only that girlfriend of his was out of the way. What can I do to get her away from him? I've got to think of something!"

CHAPTER ELEVEN

I N THE GROCERY STORE, KEVIN and another employee were hanging up lace snowflakes. The store looked like a winter wonderland, with spray paint on the windows, and tinsel on the registers. Now they were almost through decorating by tacking the snowflakes on the ceiling. Kevin stood high on a ladder, while the fellow below handed him the decorations.

Kevin rubbed his sore neck, as he reached with his other hand for the next snowflake.

"It's a good thing that you're afraid of heights," he told the boy below.

The other guy looked up with a sheepish grin on his face.

"Fear has its advantages," he said. "At least I can avoid the stiff neck."

Kevin looked back up, nodding in agreement. He was ready to call it a day. He figured he would dream about the stupid snowflakes.

When he reached down again, his hand touched something soft. He glanced down to see Hope holding up a snowflake. A coy smile played on the corners of her lips. His "friend" had made himself disappear, so Kevin could be alone with this pest of a girl!

Frowning, he took the snowflake from Hope, almost snatching it from her.

"You don't give up, do you?" he snapped.

Hope flushed in embarrassment. She gathered her best poise and smiled sweetly.

"Actually, I do give up," she answered. "I just came in here to apologize for the way I acted the last time I was in here. I was way out of line. You're just so good-looking, I forgot where I stood, and got a little out of control, I suppose."

Kevin remained on the ladder, feeling like a jerk.

"That's OK," he finally answered. "Sorry for the way I just acted; some people can't take "no" for an answer. I thought you might be one of them."

"Well, I'm glad that's out of the way. I hope you see me for what I am," Hope lied.

She extended her hand. "Friends?"

Kevin shook her hand.

"Sure," he answered.

She smiled again, then walked away. Kevin watched as she went out the door. No sooner was she gone, the other guy returned.

Kevin shook his head and made a face.

"You can be a real jerk sometimes," he joked.

"Yeah," he answered, "but it's fun seeing you squirm. Why don't you date her?"

Kevin jumped off the ladder.

"If you dated Karen, would you date her?"

The other boy pondered for a moment.

"You've got a good point," he answered.

Kevin laughed.

"Come on. Let's go take a break."

They walked away, leaving an incomplete winter scene with some snowflakes dangling in the air, while others lay in the floor, waiting for their turn at temporary glory.

*   *   *

Back at the college, Karen and Tina were decorating for the Christmas dance. Karen stood on a ladder, hanging up some silver garland. Tina stood below, helping to keep the long strand from getting tangled.

"Who's taking you to the dance, Tina?" Karen asked.

"I think Kevin's roommate, Alan's going to take me. He's already asked me three times, but I haven't given him an answer yet."

"He'd be good to go out with," Karen commented. "He could stand to lose a few pounds, but he's kind of cute."

"Cute is OK, but I'd really like someone who's spectacular," Tina said in a low voice.

Karen tacked up another foot of garland.

"What? Oh yeah, spectacular—that'd be great. Is there anybody here that can fill that definition?"

"No," Tina lied. "I don't suppose so."

Before they could carry their conversation on any further, a tall, plain-looking fellow with glasses came walking up to the ladder.

"Hi, Karen," he said. He pushed right in front of Tina as though she didn't exist.

Karen glared at him as though he had tread upon her feet.

"Do I know you?" she asked coolly.

The guy shuffled his feet, as a blush rose to his cheeks.

"I'm in your English class. My name's Chuck."

"I'm not sure if I remember you or not," Karen answered.

Chuck smiled.

"Well, that's not really important. I really just wanted to ask you out."

"No," Karen stated rudely.

"What's your problem?" Chuck growled. "You date everybody else!"

Karen started coming down the ladder. She stopped halfway, then looked Chuck over like he was just a piece of merchandise. Her face didn't hide the fact that she didn't care for what she saw.

"You have absolutely nothing about yourself that appeals to me," she snapped, sarcastically.

Tina stepped in front of him, making sure to tread on his foot.

"You're just out of luck—Chuck," she hissed.

Chuck's temper exploded in one violent eruption. He cursed Tina, and pushed her out of the way. Then he started shaking the ladder violently. Karen screamed and held to the ladder with all her strength.

One of the professors heard the commotion, and started running across the gym. He did not get there, though, before Karen fell a few feet to the floor. As Chuck turned around, Tina gave him a swift kick where it hurt. He fell to the floor, grabbing his crotch, trying not to scream in pain.

The professor bent down to check on Karen. After he'd assessed the situation, he turned and pointed his finger to Tina and Chuck.

"You two are dismissed from this project—get out!"

Tina leaned over to look at Karen, but he shouted again, "Get out!" She noticed all the other students in the gym. They'd stopped whatever they were doing, and were staring at her and Chuck in confusion. Tina bolted out of the gym, before anyone could see her cry.

Meanwhile, Chuck crawled away as best as he could, but no one offered to help him. He had made a complete fool of himself.

As the professor helped Karen to her feet, she wailed in pain. A few students came to her side to see how badly she was hurt.

"Do you need to go the hospital?" the professor asked.

Karen shook her head. "It's just a bruise. It hurts, but not enough to have been broken."

"I still think you should go and get some X-rays taken," the professor suggested.

"No, really," Karen insisted. "I'm all right."

"Well, if you get worse, or change your mind, call one of us in the office. If not the office, then at home," he said.

Karen nodded her thanks, then accepted the support of two girls who offered to help her back to her dorm.

*   *   *

Back at the dorm, Tina wiped her eyes. She felt so stupid! Why did she always have to get into the middle of things? She always had to get into fights and come out looking like some tomboy.

Why couldn't she be more like Karen? She was so graceful, so beautiful. Karen would never have behaved that way. At that thought, Tina had to grin. Maybe guys were scared to ask *her* out for fear of getting beat up. The grin faded, though, as she began to cry again.

Sounds were coming from the hallway. She could hear voices coming towards her room. Ashamed, she dashed into the bathroom, and locked the door. She turned on the shower, and sat on the toilet as she listened to the door open. People were shuffling into the room. She kept listening as Karen verified over and over again, that yes, she was all right. No, she didn't need a doctor. After a few minutes, those same sounds retreated, and the door closed behind them. Now she knew that Karen was alone in the room.

Slowly, she opened the bathroom door and peeped out. Karen was sitting on the bed, hugging her leg. She smiled meekly at Tina.

"Thank you," she whispered.

"I was pretty stupid, wasn't I?" Tina asked.

"You were very brave," Karen replied. "You always fight for what you think is right. I wish I could be more like you."

Tina laughed. "If only you knew how I'd like to be like you!"

"Maybe we can trade bodies," Karen joked.

Tina smiled, and walked over to the bed. She watched as Karen peeled off her pants, revealing a hideous bruise which covered a large portion of her leg. Gasping, she sat down beside of her friend.

"It looks bad," was all Tina could manage to say.

Karen nodded, tears welling up in her eyes. The tears were more from vanity, than from the actual pain, but it made Tina furious.

She shook her head and clenched her fists, as the first of Karen's tears rolled down her cheek.

"What in the world is his problem anyway?" Tina demanded.

"I don't know," Karen answered. "I hardly remember him from class. I had no idea he was even interested in me."

"Well, it that's interest, I'd hate to see what true love means to him," Tina said firmly.

Karen clasped Tina's hand.

"Please don't tell Kevin about this," she begged.

Tina nodded understandingly. Just then the door to their room flew open. They both jumped as Kevin burst into the room. He stalked right over to Karen and knelt down on the floor. He gingerly held her leg. When looked up at her, his eyes were filled with pain, worry, and above all, anger.

"Why?" he asked.

"How'd you find out?" she questioned in return.

"Bad news travels fast. Why did he hurt you?"

"I wouldn't go out with him—I guess the disappointment was too much," Karen joked.

Kevin slammed his fist so hard onto the mattress, that both girls jumped.

"It's not funny," he cried out. "You could have really gotten hurt!"

"I'm OK, really. It'll just hurt for a few days," Karen said.

"You shouldn't be hurting *at all*," Tina insisted. "You were minding your own business."

Karen smiled at Tina.

"Thanks," she whispered for the second time that day.

Tina nodded, then stood up.

"I've got to take a shower. Is there anything else you need?"

Karen shook her head. Satisfied, Tina went into the bathroom and closed the door. When they heard the water running, Kevin helped Karen with the rest of her clothes.

"What do you want to sleep in?" he asked.

"Just get one of my long T-shirts out of the bottom drawer."

Kevin sauntered over to Karen's dresser and opened a drawer which held impeccably folded clothes. He reached in and selected the T-shirt which he felt would fit most comfortably. She already had her arms up playfully, when he returned, and he stifled the sudden urge to make love to her there. Remembering that Tina was just a short distance away, and would be coming out at any moment, helped him to regain some control. He softly slid the shirt over her golden hair, then pulled the bedcovers back. As he helped her get into the bed, the bruise caught his attention, and he felt his anger flaring up again.

"He's not going to get away with hurting you, Karen," he vowed.

Karen shook her head in protest, while he pulled the covers back over her.

"There's nothing we can do, Kevin. One of the professors saw it all. I'm sure he'll be suspended, if not dismissed from here."

"It would serve him right," Kevin hissed.

"Please promise me that you won't do anything rash," Karen pleaded.

Kevin nodded his head reluctantly, then he kissed her on the forehead.

"Goodnight," he said.

"Goodnight, Kevin. I love you."

Quietly he got up and walked out of the room. Deep inside a fury grew, and he tried to push his hatred away. It kept burning, like a fire out of control. He walked out of the dorm, and disappeared into the night.

*　　*　　*

At the dorm where Chuck stayed, things were quiet. He limped to his room, thankful that there were no students around to see him like that. Once again he cursed that stupid Tina under his breath. He fumbled with his key, trying to ignore the throbbing sensation in his groin. Eventually he got the door opened, and glanced around the room. He gazed with disgust at his empty bed and the one next to it, empty as well.

"I don't know why that idiot roommate of mine bothers paying for a dorm—he's never in it," he grumbled. Nope his roommate wasn't here. He was out somewhere, probably getting laid, while he, Chuck, was alone again. Only this time he wasn't just alone. He was alone *and* his balls hurt!

Chuck peeled off his clothes and went into the bathroom to take a shower. In spite of his pain, he smiled as the water rushed over his body. It felt good to wash the dirt and frustrations off of his body and out of his mind. He was vigorously shampooing his hair when he thought he heard something. He stopped shampooing for a moment to listen. There was no sound now except for the water running, but he was sure he'd heard something—a kind of "thump". A solitary "thump", unlike the increasing, erratic thumping of his heart now.

Quickly he rinsed off, then threw a towel around his body. Without bothering to dry himself off, he walked to the bathroom door and threw it open. An evil silence greeted him, followed by a cold chill. He gazed across the room and noticed that the window to his first floor room was open. He hadn't noticed it before, but that was not unusual. His roommate, who was never in there, always left the window open. The guy was always overheated, but could never stay in the room long enough to appreciate the icy winds that he invited every time he opened that idiotic window.

Chuck cursed, then stalked to the window, slamming it shut. For some reason, he was still paranoid, so he turned the radio on. His arm nudged a water bottle on the stand beside of the radio. It tumbled to the floor, making him jump. He bent to pick the bottle up, thankful that the cap was still on. That's all he would need now, more crap to wipe up. He considered looking under the beds as he got the bottle, but that was a stupid thing to do, wasn't it? Nonetheless, he knelt and glanced first under one bed, then the other. The cold air was sending shivers over his drenched body, so he slammed the bottle back on the table, and retreated to the safety of the bathroom. Once there, he locked the door. He looked in the mirror, feeling sheepish about being so nervous, yet at the same time noticing how handsome he looked without his glasses.

He picked up the hairdryer, which was in its usual spot, straddled across the towel rack. He plugged it up, then flicked the "on" button. Nothing happened. He jiggled the plug. Still nothing. Cursing, he unplugged then plugged it back up again. This time when he turned the dryer on, it sputtered to life, making an odd rattling sound.

"Great," he muttered, "now it's got a short in it." That stupid roommate of his probably dropped it again. Chuck was determined that his roommate would replace the hairdryer, even if it meant using it until it just wouldn't run anymore.

He started drying his short hair, hoping the appliance would at least last long enough for him to finish his hair tonight. He was too busy fuming and grooming to notice a stream of water coming from under the crack in the door, until his feet were immersed in it. By then it was too late. Suddenly, a feeling ran through his body, like a thousand needles picking away at his flesh with incredible speed. He body shook violently, as he stood frozen glancing at his terrified face in the mirror. It was as though he had no tongue, because he could not even scream. He could only stand there trapped with the dryer in his hand, and watch himself die. The lights were flickering madly, then as they finally went out, the pain stopped, and he fell to the floor dead.

CHAPTER TWELVE

THE NEXT MORNING WAS SATURDAY. Karen and Tina were still in their beds, taking advantage of the opportunity to sleep late. Tina barely opened her eyes to look at the clock beside of her bed. Its blue neon numbers flashed 10:07. She'd stay in bed a little while longer. Smiling to herself, she pulled the covers up more around her head. In a few moments, she was asleep again.

They were awakened thirty minutes later by loud knocking on their door. Karen cursed quietly, as she got out of bed to slip on her robe. Tina forgot about a robe and simply bounded out of bed to answer the door. When she opened it, a couple of the girls from her dorm were standing there, apprehensive, in their nightgowns.

"Did you see all of the police cars and the ambulance out there?" one of them asked.

Karen had joined Tina by then, and both girls shook their heads.

"There's something going on at the freshmen boys' dorm," another girl said.

Tina, Karen, and the two other girls went over to the window to get a better look. As they peered out the window, they could see the ambulance workers carry a cloth shrouded body out of the dorm, while the police went about the building with yellow tape. Other police scurried in and out of the dorm. Some had pads out, writing down comments from some of the students. The crowd which was gathering by the dorm was growing larger and larger, the longer they stood at the window.

"We're going to see what's going on," one of the girls said.

Karen and Tina barely acknowledged the girls' exit, but instead went to get dressed themselves.

"I've got a bad feeling, a really bad feeling," Karen said, her voice trembling.

"Yeah, I do too, especially since they carried somebody out of that building," Tina agreed, almost sarcastically.

Once outside, Tina hugged herself. Though she had a coat on, the December wind sliced through the material, sending a cold chill that went straight to her bones. She dug her hands deeper into her coat pockets, yet that brought little relief. She glanced at Karen, whose porcelain face was now marked with red areas where the cold was stinging her as well. She noticed her friend, usually walking straight, slumping into her coat for warmth. Tina wondered if that was helping any, when she noticed Karen's teeth chattering.

They joined the crowd of students which had doubled since they'd first looked out from the window. Everyone was muttering in what appeared to be a mass of confusion. When the sheriff emerged from the dorm, a sudden hush spread over the crowd.

"Everybody go back to you dorms. There's been an accident here, and you'll only get in the way. We need to check the area out thoroughly, though, to make sure it was just an accident. We appreciate your cooperation."

"Sheriff," someone from the crowd shouted, "who was hurt in there?"

The sheriff inhaled deeply. It was going to be a bad weekend. When he exhaled, cold air blew from his mouth like smoke.

"Normally we don't give out that kind of information this soon, but since the family's been notified already, I can give you the basic details. Chuck Winslow was accidentally electrocuted last night while he was drying his hair."

All of the students gasped in shock. Questions started pouring out from all directions, but the sheriff shooed them away with a wave of his hand, as though they were mere flies.

"That's all I can say at this moment," he announced, before retreating to the building.

Tina turned wide-eyed to Karen to gage her reaction. Karen's face was now a sickly milky white and her mouth was gaped open. Her leg was sending arrows of pain to all parts of her body. Now this news about Chuck was just too overwhelming. She started to sway just a bit.

"Karen, are you all right?" Tina asked, concerned. She grabbed Karen's arm.

When Karen looked at her, it was as if she didn't even recognize Tina. Her eyes wore a blank expression.

"Karen?" Tina repeated, this time more urgently.

Karen never answered, for at that moment, everything went black and she fainted. She fell to the ground, taking Tina with her.

*   *   *

Two hours later, Karen woke up. Sitting straight up, she blinked her eyes and started gasping for air. The surroundings were unfamiliar and it terrified her. Suddenly she noticed a movement from the corner of her eye. She stifled a scream, then realized it was her mother walking towards her. She lay back down, watching as her mother came to sit in the chair beside the bed. Karen did not recognize the room, nor the bed. Her eyes were wide with fright, and she tried to speak. The only thing that came out at first was a small "squeak". Finally she found her voice.

"Mother, where am I?" she cried.

Her mother looked down at her with compassion.

"You're in the hospital, Dear," she answered gently. "You fainted at the college."

"Why would they put me in the hospital for fainting?" Karen asked incredulously.

"You had a fall the night before. They were afraid that the fall might have fractured your leg. You should have let them take you to the hospital then."

"It was just a bruise!" Karen persisted.

"Yes it is, but it's a bad one. You needed something for pain. When you walked on it this morning, it was too much for you."

The pain medication plus the shock of everything that had happened, took its toll on Karen. She started whimpering, while small tears ran down her face.

"I feel so responsible for all this, Mother," she cried. "You would be ashamed of me. I was so rude to Chuck that night! All he did was ask me out! I treated him like dirt, instead of just telling him 'no'!"

"He hurt you, Karen," her mother reminded her.

"I know!" Karen shrieked. "I know he hurt me, but if I would have been nicer, none of this would have happened! Chuck might even still be alive now!"

Karen's mother shook her head, and frowned.

"I know you feel guilty about what happened to that boy, Karen. It was wrong of you to be rude to him, but it was also wrong of *him* to hurt you. Nonetheless, he's dead now, and you can't go back and take away the things you said to him. I'm sure he realized you didn't really mean to act the way you did. As for Chuck still being alive now, well you had nothing to do with that. It was an accident. The sheriff said that Chuck's hairdryer had a short in it. There's nothing you could have done for him, even if you had been there. You just would have gotten killed yourself."

"It's all so terrible," Karen whispered.

"Yes it is. I can't imagine anything like that happening to you. My heart goes out to the family of that poor boy. Terrible things happen—we just don't expect them to happen to people we know."

*   *   *

In the hallway of the hospital, Tina and Kevin were waiting to hear about Karen. Kevin stared into space while Tina chewed violently on a piece of gum.

"It's hard to be in love with someone so beautiful," Kevin confessed quietly.

Tina immediately forgot about her gum and stared at Kevin.

"Leave her," she said. The words were out before she had a chance to think about what she was saying. She sat there and held her breath, waiting for the inevitable fight from Kevin.

Instead, he sighed, leaned over in his chair, and gaped at the floor.

"I can't do it," he said. "I know that sometimes I think she'd be better off without me, but I just can't do it. I don't want to ever let her go."

He looked up and his blue eyes locked into her brown ones. Tina simply nodded. As bad as she wanted to disagree, she couldn't. All that her heart and body wanted was Kevin, but she could never have him. She leaned back in her chair and closed her eyes. She tried to think of other things, anything! Kevin's cologne drifted up pleasantly, invading her mind. Inhaling, she smiled to herself. He always had this pleasant smell. It was mild, yet hypnotic. All thoughts veered back to him. It was useless to try to think of anything else with Kevin sitting right there! Tina envied Karen for being able to hold him so close. He would probably be as soft and warm as the cologne that was emitting from his beautiful body.

All of a sudden, the door next to them opened, and Karen's mother stepped out. Tina's mind was jerked out of its pleasant fantasy.

"She wants to see you," she said, looking at Kevin.

Kevin got up to talk quietly to Karen's mother for a moment. As he did, Tina felt more out of place than ever. She did not belong here with these people. Silently, she got up and stole from the hospital.

When Karen's mother had finished talking to Kevin, he stepped into the room. She turned around to speak to Tina, but the girl had vanished. She looked up and down the hallway, but there was no trace of Karen's best friend. Karen would have wanted to see her, as well. She shook her head, and sighed. Her daughter would need some time alone with Kevin. She decided to go get a cup of coffee. Alone, she strolled down the hallway.

Kevin sat beside the bed and held Karen's hand. He stared at her as she lay there. Her hair spilled around the pillow like the rays of the sun, and her face had a peaceful look now.

"I can go back to the dorm today," she said. "They just want me to rest for a couple more hours, then I can get you to drive me back."

Kevin smiled.

"You're going to be fine, because I won't ever let anything happen to you," he said.

Karen looked at him, noticing the seriousness in his eyes.

"I know," she answered. "I always feel like you're on my side."

Kevin squeezed her hand.

"I am," he admitted. "I am."

*   *   *

While Kevin was in the hospital visiting with Karen, Tina was running. She ran with an energy gathered from years of loneliness. The cold air stung her eyes and burned her throat. She closed her eyes for a few seconds, as if to blot out the physical pain. In an instant, her mind flashed back to the horrible day that had changed her life forever. She saw her aunt once more, and blinked away the impending tears. All those years alone had taught her a lesson. She'd learned that she could only depend on herself. An invisible wall had built itself around her over time. No one had been able to penetrate that barrier. Not until now. Kevin—the name that brought so much happiness and so much sorrow all at the same time. Why him? The sad thing was that he didn't know he'd gotten to her!

She tried to think of bad things about him, in a feeble attempt to make him appear less wonderful than he really was. Nothing came to mind. Her brain was like some bizarre filter. It allowed no bad thoughts of Kevin to enter. She was helpless against it.

The pain in her chest and her throat told her she'd already run too much. As she slowed to a jogging pace, she heard a car slowing down behind her. She kept jogging, not daring to look back. What if it was Karen's mother? She felt enough like a fool, without running into her now! Out of the corner of her eye, she could see that the car was pulling closer to the curb. She decided to stop and accept whatever faced her. When she turned around, she was relieved to see that it wasn't Karen's mother. In curiosity, she walked over to the unknown vehicle. The window came down, revealing the smiling face of a boy from her French class. She leaned down to look inside the car, and see what it was that had prompted him to stop.

"What are you doing out there?" he asked. "It's freezing today!"

Tina threw up her hands and looked towards the sky.

"I thought it was great exercising weather," she joked.

The guy leaned over, and opened the passenger door.

"Get in," he said. "It's at least two more miles until you get to the campus. You'll be frozen by then!"

Tina gladly accepted his offer. She got into the car, and he pulled back onto the road. The warmth from the car's heater began to envelop her. As she rubbed her hands together, to get the blood circulating, she looked at him again.

"Merci beaucoup," she said.

"Pour toi, j'ai fa tous," he answered.

Tina smiled.

"You're good at that. I'm trying hard, but it's not easy for me to pick up. It's even harder to remember!"

"What you need," he answered, "is a study partner. Do you have one?"

"Unfortunately I don't—it's just me and those stupid French tapes."

"It doesn't have to be that way," he said.

"Yeah, I know. I thought about throwing away those tapes, but I couldn't bring myself to do it."

Tina looked at him. He had such a confused look on his face, that she couldn't help but to laugh.

"I know what you meant," she said. "I'd be glad to have you as a study partner. You'll just have to be patient with me when I mess up."

"When do you want to start?" he asked.

"Gosh, you don't waste any time," Tina admitted.

"I know. So when do you want to start?"

"As soon as you tell me who you are. I apologize, but I'm not too good with names."

"It's OK," he said. "I'm Matthew Collins."

Tina nodded in remembrance. She studied the inside of the car. It was equipped with everything one could ask for, and it still had that wonderful new smell. She gingerly touched the leather seat.

"So tell me, Matthew, how did you rate this nice of a car?"

Matthew grinned.

"Actually it's a loaner—at least until I finish college. My folks gave me the car at graduation, but they won't hand over the title yet. The deal is that I finish college. I also have to have at least a 3.5 grade point average just to drive it. That's why I study so darn much. I really like the car, and it'll be mine in a little over three years."

Tina sighed.

"It seems like such a long time," she admitted.

Matthew glanced over at her.

"I know I'm gonna sound like an old fart, but you should really be enjoying your college years. It's a real pain when you get out and have to start working for a living. My older brother said that college was a party compared to work."

"I know you're right," Tina answered, "but I just can't seem to put my whole heart into it. I make good grades, but so far, it's not been any 'party' for me."

"I think that once you and I start studying, you'll see that college suits you. It can't be too fun trying to concentrate on your work with Karen running around all of the time."

Tina's eyes grew large.

"What do you mean?" she asked.

"You don't have to act like you don't know what I'm talking about," Matthew answered. "Most everybody at college knows about Karen's reputation."

Tina blushed.

"I feel so guilty about the whole situation," she confessed. "I've never seen a person so in love with someone as he is with her. I sometimes wonder if I should just tell him what she's doing behind his back."

"He'd never believe you," Matthew said, "and if he did, he'd hate you for it."

"It wouldn't be my fault, though," Tina protested.

"It wouldn't matter. He'd hate you for telling him. He'd hate you even more for not telling him sooner."

"Then I'm trapped," Tina sighed.

Matthew nodded. He turned into the driveway of the campus.

"Which dorm?"

"Over there," Tina said, as she pointed.

They stopped right in front of her dorm. An uncomfortable silence followed.

"How about meeting me in the library at 7:00 tonight?" Matthew suggested, breaking the silence.

Tina nodded, then got out of the car. As he drove away, she realized that she was relieved that the ride was over. She turned on her heels, and dashed into the building, before the warmth from the car wore off.

CHAPTER THIRTEEN

O N THE WAY FROM THE hospital, Kevin and Karen were unusually silent. Her silence was caused from the drugs; his from anger.

"She should have stayed," Kevin said, breaking the silence.

Karen sighed.

"She probably had her reasons," she commented.

Kevin slapped the steering wheel with his hand so hard, that Karen jumped in her seat.

"For crying out loud, Karen, she's supposed to be your friend! You needed her, but all she did was run out on you! Is that all that she can do—think only of herself?"

Karen rested her head against the back of the car seat, and closed her eyes. She didn't want to think now. Too much had happened in too little time. Beside of her, she could hear that steady, heated breathing of Kevin's. He had such a temper! She knew he'd never harm her, but he'd probably do God knows what to the person who ever hurt her. What if he ever found out about her liaisons? She shuddered at the thought, for she knew she'd lose him forever, plus he'd probably kill anyone who touched her.

She opened her eyes and glanced at him. His jaw was still firm; his eyes still held that proud determination. When he felt her staring, he returned the gaze. The coldness melted from his eyes, and his jaw relaxed. He even smiled that charming, comforting smile that Karen was so accustomed to. She smiled back, then reached for his hand. Satisfied, she closed her eyes, and dozed off.

*   *   *

In the dorm, Tina stood in front of her closet. She'd already been there several minutes, trying to decide on something to wear for her meeting with Matthew. He was different from anyone else she'd ever dated, not that this was even remotely close to a date. Nonetheless, everything about him spelled m-o-n-e-y. She felt inferior to him in that aspect. She remembered from seeing him walking to and from class, that he stood at least a foot taller than she did. He wore the best clothes all the time. Everything that clad his body had some designer label slapped to it. Some she didn't even recognize. That told her right away, that she'd never even approached some of the expensive clothing stores that he frequented.

As she stared glassy eyed at the drab clothing in her closet, she pondered over Matthew. She'd noticed his medium length blonde hair. She'd even been charmed by the aqua eyes that twinkled from behind gold-framed glasses. Tina guessed that he was near-sighted, for sometimes in class, he took his glasses off to read. He was not unusually handsome. In fact, in some ways he might appear plain. It was his manner and the way that he dressed which made him so attractive. He had a confidence about him that she was not used to, but she found that very appealing. Hopefully studying with him would take her mind off of Kevin.

She was still going through her closet, getting aggravated now. Nothing would look good compared to what he wore. In desperation, she went to Karen's closet. Upon opening it, she found a lot of things that were fashionable, but even Karen's wardrobe didn't compare to Matthew's. Tina had to smile at that one. Before she closed the door, something caught her eye. She reached further to the right of the closet. What she pulled out was a satiny black teddy, accented with tiny sequins on the straps. She put the item back, laughing.

"Karen, you slut," she said to herself.

Upon returning to her closet, she forced herself to make a decision, no matter what. She chose a peach sweater, a knee-length denim skirt, stockings, and brown low-heeled pumps. She threw the items on the bed, then undressed for her shower.

Once inside, Tina watched as the hot water flowed over her body. It made her skin look shiny and silky. She ran her hands over her neck, her breasts, and her legs, remembering her night with Brad. It seemed like an eternity ago since they'd made love.

She pushed thoughts of Brad aside, and let the hot water caress her skin. It felt so good! She was so relaxed, that for a moment, she faded off into a sort of trance like state. In her mind, she could see Chuck. He was in the shower. Like her, he thought that the water felt good. All of a sudden, she could imagine the lights blinking on and off, while Chuck looked around, panic-stricken. She saw smoke rising from the floor, and in vivid detail she was seeing Chuck's death. At least she saw it as she imagined it would have happened. It was enough to frighten her so badly, that she lost her balance in the shower. Her eyes opened wide as she grasped about to regain her balance. Her hands slid among the slick tiles, but she finally locked onto the soap holder. Once she realized that she was not going to fall, she remembered the horrible image. She clutched at her hair, pulling it so hard that it hurt, but the anxiety would not leave her. Her breathing was like gasping for air that wasn't to be had, and her heart pounded so fast in her chest, that it was actually painful. She wanted to run, but there was nowhere to go. Instead, she crouched down in the shower and let out one long desperate scream. This time, no one heard her.

*   *   *

Karen and Kevin finally made it to the campus. As they walked up the steps to the dorm, he prayed that Tina would not be in the room. He just didn't want to see her now, afraid he might say something harsh to her that he would later regret.

His prayer was unanswered, though, because when they opened the door, they saw Tina. She was standing, dressed, in front of her dresser mirror. She turned to them, surprised, then smiled. She looked different tonight, exceptionally beautiful, as a matter of fact. Kevin noticed her beauty, and was filled with all kinds of unexplainable emotions. His temper was the most prominent one, so he spoke before he'd had a chance to think.

"Why did you leave?" he demanded.

Tina's smile faded at once, as her face flushed in utter embarrassment.

"I-I-I couldn't stand it in there anymore," she stammered.

Karen clasped Kevin's arm in an attempt to calm him down, but it only increased his anger. He shook her hand off. In defeat, Karen sunk to her bed, her head down.

"Karen needed you today!" he shouted.

Tina's eyes filled with tears, but she refused to cry. Instead, she held her head up and looked directly at Karen.

"Please forgive me," she whispered, "I didn't mean to seem indifferent. I just felt so out of place in there. I don't know why, but I did."

Karen curled up on her bed. She nodded in understanding.

"Where are you going?" she asked Tina.

Tina looked down at her shoes, avoiding Kevin's cold stare.

"I'm meeting someone at the library. We're going to study."

"You're going to study on a Saturday?" Karen asked in amazement.

She may have been drugged up, but she remembered what day it was.

"Yeah, I'm studying on a Saturday," she said through clenched teeth.

She walked towards the door, but stopped right beside Kevin. This time she was able to look him in the eyes with a fierceness that made him shudder.

"Not everyone is fortunate enough to have naive, over-protective boyfriends!" she snapped.

She went out the door with an air of pride and dignity that Kevin had never seen in her before. He looked at Karen so say something in his defense, but she was already asleep. He exhaled in relief, then tucked her in bed. Satisfied that she was all right, he turned and left the room.

*   *   *

At the library, Matthew was helping Tina to become more fluent in her French speaking abilities. She watched him intently as he spoke.

"Ja'i va alle a Paris avec tois," he said.

"Jaaa'i va alle a Paris—avec tois," Tina repeated somewhat unsuccessfully.

Matthew grinned, and took her hand.

"Say it again," he coaxed. "This time make it sound smooth and creamy."

"Like a milkshake?" Tina teased.

"No," Matthew answered, "like your hand."

Tina fought away the blush which rose to her face, as she tried to ignore the warmth of his hands on hers.

Tina repeated the phrase, and Matthew leaned back in his chair with a look of satisfaction.

"You'll get it," he bragged.

Tina blushed again, and turned a page in her book.

"Explain this," she requested.

He leaned over and together they studied like that for two hours. Tina asking questions—Matthew answering. He pronounced; she repeated. Suddenly French seemed like a challenge to her, instead of an annoyance.

"Have you ever been there?" she asked.

"France?"

"Yes, France."

Matthew closed his eyes for a moment in reminiscence.

"Yes, I've been there. It's beautiful. It was like being in a different world. People dressed in sweaters and cotton pants—children running down cobblestone streets. They carried bread in their hands! Those long loaves like you see in the grocery store, only not as fat, but harder on the outside, and flaky on the inside. Oh, the open air markets, too! So many vendors, with so many things to see and to buy. Food everywhere! Plus there were so many castles and old buildings! It was like being in a different dimension.

"I'm going there one day," Tina said firmly.

118

Matthew looked at her.

"You won't regret it," he promised.

Just then Tina's stomach growled. It wasn't loud enough to hear, but she put her hand to her tummy, anyway.

"You know what?" she commented. "I just realized that I've not eaten supper yet. Let's go get something. It'll be my treat. It's the best way I know to repay you for your help."

Matthew held her hand again.

"I *wanted* to be with you tonight," he said. "You'll never have to 'repay' me for anytime spent with you. It just feels good having someone as pretty as you, with me."

"Thanks," Tina whispered.

"So, are you into hamburgers and junk food?" Matthew asked.

"You bet I am!" Tina answered.

They gathered all of their things and left the library. As they passed rows and rows of books, they did not realize that they were being watched.

When they left the building, Kevin stepped out from behind a bookshelf. He stared at them until they were almost out of sight. Something compelled him to follow them, and he ran out of the library.

*   *   *

Matthew and Tina were at the small restaurant across from the campus. It was the same one that she frequently visited with Karen and Kevin. They were sitting in a booth at the back. Tina glanced around while Matthew studied the menu. The place was not crowded at all. She guessed that everyone had already eaten, then had gone to the nearby clubs to get drunk.

"Why aren't you looking at the menu?" Matthew asked when he finally looked up.

Tina laughed.

"I always order the same thing! Besides, I come in here so much, that I almost have that menu memorized!"

"Next time, I'll take you to a place where you've never seen the menu," Matthew promised.

After the waitress had taken their orders, they sat there in an uncomfortable silence for the second time that day. They had spoken about French and food. Now they had run out of things to say. They stared at the surroundings in pretended interest. Finally their eyes met, and Tina laughed.

"Well," she said, "what can we talk about now?"

"Go to the Christmas dance with me," Matthew blurted out.

It was said so suddenly, that all Tina could do was stare at him. She had pretty much put the dance in the back of her mind. It seemed like an unpleasant event until now. No one had asked her yet. As least no one had gotten a chance, because of the way that she acted. Every time she thought that she was being approached by a guy who might ask her, she went the other way. If they were talking, and it happened to come up, she'd quickly changed the subject. The thought of seeing Brad with someone else, combined with the thought of seeing Kevin crooning over Karen had been too much. Now she had been asked. Matthew had done it quickly and politely. She had to answer.

Her mind said 'no', but she heard herself say, "OK, I'll go."

Matthew leaned back in the booth and smiled.

"It's just a little over two weeks away," he said.

"So are the exams," Tina reminded him.

"We'll make it," he said confidently. "We've got study partners now."

Tina was about to say something when she saw the door to the restaurant open. Kevin stepped inside and looked around. His eyes met Tina's. He saw that she was still with Matthew, so he turned to leave.

"I'll be back in a minute," Tina told Matthew. She jumped from the booth and ran after Kevin.

"Wait!" she shouted, not caring what Matthew might be thinking about her sudden departure.

Kevin pretended not to hear her, and he stepped outside. Tina threw the door open, not realizing that'd he'd stopped. She almost bumped into him. He looked at her, and was about to say something, but she spoke first.

"Kevin, I'm so sorry for what I said to you. It's been a hard day for all of us. I swear, I wish I could take it all back!"

He looked at her as though he were in a trance. His eyes were misty, and it broke her heart to think that she'd hurt his feelings.

"It's OK," he said, "but the thing about it, is that it's true. It was like a slap in the face, but it woke me up to reality. I just can't change, though."

"I don't want you to change, Kevin," Tina said.

"I'm sorry I was so hard on you," he said. "I get so wrapped up in what I want for Karen, that I tend to forget other people have feelings, too."

Tina nodded.

"You wouldn't believe the feelings that others have," she confessed.

He missed her meaning completely, then slowly turned to walk away.

"Kevin!" Tina cried.

He turned and looked at her.

"Come inside and join us—please!"

"I've spilled my guts out tonight. I think I'd better get back to the dorm."

Tina glanced back inside. Matthew was turned around in his seat. He waved to her, then pointed to the table. The food was already there.

"I've got to go," Tina said.

"I know," Kevin answered. "Let's just forget the harsh words we threw at each other in the dorm. We'll act like none of that happened."

Tina nodded, and watched as he walked away. A tear rolled down her cheek, but she rudely rubbed it away. Then she gathered herself together, put a smile on her face, and walked back inside.

"What did he want?" Matthew asked when she had gotten back to their table.

"He just wanted to talk about what had happened today," she said. "Karen had to be taken to the hospital; she fainted."

Matthew's eyes grew large as he bit into his hamburger. He pondered her words for a moment, as he swallowed his food.

"Since when do they take someone to the hospital for just fainting?"

For some reason, Tina got angry, but she restrained from saying anything spiteful. "She fell off a ladder last night, but she wouldn't go to the hospital. Today after we found out about Chuck, she fainted. They said the pain, plus the shock over Chuck's death was too much for her."

"Why would a snooty person like Karen worry about a jerk like Chuck?" Matthew asked.

"She's not snooty!" Tina snapped.

Matthew rolled his eyes. "Sorry," he said. "Let me word it differently. Why would Karen worry about Chuck?"

"He's the one who caused her to fall," Tina answered.

"He should have known better," Matthew said firmly.

"What do you mean?" Tina asked.

"I mean that she's a jinx! Anybody who does bad things to her ends up getting hurt!"

Tina squirmed uncomfortably in her seat. She tried to ignore him by concentrating on her fries.

Matthew leaned over the table, until his face was close to Tina's. "She was sleeping with Clyde, wasn't she?"

"I don't know," Tina lied.

Matthew eased back in his chair and looked at Tina smugly.

"She's your best friend. I bet you know a lot about her."

Tina's eyes took on a glassy appearance. She tried to see, but everything looked blurry. She blinked her eyes, then everything was clear again. Her stomach was hurting, badly though, as a wave of nausea came over her.

"Do you know what they're calling our college now?" Matthew asked.

Tina shook her head in an undignified manner.

"They're calling it 'Blood University'," he said.

Tina couldn't stand it anymore. She excused herself and walked quickly to the restroom. When she got in there, she stared at herself in the mirror. Her face was dripping with sweat, in spite of the cooler air in the bathroom. She hung her head down, with her eyes closed, and shook all over. Try as she might, she couldn't shake the sick feeling that was overtaking her. Her stomach rumbled, as she clutched it one more time. Finally, her body gave up the fight and she ran to the toilet to throw up.

Back in the dining area, Matthew looked at the door where he had last seen Tina disappear into. She sure had been gone a long time. He had already finished his food, and in boredom, started picking fries from her plate. As he nibbled on the lukewarm food, he thought about Tina. She was a pretty girl, but kind of strange.

"Oh well," he mumbled, "at least I've got a date for the dance."

*   *   *

A few days later, when Karen was feeling better, Tina asked her to go shopping with her. She had written her aunt, telling her about the dance. She had also asked for some money to buy a dress and some shoes. The letter she had received in return contained a check for the dress. It was not as much as she'd hoped for, but it was the best she could get. Tina figured that Karen would know the best places to go for the amount of money that she had. Karen did know of a few places, and was excited that she would be able to help Tina pick a dress. It was like dressing up a doll, only this time, it would be real.

"I know this really neat place to go!" Karen said. "It's a bridal shop. They have these really neat formal dresses that you can rent. You can buy dresses in there if you want to, but if you rent, you'll have money for all of your accessories, as well."

"That sounds good to me," Tina answered. "I need to save all the money that I can. This almost isn't enough to buy a dress, much less, accessories."

"I look like a bum," Karen said, frowning at herself in the mirror. She had on faded jeans, sneakers, and a sweater top.

"You couldn't look like a bum, if you were dressed in a potato sack!" Tina joked.

"Well, thanks," Karen said. "I just hope we don't run into anybody who means anything to me. I'm still sore, so I'm sure not in the mood to dress up yet."

Tina pulled her hair back in a ponytail and looked in the mirror. She wished that she could be as carefree as Karen and look good doing it. It seemed that she had to work harder on her appearance. Karen could get out of the bed, already looking like she was ready to go out.

"Let me put your hair in a French braid!" Karen offered.

"You know how to do that?" Tina asked in surprise.

Karen took Tina's hair out of the ponytail and began to work on it. "Yeah, I know how to do that," she said. "I'm really not that stupid. I ignore my books now and then, but I love hair and makeup."

"How'd you learn?" Tina asked.

"Well, when I was younger, my mother was a beautician. I used to sit with my dolls and watch her work. I learned a lot of things just by imitating her."

She put the finishing touches on Tina's braid, the stepped back. "Well, how do you like it?"

Tina stared at herself in awe. Her bangs fell softly over her eyebrows. She took a small mirror and turned around to see the back of her hair. It was beautiful and elegant. She returned to her position and smiled, feeling pretty.

"I love it!" she said.

Karen grabbed her purse. "Great—let's go!"

*   *   *

Back at the college cafeteria, Hope nibbled with little ambition on a chicken casserole. Allison, next to her, ate heartily, not daring to aggravate Hope. Something had really been bothering her lately. She had been almost impossible to be around. Allison shrugged to herself. When was Hope ever pleasant to be around? At least they didn't have a lot of the same classes! Next semester, maybe she'd see about getting another roommate.

What Allison did not realize, though, as she pondered upon her roommate, was that she was not well liked, either. Most of the students considered her an oversized, female bully. She was beautiful, in an exotic kind of way, with her black shoulder length hair, her olive complexion. Her beauty served little purpose, though, as she had a hard time communicating with others. Her only other outside interest, it seemed, was working out. Her physique told that at one glance. She was formed like a piece of art, chiseled. The curves of her muscles blended together like perfectly placed puzzle pieces. Perhaps it was for this reason that guys shied away from her. It was hard to keep up with a flawless body combined with a brassy, cold attitude.

"What are you wearing to the Christmas dance?" she asked Hope, more to break the silence, than from sincere curiosity.

Hope slammed her fork down so hard on the table, that some of the students sitting nearby, stared at her. She leaned over the table and glared at Allison. "You, moron," she hissed, "I've not even been asked to go yet!"

Allison just rolled her eyes. "It's still over two weeks away; I'm sure you'll be asked by then."

"Well it sure won't be Kevin who does it!" she snapped.

"What is your problem with that guy?" Allison asked. "Sure he looks great, but he's got a girlfriend. He doesn't even know you're alive! Why don't you just leave him alone and find someone else? There are plenty of other guys here who look as good, if not better. At least they'd treat you with some respect. You can't even get that out of Kevin."

"I've gotten some respect out of him," Hope argued.

"He just feels sorry for you," Allison pointed out candidly.

Hope snatched up her tray, and stood up haughtily. "You are absolutely no kind of friend. You're so pessimistic! One day I'll have him! Nothing you say or do will stop me!"

Allison sat and shook her head as she watched Hope strut out of the cafeteria. It was useless to argue with her. She started to take another bite of food when she noticed someone staring at her. It was a fellow from one of her classes. He got up from his seat, then walked over to her. She held her breath, as he asked her to go with him to the dance. With much effort, she hid her enthusiasm while she accepted. When he walked away, she smiled from ear to ear. She had a date to the dance, and Hope hadn't even been asked yet! She happily went back to finishing her meal.

*   *   *

"That looks great on you!" Karen exclaimed.

Tina stared at herself in the boutique's mirror. She was wearing a full-length crimson dress that Karen had helped her pick out. It had a straight neckline in the front, and a deep plunge in the back. The sleeves were long, but worn off the shoulders. A V-shaped waistline preceded the full skirt. The dress was made of satin, with a layer of crimson lace on the skirt. On her feet, she wore matching satin shoes that were too big for her.

"Those are just sample shoes," the saleslady explained. "We can order any shoe you want in any size. It'll take about a week for them to come in. For just an extra six dollars, they'll dye them for you at the factory."

Tina nodded. "I love this dress!" She glanced at the price tag. "What I really came for though, is to see about renting a formal dress."

"I don't have one like that, that you can rent," the saleslady answered. "I can show you some that are for rental purposes, but I don't believe you'll find one as exquisite as this one."

"How much is it for everything?" Karen asked.

"Well, it should be close to the price range that you mentioned," she answered. "Let's see what we have." She leaned over and began entering figures on the calculator. "Shoes, dress, brazier, crinoline—that'll come up to $431.28, including tax."

Tina subtracted in her head, then frowned. "That's $81.28 extra that I don't have," she said sorrowfully.

"No it's not," Karen said, reaching into her purse. She handed the saleslady a credit card. "Could you just put the extra amount on this?"

The woman smiled. "That'll be just fine! We can accommodate you there!"

Tina held up her hand in protest. "No, Karen, I can't accept that! Let me just look at something else!"

Karen looked at Tina. "Shut up, Tina. Merry Christmas!"

Tina opened her mouth to argue, but the saleslady was already ringing everything up on the cash register. Karen was grinning from ear to ear. If she talked too much, she might hurt Karen's feelings. She shifted uncomfortably from one foot to the other. No one had ever done anything like this for her. She'd never be able to repay Karen. There was nothing she could offer her that Karen didn't already have.

Karen helped Tina carry her things out to the car. As they were walking, Tina tried to express her appreciation for what her friend had just done.

"Thanks so much! I know there's nothing I can say that will prove to you what this means to me," she said sincerely.

"I know what it means to you," Karen answered. "I know for sure that you would have done it for me."

Tina nodded. She was now looking forward to the dance. Two weeks now seemed like an eternity away.

CHAPTER FOURTEEN

"ALAN, DON'T YOU BELIEVE IN picking up after yourself?" Kevin asked. He was standing in the middle of the room, frowning at the mess. Alan's clothes were scattered haphazardly all over the floor. The waste basket was overflowing with beer cans and empty potato chip bags. Alan's bed, as usual, was unmade. It appeared to have been slept in a hundred times without being made.

Alan clutched his heart, feigning a heart attack. "Oh, no!" he shouted. "You've been possessed by my mother! Where's the priest?! Where's the holy water?!"

"Very funny," Kevin said. He was pushing the clothes into a heap, which was rapidly taking the form of a small mountain.

He looked over at Alan, who still had made no attempt to move.

"Come on, man, help me!" Kevin ordered.

""What's the hurry? I always have it like this!" Alan grumbled.

Kevin laughed. "Sorry, friend, but Karen's coming over to study with me tonight. You can't expect me to expose her to this, can you?"

Alan frowned, then got up off the edge of the bed. He started picking things up. He moved slowly, though, and held everything as if it weighed a ton. Kevin patted him on the back.

"I hope you live through this," he said.

Alan grunted, and kept on with his horrendous chore. Kevin shook his head and walked off. He'd never let Karen walk through a mess like that. He wondered what a house of theirs would look like. His and Karen's. It'd be contemporary and clean, unlike this rat hole he was dwelling in now. Also, it would be large, with lots of rooms. There would have to be many rooms, because he knew he'd want children later. His and Karen's children would be beautiful! He knew that. Kevin smiled to himself at the thoughts of a life together, forever with Karen. He rummaged through his dresser drawer and took out a little box. Inside, he had some money that he'd been saving. He counted it. It might be enough for what he wanted to buy. Clutching the money in his right hand, he looked up. Yes, it would be wonderful to spend the rest of his life with her. With that pleasant thought on his mind, he grabbed his car keys and left.

$$* \quad * \quad *$$

On the way to the jewelry store, Kevin thought about the perfect ring for Karen. It would have to be one that reflected everything that she was. He wanted a diamond that would capture the cold blue crystal of her eyes. It would have to reflect the bright sun as the rays bounced off her golden hair. Also, it would have to be like her in shape. She was not tall, but she was slender and delicate. A marquise shape would suit Karen. Like her, it would be slender, but delicate on the ends. It would put other girls' rings to shame with the way it would shine. Karen was the most beautiful girl, who should wear the prettiest diamond on her creamy white hand.

Kevin smiled to himself. It seemed like an eternity ago when he was just a clumsy high school boy in love with the elusive blonde cheerleader. Sometimes he forgot about all the parties that she had gone to—parties to which he was never invited. Had he gone to any of them, he doubted that anyone would have even recognized him. "Popular" students didn't know that other people existed out of their select group. A chill when over his body as he thought about the changes he had gone through that past summer.

Obsession had driven him to work out on his body, until he trembled in exhaustion. Every time he had wanted to give up, he just looked at the picture on the wall. It was his only inspiration, but it was enough. If she would not be there in person, he was satisfied with that picture. He'd had no choice. Many days, he had sat on the edge of his bed staring at the poster sized photo. God, she was beautiful! Her small body was frozen in mid-air. Her golden mane framed her face and flowed in the blue sky like a wild bird. Her arms were held high, while her shapely legs were tucked under her body. The most awesome thing about the picture had to be her face. She was smiling at the world. Her lips and her cheeks were flushed, so that she glowed in a natural beauty. Her eyes in that picture appeared as two pools of lapis blue water. They sparkled more than any diamond, as they reflected the sky. Kevin smiled. Now that beautiful girl was his. When they had started college, he was in a small play. It was put on by the freshmen as part of Orientation Week. He'd sent Karen a dozen roses, along with an invitation. Inside the card, was a ticket, plus a note. In his letter he'd told her how beautiful he thought she was, and to please come to the play. He'd also mentioned the part he was playing. It was vital that she saw him, and he hoped she'd come.

She *did* come that night. Kevin had seen her from behind the curtain. He'd watched as she'd made her way down the aisle. She'd been alone that night. Her face held that unsure look of being in a new place and away from home for the first time. She'd glanced around at all the strange faces. It'd been so different from high school where she'd been surrounded by friends constantly. He had watched with relief while she glanced at her ticket, then took her place at the exact spot he'd wanted her to be.

When he had acted that night, he'd done his best. His whole heart and soul went into the play that night. For some reason, he had felt that if he did less than perfect, his chance of winning her would be lost forever.

After the play, he'd rushed to her before she'd had a chance to leave. His heart almost stopped when she'd accepted a dinner date with him. They had left the play together that night to get something to eat. The rest was history. For some reason, she was attracted to him, even though she'd only remembered him vaguely from school. They had spent the entire evening reminiscing about the high school days. She and her boyfriend had broken up soon after summer vacation had started. It didn't seem to bother her, because she laughed and treated Kevin as though they'd always been close friends. Maybe she was lonely and felt homesick for a familiar face. Whatever it was, Kevin had not minded. He could take being used, as long as Karen was the one using him.

That date had led to another date, and so on. Within one short month they were "boyfriend and girlfriend". Everything had happened so quickly, that it made Kevin ecstatic, yet nervous. Were they moving too fast? Maybe. Nonetheless, all thoughts of moderation quickly slipped out of his mind as he jerked the key out of the ignition. Somewhere in the shopping center, there was a ring just waiting for Karen. He was going to get it now—no matter what.

*   *   *

The night that everyone had been waiting for finally arrived. It was the night of the Christmas dance. Dorms were bustling with the sounds of people getting ready. It was mass confusion as people struggled with hair, clothes, and makeup. Everyone wanted to look perfect. It was as if there was something in the air that drove them to look their best. All of the excitement that had been building up that week, now exploded like fireworks.

At their homes away from the campus, professors were getting ready, too. They would be at the party as chaperons. Worrisome thoughts consumed them at the prospect of having so many young people in so close of a space at one time. Especially after all that had already happened thus far, they feared yet another tragedy. Would anyone get hurt? Would anyone cause trouble? One never knew when such a large crowd was gathered. It was a huge responsibility and one to definitely be nervous about. This was so different from the days not so long ago, it seemed, when they had flirted and danced. They, who had loved and laughed effortlessly, would now stand and watch. Years ago, they had ignored the feelings of their chaperons. Now they were standing in the same shoes, and it felt strange. At least there would be plenty of good food. That should soften the blow some. Whatever worries that anyone might have had, the time came to go on. All that they had planned was happening right before their eyes, and tomorrow, it would be a memory. People put the finishing touches on themselves, and it was off to the dance!

The night was beautiful! The air was cold, but the wind was not blowing. In the black sky, stars danced and sparkled like tiny gemstones. They put on a show for everyone, and each star seemed to plead silently, "Look at me! Look at me!" The towering trees bordering the campus, reached out pine-covered branches towards the students. As people passed by, the trees seemed to blow pine-scented kisses to them. The fragrance was sweet, with a slight touch of spice, and everyone inhaled approvingly.

In the lobby of her dorm, Tina took one final look at herself in the mirror. Her hair was pulled back in a French braid. Close to the bottom of the braid, was an elegant red bow. Her deep brown eyes had a healthy glow to them. They added a special beauty to her light brown skin. Red lips curved into a smile as she saw Matthew walk into the lobby. He stared at her from head to toe, then smiled in approval. This beautiful girl in red was all his tonight! She looked like a wild thing that had almost been tamed. There was still a mischievous glimmer in her eyes, though, and he was prepared for the unexpected!

Tina looked Matthew over. He was dressed in a black long-tailed tuxedo. Shiny ebony shoes peered out from under his pants. About his waist, was a red satin sash that matched her dress. He stood tall and proud, and his blonde hair shone. Tina had seen him dressed up many times, for he only wore the best. Tonight, however, his clothes exceeded anything he had ever worn. He was rich, and tonight especially, it showed.

"You're beautiful, Tina," he said, as he leaned down and kissed her on the cheek.

This time Tina did not blush, and she returned the compliment.

Matthew held out his arm. "Shall we go?" he asked.

"It's what I've been waiting for," Tina replied, as she slipped her hand through his arm.

*   *   *

Since the dance was in the gym, and the night was so lovely, many people walked. The campus was a cobweb of sidewalks, so it was really more feasible to walk, then to drive a car just a few blocks. Tina smiled to herself as she watched the other people. Everyone looked so wonderful tonight! She strained her eyes to see if she could find Karen among the crowd. Her roommate had eluded her all day, and it bothered her. Karen knew, of course, what Tina was wearing, but she'd refused to reveal anything about what she would be dressed in tonight. If only she had given Tina some clue, but all she had said was, "Wait and see!" It wasn't fair. Karen knew how much Tina hated suspense, yet she seemed to gloat in the fact that Tina was immensely curious.

Tina temporarily forgot Karen, as they got closer to the gym. The sound of music was blaring outside, drawing students to the doors. It was clear and loud, and Tina could already feel it thumping through her veins. When they entered, she gasped. It was so beautiful! Though she had helped decorate, she had not expected the beauty that met her eyes. The gym was completely unrecognizable. She felt as though she had stepped into another dimension. The center attraction was a twenty foot Christmas tree. A rainbow of blinking colors cascaded down its pine dress. Tinsel glittered like millions of tiny icicles. The round glass ornaments dangled majestically from the branches. At the top, in the place of honor, was an elegant gold star.

Above the tree, was a panorama of color. Crepe ribbons stretched and dipped in a beautiful web. They were complimented by delicate lace snowflakes, which hung daintily from the ceiling. It appeared as though the sky had sent a myriad of colors, not to reach the ground, but to pause here on the ceiling and please all who saw it.

To the right of the tree, was a hors d'oeuvres table. It stretched the length of half of the gym. On it rested so many tempting foods, that it would take several plates, should anyone even try to taste a little of everything. Already, students were slithering down the line, modestly picking all of the good things that they could fit on their plates.

The cafeteria staff smiled, glad to be out of their white uniforms for a change. They laughed and chatted with the students while making sure that the food stayed well stocked. Under the table were more trays, nestled on small carts. In the event that they needed even more than that, the coolers in the kitchen were stocked to capacity.

At the end of the table, waiting for the students, sat an enormous punch bowl. In it was a sea of red, citrus scented punch, topped with strawberries floating about in a scalloped ice ring. Inez was in charge of the punch, and she grinned as she poured punch for the students. She looked quite refreshing in an emerald green dress that she wore over her rounded figure. She wore makeup tonight, and when she smiled, she was pretty. Most of the students knew her, and she beamed more and more with each compliment.

Angled in the left hand corner of the gym, was a stage that the students had constructed for the dance. This band was larger than the usual bands that were normally hired. There were a few musicians playing wind instruments, a pianist, and other musicians playing the string instruments. They played old and new songs, frequently throwing in much loved Christmas carols. There were two singers, a man and a woman. They were both dressed in midnight blue. She was in a sequined gown, he in a satin tux. Together they set the mood for this event. Her soprano voice rose above everything, and people paused to gaze at her. She was beautiful! Her slender oval face was creamy white, and offset with wide almond shaped hazel eyes. Her black hair was swept up and held in place with a sequined comb. Her long, graceful neck seemed to flow to her bosom, which was partially revealed by the v-shaped neckline. Her body was tall and lean, yet amply blessed with feminine curves.

The man beside her seemed unaffected by her beauty as he sang with her. His chocolate brown eyes sometimes closed as he let himself get completely involved in his singing. His body towered about a foot over the woman. As he sang, he tried to ignore the stares from the mesmerized girls below, but it was hard. Nonetheless, he had a job to do, and he did it well.

"Oh, Matthew, this is beautiful!" Tina cried.

He nodded. "Word has it, that this is the most they've ever spent on a dance in the history of this college."

"I believe it," Tina agreed, as she glanced about.

They continued towards the tables of hors d'oeuvres. Tina's eyes grew large. There was so much! How could she eat without looking like a complete hog? She helped herself to many things she wanted, and at the same time passed up a lot of other things she would have liked to have sampled. Once she reached for a cracker, and her hand collided with Matthew's. They looked at one another, and laughed, after which he quickly kissed her on the cheek. They moved on with the others, this time a little more carefully. When they reached the punch bowl, Inez gleamed at her helper.

"Tina, child," she cried, "you look so pretty tonight!"

"Thanks, Inez," Tina answered. "You look very pretty, too!"

"Where's the other half?" Inez asked.

"If you're referring to Karen," Tina answered, "I haven't seen her all day."

"Well, child, you'll see her tonight! Ain't nobody missing this!"

Tina nodded. "I know that's a fact! See you later, Inez!"

"Bye, child!"

Tina and Matthew walked away from the tables. They found two chairs close to the right hand corner of the gym. When they had seated themselves, Tina tasted of the punch. She smiled in relief; it hadn't been spiked yet. She bit into a Christmas cookie shaped like a star. The sweet pink cherry frosting practically melted on her tongue. That cookie was soon gone, and the only thing left behind was its delicious memory.

They had finished eating without Tina ever seeing a trace of Karen or Kevin. She wondered if anything was wrong. Maybe they were just running late. Perhaps they'd had a wreck! God, please, no! Suppose they had fought tonight? It could happen. Then that could mean that there was a chance that they had brok...

"Do you want to dance?" Matthew asked, unwittingly interrupting her thoughts.

Tina pushed Karen and Kevin to the back of her mind. She nodded at Matthew, who took her plate and cup. On the way to the dance floor, when he threw everything away, he took her hand in his. They reached the others, and he pulled her close to him. A slow, haunting melody was playing. As they danced, Tina became acutely aware of the warmth of his body. They'd never gotten this close to each other physically, since they'd started spending time together. It was an overwhelming feeling, but one she could not distinguish. She relaxed, then rested her head on his chest. A mild, pleasant smell drifted up. She'd never smelled that cologne before, and instantly knew she'd always associate that wonderful scent with Matthew. She inhaled softly, again and again, trying to guess what it was that he had on.

"You're not one for words, are you, Tina?" Matthew asked. He was amused at her silence. Seldom did he meet a girl who was at a loss for words. It surprised him, and made her even more attractive to him. He knew that her mind must be racing, and it drove him crazy with pleasure, anticipating what she might be thinking.

"I'm not one for many words," Tina admitted. She stared into his eyes. "When I do talk, though, it's true, and completely from the heart."

Matthew didn't say anything, but watched as Tina burst out laughing.

"What's so funny?" he asked.

"I just realized how stupid I sounded," she confessed.

Matthew stopped dancing, and held both of her hands in his.

"If you say something stupid, I'll tell you."

Tina started to say something in response, but the sound of people suddenly talking excitedly distracted her. She turned to see a group of students making a fuss over a couple who had just walked in. In between everyone, she caught a glimpse of Karen and Kevin. She shook herself away from Matthew and went to see her friends. She stood there with the others and stared. Karen and Kevin appeared as though they were at the wrong event. They were too beautiful for tonight! They looked like movie stars, instead of college students. Karen's shiny blonde hair fell to her waist in a mass of waves and curls. Above her blue eyes, blonde hair swept back, generously revealing her smooth forehead and her blondish-brown eyebrows. Her face was as radiant as a bright candle. It out shined all the other faces.

On her tiny figure, she wore a white dress. It had a rounded neckline that was decorated with tiny sequins. The dress was simple; it merely flowed like milk from her neck to her feet. Tina noticed enviously that it was not even gathered at the waist. She guessed that the dress must be no more than a size 5.

On her upper body, she wore a jacket of sequins. With each slight movement, people's eyes met a kaleidoscope of colors. She looked like an angel, with her porcelain skin and white dress.

Tina looked down at her own dress, and suddenly felt childish. If only she had chosen an elegant dress like Karen's! She was still looking critically at herself when Karen noticed her. She tapped Kevin on the arm, and pushed her way through the crowd.

"Tina," she cried, "you're so beautiful tonight!" Karen hugged her friend, then pulled back to admire her. Tina grinned sheepishly as she noticed Kevin standing behind Karen. He was dressed in a white long-tailed tuxedo. She thought that he looked as if he was getting married, and she wished desperately that when he did, she could be his bride.

"You both look wonderful tonight," Tina finally managed. She wondered if she had sounded sincere. They both *did* look wonderful, but it hurt her pride to admit it. She wanted to look beautiful to Kevin, but now she felt as though she had lost all chances to impress him.

Karen stepped around Tina, and hugged Matthew. He seemed happy that he had finally been noticed. Guilt overcame Tina at the ease with which she'd abandoned him. Until Karen noticed Matthew, she'd forgotten all about him!

"You look good tonight, too," Karen told Matthew. He beamed at the compliment, and Tina had to fight the urge to slap him, *and* Karen. Why didn't she just go back to Kevin and leave Matthew alone? Wasn't she satisfied having the best guy in the world? Why did she have to gush over another girl's date?

Tina wondered why Karen was acting so elated. It was out of character for her to hug someone she was not involved with.

Tina glanced at Matthew for a moment as a terrible thought crossed her mind, but she quickly dismissed it. It had not been an erotic hug that he'd received, but rather one of sheer joy. She was still contemplating what had come over Karen, when Karen grabbed her by the wrist. In her excitement, she did not notice that she was practically cutting the blood circulation from Tina's arm. She drew her friend back into her little crowd, with Kevin right beside her.

"I've got some wonderful news!" she announced. She was still holding Tina's wrist in one hand and Kevin's hand in the other.

Tina glared at her, annoyed. Couldn't she tell that her vice-like grip was unwanted?

All of a sudden, Karen released Tina's arm. She thrust out her hand to the crowd. On the ring finger of her left hand was a diamond. It was not huge, but it was a diamond! Tina stared at it, a feeling of repulsion overcoming her. "God, please don't let her say it . . . . *please*," she begged silently.

As if she'd received a slap in her face to her prayer, Karen said the dreaded words. She said it so loud and so clear, that the words seemed to burn Tina's ears. "Kevin's asked me to marry him, and I've said 'yes'."

As people oohed and ahhed and gave their words of congratulations, Tina felt herself getting fainter. In the one minute that she remained there, she felt as though her life had stopped. All that was left was this horrible moment that was seemingly going on forever. She looked through blurred eyes at the happy faces of those around her. People were hugging Karen and shaking Kevin's hand. "This is so stupid!" Tina thought. "Don't they know that it won't work out? They haven't even been dating a year!"

No one noticed her until Karen turned to her. Tina knew that her friend expected words of congratulations. Fighting a wave of nausea, she managed a smile. It was a beautiful smile, which belied her true feelings. Everyone got quiet, for they knew that whatever Tina had to say, would be of utmost importance to Karen. After all, Tina was her best friend.

"Nothing I can say can express the way I feel for you tonight!" she managed. "Congratulations!" There. It was said.

Karen beamed, missing the double meaning of Tina's words. She threw her arms around Tina's neck. "I love you, girl!"

Tina smiled again, and fearing that her eyes would betray her, she slowly withdrew from the small crowd. Matthew followed her, and they sat down again.

"Tonight's full of surprises, isn't it?" he asked.

Tina looked at him and simply nodded. This time her smile was almost non-existent. Was he stupid?! Could he not see that her world had come to an end? Nothing would ever be the same again. Now until the end of the school year, she would have to hear endless talk about wedding plans. Depending upon the length of the engagement, the torture could go on indefinitely. There would be constant talk of the wedding. Surely no day would go by without Karen raving about it or asking her to go shopping with her. Closed mouthed, she have to sit through endless sessions of hearing Karen ramble on about napkins, decorations, invitations, and so on.

She cringed at the thought of seeing Karen choose a wedding dress. She'd have to stand there, coy and polite, while Karen's mother and the salespeople made a fuss over how beautiful a bride she would be. She could see it now: Karen in front of triple mirrors, smiling and looking like a goddess. It would be too much!

She looked at Matthew. He was smiling at her, and again, she had the urge to slap his face. Instead, she excused herself, and went to the restroom. The crowd of students had grown very large by now, but she paid them little attention. They were merely a sea of blurred faces that seemed to dissolve right before her eyes. Finally she made it to the restrooms. As soon as she walked through the door, some of the anxiety left. She sucked in the cool air, for the room wasn't very well heated. Her hand rested on her breasts as she breathed heavily, hungrily, as though she'd been under water for a long time, and was just now getting relief. Where her hand rested, a stabbing pain grew. It was as though a knife was lodged in her heart.

She walked over to the long row of basins and viewed her reflection in the mirror. The face looking back at her was beautiful, yet sad. She blinked back tears. Her mother was gone.

Her father, too, was gone. Now the only other person that she really wanted to spend the rest of her life with was out of her grasp. Sure he wasn't dead, but once married, he'd be almost just as elusive. He'd be unreachable. More so than he was now.

She hung her head down. "Oh, Kevin," she whispered, "why did you do it?"

There was no response, except for the showers in the back. They dripped slowly and constantly. Each drop that fell seemed to moan to her, "Gone, gone, gone....". She stood there listening to them until she felt that she would go crazy if she stayed another minute. She had to get out, and she had to do it now.

She slammed her fist against the rim of the basin. She had to do something about Matthew. It would be rude to just leave him. Gathering her emotions together, she managed a phony smile, and went back out into the crowd to find Matthew.

Matthew was at the punch bowl. He wasn't thirsty, but it beat sitting there looking stupid, while Tina took forever to get out of the bathroom. He wondered why she had looked so strange when Karen had flashed her ring. All of a sudden, shame overtook him. Surely Tina must have felt embarrassed that he had not gotten her a gift for the evening. He had given her a lovely corsage, but he should have at least brought her a small gift, as well. Tonight would probably be the last time he saw her until after the holidays. He silently cursed himself for his stupidity. He'd have to find out exactly when she was leaving. She had told him that she would be spending the holidays with her aunt in Florida. Perhaps he could call the jewelry store and order something special to be delivered to her dorm. He was one of their regular customers, plus he had a charge account. That's what he'd do. He'd call Cindy Morrow, the attractive red-haired manager, and have her send something to Tina's dorm. He'd see to it that Cindy was well paid for her troubles.

He looked around, and saw that Tina had beaten him back to their chairs. Quickly, he approached and handed her some punch. She appeared as though she was not feeling well. She accepted the punch, and he watched as she drank. When it was all gone, she looked up at him.

"Matthew, I don't know how to say this, but I've got to go. I'm not feeling well. I think all the excitement, plus the fatigue from the exams, has gotten to me."

She stood up, and he took her by the hand. "OK," he said, "we can go. I've about had enough for tonight, too."

Tina shook her head. "I can walk myself to the dorm."

He wouldn't hear of such a thing, and promised her that if he wanted to go back to the dance, he would. So Tina had to spend even more time acting happy. Not even the darkness would hide her face, because lights were all over the campus. They walked in silence, each wondering what the other was thinking. Tina tried not to walk too fast, though she wanted to break free and run. She didn't want to hurt Matthew's feelings, though, so she kept her pace at a painfully slow stroll. She wondered if she would ever find relief, and if this eternal night would come to an end.

Just when she thought she couldn't stand it any longer, they reached the dorm. They walked quietly to her floor, and she took out her key. After apologizing once more, she kissed Matthew, and tried to convince him, that she really had a good time. He stood as she went inside and closed the door. He did not know that she was leaning against the door, listening for his retreating footsteps. He walked away slowly, wondering if she would be all right. She had apologized, and she *seemed* to have been telling the truth. Still something was out of place, but he couldn't figure it out. He'd just go back to the dance. If he tried to go to bed now, he'd just toss and turn, wondering what it was that he had done wrong.

As soon as she heard Matthew walk away, Tina let the tears flow. They came as though a dam had broken, and her body shook violently. Again and again she beat her sore fist on the wall. Once she let out a cry of defeat. It rose through the air, and drifted down the hall. Not one person heard it; there was no one there.

After she had run out of tears, she got undressed. Her body shook with sobs, and her make-up was streaked. Unceremoniously, she dumped her expensive clothes to the floor. She reached into the drawer for her soft cotton gown. As she slipped it over her head, she started feeling better. It was a familiar item, unlike the dress she'd worn this evening.

As the gown went over her head, she saw her stuffed bear in the corner. As childish as it seemed, almost all of the girls on campus had at least one stuffed animal in their rooms. Tina bent down to pick it up. She smiled at it, then held it to her breast. This toy had been with her for as long as she could remember. She wiped her tears on its plush head, and held it up so that its eyes faced hers.

"You understand what I've gone through, don't you?" she asked.

The bear just seemed to stare back at her in a trance, and she held back a sob. After rubbing its soft head for a few moments, she took it to bed with her. She snuggled under the covers, reaching up momentarily to turn off the bedside lamp. Now that she'd stopped crying, she realized just how deathly quiet the place was. Her only consolation was that she'd be leaving in a couple of days.

As much unhappiness as Florida's memories held for her, she still missed it. Orlando's bright sunshine and balmy winds were home to her. She was stupid to think that things would be better here. She would never be able to get used to the cold, and she missed the beautiful, timeless ocean. In a couple of days, she'd be back at her aunt's home. She'd throw her things in the car when she got there, then she'd drive out to the coast. With that pleasant thought on her mind, she drifted off to sleep.

A few hours later, Kevin brought Karen back to the dorm. In all of their excitement, they had forgotten about Tina. It was only when they'd seen Matthew dancing with another girl, that they'd found out about her early departure. By then, it was too late, for the party was almost over. Now as they peeped in the door, they could see her sleeping peacefully. Karen grinned when she saw the bear clutched tightly in Tina's arm. Kevin smiled, too, but neither of them laughed at her. They embraced in the hallway, then Kevin walked off. Karen closed the door behind her, and stood there for a moment. She held out her hand. The ring sparkled even in the small amount of light that seeped into the room.

She smiled to herself. Soon she would be Kevin's wife. She knew that deep in her heart, that all her fooling around would have to stop. There would be no more dating other guys. A chill went over her body at the thought, and for the first time that night, she began to realize what she'd gotten herself into. Part of her felt ready for a commitment, but the other part was extremely fearful of it. She wondered if she would be able to resist the temptation of others. Once again the ring caught her eye, and she stared down at it. "Yes," she thought, "I can be faithful. Maybe it won't be that hard to do. I'm engaged now to a person I love very much."

With that on her mind, she undressed and got ready for bed. On the outside, she appeared sure of her impending vows, but on the inside, she was very nervous. She pushed the thought away, making excuses for the way that she felt. It had been a long day. She was tired. After a good night's sleep, she'd see things more clearly.

CHAPTER FIFTEEN

THE DAY CAME TO LEAVE for the holidays with blinding sun and cutting wind. Tina watched from her window as Karen was escorted to her car by Kevin. He struggled with a couple of large suitcases. She strolled beside him carrying an overnight bag and her purse. Karen opened the trunk of her car, while Kevin stood by gazing at her in ridiculous wonder. He placed the suitcases in the trunk, then gently took the overnight bag from Karen. He fit the bag on top of the suitcases, and shut the trunk.

"That's it, Kevin," Tina muttered, "don't let her strain her back."

She glanced at her own suitcases, which she would be carrying out herself.

"Oh, well," she thought, "such is my destiny."

As she returned to the window, her stomach knotted up, as Kevin took Karen into his arms. He kissed her passionately, while Karen gladly returned the kiss.

"This is *way* too much," she stated, as she turned away from the window. She checked the room once more for any items she may have forgotten to pack. It felt too quiet in the room, and the dorm was beginning to take on the same aura, as more and more students left. There was something very unnatural about a once life-filled building becoming quiet. It made everything sound too loud.

Tina fought off a chill, then bent down to get her suitcases. She carried them to the door, set them in the hallway, and stared once more at the empty room. With a sign, she closed the door and locked it.

*   *   *

The airport was bustling with people. Tina sat in a café, sipping on a cup of coffee, watching the crowds. It was actually a pleasant distraction. The airport's many shops were a kaleidoscope of brightly lit Christmas colors. Children, holding on tightly to parents' hands, were gazing in awe at the sheer largeness of the airport. Announcements were coming through the intercom, almost back to back, as planes were boarding the unusually high number of travelers.

Tina glanced at her watch. Soon, she would have to make her way to her gate. It was just so relaxing where she sat, and the hot coffee tasted so good, that she'd wait a little longer.

When the coffee was finished, Tina made her way to the waiting area for her departing flight. The lobby was practically full with other passengers who'd be sharing the next couple of hours in close proximity to her. Most seemed to be families or couples, and for the first time since she'd arrived at the airport, she felt a pang of loneliness. If only someone she knew was traveling on the same flight! Others had apparently chosen other routes, while many had simple decided to drive.

She didn't have much time to wallow in her loneliness, for at that moment, one of the flight attendants announced that it was time to board. This was the moment that nervous anticipation hit her. She was relatively comfortable with flying, but always had the fear in the back of her mind about something going wrong with the plane. She shrugged the feeling off, got in line behind the other passengers, and presented her ticket to the flight attendant.

*   *   *

Later, from the sky, Tina stared out of her window in awe. No matter how many times she would fly, she would never be able to get over the view from a jet at altitude. The clouds passed underneath her and beside of her, occasionally giving breaks which allowed her a view of the earth below. The landscape appeared to be one gigantic map of green and brown.

"Would you like something to drink?"

The voice of the flight attendant interrupted her thoughts. Tina glanced up to see a brunette haired woman standing there.

"Yes, I would," Tina said. "A soft drink would be great!"

The attendant handed Tina a clear plastic cup filled with ice, then she popped open the tab on a soft drink. She poured the drink over the ice, and left the remainder of the can on Tina's tray.

Tina sipped quietly, while she resumed gazing out of the window. The cold drink felt good on her stomach. Air travel had a tendency to make her queasy. She was sure the passenger next to her would really *not* appreciate it if she were to get sick! She pushed the thought away, and resumed gazing outside.

When she was done with the drink, and the trash had been collected, she laid back in her seat. She closed her eyes and fell asleep to the roar of the jet engines. There were dreams, but they were sporadic and senseless, and filled with the hum of the air hissing from the vent, and the mumble of other passengers.

*   *   *

When Tina landed at the airport, she went straight to the baggage claim area. The crowd was so thick, that she had a moment where it was difficult to breath. It was hard not to feel some anxiety in such a large crowd! The trip had left her feeling tired and a bit nauseated. She was so prone to getting airsick! It would feel wonderful to get her bags and go home!

She stood by the conveyor belt and waited. In a few minutes an alarm sounded and the belt began moaning and screeching as it turned. It moved along slowly, like a giant snake. Before long, suitcases were covering it, moving with the same slow indifference. Tina scanned the area for her bags, as other passengers pulled their belongings off.

When she finally reached out for her bags, she heard her aunt calling her. Tina turned around to see her Aunt Beth walking quickly towards her. A big smile came across her face, as she watched her aunt. Beth was dressed in jeans and a pretty knit top. She had her purse in one hand, while she waved with the other. When she reached Tina, they embraced.

"Sweetie, I'm sorry I'm late," she said. "The parking was impossible! We'll need to take another plane just to get to the car!"

Tina laughed. "After flying, I can use some walking."

Beth stared at her, concerned, "Airsick?"

Tina nodded. "I guess I'd better be glad that it wasn't a cross country flight!"

Her aunt nodded. "Here, Darling, let me help you with these." She reached down and took one of the suitcases. Tina was glad that this time she didn't have to deal with them by herself. They went through the airport and out into the bright Florida sunshine.

Beth put on her sunglasses, as she scanned the parking lot.

"I can never remember where I park," she complained, as she dug through her purse and produced a scrap piece of paper with the parking lane number on it.

"OK, here it is!" she cried out.

They walked for what seemed like a mile, until they reached Aunt Beth's car. Together they loaded the suitcases in the trunk, then got into the car.

As they paid the parking lot attendant, Aunt Beth turned to Tina.

"I thought that we'd just go get something to eat, if you feel like it."

Tina put her hand on her stomach. "I think I want to eat. It's hard to tell, though. I feel that if I eat, I'll get sick, but if I don't I'll get sicker."

We'll make it simple," Beth stated.

Tina nodded, and leaned back in the car seat, while her aunt drove to a hamburger restaurant. They didn't even have to get out of the car, as the employees rode skates to the customer's car to take orders and bring the food!

"When did this place open up?" Tina asked later, as she bit into a sinfully juicy hamburger.

"About three weeks ago," Beth answered. "It's supposed to serve the best hamburgers in the city."

"It does," Tina agreed, as she wiped her mouth with a napkin. The food was delicious!

They ate in quiet contentment, and pretty soon, the aches in Tina's stomach subsided. Full and satisfied, she took the trash and threw it into a nearby can.

When she returned to the car, Beth smiled at her. "Ready to go home?" she asked.

Tina smiled back. She was no longer hungry, and the food was making her sleepy.

"Yes," she answered. "Let's go home."

*   *   *

Later that evening, Aunt Beth stared at Tina from across the table. She pulled her glasses off. With her deep brown eyes, she studied her niece. Tina was not the same girl who had left for college a few months ago. The girl who had left her home was a bubbling, innocent, bright-eyed child. Now Beth saw a girl who seemed withdrawn. The gleam was somewhat gone from her eyes, and her face was pale. She noticed that Tina has lost some weight, from her already slender figure. Even now she piddled with her food, as though in a trance.

Tina looked up from her plate, and noticed her aunt watching her. Aunt Beth immediately lowered her eyes. An uncomfortable silence followed, while each resumed the task of eating.

After she'd composed herself, Tina stole another glance at her aunt. Beth was a pretty woman. Though Tina guessed that her aunt was up in her years, she really didn't know how old Beth actually was. Aunt Beth had never discussed her age, and Tina had not embarrassed her by prying. She looked to be about thirty-five, but Tina knew she was much older. Her aunt had taken good care of herself, and now it was paying off. Her light-brown hair fell into soft, full curls at the bottom of her neck. Her skin which used to be tanned, now had taken on a more alabaster appearance. It had been years since she'd exposed herself to sunbathing. The most she got out of the Florida sunshine was her daily walks. Aunt Beth was a fanatic for sunsets, so she walked every evening to enjoy the view.

Her manner of dress was usually casual; she either wore cotton shorts or comfortable jeans. She was known to dress elegantly, though, when the occasion called for it. Tina remembered times when her aunt was the envy of a lot of other women. The few parties that she had been allowed to attend as a child, were like golden memories in her mind. She remembered men making all kind of fusses over Beth. At the time, it used to bother her, because her aunt was unmarried, and never returned the advances. Tina used to wonder why, but as the years wore on, it became something as common as her own reflection in the mirror.

She had caught bits and pieces of rumors that her aunt had come very close to being a bride. It was when Beth was eighteen, Tina's mother had said, and her father had heartily disapproved of the young man. Like most parents, they felt that he was not good enough for their daughter. He appeared to be a rough neck, without a promising future, spending his afternoons working at a garage. Not that Beth's family was above his status, because they were a middle-class family, also. They just had their own ways, and felt that his ambitions were limited. Like most people in love, though, Beth was consumed with the young man, to the point of oblivion. Beth argued with her parents almost constantly, despising her father, and hurting her mother with her rebellious words.

She was smitten with the young man, and would hear nothing negative in regard to him. He was tall and the most handsome thing she'd ever seen. His jet black hair, swept to the side, in the style of the day, was the most luxurious thing she'd ever touched. His eyes were gray, like pinpoints of ice on the edge of a snowstorm. When he held her in his arms, her mundane world ceased to exist, as she created a new life around him.

Word had it that Beth went against her father's wishes, and made plans to marry her boyfriend. When her father suspected her plans to do this, he became livid. He threatened to move the family away, to have the boy arrested, and a number of other threats a parent makes in desperation. Beth, forced to choose between the love of her life, and her parents' wishes, made a drastic choice. She'd left home, with a couple of suitcases and all of the money she'd saved since she was a child. She boarded a bus to Florida, where she and her love would meet. She would establish herself in an apartment and a job, while he stayed behind for a few weeks. Hopefully, the volatile situation at home would become calmer, and he could appease the ongoing bitterness of her parents. With time, perhaps Beth's parents could accept that she was no longer a helpless child, and that her boyfriend was indeed worthy of her. She would have a good job and a lovely place to call her own. Then, when he came to join her, they would get married, with or without her parents' blessings.

She'd found a furnished apartment, bought some pretty things for it, and fixed it up for them. Each novelty or item she purchased was bought with love and in consideration of him. Anything to make the place a home was her daily endeavor. Soon, she even went around to bridal shops to try different gowns, in eager anticipation for her upcoming marriage. Had she had the funds, she would have had a gown waiting, as well, but she had to be careful. It wouldn't do for him to arrive and find her penniless! Each day that passed was torture for her, but it only meant that it was another day closer to the time when they would be together, again. Every night, in the strange city and room all alone, she closed her eyes, seeing his beautiful face. Her body tingled with anticipation, as she waited for her boyfriend to join her.

Days turned into weeks, then the weeks turned into almost three months. He never came. His love and devotion for her was fleeting and shallow. While she was getting everything ready in Orlando, he was back home making a play for one of her "friends". When she'd confronted him about his delay in coming to her, he'd broken down in tears. He admitted that things had moved too fast, that he wasn't ready for a commitment. He was too young, too unsure, and wasn't really ready to leave home, as he thought he'd been. In the next breath he confessed to having had an affair with her friend. Oh no, he wasn't in love; he was just lonely and gave in at a weak moment!

Even then, Beth was so desperate and frightened of her sudden independence, that she offered forgiveness should he choose to still join her. She had been ready to make this move, but never had anticipated making it alone. The fear of having no one near was more than she could bear! She was ready to swallow what was left of her pride. When he hedged in regard to her offer for forgiveness, she begged and pleaded with him. Still he refused. By then, Beth knew that he had indeed fallen in love with the other girl. His marriage a few months later rudely confirmed the horrible revelation.

Pride and hurt had prevented Beth from returning home. There would be no way she could face her family and her friends. In the few weeks that she'd been alone, she'd established a job, and had found consolation in the beautiful city of Orlando. No one there knew her personal life, so there was no shame. She could start a new life for herself, albeit alone. There would be no embarrassing questions to answer, because no one would know what to ask.

In her new environment, she found a sanctuary. There was something about the way the wind whispered through the palm trees at night, that make her feel surrounded by angels. She'd found a tiny slice of heaven in her sad life. Though the hurt faded a little each day, her trust in romantic love was shattered. Many people get past heartbreak numerous times. For Beth, it was just too much. She never planned to remain alone; it just happened.

Years later, a little older, and much wiser, Beth had worked her way up to an executive secretary position. In the earlier days, her only means of earning money was by working in offices, typing. It was something she almost didn't even have to think about, as the talent came naturally. She was faster and more accurate than a lot of the other girls. As her experience grew, she moved into an office in a larger corporation. At first, she felt guilty for making good money for something that she loved doing. Soon, though, she realized the company's need for someone like her. Her responsibilities increased along with her titles and her salaries. By the time she'd retired, she had a home of her own, completely paid for, a generous savings account, and a pretty comfortable pension.

Her home was not large, but it was perfect for her. It was a one-floor home with two bedrooms, one and a half bathrooms, dining room, living room, kitchen. It had a lovely garden with lots of flowers and a couple of towering palm trees.

It was a peaceful neighborhood, and many evenings were spent outside, sitting in the swing, watching the sun go down. Beth had made her peace many years ago, with her parents, but she had chosen to remain in this beautiful place. It was home to her, and where she belonged. Though she was alone, she had learned to become independent and happy. It felt good to depend on herself. She knew she'd never be hurt again by doing so.

Years ago, she never imagined that she would share the home with anybody, but then her sister and brother-in-law were killed in that terrible accident. Tina used to stay there every time her parents went away. They lived about an hour and a half away in Daytona, so Aunt Beth was the closest relative. Without planning it, Beth became a "parent" overnight. Now that Tina had spent most of her life with her in this house, it seemed as though she were her own daughter. That is why she was so concerned with her niece. She knew something was wrong with her.

"Do you not like the food?" she asked, breaking the silence.

Tina smiled. "The food is great, Aunt Beth. You know I love your fried chicken. I'm just a little tired from exams."

"Exams were over a few days ago, weren't they?" Beth noted.

Tina blushed as she always did when she was caught in a lie. "Yes, they were. Perhaps I've got jet lag."

Aunt Beth did not press Tina on any further. In four days, it would be Christmas. Surely her niece would cheer up by then.

"I thought I'd take the car and go to the beach for a day," Tina commented.

"That's a good idea. A day of rest at the beach would be an excellent cure for your jet lag."

Tina ignored the implication that she'd been caught in another lie, and simply smiled. The beach was waiting for her.

She could let its tide carry her sorrows away. Her skin tingled in anticipation of the salty air, the white sand, and the blue ocean.

"What's his name?" Aunt Beth asked, interrupting Tina's thoughts.

"What?" Tina asked in surprise.

"I asked you what his name was," Beth answered mildly.

Tina laid her fork down, and stared right at her. "You don't miss anything, do you?"

"It's in my blood, I guess," she sighed. "Well, whatever his name is, if he's worth keeping, don't let him go."

Tina glanced at her aunt, and noticed the faraway look in her eyes. It was a look of regret, of giving up too easily and never having had a second chance. She couldn't tell Beth everything that was bothering her; they had never been too intimate with each other. They had a friendly, semi-formal relationship, even though they shared the same house. That was the extent of it. There was mutual respect and love, but not much sharing of secrets. Besides, Beth would be shocked to learn that Tina wanted a fellow who belonged to someone else! He was her best friend's fiancé! Tina resumed picking at her food. "What a horrible, disgusting snake I am!" she thought to herself bitterly. Right then she made a promise to herself to use this vacation time wisely. She would strengthen herself against any admiration she might have for Kevin. She had to shut off her feelings if she was to continue going to college and living with Karen. If she didn't, she would surely go insane! Each day she experienced the unreturned love from him, was another day that her self-esteem would plummet. It would do nothing but hurt her to see Karen and Kevin developing their relationship. It was already hurtful and annoying! Especially now, with all this talk of a wedding! How could she expect to last, if she didn't get a grip on her feelings? She would have to be more responsible, if she intended to survive in peace. She didn't even know if Karen would ask her to be a bridesmaid! Even so, she'd be expected to be at the wedding one way, or another. It was almost too much to think about. She set her goal to release her feelings for Kevin firmly then, and in her mind, he was a picture slowly dissolving. *Very* slowly. Maybe by the time she went back to school, he would be completely out of her mind.

As she looked back at her plate of food, she noticed the onyx ring on the finger of her right hand. Why Matthew had chosen to give her such a nice Christmas gift, was beyond her understanding. She had completely ruined the evening of the dance for him, even if he refused to admit it. What did he do in return? He had a beautiful heart-shaped onyx ring delivered to her dorm. When she had first seen the attractive red-haired lady standing at the door, Tina had thought that there had been some kind of mistake. The lady had insisted that she was at the right place, with the right gift, for the right girl. Tina, shocked and embarrassed, had taken the gift. When the woman had gone, she had torn into the package. Karen had stood by, a huge grin on her face, as Tina opened the small velvet box. When they saw what was inside, Karen had thrown her arms around Tina, as if the present was from her instead of from Matthew. She had cried to Tina, "Now we both have rings!"

As Tina gazed on it now, she smiled. It was beautiful, but she could not seem to attribute any sentimental value to it. Perhaps that would come in due time. She was glad that her aunt had not noticed it, or at least had pretended not to notice it. She was not ready to give an explanation of its origin. She could only hope that Matthew did not expect her to be obligated to him. She just didn't want any serious relationships right now. Well, she wanted Kevin, but she'd just made a vow to forget him! Matthew was nice, but there seemed to be an invisible wall that kept them from getting too emotionally close to each other. Tina silently thanked that "wall", and without knowing why, she hoped that it would stay there. They hadn't even made love yet. She was sure that she could have Matthew whenever she wanted to, but she kept holding off. The feelings just weren't there. Matthew, always unsure of what Tina wanted, did not try too hard to pressure her.

*   *   *

The next day arrived, and with it came an abundance of sunshine. The air was very agreeable for late December, and as Tina stood by the car, she inhaled deeply. The night before had been filled with a peaceful slumber, and now she felt refreshed. She wore a blue cotton T-shirt tucked in white shorts. Her feet were bare; she seldom wore shoes when she was at home. The cool concrete beneath her feet felt soothing, and she wriggled her toes in excitement. Throwing her shoulder bag into the car, she adjusted her sunglasses and sun visor. Aunt Beth came out of the house carrying a small picnic basket. She handed it to Tina, who looked inside it. She squealed in delight like a child. There were so many good things in there! There were assorted breads and sliced meats, fruits and vegetables, hard boiled eggs, canned drinks, condiments, and candy.

"Aunt Beth," she cried, "I'll never be able to eat all of this! Why did you pack so much?"

"Well," Beth answered, flustered, "I thought if you met somebody interesting, you might want to share."

Tina hugged her aunt. "You're a very trusting person. I don't think I'll find someone to share this with. I just won't come home until I finish all of it!"

They both laughed, then Tina got into the car and drove away. Beth went inside the house feeling old-fashioned. She hoped Tina had the good sense to know who to talk to and who to avoid. Maybe the overloaded picnic basket was a bad idea. She paused for a moment, then shook her head. Tina was capable of taking care of herself—she hoped.

Tina drove down the highway with the window rolled down and the radio playing loudly. For the first time in months, she felt relieved of a burden. Her unreturned love for Kevin was a heavy load to carry. As she drove, her foot heavy on the accelerator, thoughts of him seemed to drift out of the window. She inhaled deeply. The air close to the beach always had a certain smell. It beckoned to her, and she increased her speed.

*   *   *

When she got to the beach, she took her bag and her picnic basket out of the car. She was familiar with the area, so she picked a spot that was not usually too crowded. There were more people than usual, because of the holiday, but she didn't care. It was her beach in her mind. Nobody could spoil it for her.

She found a comfortable spot, and spread her towel down. As she sat on the towel, the sand gave way like a soft mattress. She could always sleep so good on the beach, but she would save that for later. After taking off her outer clothes, she adjusted the straps on her one-piece white bathing suit. She reached into her bag and pulled out a book of poetry. Poetry always seemed silly to her to read unless she was at the beach. It was tranquil to read the beautiful words at the ocean, for the sea was tranquility in the purest form. She read slowly and silently, pausing to reflect now and then. The waves were her music, the sand her bed.

When she grew tired of reading, she went for a walk along the beach. The wet sand and the cool water felt good on her feet. She had been looking down, when she heard the shrill laughter of a child. Glancing up, she saw a little girl a few yards away. The child danced and skipped by the water like a little fairy. Her blonde hair flowed in the wind like long gold ribbons. As Tina watched her, a strange feeling came over her. She was happy, yet sad at the same time. She rejoiced silently at the innocence of this glad child. How wonderful it must be to play at the ocean all day long without worrying about stupid problems. Tina's eyes misted as she realized that she could never go back to being a child. How simple life was then! She remembered friends who were in such a hurry to grow up. She had been different; she'd clung to her youth with all of her strength. As expected, though, time had loosened her grasp, and had snatched childhood away from her. The time had come to become responsible. It had seemed that one moment, people had let her alone, then before she knew it, she was pressured into making decisions about her life. Everyone had that problem at one time or another, it seemed, but it did nothing to console her. If life was so confusing now, what would the future bring? It was very frightening to think about it.

As Tina got closer, the child stopped dancing and stared at her. She smiled at Tina, then playfully bent over and scooped up water in her tiny hands. She threw water up at Tina, and laughed loudly. Tina looked at the little girl in surprise, then returned the greeting. She glanced, and saw the mother sitting several yards away. The woman had her face buried in a magazine, apparently comfortable hearing the voice of her child.

Tina and the girl chased each other around, each trying to get the other one wet. As an only child, Tina found babies and children fascinating. Her laughter pealed, as she played with the girl. She looked back and noticed that the mother had put down her magazine. "Maybe she thinks I'm a pervert," Tina thought in horror. She pushed the terrible thought to the back of her mind and continued to chase the little girl.

When they had both run as much as they could, they stopped to catch their breath. Tina glanced down at the little girl. She looked like a miniature model of Karen, glancing up at Tina with innocent blue eyes and smiling. Tina smiled back.

"You remind me of a friend that I have at college," Tina remarked.

"What's her name?" the girl asked.

"Karen."

"Oh," the girl said, "my name's Amber."

"That's a pretty name," Tina commented.

Just then, Amber's mother called for her daughter, and the conversation was cut short. Before she left to go to her mother, Amber placed a seashell into Tina's hand. Then she smiled in spite of herself, and ran off.

With the seashell clasped in her hand, Tina walked slowly back to her towel. She sat down and fixed herself a sandwich. Food always tasted better at the ocean, and she ate slowly, fully enjoying each bite. As she looked at the ocean, she saw two lovers strolling absent-mindedly hand in hand. A sharp pang pierced her heart, and she tried to look away. As if her head was glued to the spot, she could not move. She watched them, instead, until they were out of sight. Once, she closed her eyes and imagined that the two people were she and Kevin. Reality and self-discipline slapped her in the face, and she was overcome with guilt. Would she have to leave the country to escape Kevin's haunting memory? No—even that would not be good enough. It was her problem, and she would have to deal with it. Never in all of her life had she known frustration such as this. She finished the sandwich, and washed it down with one of the soft drinks that Aunt Beth had packed.

She yawned, for eating often made her sleepy. She lay down on the towel. The sky seemed to become darker. It was the last thing she saw before she fell asleep.

An eerie feeling came over her, and deep in her mind, she knew that she was dreaming. It was so cold! Her body shivered as the wind whipped through her hair. It slapped against her face, and each time she moved her hair, it came back to slap her even harder. She sat up on the towel, and looked up and down the beach. Where had all the people gone? She stood up with great difficulty, for it was as though her body weighed hundreds of pounds. She tried walking. Each step made her so tired! The wind was picking up speed, and she had to brace herself against a palm tree. As she let go to move on, the tree crashed behind her. She turned to look at it, and saw a small figure a hundred yards down the beach. It skipped slowly and hauntingly, its little arms behind its back. As it got closer, Tina recognized it as Amber. Something was wrong, though, for her eyes were milky, and her face was like stone.

"Amber!" Tina cried, glad to see some form of life emerge from the deserted beach. She stood with her arms out to receive the child. As she smiled, she noticed a movement out of the corner of her eye. In slow motion, she turned her head. Her happy expression took on a look of horror, for only a few feet away, stood Chuck and Clyde. They grinned evilly at her, holding out their arms, mocking her. Chuck was standing in a pool of blood, and as she watched, blood dripped freely from his gaping mouth. It trailed down his ashen body, lying to rest by his feet, instead of sinking into the sand. Tina noticed with horror that his feet were almost covered up, and the blood was rising to his ankles.

Clyde stood beside him, singed from head to foot. His eyes were rolled back in his head. Little layers of burnt, rotting flesh peeled off of his face and body. He pointed at the ocean.

"Let's go for a swim, Tina," he said. His voice was deep and scratchy.

Tina, whose arms had dropped, shook her head violently from side to side, in silent protest. Her face felt wetter and wetter, and she brushed at her skin with her hand. As she pulled her hand down, she noticed that it was full of blood. She screamed, while Chuck and Clyde laughed at her. As she was about to run away, she thought about Amber.

"My God," she thought, "I've got to get Amber out of here!"

She turned, then about died of fright, for Amber now stood behind her. Her face up close was almost blue, and her eyes still held that milky color to them. Only this time, Tina noticed that the child's pupils were gone.

"We've got to get out of here!" Tina cried. As she reached for Amber's hand, she felt a sharp pang. She jerked her hand back and noticed a big gash in it. As she looked at Amber in shock, the child drew back her arm. In her hand was a long knife, dripping with the blood from Tina's hand. Tina looked to the sky, and let out a bloodcurdling scream as the child laughed like a demon. Her face felt wetter and wetter. Suddenly something grabbed her, trapping her arms behind her back. Without looking, she knew that it was Chuck, because his cold blood ran down her face.

"We want you to join us!" he hissed.

"No!!!" Tina screamed. As she did, she saw Amber's hand stiffen around the knife. Just as it came down, Tina yelled, and her body jerked her into consciousness. She sat up on the towel, gasping for breath. Recovering from the nightmare, she greedily sucked in the cool air. It was raining hard now, and in the background, she could hear thunder. Grabbing her things, she ran to the car. It wasn't until she was locked inside, driving down the highway at a high rate of speed, that she actually felt safe.

CHAPTER SIXTEEN

"I'D LIKE TO MAKE A toast to Karen and Kevin!" boomed Karen's father. "I wish them all the happiness that the future will bring!"

Karen and her parents, Kevin and his, all stood and touched glasses. The air resounded with a pleasant tinkling of crystal. It was Christmas Eve, and everyone had gathered to celebrate the engagement.

"What a wonderful way to celebrate Christmas!" cried Karen's mother.

Kevin's mother, Ann, gave him a kiss on the cheek. His father, Glenn hugged him. They were so proud of their son tonight!

"You sure know how to pick a beautiful woman!" raved Glenn, as he embraced Karen also.

"I know, Dad," replied Kevin. He kissed his future bride, who was blushing at all the attention.

"When is the wedding, dear?" asked Karen's mother.

"Well," Karen answered carefully, glancing at Kevin, "we've got our hearts set on May, but we've not set a date yet."

"You've got quite a bit of planning to do," Ann said nervously.

"Yes," agreed Karen, "but together, Kevin and I will be able to handle it."

"Will you be able to handle the studying, too?" Karen's mother asked her.

Kevin giggled to himself, and Karen nonchalantly elbowed him in the side. They were both aware of Karen's short attention span. It would be even harder to study now with wedding plans on her mind. She put on her most charming smile, then looked at all of them sincerely.

"Studying is going to be top priority, as always," she lied. "With everyone helping, I'm sure it'll ease the burden, making things easier for Kevin and me."

Fortunately, they seemed to believe her. Satisfied that their children would still be able to keep their grades up, the two women went to the kitchen. The men went to shoot a game of pool while they waited for dinner to be fixed. Karen and Kevin were at last alone. Karen poured some more champagne, then they sat down.

"We've won them over!" she whispered to Kevin.

He gazed into her sparkling blue eyes and smiled at her.

"With you charming them, how could we lose?" he asked.

"Well I had my doubts, didn't you?"

"Never!"

Karen tilted her glass up and drank until it was empty. She set the glass down as she seductively licked her lips. "Pour me some more!" she requested.

Kevin gave her an awkward glance, but did as she'd asked. "You'd better not get too drunk in front of our parents," he warned.

"I won't let it show if I do," she promised, "besides, you know that drinking makes it better."

"Are you referring to sex?" Kevin asked.

Karen clasped her hands to her breasts and put on a look of feigned innocence. "Me? Talk about sex? Yes! I'm talking about sex and you know it—you know drinking makes me ready!"

"How would I know?" Kevin asked, playing along with her game.

"If you don't know, then who was it the other night?" Karen retorted.

"All right, I give," Kevin laughed. "As usual, you win."

"I always do," she teased, then quickly nipped at his ear.

They sat there for a while, drinking, talking, and just simply enjoying each other's company. When their mothers returned from the kitchen, Karen pretended to be completely sober. This caused Kevin to laugh silently, his body occasionally shaking.

Karen kept pinching his leg under the table, but it only made him shake more. If their mothers noticed, they said nothing. They just kept on bringing out food. Soon the table was set with all kinds of delicious choices. The men stopped playing pool, and everyone was gathered at the table again.

After dinner, the parents took their glasses and retreated to the game room. Their laughter was loud at first, but got quieter as they walked down the hallway. Karen and Kevin sat there for a moment, listening. All of a sudden, Karen took Kevin's hand and they walked upstairs together. When they got to her bedroom, she pulled him inside, then locked the door. She removed her sweater and threw it to the floor. As Kevin looked on, stunned, she began unbuttoning her blouse.

"What on earth are you doing?" he gasped.

"I'm doing the same thing we usually do. I'm just doing it in a different place," she answered confidently.

Kevin looked around. Karen wanted to make love in her bedroom! Their parents were downstairs, liable to notice them missing at any given moment! He didn't think he could do this. They usually had sex in his room at college. He never expected to make love to her in this room of pink! It screamed of little girl innocence with its stuffed animals, dolls, and posters. Gathering every ounce of his self-control, he grabbed Karen's wrists. She stood there barefooted in nothing but her bra and panties.

"Get your clothes back on!" he whispered frantically.

Karen threw her head back and laughed. She pulled her wrists from Kevin's wavering grip, took off her bra, and wrapped it around Kevin's neck. He was a willing victim as she pulled the ends of the satin material, bringing his face just mere inches away from hers. The softness of the bra caressed the back of his neck, and he closed his eyes. It was too late, though, for he had already caught a glimpse of her alabaster breasts. He knew before he touched them, how soft they would be. His blood seemed to be on fire, as his pulse raced at a maddening speed.

Karen brushed his ear with her lips. "My parents never invade my privacy," she assured him. "Besides, they're playing pool, and it usually takes them a couple of hours to get tired of it."

As she whispered into his ear, he was oblivious to his clothing being removed. It was only when he was nude, the cool air hitting him, that he gave in. He grabbed her into his arms and kissed her with a starving, savage hunger. Her lips were like nourishment to him, her moans like an intoxicating wine. They fell into the bed together, and made love. Even in the heat of passion, he kept his ears open for any sound in the hallway. He was thankful that the door had a lock on it. He couldn't have begun to do this, had there been no lock at all.

When they were finished, they lay there for a moment in each other's arms. He gazed into her blue eyes, and it was as if he were looking into his own. That was the only thing they had in common physically, but it was such a wonderful thing! It was almost magical to see her staring at him with eyes that matched his own. He kissed her warm lips once more, this time slowly. They got up and got dressed, going downstairs as if nothing had happened. The only clue to their lovemaking was their two hands, entwined, and a glow in their eyes.

*   *   *

Late Christmas morning, Karen trudged upstairs with all of her presents. When she made it to her room, she threw the opened packages on her bed. She had so many new clothes! The garments were pulled out piece by piece and examined again. Clothes were wonderful! Greedily, she caressed each fabric, then inhaled of their new fragrance. There was something exciting about the way new clothes smelled. Each crisp outfit demanded to be worn first, as she stared in utter confusion. She was debating between a white silk blouse and a peach wool sweater, when she remembered her other presents. Running downstairs, Karen snatched the rest of her things, and returned to her bedroom. There were leather shoes, purses, a wallet, and a jacket. How fortunate to be the only child at Christmas, she thought selfishly! It made the rest of the lonely year seem well worth it.

"Karen!" cried her mother from the kitchen downstairs. Karen forgot her presents for the moment. It was breakfast time! She didn't know how the tradition got started, but every Christmas, after opening presents, the three of them sat down to a pancake breakfast. There were fluffy flapjacks, thick, sweet maple syrup, and cold foamy milk. Oh, how she'd missed her mother's cooking! She bounded down the stairs, two at a time, and joined her parents at the table. Christmas seemed one of the few appropriate times when one could behave as a child, and Karen took full advantage of it. It was good to be home again!

*   *   *

"Thanks, Aunt Beth," Tina said as she hugged her aunt. "I love these new clothes! You remembered how quickly I get tired of wearing the same things!"

Beth smiled at her niece, then started picking up the wrapping paper that was dominating the floor. She loved Christmas, but hated the mess that usually followed. Her only remedy was to pick things up as soon as they hit the floor. Tina, her arms full, threw a backward glance at her aunt, and laughed out loud.

"I'll be back to help you," she promised.

Beth nodded, but continued her task. She got to the box that held the beautiful pink sweater in it. Picking it up, she held it to her body. She loved pink! It wasn't really a womanly color, but what the heck? It was one of the few girlish things left in her blood. Pink towels, linens, and curtains accented her home. There was just something so soothing and tranquil about the color!

She bent down and picked up the porcelain doll that Tina had bought her for her collection. Dolls and pink accessories for an old maid like her! Her family would laugh if they could see her now! She sighed, for there was not much of a family anymore. Many of her kin people had died. It was strange how death hovered over the holidays. Once someone died, special occasions were never the same. Children grew up, old people died, and the living still made an effort to celebrate. She knew even now without looking, that Tina was holding her family portrait in her young hands. She did it every year. It was the only way she could celebrate Christmas with her mother and her father—to hold the small 5 x 7 in her hands, and to meditate quietly for a few moments. Once, years ago, Aunt Beth had spied on Tina to see what she was doing after they'd opened presents. Filled with a curiosity that out-weighed her shame, she'd watched Tina hold the photo and whisper to it. Beth was not stupid, nor did she ruin the moment by announcing her presence. Instead, she had quietly retreated, returning to her task of cleaning up scattered wrapping paper.

Tina came back into the room. This year there were no tears. There had been no crying for many years now. The tears had been replaced with a tranquil, but sorrowful look on the pretty brown face. She bent down and helped her aunt with the remainder of the cleaning up.

When Tina was through, she walked outside into the bright sunshine. It was so peaceful on Christmas morning! Already the sun warmed the outdoors. The lush green plants in the yard, guarded tender blades of grass from the sun. Tina sat on a bench under one of the trees. As she gazed up at the baby blue sky, she realized just how much she missed Karen and Kevin. A sudden sickness washed over her body, causing her to shudder. Strange as it seemed, she was ready to go back to college. "Two more weeks to wait," she thought. Suddenly Christmas break seemed like an eternity, and she wondered how she would survive.

*   *   *

The next day, Aunt Beth picked up the telephone. Tina was stretched out on the sofa, trying to read a book. Her heart wasn't in it, though, therefore many of the words meant nothing to her. Beth had to call her name twice before she heard. Startled, she looked up, and saw her aunt holding the phone out to her. She leapt off the sofa and walked quickly to the phone.

"Hello?"

"Hey, Babe! Boy, it sure is good to hear your voice!"

Tina cried out loud, "Chris!"

"That's right, Doll, it's me. How're you enjoying your time off from college?"

"It's great!" Tina lied.

"That's too bad," Chris commented, "because if you were bored, I was going to take you to the beach today."

"Oh, Chris! I'm bored! I swear I'm bored! Oh! Sorry Aunt Beth, don't take that wrong! Yes, please take me to the beach! Can I be ready in twenty minutes? Yes, of course! See ya!"

She hung up the phone and pirouetted around the kitchen.

"Aunt Beth, why didn't you tell me that Chris was home from college?"

Beth looked at her niece skeptically. "Well, Honey, I thought that you would have figured it out. Just because a guy doesn't get along well with his parents, doesn't mean that he's going to avoid them at Christmas."

Tina ran down the hall in her socked feet. She almost fell as she skidded to a halt in front of the bathroom. She ran inside and shut the door. Thank God, she looked OK! She just needed to freshen her make-up. As she put the final touches on her face, her body tingled with eager anticipation of Chris's arrival. Chris Collins was her first friend when she'd moved in with Aunt Beth. Before that, he was the boy who peeked shyly at her while she played in the yard on one of her regular visits as a child. Chris was a blonde-haired little angel then. Since that time when his shyness had finally melted away, they'd become the best of friends. Together they had grown up. They had nursed each other's wounds, whether they were physical or psychological.

When they were in their mid-teens, Chris's father bought a larger house in one of the better neighborhoods. It was not far away, just a couple of miles, but it broke the two teenagers' hearts. Chris had decided stubbornly to run away, but Tina had talked him out of it. Instead, they'd put their money together and had bought a sleek red ten-speed bike for Chris. He was to use it to visit Tina until he got a car of his own.

The day that he left for his new home, he had grabbed Tina and kissed her on the lips. The kiss was soft, though salty from his sweat. It was the only time that they had ever kissed. Their relationship went beyond sexual. If was that of two people who understood each other completely. Together, they were free to be themselves, without fraud.

Distance had only proved to make their friendship stronger. Each day, Chris had arrived on his bicycle for another day of adventure. As their bodies began to blossom into adulthood, Tina began to notice his muscles every time he visited. He too, noticed her womanly figure, the supple rise of her breasts and the curve of her waist. Somehow, though, they respected each other, and avoided the physical temptation that could easily ruin their union.

It was not unusual for them to go dancing together, but to leave with different people. They had no bonds on each other, and they confided in one another frequently. They had laughed at accounts of their first awkward kisses, and they had cried together during their first heartbreaks.

Now he was coming to see her again! She smiled deeply and glowed on the inside. Her happiness of arriving in Florida was minute compared to the way that she felt now. Tina wondered in eager anticipation what Chris looked like since she had seen him last. It had been several months since their last good-bye. Oh, if only he would have gone to the same college that she was going to! Chris was not like that. He had insisted on going all the way across the continent to California. Even though he could have gone to college in Florida, Tina understood his reasons. His domineering father had pretty much run him off. He had actually seemed glad that Chris had chosen a college so far away! Tina's eyes watered, and she felt a little sadness for the father who just could not get close to his son. Chris was such a special person! How anyone could treat him with anything except the utmost respect was beyond Tina's comprehension.

Quickly she grabbed a large duffel bag and began stuffing things into it. Her swimsuit, towels, toiletries, and cassettes were among the things that she packed. Tina bit her nails as she pondered on whether to take an evening dress. A day at the beach was usually followed with a night of dining and dancing. She went to her closet and chose a dark blue cotton dress, a shiny black belt, and black patent pumps. Then she searched through her drawers for her stockings. As usual, they were buried under dozens of socks. As she snatched them out of the drawer, she heard Chris's car pull up. She grabbed her bag and ran down the hall. Aunt Beth stood there with a quickly made basket of food, and Tina kissed her on the cheek. They had done this many times before Tina had left for college, so Aunt Beth didn't have to ask where they were going. For some reason, she trusted Chris with Tina's very life. Perhaps it was because she'd known him since he was a toddler. Nonetheless, she watched as Tina raced out of the house, then she retreated into the kitchen to pick up the mess she had made while putting together the picnic basket.

As Tina ran down the driveway, Chris got out of his car. She squealed with delight at the sight of him, and he grinned from ear to ear. When she reached him, she almost threw her things down. Chris snatched her up in his arms, swinging her around and around.

"It sure is good to see a beautiful dark-haired woman!" he cried. "God knows I've seen my share of blondes lately!"

He put her down, then took both of her hands in his. He shouted a happy swear and gathered her into his arms. Tina held him tightly, too, for he seemed like a refuge. He was like the port to the weary sailor, the food to the hungry person. She remained in his arms while he stroked her hair. He seemed to indulge in its silkiness, so she didn't push him away.

"Chris, I've missed you so much!" Tina whispered.

He leaned back a little, and tilted up her face so that her eyes were locked into his. The sight of her tanned face and deep brown eyes stirred a burning passion in him. He wanted badly to crush his lips into hers, to taste her sweet mouth. Fearing that he would ruin the moment, he kept his desire to himself, though it was near impossible. This was his childhood friend, he reminded himself, his "sister" in spirit. She might never forgive him if he made moves that were too fast.

"I've missed you too, Babe. I even think that you've changed a little, but I'm not sure how. Have I changed any?"

"If you did, it's only for the better," Tina answered. "I do see a wilder look in those green eyes, though!"

Chris released his grip, and took Tina's things. "Do you think that you can survive a day with a wild green-eyed creature?"

He held the door open, and Tina hopped in the passenger side. "I've survived other days with you," she answered. "I'm sure I can handle myself once more."

On the way to the beach, they stopped at a drive-through window to get some breakfast. Tina bit into her ham biscuit. She tried to stay away from foods like that, but it was fun to cheat once in a while. Her tongue tingled from its saltiness, and she knew that she'd regret eating it. It always made her so thirsty! She sipped on her juice to quench her thirst.

"Tell me about college, Tina," Chris urged.

Tina nodded, then swallowed a mouthful of food. "It's different than what I expected," she confessed. "In high school, the teachers seemed to be with you every step of the way. If you were doing badly, they took you to the side and asked you if you were having problems at home or whatever. At my college, they don't seem concerned unless you're really going downhill, which fortunately I haven't been. I've yet to see an instructor who's worried about your emotional state. They only seem to be interested in seeing all of your work turned in—on time! I guess there are so many more students to deal with in college, that it's impossible for them to get too involved in others' personal problems. Sometimes, though, I miss the shelter of high school. I used to think that high school teachers were jerks, but at least they seemed to be human."

"I guess in college, they figure if you don't like the class, or can't handle it, you'll drop it," Chris commented.

"Yes, that's probably true, but it seems like such a shock to have so much responsibility."

"Wait until you get out into the world!" Chris warned.

Tina swallowed another bite, then wiped her mouth gently. "I've heard that before, and if you ask me, the 'real world' doesn't seem too appealing right now."

Chris laughed and put a reassuring arm about her shoulders.

"You'll be fine, Babe," he said, "because you're a really strong lady."

"Well how is college treating you?" Tina asked.

"It's keeping me away from my father, isn't it?" he asked jokingly.

"Chris!" Tina cried.

"Well it's true," he said. "Anyhow I love it! It's like this really intense competition all of the time. I'm in these classes with so many other people, and we're busting our tails to make these ludicrously high grades. I know you probably won't believe this, but I study hard. Don't look at me that way; I really do! I want to show that jerk of a dad, that I can make it in the world! You know what—it's fun in a weird sort of way. It's like my mind is this sponge, and I can keep soaking and soaking it with information. It's a natural high!"

Tina looked at him with great admiration. Even Matthew didn't seem to have the zest for learning that Chris had. His enthusiasm was contagious, so she made a promise to herself to be more like Chris. She'd try to make the best grades possible. It would definitely keep her mind occupied. She leaned back in the seat and propped her feet on the dash. It was little things like this that made being with Chris enjoyable. Any other guy would have gone into cardiac arrest at seeing her do that to his car!

"So, Babe, have you taken that big leap yet?" Chris asked.

Tina blushed, for she knew that Chris was referring to her virginity, which was now a thing of the past.

"What do you mean?" she asked quietly.

Chris glanced over at her, and one of his eyebrows shot up.

"You know what I mean," he said firmly. "Do you want me to say it point blank?"

Tina looked away, and immediately Chris felt sorry for her.

"Darling, I didn't mean it the way it came out," he explained. "We've always shared everything, but I can understand it if you don't want to talk about it. I guess sex is a bit harder to discuss than a first kiss."

Tina turned to him, and he was taken aback by the blank look on her face.

"It was painful," she said in a low voice. "It was painful more physically than mentally, and mentally, it hurt like hell. I thought he was what I wanted at the time. I thought he could get my mind off of . . . ."

She stopped suddenly, afraid to even say his name. If only she had waited, but now she could never go back. She had used Brad for a crutch, and that was wrong. She did not plan to make the same mistake with Matthew, or anyone else. When she fell in love, then it would be right. She clenched her fists. Why did she have such a conscience? Karen made love with guys, like married women made desserts, without much thought, and no guilt.

"You thought he could get your mind off of who?" Chris asked, interrupting her thoughts.

"Kevin!" Tina finally cried out. It was as if a huge burden were suddenly lifted from her chest, and she started to relax again.

"What's the deal with this Kevin?"

Tina, finally realizing that she could tell the truth, blurted everything out.

"There's this really wonderful guy that I go to college with! He's amazing, but he's got this exceptionally beautiful girlfriend, who happens to be my roommate. She screws around on him—a lot. I don't know what his problem is. Maybe he doesn't know; maybe he just refuses to believe. Anyway, I'm crazy for him! I'd die for this guy, Chris, but he hardly knows that I'm alive! Then I've got guilty feelings, because I'm a friend of his girlfriend's! It's like this crazy triangle, and I can't seem to work things out!"

Chris was silent for a moment, reflecting on everything that Tina had told him. He parked his car near the beach, then they got out. He was still silent as they walked towards the ocean.

"Is this spot OK with you?" he asked her.

She nodded, and they put everything down. He put his hands on her, then turned her around to face him. He looked deep into her eyes. They seemed to go on forever—those eyes. How any guy could resist the charm of her face was beyond him.

"He's naive and stupid for rejecting you," he said at last.

Tina shuddered at his sudden seriousness, but then she realized that Chris had never seen Karen. She bent down and fumbled in her duffel bag. Inside was a wallet with a photograph of Karen and Kevin. He would understand when he saw it.

"This is what I'm up against," she said, holding the photo before his eyes.

He looked for a moment, then gently pushed her hand down.

"She *is* beautiful, but beauty only goes so far, Tina. When someone is able to look beyond the face and really see what is inside of a person, then the truth is revealed. Think of someone's inside as being a garden. If it's someone like this girl here, it's probably full of weeds. Your inside has nothing but roses, Tina. I know that sounds ridiculous coming out of my mouth, but it's true. I've known you for years, and you're good, deep down where it really counts. You're also beautiful, though you'd die rather than admit it. Don't blush; it's true."

Tina smiled, as the color rose to her cheeks. She could say nothing. Instead, she busied herself with fixing the blanket and finding a comfortable spot. Chris followed her lead. When they had lain down, Tina asked, "Have you met any interesting women at your college?"

He smiled and gazed up at the sky. "Yes, as a matter of fact, I have. There's plenty of beautiful girls at my college. There's even more in other parts of California. I've found many of them to have a phony personality, though. Most of the one's I've dated have just wanted something from me."

"Your body?" Tina asked.

Chris turned and looked at her in pretended shock. "Yeah, what else would they want?"

Tina laughed at his bluntness. She knew that Chris would be more than happy to share his bed with beautiful women.

"Haven't you met anyone special?" She inquired seriously.

"No one I've met is as special as you," he answered. He rolled over on one elbow, and leaned towards her. His face was only inches away from hers, and he wanted badly to kiss her like he kissed other girls.

"Let me kiss you, Tina," he said softly.

Tina put her hands on his bare chest and pushed him away.

"It'll just ruin things between us, Chris."

His hand went to his forehead, as he dealt with the rejection. "You're a hard woman, Tina," he commented.

"I have to be," she answered softly, "you're my best friend."

As he nestled down for a nap in the sun, Tina nudged him. "Are you ever afraid to go to sleep?"

He looked at her in surprise. "Of course I'm not afraid to go to sleep! Why in the world would you ask that?"

She took a deep breath. "I had a nightmare the last time I fell asleep on the beach, Chris. It really scared me! Now I'm afraid to sleep on the beach again."

Overcome with sympathy, he took her hand in his. "Don't ever be afraid to sleep while I'm with you, Babe. Nothing is going to happen to you. I'd die before I'd let anything hurt you. You just leave you hand in mine. If you so much as twitch, I'll wake up to take care of you. Does that sound all right?"

Tina nodded and moved closer to Chris. She closed her eyes, security washing over her, by being so near to him. When she fell asleep, a hint of a smile was on her face. The sun warmed her body, while the waves and the wind sung nature's lullaby. This time only pleasant dreams awaited her, and she slept in peace.

CHAPTER SEVENTEEN

As Tina had suspected, the day with Chris was followed by an evening out. They drove to the nearest hotel, and changed in the restrooms adjacent to the lobby. When they met outside, Chris wore his best "We didn't get caught" grin, along with a royal blue dress shirt and black pants. Tina laughed as he whistled at her.

"How can you look so good, so fast?" he questioned. "You've got a look of a woman who took an hour to get ready, but I've clocked you at ten minutes!"

"Enter me in a race, Coach," Tina teased. "I bet I could even beat that record!"

"I know you could," Chris commented, as he kissed her on the cheek. "So are you hungry?"

"I'm ravenous," Tina admitted. "Something about the beach makes me want to eat constantly!"

"It must be that fish smell," Chris joked, while he dodged a punch that Tina had directed at his arm. "Seriously, where do you want to go?"

"You pick," Tina said.

Chris agreed and he took them to a restaurant on a pier. It was a lovely place, surrounded by windows, candlelight, and beach decor. They were seated at a table by one of the windows, and Tina gazed outside. The moon was full, casting its reflection on the black ocean below. The waves caught its light in their motion, breaking it into thousands of dancing diamonds. Inside the restaurant, soft music played, accompanied by the eternal crashing of the waves.

Tina was held captive by the beauty that surrounded her, when she felt a gentle tap on her shoulder. She was startled to see Chris and the waiter staring at her.

"What do you want to drink?" Chris asked her, stifling a laugh.

Tina blushed, then ordered her drink. When the waiter had left, she looked back out the window.

"It's so beautiful, Chris!" she commented.

"Yes, it is," he agreed, though he gazed at her, and not the sight outside. As usual, she missed his meaning. When she turned back to him, he was studying the menu.

After they'd ordered their food, Chris took her by the hand.

"Come with me," he said.

"What?" Tina asked, but he simply put a finger to her lips as he led her out of the restaurant. Tina sucked in her breath and hugged herself as the cold ocean air hit her.

"Chris, why are we outside, freezing?" she questioned.

He remained silent. They strolled to a part of the pier that opened to an outdoor dining area. The place was vacant, but music drifted out of the speakers above them.

"Dance with me?" he offered.

Tina obliged, allowing herself to lean into him, as he took her hand in his. He put his other arm about her, and nuzzled her hair.

"You smell wonderful," he confessed thickly.

"You too," Tina admitted.

They danced quietly for what seemed like an eternity. It was like a dream, with the moon and the sounds of the ocean. Tina forgot that she was cold, so comfortable was she in his arms.

"Tina, do you think we'll ever be together?" Chris whispered in her ear.

Tina fought a rising desire, as she shuddered. "Shut up, Chris," she said, with very little enthusiasm.

He started to retort, but the waiter chose that moment to open the door to the pier and announce that their food was ready.

"What timing," Chris grumbled.

Tina laughed, relieved.

They retreated to the warmth of the restaurant and had a lovely dinner. When Chris drove Tina home, he'd already lined up a date with her for New Year's Eve. Tina watched him drive away, thankful that they hadn't crossed the line between friends and lovers. She just didn't know what she'd do if they ruined their friendship. Satisfied, she strolled into the house, humming a song from their dance on the pier.

*   *   *

It was New Year's Eve, Tina's last night with Chris. He was leaving the next day. A deep sorrow seeped through her body and seemed to cling to her bones. She knew that he wanted a few days to relax before school started again. It was important that she give him a good time tonight. She took him out to eat at one of his favorite restaurants. Though it was costing her a fortune, he was worth it.

Tina watched him from across the table. The candle burning in the lantern cast a warm glow on his young face. Tonight his eyes were deep green, his hair bright gold. He wore a crisp white dress shirt tucked into black pants. He was extremely handsome, and Tina was proud to be with him tonight.

She took a bite of her broiled fish, careful not to spill anything on her dress. She wore black tonight, also. It was not a color that she wore often. She usually preferred blue, but Chris had begged her over the phone to wear something black.

"You look sexy tonight," he complimented.

Tina felt sexy, and she smiled. They touched glasses in a silent toast, then slowly drank their wine. Wine always warmed her body and made her skin tingle. She could close her eyes, imagining rows of vines loaded with succulent grapes. They waited to be turned into the delicious drink that she was enjoying tonight.

When they were through with the main course, the waiter rolled out the dessert cart. It was Tina's favorite part of the meal to see the rich, colorful desserts presented before her. Each one looked better than the one beside it, and it was always so hard to choose. They both settled on strawberry cheesecake.

"This might make you fat!" Chris warned.

Tina held up her dessert fork and smiled greedily. "I don't care tonight! I plan to eat and drink all that I want! I'm so tired of watching what I eat! Tonight I want to splurge!"

He laughed at her carelessness. "Splurge on me, Tina. Use me!"

"Chris, finish you dessert!" Tina said firmly.

He rolled his eyes. Trying to get Tina's body was going to be a losing battle. He was her friend, but he couldn't help it! He was a man also, and he'd be glad to get back to California! If she would only be his girlfriend, he felt that he could forget all the other girls. They had such a stable relationship, and Tina really understood him. If he had her, he felt sure that he'd never want another woman.

"Marry me," he said in a feeble attempt.

"Get serious, Chris," Tina reprimanded.

"Well, I've tried everything else. I thought that this one might work," he said jokingly.

"Chris, if we made love, I'd fall for you. I'd fall really hard. You'd date other girls. I'd go crazy, then we'd fight. After that I'd never see you again, and our friendship would be finished."

"Why do you plan everything out in such detail?" he grumbled.

Tina sighed. "I don't know. It really gets on my nerves. Let's talk about something else. Where do you want to go to party?"

"Some of the hotels are having really big parties. I thought that we'd check some of them out."

"That sounds good. Are you ready to leave?"

He put his napkin down, and nodded. Then he took her by the hand, and they left.

*   *   *

Back in North Carolina, Karen and Kevin sat in his car at the mall. The stereo was playing soft music, as they sat there looking at the black sky. They waited patiently for the fireworks show to begin. Outside it was cloudy and icy cold, but in the car, they were warm.

Their New Year's Eve had been celebrated with a quiet dinner. Karen respected Kevin's negative opinion about nightclubs. Memories of the terrible night that he and Clyde had fought over her, deterred her from going to any place like that tonight.

With hands clasped, they watched as the fireworks began to burst in the sky. Bright sparks of blues, reds, greens, and yellows met their expectant eyes. On the radio, the announcer was counting down the time until the New Year should arrive. Karen and Kevin kissed long and passionately until the old year was gone.

"You're the first guy I've kissed this year!" Karen cried happily.

Kevin held her hand up to his face and pretended to bite her fingers. She laughed and tried to pull away, but he did not let go.

"I better be the only guy that you kiss this year," he said.

She looked into his eyes, and saw that they were dancing. A big smile broke over his face, then he quickly kissed her again.

"You'll be the only person I kiss this year, and many years to follow," she said. As soon as the words were out, she began to worry. A lifetime was a long time to be with someone. She looked into his face again, and for the first time since she had dated him, she was afraid of the future.

Her look of apprehension was unnoticed by him, and he turned to start the car up. After the long awaited countdown, it was hard to think of something else to do. Her parents had gone to a party, so he drove to her house.

This time when they made love upstairs, he was not worried. They were totally alone. Everything that he wanted to express, he could, for he had no reservations tonight. Karen lay in his arms, hardly paying any attention. Her mind was in a whirlwind of confused emotions. She loved Kevin, but now she was unsure of marriage. The impact of her youth hit her like a speeding train. She could wait to get married. Maybe in a few years after they had finished college, she could make that big step. Her mouth opened to tell Kevin about her wishes, but she caught a glimpse of his face. It was an intoxicated look that he wore, when he looked down at her. His eyes were full of love. She closed her eyes, instead.

"I'm just nervous," she thought to herself. "I really want to get married. I date him steady anyway, so why not get married."

With those thoughts, she pushed her doubts to the back of her mind and buried them there. She would just not think bad things anymore.

After he'd left her, she sat up in bed most of the night looking at bridal magazines. There were so many beautiful things to choose from! The last thing that she saw before drifting off to sleep was the smiling face of a model in a wedding dress.

*   *   *

That same night, after Tina had come home, she wandered through the kitchen. Tears streamed down her face, making everything look like it was under water. She opened the refrigerator and stood there in a trance. The cool air from the open door felt good on her burning face. Unaware of time, she stayed there until her feet began to hurt. Quietly, she reached inside for the remainder of a coconut cake that her aunt had baked. There was enough there for at least another three helpings, or more. Tina took the platter, shut the door, and reached into the silverware drawer for a fork. With the fork and the cake in one hand, she used the other hand to open a cabinet. She knew before she saw it, that the brandy would be in there. Aunt Beth always kept a bottle of brandy in her house. She said that it helped her to go to sleep.

As Tina sat on the couch in the living room, she hoped that a drink would obliterate her pain. When she had brought Chris home, it had taken all of her strength not to cry on his shoulder. She knew that she would see him again, but when? They probably wouldn't meet again until the end of the school year, and now that seemed like an eternity away. She greedily munched on the cake as if that would help her to forget him. She had never realized until tonight just how much of a friend she had in Chris. He understood her so well! If only Karen or Kevin were like him! She knew that now she would seem like a lost soul when she returned to college. Taking a large swallow of brandy, she squinted her eyes. Another pain was eating at her heart, and now she remembered what it was. She knew it was more than the temporary loss of Chris bothering her. It was the permanent loss of Kevin that hurt worse than anything. The night had done nothing but resurrect the hurt that she had felt the night of the dance.

She felt with her fork for another piece of cake. When nothing came to her mouth, she looked down in surprise. Only a few crumbs remained. She leaned down to make sure that she hadn't dropped any. Surely she hadn't eaten all of that! The floor however, yielded nothing, and when she sat back up, she became dizzy. Without thinking, she put the bottle on the coffee table. As she stood up, the cake plate slid to the floor, but she didn't notice it. All she wanted to do was to go to bed. She clutched her head as she walked shakily down the dark hallway. The bedroom finally loomed before her, and her feet quickly shuffled to it. With her last bit of energy, she collapsed on the bed and fell asleep with her clothes on.

*   *   *

The morning brought with it bright sunshine. It slipped through Tina's curtains and caressed her face. As she slowly woke up, she became aware of a terrible pain in her head. She moaned and tried to move. Her body was sore from sleeping in a cramped position all night. She sat up and realized that she'd slept with her dress clothes on. As she sat there, she heard footsteps coming up the hallway to her room. Too embarrassed to be seen, but too tired to move, she sat there in a stupor.

Aunt Beth walked into the room with a tray of food. Her eyes avoided Tina's as she set the tray down.

"This won't cure you, but it'll help. I'm sure that you don't make a habit out of getting into this condition, so I'm sure it won't happen again."

With that, she walked out of the room. Tina stared at the door in stunned silence. Harsh words would have been understandable, but Beth's matter-of-fact tone surprised her. She looked down at the tray. On it were hash browns, toast, poached eggs, fresh fruit, coffee, and juice. Tina grabbed the juice, realizing just how parched her throat really was. The liquid was cool, and she did not put the glass down until it was finished.

In the living room, Beth picked up the mess that Tina had made. She knew in her heart that Tina was not a habitual drinker. She also knew that she could not punish Tina for something that she had done herself in the past.

*   *   *

All too soon, the Christmas break was over. Aunt Beth drove Tina to the airport, wondering what she could do to alleviate the lost look on her niece's face.

"You know you could transfer to a college over here," she offered.

Tina smiled, and put a reassuring hand on her aunt's shoulder.

"I know," she admitted, "but I really want to finish this year out. I've got friends that I miss, too."

Beth nodded, but she wasn't satisfied. Her sister's child was so hard to understand. Later as she'd watch the plane leave, she'd feel as though she'd sent a babe amongst wolves.

CHAPTER EIGHTEEN

"TINA, ARE YOU ASLEEP?" KAREN asked.

Tina rolled over in her bed and looked at Karen. It had only been a week since college had started back, yet she felt as though it had been months. The long days of classes, followed by evenings studying, left her fatigued. She gazed at Karen through sleepy eyes, half-opened. The moon shone through the window. It cast an eerie blue glow over the entire room, giving Karen's face an even paler appearance.

"No," she answered. "It's going to be one of those nights."

Karen inhaled softly, then pulled the covers up to her chin. She lay flat on her back and stared at the ceiling. "Have you ever had any fantasies, Tina?"

"What do you mean?"

"I mean, have you ever had any dreams? You know, dreams that can't possibly come true—stuff like that."

Tina laughed. "As a child, I used to think that one day I'd find a unicorn. I really believed in them for so long. I'd imagine that I'd be in the woods somewhere, find one, and have all my wishes come true. What about you?"

"When I was little, I used to think that I was really a mermaid," Karen said, waiting for Tina to stop giggling. "Seriously, I used to think about how beautiful it would be to live underwater."

"I used to wonder what it would be like to get laid by someone from another planet," Tina said playfully.

Karen cursed quietly, which brought even more laughter from Tina. "I'm sorry," she said between giggles. "Seriously, I think that everybody has fantasies when they're very young. Then we get older, and we realize that life sometimes stinks."

Karen, startled, stared at her friend. There was a sad, distant look on Tina's face, which Karen could not figure out.

"I still have fantasies," she confessed. "I dream about being invisible and raiding the most elite boutique in town."

Tina laughed again, and the sad look on her face vanished. "You're weird, Karen," she admitted.

"Thanks," she answered in a mocking tone.

There was silence for a few moments, then Tina spoke. "Karen?"

"What?"

"Karen!"

"What?!"

"Goodnight."

"You're weird, too, Tina," Karen answered.

Tina rolled over and snuggled under her blanket. "I know," she confessed, then she drifted off to sleep.

Karen lay there for a long time staring at the window. The moonlight penetrated the darkness of the room, bathing it in a comforting glow. She liked the light. Darkness was always so uncertain. Like her future. Things had seemed normal since she'd returned to college, yet she felt a little twinge of uneasiness. Kevin's excitement over their engagement and the happy reaction from their friends was a bit overwhelming for her. As she'd done many times lately, she pushed the thought to the back of her mind. She focused on the sound of Tina's soft breathing coming from the next bed. She began to breathe in sync with her friend, softly, easily. Finally sweet rest came to her, as the darkness covered her like a warm blanket.

*   *   *

In another dorm, someone else was having difficulty sleeping. Hope sat in a chair by the window, as she gazed out on the campus grounds. The side of her pretty face was pressed against the glass. She wore nothing but a blue long-sleeved shirt.

As she stared out the window, a tiny tear rolled down her cheek. Why didn't Kevin want her? It was torture to see him back at college with that uppity girlfriend of his sporting that diamond! Couldn't he see that she would be so much better for him, than Karen? Another tear followed the first, and she rubbed it rudely away with the back of her hand.

She glanced at Allison who was softly snoring in her bed. Her useless friend hadn't a care in the world! She faced the window once more. Clutching her fist tightly, she vowed quietly. "You'll be mine, Kevin! If I have to go through hell and back to get you, I'll do it! I swear I won't be happy until then!"

Allison stirred in her bed, and Hope, fearful of having her words overheard, stopped whispering. She got up to go to her bed, but on the way, she stopped at the mirror over her dresser. Her short, boyish haircut was slightly tousled. Even without makeup on, her full lips were dark, almost red. Her large, brown eyes stared back at her. They looked at her in self-pity. In defeat, she hung her head down, and retreated to the comfort of her bed.

*   *   *

The following day, Kevin began experiencing his share of problems. It hadn't been a week since school started back, and now he wished desperately for another break. He was trying out for a play, but his instructor was insisting that he try for a more important role. The starring role of this particular play called for the actor to kiss the leading lady. Kevin had repeatedly declined his teacher's advice to try for the part. As a result of his beliefs, Kevin was now backstage arguing with Ed Foster.

Ed paced the floor, sucking greedily at his pipe. He was a middle-aged man who seemed to be able to fit in well with younger people. Twice divorced, he found it difficult to live with Kevin's lack of desire to play a starring role. Kevin was pure talent on two feet, and Ed wanted to display his student as best as he could. When Kevin had refused the role because it called for him to kiss his costar, Ed had been shocked. Had it been someone else, he may have understood, but he was refusing Carmen! Beautiful, dark-haired Carmen, with the full lips and the alluring eyes was being noticeably rejected! Ed shook his head and threw his hands up in the air.

"I can't believe you're not going for this, Kevin," he said for what seemed like the hundredth time, pipe shoved to the side of his mouth.

Kevin rolled his eyes, and inhaled deeply. He was growing tired of his professor, and was on the verge of walking out.

"I'm engaged," he argued. "I told you that I'm not kissing anybody, especially Carmen."

Ed removed his pipe, then took Kevin by the shoulders. He looked at him with pleading eyes. It was his last desperate attempt to talk sense into Kevin's stubborn head.

"I know you're engaged! I'm happy for both of you, but I don't understand you! How can you be an actor with this attitude? People in the movies are usually seeing someone, or are even married! That doesn't stop them from doing romantic scenes, even nude ones, with other people. It's just acting! I thought you knew that, but your medieval ideas tell me differently! Cut loose and grow up, for once, Kevin! I want you to have a great part this time! Aren't you tired of playing secondary characters, when you should be the one who shines? If Karen is any kind of a girlfriend, she'll understand!"

At the mention of Karen's name, Kevin stiffened up. The mere insinuation that Karen was less than perfect made his blood boil. His jaw was set so firmly, that his teeth began to ache. Roughly, he shook Ed's hands off his shoulders, and snatched his script off a table.

"I'm trying for this part and nothing else!" he bellowed. His eyes challenged Ed.

"I'll flunk you," Ed threatened.

"No you won't!" Kevin snapped. "This has almost as many lines as the starring role! You know good and well that I don't have to play certain parts; I just have to do a certain amount of projects!"

Ed watched as Kevin stormed out. He had lost the battle. He put the pipe back in his mouth and inhaled deeply, wondering why Kevin was so devoted. The only hope he had for him was the possibility of a lasting marriage.

Kevin stalked back into the auditorium to join the other students. The shunned Carmen shot him a look of hatred. Any other guy would have paid for the chance to kiss her! She knew that the other students were aware of Kevin's hesitation to play opposite her, and she was filled with embarrassment.

Kevin took his seat as though nothing had happened. He was so satisfied with his decision that he was beyond any shame. He sat there thinking how proud Karen would be at the way he had handled today's situation.

*   *   *

Karen sat on her bed with a robe on her body and a towel on her head. She painted her toenails as she chewed nosily on some bubblegum. Tina had been studying hard ever since school had started back, and it was beginning to wear on Karen's nerves. She was bustling with excitement, wanting to have fun, but she was living with what appeared to be a recluse. Tina had been buried in books lately, her pen moving fervently jotting down notes. The only conversation that she was good for lately was to answer "yes" or "no" questions.

Tina was trying hard to concentrate on her work, but it was very hard. Karen's heavy sighs and that incessant bubble popping was taking its toll on her mind. She held her pen to her lips and nibbled on the end of it to calm her nerves. She cut her eyes at Karen in hopes to get some quiet. Instead, Karen saw an opportunity for conversation.

"Don't your hands ever get tired?' she asked Tina.

Tina shook her head and tried to read again, but Karen was walking towards her now. She balanced herself on her heels to keep from messing up her polish. The towel and the robe, plus the funny walk, brought a smile to Tina's face. Karen saw the smile and wobbled over faster. She plopped down on Tina's bed, and tried to close the enormous textbook that Tina held.

"Let's have fun today, please!" she begged.

Tina reopened the book and shook her head. "I've got to study, Karen," she said firmly.

Karen pouted. "You've been studying ever since you got back from Christmas break! If you don't know it now, you never will!"

"Don't be silly, Karen," Tina answered. "There's something different every day. Besides, I work part-time, so I have to study harder in my free time."

"Liar!" Karen cried. "You use your free time to pump iron and run around that stupid track!"

"Well, if you knew what was good for you, you'd do it, too. Your body knows no exercise except for climbing the steps to this room."

"That's a lot of steps!" Karen cried.

Tina laughed, and Karen took the book out of her hands.

"Come on," she said to Tina. "Give your mind a rest today, and let's go get something to eat! Maybe we can go to a movie. Kevin's working tonight, and I'll go crazy if I have to stay in this room!"

Tina rolled her eyes. "All right, you win. Just don't try to do this every day, because I'll fail in a week if you do."

Karen laughed with delight and ran to the bathroom to dry her hair.

*   *   *

For the first time since she had been back, Tina had a really good time. Just being alone with Karen was so much fun! Karen acted like a child, her face glowing, her heart happy. Karen found it so hard to get close to other girls, but with Tina, it was different. Tina was everything good and right. She was like a solid building in which Karen felt safe. Her eyes were sometimes strange, though, like her guilt with sin. Karen knew that if she were in Tina's shoes, she would do things differently. Tina had no steady boyfriend. Karen saw that as an opportunity for guiltless lovemaking, and she wondered why Tina didn't take advantage of it.

They ate pizza that night, enjoying the longing glances that other guys were giving them. Every time they went out, they were usually with Kevin. Now without a young man present, the other guys were more obvious in their flirtations.

Tina was surprised to find herself happy with Karen's engagement. It meant double the attention for herself as soon as the fellows saw Karen's sparkling ring. For once, she was proud to place her bare fingers on the table.

After they had eaten and had gone to a movie, they went back to the dorm. Tina was filled with so much energy, that she found it hard to sleep. Karen was in the other bed, her body still, her face peaceful.

Tina quietly got out of bed and walked to the window. The lights from the football field rose above the pines and beckoned to her. She touched the window and shivered at the cold. Without thinking about the sleep that she needed, she began to get dressed.

Outside, her breath became visible like smoke. The campus was deathly quiet, its silence broken by an occasional breeze. There were no stars shining tonight, and where there were no streetlights, blackness abounded.

She reached the top of the bleachers, then looked down at the track. It was generously lit by the stadium floodlights. Tina seemed to be the only thing living, and she shuddered at the feeling. It was so deathly quiet, that she could hear nothing but her breathing. Her heart rate had already begun to increase. The *thump, thump, thump* of it drummed in her ears, which were getting very cold. She pulled her cap further down over her head. Her gloved hands were feeling the nip in the air, also, so she put them to her lips. She breathed on them, trying to warm them.

Once on the track, she ran with an unusual energy. Her body seemed to be on a natural high. She'd had fun tonight, and now all of her tension was melting away. How could she have forgotten how to have a good time? It seemed strange to her now. She found herself wishing for more outings with Karen.

She'd lost track of how many times she'd been around the track. A movement out of the corner of her right eye, brought her back to reality. As she slowed down, she looked up towards the top of the bleachers. She was sure that she'd seen a movement! Suddenly she was aware of how vulnerable a position she'd let herself get into! She was alone. If someone chose to harm her, she'd be helpless.

She came to a complete stop and strained her eyes. Sure enough, there was another movement! Someone had been watching her! How long that person had been there was a mystery to her. She looked for a place to run, should the person come after her. With relief, she noticed the figure retreat into the shadows, then she heard the sound of running feet.

For what seemed like hours, she waited in the stadium, hidden under the bleachers. When it seemed that the person was not coming back, she got up to leave. Using a different route, she ran with all her strength to her dorm. She didn't rest until she was locked safely in her room. Quietly pulling her jacket off, she lay in her bed in her jogging clothes and drew the covers over her head. There would be no more late night jogs for her!

CHAPTER NINETEEN

"TINA, 'CHILD', WHAT HAVE YOU done with my knife?" Inez asked as she rummaged through the kitchen. Her body moved slowly, and there was a frown on her dark face.

"I've not used your knife," Tina replied. The item in question was about twelve inches long, and used for cutting vegetables. It was Inez's favorite knife, so no one in the cafeteria dared to use it, for fear of incurring a tongue lashing.

"Can't leave anything lying around anymore!" Inez grumbled.

Tina just shook her head while she continued cleaning the kitchen counters. Though it was winter, her uniform was moist with perspiration. It stuck to her body, aggravating her. All she wanted to do was to take a shower. She could have helped Inez search for the knife, but she wasn't in the mood to do that.

Suddenly the dishwasher walked into the kitchen. He hadn't stepped two feet into the room, before Inez started interrogating him, as well. Tina glanced at the boy and rolled her eyes. Sometimes Inez could be a real pain.

"You sure you ain't seen my knife?" Inez asked the fellow again.

Before he had a chance to answer, Tina turned around. Inez apparently was not going to shut up until someone produced one for her.

"Let me go buy another knife for you, Inez," she offered. "It'll be you own, then. You can even take it home with you, if you want. At least that way nobody would steal it."

Inez stood there contemplating. Maybe a new knife would be good. The other one was getting a little dull. If it were hers, then she *could* see to it personally that nobody took it.

"You sure you don't mind, Child?" she asked Tina.

Tina, relieved that Inez had paused complaining, answered, "No, I don't mind. You deserve another one. I can have it for you by tomorrow. I saw a steak knife in the silverware tray, if you want to use that for now. It should work."

Inez strolled to the tray, happy that things were going to go her way. She started humming to herself, forgetting about her old knife.

As Tina wiped the counter, she tried to think of what could have happened to the knife. It was always stored in a drawer in the kitchen, so it was strange that it should have disappeared.

"What would anybody want with that stupid knife, anyway?" she thought to herself. No answer came to mind, and she continued working.

*   *   *

"I'm sorry you didn't get the part," Allison said to Hope. They were sitting in their dorm, getting ready to study for an English Literature test.

"It wouldn't have been worth having," Hope grumbled. "Kevin didn't even try out for the lead. I figured if he wouldn't kiss me in real life, he might do it in a play. Besides, Carmen got the part, and he wouldn't even try it, because he didn't want to cheat on that slut, Karen. Why does he have to act like such a saint?"

"Well," Allison pointed out, "he *is* engaged."

Hope glared at her roommate. "I don't care if he's married with children!" she snapped.

"Why don't you date someone else?" Allison offered. "You'd feel better if you'd get your mind off of Kevin."

"What kind of a friend are you?" Hope cried. "You told me you'd help me get Kevin, but you don't even try!"

Allison slammed her pen down on her desk. "What do you want out of me?" she shouted. "I can't force the guy to want you!"

Hope bowed her head in defeat. She knew that Allison was speaking the truth. If only she could accept rejection, it would be easy. She'd just never had an incident in which she'd never gotten what she'd wanted. She supposed she'd just stay miserable, until Kevin came to his senses.

"I'm going to the store," she said.

"I wish I had the money that you've wasted in that store," Allison commented.

Hope ignored her and left. If she wanted to spend money, it was her own business.

*   *   *

"Here she comes!" one of the stock boys cried.

"That's ten bucks for me!" another one shouted.

Kevin turned a deep shade of red, then disappeared to the back of the store. It was bad when the employees resorted to making bets on whether or not Hope was coming to the store. She was almost as regular a sight as the employees who worked there.

Hope walked to one of the bag boys. He had a smug grin on his face, which annoyed her immensely.

"Where's Kevin?" she demanded, conscious of the cashiers eavesdropping on her conversation.

"He's on break, Babe," the fellow answered.

"Thank you," she replied sarcastically. "Now how about getting the stupid smile off of your face?"

At that, the other employees within hearing distance roared with laughter, as Hope strutted off.

"What a *nice* girl!" one of the cashiers cried.

Hope blushed, but pretended not to hear. She'd just shop until Kevin was finished with his break. There was no way she was going to spend her money if Kevin was not going to be the one to bag her purchases.

Kevin sat in the break room, staring at the clock. If he didn't like working at this store, he'd quit. Hope had become such a pest! He wished she'd leave him alone!

Suddenly the door to the break room swung open, and one of the bag boys walked in. He lit a cigarette, then bought a drink out of the machine.

"You might as well go back," he said. "She's not going to leave until she's seen you."

Kevin glared at the fellow, and stood up to leave.

"You ought to be flattered, Kevin. She's gorgeous!"

Kevin ignored his co-worker, as he left the break room. He'd be glad when it was time to clock out. He'd walked only a little way, when he heard his name.

"Kevin!" Hope called out, waving furiously from the other side of the store.

He threw up his hand, picked up his pace, then headed for the checkouts. Perhaps he'd find refuge there for a little while.

Hope fumed inside as she watched Kevin walk away. He had some nerve being so rude to her! She snatched a couple more things off the counter, and made her way to the registers. The whole time she was there, Kevin averted her glance. Had she not bought many things, he probably wouldn't have spoken to her. As it was, he had to carry the things out to her car, so speaking to her was inevitable.

"Congratulations on getting the part you tried out for!" Hope said cheerfully, as they stepped outside.

"Thanks," Kevin mumbled. "Did you get anything?"

Hope shook her head. "I guess I wasn't right for them."

"There's always another time," Kevin offered.

"Why didn't you try out for the lead part?" Hope asked.

"I didn't feel like kissing the illustrious Carmen," he answered sarcastically.

"I think that's very admirable of you, Kevin," Hope lied.

Kevin stared at Hope, as though she'd gone mad. He certainly hadn't expected her, of all people, to approve of his decision!

"Thank you," he said, letting his guard down. "That means a lot to me."

"Well," Hope said, as she watched him close the trunk of her car, "you have to draw the line somewhere. They say acting is only acting, but look at the divorce rate in Hollywood."

"You've got a point there," Kevin admitted. He stepped back so she could get to the driver's side.

Hope told him good-bye, then got into her car. He actually believed her! She'd made some positive steps by pretending to be on his side! That was it! That's how she could win his affections! Why hadn't she thought of it before? It had been so simple and right there before her, yet she'd overlooked it all this time! With renewed joy, she hit the accelerator and sped back to the dorm.

*   *   *

That night it snowed. Tina gazed out of the window in a happy daze. She'd never seen snow until a couple of months ago, and it still fascinated her. She stood, her nose pressed against the window pane.

"It's as soft as it looks," she commented.

"You really like snow, don't you?" Karen asked. She was so used to it, that it ceased to impress her. Now she found delight in Tina's interest in it.

"I love snow! I love to watch it fall!" Tina admitted.

"Have you ever caught a snowflake on your tongue?" Karen asked playfully.

Tina looked at her and shook her head.

"What about snow cream? Have you ever tried that?"

Again Tina shook her head.

Karen grabbed their coats and a couple of cups. "You've not lived yet!" she cried. "Let's go out!"

Tina threw her coat on, and they ran outside like two children. Karen looked so funny with her tongue out, her blonde hair flapping in the wind. Tina laughed at her, while Karen made a snowball. She threw it, *smack*, into Tina's side. Tina returned the throw, barely missing Karen. When she reached down to make another one, Karen squealed, then ran. They chased one another around the campus. Other students leaving classes, saw them. They joined in on the fun, until there were dozens of snowballs zigzagging through the air. The atmosphere rang with the laughter of students acting like children again.

Out of nowhere, a snowball flew and hit Tina on her back. As she whirled around to see who her assailant was, Matthew stole a kiss. Karen laughed as Tina instinctively put her gloved hand to her lips.

"You're not going to wipe my kiss off, are you?" Matthew teased. He stood tall and proud, dressed in fashionable winter clothes and a suede coat.

"No, I'm not going to wipe it off," Tina answered, "but I am going to get you back!" She bent down and scooped up some snow. When she stood back up, Matthew was running away. Laughing, she followed him, leaving Karen behind.

Matthew was not used to running; Tina was. She was almost upon him, when he slipped in the snow. Tina tried to stop, so she would avoid stepping on him. It was no use. She slid, and as she fell, he rolled over.

"What do you weigh?" Matthew asked.

"A hundred and ten," she answered.

"It's a good thing I got out of the way; you might have killed me!" he joked.

Tina picked up a fist full of snow, and shoved it in his face. She got back on her feet, then looked down at Matthew. He held up his hands in submission.

"Help me up," he said.

She put out a hand, but he grabbed it, pulling her back into the snow. She lay on her stomach, laughing, her breath coming out in little clouds. Matthew stared at her, then began laughing, too.

"I'm freezing!" he gasped.

"That's what happens when you lay in the snow!" Tina cried.

They helped each other up, then wiped off their clothes.

"Isn't it traditional to drink hot chocolate after falling into the snow?" Tina asked playfully.

"Yes, I suppose it is. Are you hungry?"

Tina nodded. "When am I not hungry?"

Matthew put his arm around her waist. "Sorry," he commented. "I forgot about your enormous appetite!"

"Don't apologize! Get me something to eat!" she teased.

They walked away together, talking about the past holiday break. Tina, in her excitement at seeing Matthew for the first time in weeks, had completely forgotten about Karen.

Karen stood on the campus watching Tina and Matthew walk away. Her head was held high, though her pride was hurt. Had it been her and Kevin, she would have invited Tina to come along. Now Tina walked away, as she stood in the snow with her hands crammed into her coat pockets. She became aware of her feet getting uncomfortably numb, so she headed back to her dorm, alone.

*　　*　　*

In the restaurant, Matthew and Tina sipped their hot chocolate. On the grill, two hamburgers were being cooked up just for them. The smell of food drifted throughout the air. Outside it was cold and wet, but inside it was cozy and dry. People chattered happily, and the employees walked on light feet.

"So how are the wedding plans coming along?" Matthew asked Tina.

At the mention of the wedding, Tina remembered Karen. She almost choked on her drink. Matthew reached over to pat her on her back.

"Are you all right?" he asked, concerned.

"I've got to go!" Tina cried. "How could I have been so stupid?!"

"What are you talking about?" he asked.

"I left Karen standing outside in the snow. She was going to show me how to make snow cream, then I ran off with you and left her!"

"Karen's a big girl," Matthew noted. "You might as well stay long enough to eat your food. A few more minutes won't hurt."

"I've really got to go!" Tina said, as she stood up.

Matthew put a reassuring hand on hers and beckoned to her to sit back down. "I'll show you how to make snow cream, then you can take some to Karen."

Reluctantly, Tina sat down. Matthew was right. The damage had been done, and a few more minutes probably wouldn't make a big difference. Guilt crept through her soul, so she ordered a sandwich and fries to go, for Karen.

*   *   *

Back at the dorm, Karen opened a book and tried to study for a test. She read one paragraph at a time, then closed her eyes to concentrate on what she'd just read. It was the easiest way for her to study, instead of jumbling everything together at once. After a while, she put the book down, and looked through Tina's notes. They were orderly and neat. She got her notebook, and started taking notes, too. It soon bored her, though, so she put her pen down and tried reading again.

The door to the room opened slowly, and Karen glanced up. Tina crept into the room, a sheepish grin on her face. She held out a container and a cup.

"I got you something to eat," she offered.

"I'm not hungry," Karen lied.

"Karen, I feel like a real jerk right now. Could you at least take a bite out of this food? I even made you some snow cream."

"Snow cream?" Karen repeated, her interest growing.

"Yes," she said. "I'm sorry for running off like that. "Forgive me?"

Karen took the container and opened it. As she bit into the juicy hamburger, she nodded. Her hurt faded as her hunger became satisfied.

"Did you have a good time?" Karen asked when she'd polished off the last of the hamburger.

"I did until I remembered about you," Tina commented.

Just then there was a knock on the door. Karen jumped up and ran to answer it. Kevin was standing in the doorway, his face tired, his shoulders slumped.

"I'm starving, Karen," he said. "Let's go get something to eat."

"All right," Karen said, ignoring the peculiar glance that Tina was giving her.

As she walked to the closet to get her coat, Tina whispered. "I hope you can find room in there."

Karen touched her full belly. "I hope so, too," she whispered back.

Before she left, she looked up at Tina. "Want to come along?"

Tina held up the empty container. "I couldn't eat another bite," she said.

Both girls burst into laughter. Karen put her arm through Kevin's, as he led them out of the room. He looked at them, perplexed, as he closed the door behind them.

*   *   *

The next day, Tina provided Inez with her new knife. The older woman smiled and held it up to the light.

"Thanks, Child," she said. "You know you didn't have to do this."

"I know," Tina said, "but I wanted you to be happy."

"You're a sweet girl," Inez cooed. She walked into the kitchen to start cutting vegetables with her new knife. As she walked away, she hummed to herself. Inez was happy again.

The old knife never did turn up, and nobody mentioned it again. Tina felt strange about it, but she kept her thoughts to herself. She pulled her hair into a ponytail, then went out front to help in the cafeteria line.

From where she stood every day, she saw many things. Being behind the counter was somewhat like watching a soap opera. She knew without being told, who was dating whom, and who had broken up.

Today she did not like what she saw. She watched with disapproving eyes as Karen's gaze met that of another guy's. Kevin was in front of her, totally unaware of what was taking place. The other fellow, who Tina did not recognize, was small in height. His features were dark, like a Native American. As he caught Karen's glance, he winked at her. She smiled back and lowered her head.

Tina's blood began to boil. She started scooping out food without watching what she was doing.

"Hey, Tina, this is going to take me all day to eat this!" a student exclaimed.

Tina looked down. The food that she had just served was covering most of the plate. She glanced to her side, and caught a stern look from one of the veteran cafeteria employees.

"I'm sorry," Tina said, giving her most charming smile. She took the plate, and gave the student a fresh, but smaller serving. She avoided looking into the eyes of the other employee. It was bad enough to see Karen flirting with another guy; she could not bear to be scolded by the older woman now.

When Karen and Kevin left the food line, the winking fellow watched Karen walk. He whistled to himself, his eyes fixed on her body. This made Tina furious. She slammed his food onto his plate so hard, that it made a loud noise. People looked up. The older employee frowned again. Tina wanted to disappear, but she could only stand there and blush. The flirtatious guy looked Tina up and down, smiling evilly, and then he left to find a table within view of Karen.

*   *   *

"Do you know a student who's part Native American?" Tina asked Matthew later that day. They had met in the library to study, and Tina hoped that Matthew might know the fellow.

"I know one," said Matthew. "Why do you want to know?"

"I think he's after Karen," Tina confided.

Matthew laughed rudely. "It shouldn't take him long to get her in bed. He's got a thing for women, especially promiscuous ones."

Tina grew angry and she snapped. "I didn't ask you to comment on Karen; I asked you if you knew the guy!"

Matthew softened and took Tina's hands in his. "I'm sorry, my loyal, little Tina, if I offended you in any way. I'll keep my comments to myself today in regard to Karen. The guy you're asking about is Danny. I don't know his last name. He's a sophomore, but he acts more like a freshman. He was in one of my classes at the beginning of the semester, but he dropped it. I think he had trouble with the professor. That's about all I know."

"I sure don't like the way he looked at Karen," Tina confessed.

"You sure are protective. What does the glamorous Karen do to deserve your friendship?"

Tina slammed her book shut and stood up. She pointed her finger at Matthew, taking no care to lower her voice.

"I'm tired of your sarcasm!" she cried. "You sit there like you're so much better than anybody else! She's my best friend, and that should be enough to earn your respect!"

Matthew crouched in his seat. He tried to fight the blush, which was creeping into his face. He looked up at Tina, who was trembling, and holding back tears. Part of him wanted to grab her, to hold her, and he almost did that. Suddenly an image of Karen flashed in his mind, disgusting him. How someone like Tina could practically worship trash like Karen was beyond him. He just sat there and let her walk away, but before she was gone, he called out, "Your friendship won't change her ways."

She heard, and he knew that she had, because she stood there for a moment, her hand on the door. Then violently, she threw the door open and ran out.

Tina was just outside of the library when she collided with Kevin. Books and papers fell all over the place. Tina muttered a soft curse, then rushed to pick her things up. When Kevin bent down to help her, their eyes met. Tina flushed, as she realized who she'd bumped into. Immediately her hand flew to her face to wipe away a tear, but it was too late. Kevin had seen it, and now he would want an explanation.

"Tina, what's wrong?" he asked, concern clouding his blue eyes.

Tina, still bent down, tried to straighten her papers and books. She hoped that if she ignored him, he would just go away. She stood up, and he followed suit.

"What's wrong?" he repeated.

"Nothing's wrong, Kevin," Tina cried. "Please just leave me alone!"

As he stared at her, Kevin noticed how pretty and vulnerable she looked. He'd seldom seen Karen cry, and he felt hopeless now.

"Did somebody hurt you?" he asked urgently.

Tina shook her head violently, as she choked back a sob. She faced Kevin but her eyes avoided him. Suddenly she caught a movement from the side. She turned and saw Matthew walking quickly towards them. She took a step to go, but Kevin caught her by the arm.

"What'd he do to you?" he demanded. His eyes were flashing in a way that Tina had never seen. The mere thought of Kevin protecting her brought all of her pent up passion to the surface. She closed her eyes for a moment, and tried to calm her beating heart. When she opened them, she felt stronger.

"I've got to go, Kevin," she said. "You should go, too. Karen needs you."

Reluctantly he let go of her arm, and watched her run away. Her words had been strange, but he did not grasp the meaning behind them. Matthew called to Tina, but she kept running, without looking back.

Kevin turned and glared at Matthew.

"You're stupider than you look," he hissed. "I don't know what you did or said to her, but it must have been terrible!"

Matthew only stood there in a stupor. All his braveness melted in the angry face of Kevin. He could slander Karen anywhere, except in the presence of the one he was confronting now.

"Aren't you going after her?" Kevin snapped.

Matthew lowered his head. "There's nothing I can do now," he said quietly.

"You coward," Kevin spat hatefully. He went down the library steps, then ran to catch up with Tina.

She was nowhere to be found, so Kevin went to Karen's dorm. When no one answered, he headed back to the library.

That night the phone kept ringing. Karen stretched in bed lazily, and reached for the phone. She had been trying to watch TV, but the phone kept ringing. She wished that Tina would talk to Matthew, but she refused every time.

"Hello," she said. "Wait a minute, and I'll see."

She held the phone out to Tina. "It's him again," she whispered.

Tina kept her eyes on the television screen. Once again, she shook her head.

"Look, Matthew," Karen said, when she'd gotten back on the phone, "Tina doesn't want to talk to you. I'm tired of answering this thing, and I'll just unplug it, if you keep bothering us. I don't know what you did, but you did it good. Promise me that you won't call anymore tonight. Good. See you later. OK. Bye."

She hung up the phone, then looked at Tina. Tina smiled in spite of herself, and lay down on the bed. "He's a pest, isn't he?" she commented.

"That's not the word I would have used," Karen confessed, "but it'll do."

Tina giggled and snuggled down in the covers. She was glad that Karen did not keep prying. She had asked once, but when Tina had not discussed it, she had respected her wishes. She closed her eyes, and hoped that Kevin would forget it, too.

CHAPTER TWENTY

A COUPLE OF WEEKS LATER, TINA returned to the dorm after working in the cafeteria. She found Karen sitting on the bed, crying. When Karen saw Tina, she jumped up from the bed and grabbed her by the shoulders.

"Tina, you've got to help me!" she cried.

Tina put her purse down, and looked curiously at Karen.

"What happened?" she asked, concerned. If anything had happened to Kevin, she would die!

"It's my ring," Karen sobbed. "It's gone!"

Tina looked down at the bare hand in shock. Immediately, her organized persona took control. She fell to the floor on her hands and knees, then started searching in the carpet.

Karen sat on the floor quickly, and touched Tina.

Exasperated, Tina cried out, "Help me look, Karen! Maybe we can find it before Kevin finds out!"

Karen continued to sit on the floor in a daze. "It's not there," she mumbled.

"What'd you say?" Tina asked, her eyes to the floor, her hands combing the carpet.

"It's not there!" Karen cried.

Tina looked at her incredulously. "Where is it, Karen? Do you remember where you lost it?" she asked calmly.

"Danny's got it," Karen said softly.

Tina stood up, not understanding completely. "Well get it back from him, Karen! If Kevin sees that ring missing, he'll kill Danny *and* you!"

Karen stood up shakily. She glared at Tina, her eyes flashing. "Do you think I'm stupid, Tina?" she snapped. "He won't give it back. He wants me for his girlfriend, and he says he's going to show the ring to Kevin! He's going to tell Kevin how he got it!" She sobbed uncontrollably. "I'm going to lose Kevin now!"

Tina closed her eyes, trying not to imagine the worst. The worst had become reality, though, and she opened her eyes again. Taking a deep breath, she asked Karen, "How did he get that ring?"

Karen sat on the edge of the bed. She began spilling out the truth, as if that would help her now.

"I've been seeing Danny on and off for a couple of weeks," she confessed.

Tina stood there remembering the evenings that Karen had left the dorm. Now she remembered how strangely Karen had acted, with her eyes downcast, her conversations brief. How could she have been fooled? Didn't she know that look by now?

Karen continued, "I've been with him a few times. He always asks me to take off my ring. He says that he can't concentrate if I wear another guy's ring. Last night I forgot it in his room. When I went there this morning and asked for it, he wouldn't let me have it back. He said that he's in love with me, and that I've got to end it with Kevin. When I refused, he threatened to tell everything! If I don't break up with Kevin, he'll tell Kevin all about us!"

Tina shook her head, and swore quietly. "Where is Danny now?" she asked.

"He's supposed to be in class."

"Do you think the ring is in his room?" Tina asked.

Karen shrugged her shoulders, and then began whimpering again, "I don't know! I think so, but I'm not sure! Oh Tina, what am I going to do?"

Tina grabbed Karen by the shoulders, and gave her a shake. "Look, Karen, we don't have much time! I need you for once to be strong! Now get a backbone, and stop crying for one minute!"

Karen's hand flew to her face. As she tried to wipe away tears, Tina began rummaging through the closet. She pulled out one of Karen's black teddies, and held it to herself.

"Can I borrow this?" she asked.

Karen nodded in confusion, while Tina jerked off her uniform, and replaced it with the sexy lingerie. She selected a tight black skirt from the closet, slid it on, and then put on some black high-heeled shoes. Walking quickly to the bathroom, she let her hair down. She brushed her teeth and applied make-up. Looking into the mirror, she frowned. She hated a lot of make-up; she'd be glad to get back and take it off.

Karen's gaze met hers in the mirror. "What are you doing?" she asked.

"I'm sorry, Karen, but right now I don't have time for twenty questions," Tina commented hastily. She brushed past Karen, and grabbed one of the longer coats from the closet. While she fastened the buttons, she got Danny's building and room information from Karen.

As she opened the door, she glanced over her shoulder. "If I'm not back in thirty minutes, send some help," she said firmly.

Karen nodded again, and looked at the clock. Tina was worrying her. She wondered what she was up to.

It was freezing outside, and Tina regretted choosing the skirt. She crammed her hands into her coat pockets, and tried to ignore the wind that cut through her clothes and stung her body. It was so cold, that she didn't try to look nonchalant. Instead, she steadily made her way to Danny's dorm.

Down on the other end of the campus, Kevin watched Tina. Had she been walking towards Matthew's dorm, he wouldn't have thought much about it. He knew from looking at her high heels, that she usually didn't dress that flashy, especially in the middle of the afternoon. He glanced down at his watch. He had a while before his next class began, so he followed.

Inside the lobby of Danny's dorm, Tina looked around uncomfortably. The student in charge walked up to her.

"Can I help you?" he asked.

"Can you point me to the direction of room 443?" she asked.

"That'll be on the left side over there," the fellow said. "The steps are right behind that door."

"Thank you," Tina said. As she walked off, the guy stared at her. He'd have to talk with Danny. Maybe he would share some of his secrets for getting all these beautiful girls to come see him lately.

Upstairs, Tina walked slowly to the room. Guys were walking by and whistling. Unaccustomed to so much attention, Tina blushed. She reached the door, gathered her poise, and knocked.

The guy who answered was not much taller than Danny. His blonde hair was long and silky. He looked Tina up and down, and stepped into the hall.

"Is this Danny's room?" Tina asked, before he had a chance to speak.

"Yeah it is? Who are you?"

"I'm a friend," Tina lied. "Danny told me to meet him here. He said he'd leave the key right here by the door, but I didn't see it."

She unbuttoned her coat, then opened it just enough for him to get a good look. As he stood gaping, she walked by him, gazing over her shoulder, pouting slightly.

"He told me nobody would be here when I arrived," Tina stated, looking at the young man disappointedly.

"H-he forgot to tell me he was having a guest," the guy stammered, embarrassed. "Usually one of us leaves if the other one is having a girl over."

Tina turned around, and strolled over to him. "*Usually?*"

"Well, what I mean is—" the fellow began.

She put her hands on his bare chest, leaned up, and kissed him squarely on the mouth.

"Danny didn't tell me he had such a good-looking roommate," she cooed.

The guy turned a brilliant shade of red, and then darted into the room to get the rest of his clothes. "Yeah, it's too bad he found you first," he said as he got dressed. "If you two don't hit it off, look me up. I'd ask you out now, but Danny'd kill me. He's got a horrible temper!"

"I understand," Tina answered. "It was nice meeting you, anyway."

The nervous guy bolted out the door, and Tina quickly locked it. Her hands shook, and she felt like it had gotten to about one hundred degrees in the room. She tossed the coat onto the bed. Precious time had been wasted trying to get rid of Danny's roommate. She jerked the dresser drawers open, and searched through them. Nothing turned up, and she thought she would die from the stress. Every few seconds, she turned to look at the locked door. A couple of times, she thought she'd heard it open, but then realized that it was another door in the building.

When nothing turned up in the dressers, she went to the bathroom, and searched through the cabinets. Again, her search was futile. She twisted about to face the bedroom, leaned against the door frame, and tried not to cry in frustration. As she willed herself to be strong, her eyes landed on a small desk. It was the only place that she hadn't looked yet. Her knees trembled as she walked rapidly to the desk. She wrapped her trembling fingers around the curve in the front drawer, took a deep breath, and pulled. Nothing! She sighed as she closed the drawer. It obviously was not in the room. Suddenly, she remembered the closets. She turned to go to them, then came face to face with Danny! Her mouth flew open, and she cried out in pain, as he grabbed both of her arms.

"What're you looking, for Tina?" he hissed.

"You know exactly what I want," she said, trying not to tremble. "Give the ring to me!"

"You're a demanding little witch, aren't you?" Danny said. He leaned his face closer to hers, and she spit in it.

Her spit on his face was like gas ignited, as he released her, then cursed loudly. His hand drew back to hit her face. When he failed to get the look of fear that he desired, he put his hand down, looked up at the ceiling and laughed.

"I bet nobody knows you're here," he taunted.

Tina's eyes widened, and she started backing away, but not before he grabbed her again. He jerked her to him, and kissed her violently. Her mouth hurt, and she began to feel faint. Suddenly, her will to get out of the room overcame her. She used that rush of frightened energy to draw her knee back and slam it into his groin.

Danny doubled over as he cried out in agony. While he was bent over, Tina noticed the ring dangling from his necklace. She reached for it, but he grabbed her hand. Straightening up, he put his other hand around her throat. She began to gag and cry, but he only smiled.

"Don't you know I can kill you in a minute?" he asked hatefully.

"Please .... Danny .... stop," Tina gasped.

His grip only tightened. In her despair, she tried again to reach for the necklace.

His grip loosened, and she fell to the floor, gasping, her hand on her throat.

"You are *pathetic*," Danny sneered. He stared at her, shook his head, and reached into his pocket. When his hand reemerged, he was holding something. He pushed a button, and a click followed by a sickening flash of metal came into view.

Tina stared up at him, frozen, her hand still on her throat.

"I'm going to cut your pretty face so much, even your own mother won't recognize you!"

Tina gasped. He was serious! She stared at him in fear and disbelief, and began backing up. She remembered that there were other people in the building. She opened her mouth to scream, but before any sound came out, a bottle was smashed over Danny's head. Danny fell to the floor, as the odor of alcohol filled the room.

Tina looked up and saw Kevin standing there with the other half of a vodka bottle. He tossed the remnant aside, then leaned down to pick up the knife. He closed it, put it in his pocket, and stared at Tina. His eyes demanded an explanation.

Tina pointed at his necklace. "He stole Karen's ring," she said weakly, then she fainted.

*   *   *

When she woke up, she was lying in her own bed. Everything was blurry, and she blinked her eyes to see better. When her vision cleared, she saw Kevin sitting on Karen's bed. His face was full of concern. When he saw that she had awakened, he walked over to her bed.

Tina smiled. "How come you're always there when I need you?" she asked.

"I've got a talent for that," Kevin answered. "Now tell me what you were doing there. I thought you had more sense than that."

"I had to get Karen's ring; he stole it," Tina croaked.

"You should have called the police, Tina, then he would have been arrested."

"We were afraid you'd get mad," Tina explained.

"Of course I'm mad," Kevin said. "He shouldn't go around stealing things. When he found it on the desk in the library, he should have turned it in to the 'Lost and Found Department.'"

"*What?*" Tina asked, confused.

"Karen explained everything to me," Kevin said. "Just promise me that you won't do anything like that again."

Tina nodded. She had no idea what Kevin was talking about, but she had a feeling that she should keep her mouth shut for now.

The door to the room opened, and Karen walked into the room, a box of pizza in her hands. She looked at Tina, and smiled anxiously.

"How're you doing?" she asked.

"I'm alright."

"We didn't know when you were going to wake up. We were getting hungry, so I got a large pizza for all of us." She put the pizza down, and then got out paper plates for each of them.

Tina sat up in bed, and accepted the plate that Karen handed her. She held it with shaky hands, as Karen put a slice on there for her. Tina looked down at herself, confused. She was still wearing the skimpy clothes she'd put on earlier.

"How did I get back here?" she asked.

"I helped you get back after you fainted," Kevin said. "Of course I had to go the long way. People would have asked questions if they'd seen me carrying you in the middle of the campus."

He took the pizza that Karen offered him, and waited as she got three canned drinks out of the refrigerator. When she got back, he slid over for her, and helped her open them. He handed Tina her drink, and she took a cautious sip. Her throat felt like sandpaper.

"I fainted?"

"Yes, but it's no wonder you did. He practically choked the life out of you," Kevin answered.

They ate quietly, and when they were finished, Kevin stood up.

"If you two feel safe, I need to get back to my dorm. I went ahead and reported off at work. I might as well use the time to catch up on some studying."

Karen walked him to the door, and kissed him.

"Don't take that ring off your finger anymore," Kevin said, smiling at her.

"I won't," Karen said reassuringly.

She closed the door behind him, and listened as he walked away.

"What's going on?" Tina demanded.

"I lied, Tina."

"Well I figured out as much," Tina replied sarcastically. "What did you tell him?"

"I told him that when I was in the library studying, I took my ring off to put lotion on my hands. Then I said that I went to get a drink of water, forgetting my ring on the table. I told him that when I got back, I noticed that my ring was gone. I said that I saw Danny walking out of the library very fast. I also said that he was the only one around at the time, and that I was sure he'd taken my ring. I told Kevin that when I told you about it, you got mad. Then I said that while I was in the bathroom, you left, and that I didn't know where you had gone."

"You should be an actress," Tina said disgustedly.

"It was the only thing I could think of!" Karen cried. "I was so shocked when he brought you back and he told me that he had the ring! I had to do some fast talking to save my hide!"

"Did you save it?" Tina questioned.

"Yes, I believe so. Thank goodness. Now I just have to hope that Kevin believes me instead of Danny. You know he's going to blabber everything!"

"I'm sure he will," Tina admitted. "Now I'll have to go the rest of the year wondering if he's on my trail. He wanted to cut me, Karen!"

"I know," Karen said sincerely. "I am so sorry! Maybe he won't hurt you now. From what Kevin told me, Danny took a pretty hard lick."

"You're not a realistic person," Tina said. She got up and changed into her work-out clothes.

"What're you doing?" Karen asked her.

"I'm going to work out. That's probably the only place that I can go where Danny won't find me."

"What if he does find you?" Karen asked, concerned.

Tina flicked the switchblade knife that Kevin had left by the bedside. "If he finds me, I'll just give him his knife back," she said tartly. She tucked the knife into her bra, turned on her heels, and walked out.

Karen made sure the door was locked. She suddenly felt scared and alone. She paused by the window, her hands on the curtains.

"What have I done?" she whispered to the empty room. She drew the curtains, and went to bed. She pulled the covers over her, curled up, then closed her eyes.

*   *   *

Under some trees a distance from the baseball field, Danny and his roommate were parked. Danny lit a joint and smoked it, then passed it on to his friend. While his roommate inhaled, Danny took a large swallow of whiskey. He would have preferred the vodka, but that had been busted over his head by some unseen enemy. His head was wrapped in a makeshift bandage. It throbbed with pain, and he took another drink to try to ease the pain.

"When I find out who hit me, Randy," he growled, "they're dead!"

"How're you going to find out?" he asked.

"I'm going to make that girl talk. If I have to rip her arms out of their sockets, I'll do it!"

Randy sighed. "Who woulda thought? She sure was pretty," he admitted.

Danny exhaled. "Well, she's going to be in a lot of pain if she doesn't talk. I about cut her face today. Now my knife is gone!"

"Are you crazy? You could have gone to jail!" Randy cried, trying not to choke on the smoke he'd been holding in.

"She would have been too scared to turn me in to the police," Danny answered smugly.

The stereo in the car was playing loudly. They were parked in an obscure location, and both boys were now very high. The car they were in was an old seventies relic that Danny had bought from his grandfather. Inside the seats were worn and shabby, and outside, the olive green paint was chipped. The handles on the car were the kind that one opened with the hand and the thumb.

Just as he was about to take another toke off the joint, someone jumped on the hood of the car. Danny cursed, and Randy choked on his drink. Danny turned on his car lights to see better. The person on the hood was dressed in a black sweatshirt, pants, and socks, but wore no shoes. On the head was a dark pillowcase, with the eyes cut out. It was tied loosely at the neck with a crude rope. The stance of the person conveyed absolutely no fear, as eyes peered out, challenging.

Danny's initial fear turned to rage. "So someone forgot Halloween is already past," he shouted at the figure. "I'm coming out to remind you what day it *really* is!"

The stranger jumped off of the hood, and ran towards Danny's side of the car. Danny pulled the handle, then looked down, confused. The door only opened a few scant inches, then stopped. He slammed his body against it, but it would not budge any further. Looking out the small opening, he saw that a rope similar to the one worn by the freak who'd crashed his party, was wrapped around his outside door handle, and secured to the back door handle. From his point of view, he could see his gas tank, open, with a small rag hanging from the opening. Danny watched in horror, as the figure lit a match and put it against the rag.

"Noooooooooo!" Danny screamed, trying harder to force the door open. "He's going to blow this car up!!!!!"

Randy was struggling with his door, too, but it would not open either. It was tied tightly, just like Danny's door. When he heard Danny screaming, he jerked out his knife and tried to cut the rope.

Danny, crying and cursing, leaned back down in the seat and drew his legs back. He raised his feet to kick out the front window. It was too late, though, for the car exploded into an inferno. The individual who had set the car on fire, had been running away. At the sound of the explosion, the figure turned around, and watched as the car and its occupants burned. Satisfied, the person ran away into the darkness.

CHAPTER TWENTY-ONE

F EBRUARY CAME WITH A VENGEANCE. Cold winds and icy rains
kept most of the people on campus very miserable. When
one flu was almost through being passed around, another
strain took its place. Attendance was at a very low percentage,
because many of the students were sick. Everywhere, everyone
complained about the weather. People were ready for spring.
Their eyes grew tired of the bare trees and the dead leaves. The
short days caused depression, and the freezing nights added to
that depression.

When March arrived, peoples' spirits started rising. The
weather was milder, and on some days, it was even a little warm.
Spring was just around the corner, and a certain excitement
filled the air.

On one of those warmer days, Tina walked slowly to her
dorm. It was her birthday, and deep inside, she was excited.
Her birthdays always made her happy, because it was her own
special day. She knew that there would be a package from Aunt
Beth waiting on her when she got to her room.

Outside of her dorm room she saw it; her package. Gently she
lifted it and carried it into the empty room. She sat on the bed,
then opened the card that her aunt had sent. Smiling to herself,
she tore at the paper, and opened her present excitedly. Inside
the box was a beautiful spring dress. It was pale blue, with a
satin floral pattern all over. Inside the box, also, was a matching
purse and sequined, strappy sandals. Tina stood up and held the
garment to herself. The reflection in the mirror was of a happy,
pretty girl. The blue material brought out the darkness of her

skin and her eyes. She slipped on her shoes, and still holding the dress, she danced around the room. Spring was almost here! The season was her favorite, and she wished that it would last forever!

She was still swaying, when she heard a laugh. Startled, she stopped and turned around. Karen was standing in the room, and Tina wondered in embarrassment how long she had been there.

"That's a pretty dress," Karen commented.

"Thanks," Tina said. "My aunt sent it to me."

"Is it your birthday?" Karen asked.

Tina nodded, and went to hang the dress up.

"Happy birthday," Karen said.

"Thanks."

"So what are your plans for tonight?"

"I don't have any," Tina confessed.

Karen slithered up to Tina and put her arm on Tina's shoulder. "I'm starving. Why don't we get ready and go get a little something to eat?"

"Well, I guess that'd be good," Tina answered.

They took their showers and got dressed, and then Karen drove Tina to the little grill near the campus. They got out of the car and walked up to the front door of the restaurant. As Karen held the door open for Tina, she commented, "I think I'd like some pizza."

Tina halted and looked at Karen. "They don't have pizza here, Karen."

Karen smiled and gently pushed Tina inside. "They do tonight!" she cried.

Tina stumbled in and noticed a crowd in a small room to the right of the main dining area. When they saw her, they shouted, "Happy birthday!"

She stood there, dumbfounded, as Karen took her by the arm and led her into the room.

"I reserved this area for your birthday party tonight," Karen said proudly.

Tina smiled. She knew some of the people, but not all of them. They sat chattering under blue and white streamers. A bittersweet feeling came over her. Matthew was not amongst them, but what did she expect? She pushed the feeling aside, and looked about the room. A few presents were spread out on one of the tables. On another table there was a long sheet cake with candles on it. Nobody had ever thrown her a surprise birthday party, and she choked back happy tears. She threw her arms around Karen, then stepped back.

"Karen, thank you!" she cried jubilantly.

Kevin stood up and motioned for Tina and Karen to sit down. They walked over to the table, and Kevin opened up all of the boxes of pizza. Everybody dug in, joking and laughing. They ate until they felt they would burst.

As she blew out the candles on her cake, Tina felt at home for the first time. She was surrounded by friends, and it was a comforting feeling. She glanced up at Karen and smiled. Karen held her diamond up and winked at Tina. Their eyes met in mutual thankfulness and friendship, and Tina knew then that their friendship would last forever.

When Tina was almost finished opening her presents, Karen handed her a brightly colored package.

"Happy birthday, Tina," she said.

Tina took the present gently from Karen. "You've already done so much!" she cried.

Karen smiled and watched as Tina opened the present. She tore the paper off, and looking into the small box, she gasped. Gingerly, she pulled out a porcelain unicorn and held it up to her face. It was beautiful, as no other she had ever seen.

"Keep dreaming, Tina," Karen said softly.

Tina smiled, filled with emotion, as she admired the unicorn.

* * *

When the party was over, Karen and Kevin helped Tina carry her things back to the dorm. She put everything up, but put the unicorn in a special spot on her dresser. It stood there with its front legs thrown up in the air. Its head was held high, and its mane seemed to float in the air. It appeared to have a magical air about it, and Tina gazed at it from her bed.

That night she dreamed about her childhood. She was riding a pony in a bright green pasture. Her parents stood nearby, watching over her. In reality, she had fallen off of a pony as a child, but in her dreams, she never fell off. She rode with the wind flowing through her hair, and the pony's hooves beating in time with her heart. The dream was always interrupted when the alarm woke her up. Today was no exception. She was riding into infinity when loud music came blasting from her clock radio. Drowsily, she rolled over in the bed and glanced over at Karen's bed. It was empty, and Tina knew that Karen had spent the night with Kevin. She rubbed her head, not bothering to turn off the radio. As she lay in bed, the memories of the past months went though her mind like a slow motion film. She saw herself, Karen, and Kevin on one of their many long walks. She saw herself swaying in the autumn leaves as the sun went down.

Later that morning, as she was walking with a crowd of students, she saw Kevin coming towards her. His eyes lit up, and she smiled, throwing up her hand. When they got closer to each other, he walked right by, not seeing her. She kept walking, turning to look at him. He strolled up to Karen, who she had not even seen, and embraced her. Tina blushed. She looked down, and just shook her head and walked on. She should have known better.

* * *

Hope sat in the back of the auditorium and watched the rehearsals for the play. She paid little attention to anyone, except Kevin. He was so full of passion and grace as he merged from one point to another, that he sometimes made her forget that it was just a play.

She almost knew all of the words to all of the lines. Sitting and watching was paying off for her in a small way. She wished desperately, that one of the girls would get sick. With her knowledge of the material, she would certainly get a part.

A student came into the auditorium and sat down beside of her. She cut her eyes in his direction and sighed. It was Paul Morgan. If Kevin gave her a third of the affection that Paul gave her, she'd be in complete bliss.

"How're you doing, Hope?"

"Fine," she said. She looked over at him. He was a tall, sturdy Pennsylvania boy, knocked off his feet by the southern beauty in Hope. Though he was not drop dead gorgeous, his hair was like molten gold, and his eyes were like slate. Had she not been so involved in her daydreams of Kevin, she would have noticed the translucent skin and the intriguing smile that Paul possessed.

"She's pretty, isn't she?" he asked as he pointed to one of the actresses on the stage. If Hope was going to snob him, he was going to try to get another girl. At least he might succeed in provoking Hope, as much as she provoked him.

Hope frowned and started to say something hateful about the dark-haired actress. Suddenly, an evil plan entered her mind. It was horrible and cruel, but it made Hope happy at the thought. She smiled in a most charming way and pointed at the girl.

"Do you mean that girl?" she asked sweetly.

Paul nodded.

"I don't ever see her with anybody," Hope lied. "Why don't you ask her out?"

"I don't even know her. I've seen her around, but I don't even know her name."

"Would you go out with her?" Hope asked.

Paul rolled his eyes. "Of course I'd go out with her, but she'd never give me the time of day. Just *look* at her!"

Again Hope bit her tongue. He'd asked her out too many times for her to count, yet he felt intimidated by that simpleton on the stage! How dare him!

Once she regained her composure, she turned in her seat and looked him right in the eyes.

"I could set you up with all kinds of beautiful girls, Paul. I could even pay you to go out with her."

"What are you talking about?" he asked sharply.

"I want in this play, and I want you to help me!"

"I can't do anything for you, Hope. They've already got who they want, besides, the play's in a week!"

Hope stood up and took Paul by the arm. He stood up also, and they walked into the hallway.

"Just go now," she said. "I'll be in touch with you later. You'll have a date with that girl, and I'll get in that play."

Paul shook his head. "Forget it, Hope!" he snapped. "I don't know what you're up to, but it doesn't smell right at all. Count me out!"

"I'll *pay* you to date her," she offered.

Paul shook her hand off of his arm. "I don't want your money," he scoffed. She started to argue, but he grinned at her.

"I'll take something else, though," he said, gazing at her up and down, and stroking her arm with the tip of his finger. He felt emboldened by the events turning in his favor.

Hope looked at him, disgustedly. "You're just as wicked as I am, aren't you?"

He nodded, and put his arm around her waist. "You work with me, and I'll work with you," he stated plainly.

They walked out of the building together. Hope glanced at her watch. She'd have to make it quick if she was to get back before rehearsal was over.

Less than an hour later, Hope walked back into the auditorium. She was almost too late, for the students were gathering their things, and listening to suggestions from the director. She watched until they were dismissed, then she walked down towards the stage.

Kevin did not see her as he put on his coat. She watched longingly, afraid to ruin the moment. He turned around and saw her before she spoke. Surprisingly, he smiled at her, and she felt suddenly high.

"You're doing a great job!" Hope commented.

Kevin jumped down off of the stage. "You really think so?" he asked, flattered at her admiration.

Hope nodded. "That's not why I came here, though," she said.

"What is it?" Kevin asked cautiously.

"Relax, it's not me this time," Hope said. "I admit defeat. I do, however, have this friend who would really love to date one of your costars."

"Who is it?" Kevin asked.

"His name is Paul," Hope answered, and he'd love to go out with that girl."

Kevin looked in the direction that Hope pointed to. "Oh, that's Christy. She's nice."

"My friend thinks so too, but he's kind of shy. He was wondering if you'd ask her for him."

Kevin shrugged. "I guess I could do that. Did he give you a number that Christy could call?"

"He sure did," Hope said as she dug through her purse. She handed Kevin a piece of paper with the number on it.

"I really appreciate this," she said.

"No problem," Kevin assured her, as he climbed back up to the stage, and walked over to Christy.

Hope smiled and walked out of the auditorium. Before she left the building, she turned around and stared at Christy. The girl was smiling as Kevin spoke to her. Excitement overwhelmed Hope, and she felt as though she could shout.

"This is going to be easy!" she cried as she left the building.

*   *   *

The night of the play had arrived, and the students were in the auditorium getting into their costumes. The director, Steve White, paced the floor nervously. Christy had not shown up, and she had never been late in the past.

"Has anybody heard from Christy?" he cried for the tenth time. All of the students shook their heads, and avoided his icy stare. They listened as he cursed and began dialing numbers to contact her. They cringed as he slammed the phone down with each disappointment.

A ragged looking student ran into the building and onto the stage. Steve glared at the youth with the unkempt hair.

"Well?" he prodded.

"She's not in her dorm," the boy answered. "Nobody has seen her! I've notified security, but I don't know if they'll be able to find her in time!"

The director put his head down, and rubbed his temples firmly.

"She better be late or dead," he muttered to himself.

*   *   *

Back at Paul's dorm, Christy lay on his bed, unconscious. Hope stood in the corner smiling evilly. She took five twenty dollar bills out of her purse and handed them to Paul.

"You've done a good job. Are you sure you put enough drugs in her drink?"

Paul smiled. "She's going to be out of it for a long time," he promised. "That early supper date was a good idea. I convinced her to drink one glass of wine. I told her that it'd calm her nerves for the play. She'll never know it was drugged. She'll probably wake up with one really huge migraine, and think it's a hangover."

"It won't kill her, will it?" Hope asked, nervously.

"Nope," Paul said. "It'll just make her sleep through the first act, at least."

"Well, by then, it'll be too late," Hope said. "I'll have taken her place in the play by then."

"It was nice doing business with you," Paul said. "Call me if you ever want to get naked or just hand over your cash to me."

Hope's lips curled into a sneer. "Don't hold your breath!" she hissed. She spun on her heels and stomped out the door. Her destination was the auditorium, and her dream was going to come true. She was going to be in the play!

Hope stepped backstage to hear Steve White and Ed Foster shouting at each other. She found Kevin standing with a couple of the other students in a corner, so she walked over to them.

"I came to wish you luck," she lied. She pointed to the two shouting men. "What's wrong with them?"

"They can't find Christy. She's over an hour late. The play starts in less than two hours, but nobody can find her," Kevin said.

Hope put on a look of concern. "What are they going to do if she doesn't show up?" she asked.

Kevin shrugged. "I don't know. It doesn't look good, though. The understudies only memorized lines for the lead characters. One of them might be able to fake some of Christy's lines, but it probably would be terrible. We've already sold a lot of tickets for tonight. I think we may have to cancel tonight's performance."

Hope held up her hands in horror. "Oh, no! That'd be terrible! Think of all the work—all the people who are coming!"

"Well," Kevin answered, "it's kind of unavoidable if she doesn't get here. She's not a lead character, but she does have a lot of lines. We don't have time to get ready for a fill-in."

"I could fill in for Christy until she shows up!" Hope cried.

"That's insane!" Kevin responded.

"No it's not," Hope said. "You *know* I came to watch rehearsals all of the time! I practically have this play memorized!"

Kevin looked at Hope thoughtfully. "Maybe you've got a point," he admitted.

He took her by the arm and led her to Ed and Steve.

"Excuse me!" he said loudly.

They stopped arguing for a moment and glared at Kevin.

"I've got a back-up plan," Kevin offered.

They stared at him in interest, as he continued. "This student has been to quite a few rehearsals. Actually, she's been to *many*, many rehearsals. She knows the lines very well!"

Ed looked skeptical, so Hope stood to the side and rattled off a few of Christy's lines. She also made sure to use the same facial expressions that she'd seen Christy using.

The director exhaled in relief. Maybe tonight's performance wouldn't go all the way to hell in a hand basket, after all.

"All right," he stated. "You take Christy's place until she shows up, *if* she shows up. Everyone get into place! We're going to run through this one quick time, with . . . what's your name?"

"Hope."

"We're going to run through this with Hope. If Christy doesn't get here, then what you see is what you get. Try to make sure you get it right!"

They rehearsed the play, and Ed found Hope true to her word. She did know the lines and was doing an excellent job. He vaguely remembered her auditioning for the play, and now he wondered why he hadn't noticed her before. She was incredible!

Watching from the side stage as the play went on that night, Ed and Steve were filled with gratitude towards Hope. The slim, beautiful girl was putting her soul into a part that had previously been denied to her. Her eyes reflected all of the necessary emotions, and her voice was like clear liquid.

The play ended with great applause, and the students took their bows. As they headed backstage, Ed walked over to Hope and smiled approvingly.

"You did a wonderful job out there!" he said. He hugged her, and stood back to look at her.

"Did you ever get in touch with Christy?" Hope asked innocently.

Ed shook his head. "No, and I'm worried about her. Either way, we can't count on her to be in this production. If we find out she's all right, great . . . nobody wants anything bad to happen to her. If she was too sick to make it tonight, then she'll obviously be in no condition to perform. If something's happened to her . . . ." he trailed off.

"I'm sure there's a logical explanation for this," Hope offered. "I just hope she's all right."

"So do I," Ed sighed. "Regardless, you can be sure of more parts in the future. You do know that you get bonus points for extracurricular work, don't you?"

Hope blushed. "Yes, I know that," she said. "I'd be glad to help in any way I can. I'll finish the week with this play."

Ed smiled and patted her on the back. He turned and went to compliment the other students.

Hope was so filled with excitement, that for once she forgot about Kevin. She strolled happily out of the auditorium and headed towards her dorm. As she gazed at the stars in the black sky, she smiled to herself. The school year was looking better for her, and she knew it was only the beginning of her good fortune.

CHAPTER TWENTY-TWO

A S SPRING BREAK APPROACHED, TINA studied twice as hard. Her head was bent down at her desk; her hand wrote furiously. Though she had improved, she wanted to get even better in college. Good grades had meant confidence and prestige for her. Instructors were beginning to take notice of the quiet, dark-haired girl. Students were beginning to accept her more.

Where Tina spent many hours studying, Karen spent many hours cheating on Kevin. She ignored the icy stares that she got from Tina every time she left the dorm to go out. Tina was starting to wear on her nerves, and she had to bite her tongue to keep from telling her off. It was none of Tina's business what she did in her spare time. She reasoned with herself that Tina gave her a difficult time because of jealously. Karen attracted boys like honey attracted bees. It was not her fault that she was sensual; rather she considered it a gift that Tina could not possess.

The time passed by, and the two friends grew apart. They were like estranged people living under the same roof. Days began to pass in which neither girl spoke to the other. The days that they used to go out as a threesome, were becoming a foggy memory. When Kevin questioned Karen about Tina, he was only given short, vague answers. He didn't know what the problem was, and since Tina seemed to annoy Karen now, he didn't pursue the subject further.

* * *

Tina was glad when mid-terms were over and spring break had arrived. Karen and Kevin had each gone to spend time at home with their parents. The campus was spotted with only a few students who chose to stay, either because they wanted to, or couldn't afford the traveling expenses.

The week was peaceful, drenched with plenty of sun and fragrant flowers. Tina sat outside most of the time, her books spread out before her. She loved spring, and all the frustration that she had felt with Karen slowly left her. She felt good all over. Her cheeks glowed, and her eyes sparkled.

When spring break was almost at an end, Tina did something in haste. She didn't know why she did it, but she did it anyway. She was coming out of the cafeteria when she saw Kevin walking towards his dorm. He had come back from his parents, and he was alone for once.

Tina's heart raced in her chest, and she was filled with emotion. The secret that she had been wanting to share with Kevin was overwhelming her. It was something that she had been desperate to tell him for so long. Now she felt if she kept silent a moment longer, she would go crazy. Dropping her books on the ground, she ran as fast as she could to Kevin. As he heard her running up behind him, he turned around to look. When he saw who it was, he smiled.

His blue eyes searching hers, caused Tina to stand there speechless. She was out of breath, not from running, but from all the pent up energy leaving her body. She breathed in and out rapidly and stared at Kevin. He opened his mouth to speak, but whatever he was planning to say was lost, for Tina started talking.

"Kevin," she blurted, "I love you! I've loved you all year, but I couldn't tell you! I can tell you now, though, because Karen's not doing right by you! It's been going on so long, and I've been keeping so many things secret! I've felt bad for not telling you, but you've got to know that I *couldn't*! You have no idea how hard it's been for me to watch all of this, and keep quiet about it! Surely you've got some clue as to what's been going on! You don't deserve that, Kevin! It's me! *I'm* the one who loves you!"

Kevin reeled back in shock. He stood there dumbfounded, trying to absorb the disturbing things he'd just heard. When he regained his senses, his eyes reflected deep hurt, and his voice was trembling with anger.

"How can you even *begin* to talk that way?" he snapped. "How can you say those things about Karen? She'd die if she knew what you just said to me about her! You're supposed to be her best friend, and here you are trying to seduce me with lies!"

Tina stood there, too humiliated and hurt to move. How could she have said those things? Now she had ruined everything! A pain tore through her body, and a wounded cry escaped her lips. She threw her hand up to stifle it, but it had come, just the same. Now she could feel the tears filling her eyes, and she hated herself for breaking down in front of him! As sorry as she was, she couldn't bring herself to apologize. She just stood there, staring in pain at Kevin.

At the sight of the tears, Kevin softened. He never could stand to see anyone cry, especially Tina. He stepped forward and put his hand on her shoulder.

"Don't cry," he pleaded gently. "I know you didn't mean those things. I'm aware that there have been problems between Karen and you lately, and that you've been studying too hard. I really think you've stressed yourself out. I won't tell anyone about this."

When the tears would not vanish, Kevin got nervous.

"Tina, if you stop crying, I'll show you something no one else knows about. You'll really like it."

Tina wiped at her face and nodded. "I'm OK, now," she said. "I'm just really embarrassed."

"Don't be," Kevin said. Satisfied that she had stopped crying, he took her by the wrist. They walked a few feet, and when he was sure that she would follow, he let go. They went past all of the dorms, and beyond the football field. Tina wondered if they were going anywhere at all. It seemed like Kevin just wanted to walk on forever.

"Are we actually going anywhere, Kevin?" Tina asked nervously.

Kevin looked at her and laughed. "I know *you're* not getting tired. Anybody who can run around that track in the middle of the night is in excellent shape!"

"How do you know about that?" Tina asked sharply.

Kevin stared down at his feet. He had forgotten that Tina hadn't recognized him that night.

"I was there that night," he admitted. "I'd gone to the football field to clear my head, and there you were. I didn't mean to spy on you or to frighten you, but I guess I did anyway."

Tina nodded. "Yeah, you really gave me the creeps that night. I've not been back since."

"I'm sorry."

"It's OK," Tina said. "You probably saved me from a real maniac."

She looked back. The dorms were now tiny, blurry specks. She wondered how they housed so many students when they looked so small now.

"We're almost there," Kevin commented, interrupting her thoughts.

Tina turned her head. They were about to enter dense woods, and she stopped at the entrance. Kevin walked several feet before he realized he was alone. He turned around and motioned for Tina.

"Come on, Tina," he called.

Tina stood there, uncertain. The trees seemed to form webs of wood, from which she feared entanglement. Sounds which she could not identify emerged from the denseness.

"Tina, come on!" Kevin cried.

"I don't know, Kevin. I've got this thing about being eaten alive by wild animals!"

Kevin walked back to where Tina stood. He looked down at her and deep into her eyes. She was so hypnotized by those eyes penetrating hers, that she barely felt him take her hand in his.

"What's happened to the brave girl who punched another guy in the face?" he asked her. "You said you were different. Don't play 'coward' on me now."

Tina surrendered and let Kevin lead her into the woods. Again, it seemed as though they were walking on forever. The sun tried unsuccessfully to penetrate the thick branches that hung over their heads. As they went farther into the woods, the sun lost its battle, and the trees won. Tina felt a chill go over her body, and she trembled a little.

"You want my shirt?" Kevin asked her.

Tina shook her head. She knew she would go mad if he removed any clothing, and then everything would be ruined. He seemed to have forgotten about her earlier outburst, but she doubted he'd forget another one.

"I'm alright. It just felt a little cool," she assured him.

"Are you scared?" he asked her.

"No," she lied.

He stopped walking so suddenly that she almost bumped into him.

"We're here," he announced.

Tina glanced around. The trees had thinned out some, and the sun felt good on her face. Other than that, she saw nothing special about the area.

"Is this what you made me walk a mile for?" she asked.

Kevin ignored her remark. His eyes were closed and he was inhaling deeply.

"Listen," he told her.

She obeyed, and a pleasant trickling sound met her ears.

"Water!" she cried.

Kevin nodded. "That's right. That's how you know you're here—you listen for the water. The next step is to go down this hill without killing yourself."

"I'm glad this was a straight shot," Tina commented. "I'd never find my way out of here, if there had been a lot of turns."

Kevin squatted down, and scrambled down a steep hill. When he got to the bottom, he reached for Tina and helped her down. At the bottom was a small creek, flanked by bushes. Kevin found a log and pulled it forward for Tina.

"Want to sit?" he asked.

Tina nodded and sat down. It felt good to rest her feet. She sat there enjoying the water and the sunshine, listening to the birds singing in the trees above.

"This is where I come when I really need to get away from it all," he said.

"It's beautiful," Tina commented. "How did you find it?"

"It was by accident, of course," Kevin said. "One day I was fed up with things and I started walking. As you can tell, I walked a long time. When I heard water, I wanted to see where it was. I about broke my neck that first time, because I didn't know about that hill. It kind of snuck up on me! Anyway, when I got to the bottom, I was in this place. I sat here for hours, and it felt so good! Now I know this place like the back of my hand. I come here quite a bit."

"I can't blame you," Tina said. "Does anyone else know about this place?"

"Maybe some local people," Kevin answered, "but I've never seen anybody else here. I make sure nobody sees me when I come. I like it here alone."

He looked at Tina seriously.

"Karen doesn't even know about it," he told her.

Tina's heart raced in her chest. Kevin had taken her to a place that nobody else knew about! She knew he must really have respect for her to trust her like he did. She didn't say anything in return; rather, she sat there and enjoyed the peacefulness that Kevin had introduced to her.

Their tranquility was broken in a few moments, though, because they heard twigs snap. Kevin rushed up the side of the hill, and looked around.

"Who's there?" Tina asked, getting up from her place on the log.

Kevin strained his eyes. He could see nothing, but he knew that something had been there.

"It must have been a deer," he said, unconvincingly.

Tina joined him, and hugged herself as she searched the area. From the corner of her eye, she could see Kevin's sturdy body. The cologne he always wore drifted up her nostrils pleasantly. She was overcome with a desire to roll in the leaves with him and make love. Knowing that it was an absurd idea, she closed her eyes, and tried to think about something else. When she felt him leaving her side, she opened her eyes, and walked back down the hill to the log.

They stayed there for a couple of hours, talking and laughing about things that had happened in the past. They seemed at the moment, to have reached an important part in their relationship. It was just the two of them this time, without Karen, and they appeared to be more relaxed with each other.

When the sun started going down, and the air started getting cooler, Kevin walked back to the side of the hill.

"I guess we'd better go now," he said. "I've never been here after dark."

Tina nodded, and Kevin helped her climb up. They walked silently until they reached Kevin's dorm.

"Do you want me to walk you to your dorm?" he asked Tina.

"No," Tina laughed. "I'll be fine."

They were silent again, and when Tina looked back at Kevin, her eyes were serious.

"Thanks, Kevin," she said.

He smiled and nodded, then watched her walk away. He didn't know why, but he felt a little sad as he watched her go. It was as if a part of him was leaving with her, and for the first time in months, he felt lonely.

*   *   *

Later that week, Tina sat on her bed, pretending to read, while Karen brushed her hair. When she was convinced that Karen wasn't looking, she stared long and hard. The luxuriant hair seemed to grow richer with each stroke of the brush. Tina fondled her hair, wishing desperately that it was long, too.

Karen put the brush down and checked her make-up in the mirror. The expression on her face was one of confidence and satisfaction. She bent down a little and adjusted her skirt. It was short, but that was Karen's style. If she showed her legs, she wanted to show as much as possible. She wasn't a tall girl, but she was proud of her curvaceous legs.

"Where are you going?" Tina asked Karen. They were the first words that she had spoken to Karen in a couple of days.

Karen turned around, indifferently, and stared at Tina. Her eyes were filled with a variety of emotions that Tina could not read. The only thing she was sure of in those eyes, was an air of mockery. Karen didn't even look at Tina as though she knew her anymore. She stared at Tina as though she were a complete stranger.

"Is it any of your business?" Karen asked rudely.

Tina sighed. This conversation was starting in the wrong direction. As much as she wanted to hate Karen for the things she did, she couldn't.

"No," she said softly, "I don't suppose it is." She glanced back down at her book and tried to read again.

Karen, sensing victory, walked over to Tina's bed.

"Unlike you, *I'm* going out," she sneered. "I'm being taken to this really expensive restaurant outside of town."

Tina felt the heat rise to her neck. She willed herself not to get angry.

"You probably want to know the name of the place," Karen chided, "but since you'll probably never step foot in it, there's no point, is there?"

Tina closed her book and looked at Karen. She felt her temper growing inside of her like a monster.

"Why are you acting this way, Karen?" she tried.

Karen smirked. "I'm not acting any way. I'm just tired of your judgmental attitude."

"Then it isn't Kevin taking you out tonight, is it?" Tina confronted.

"No," Karen snarled, "it's not, but you don't need to sit there and act self-righteous about my life."

"I'm not being self-righteous," Tina argued.

"Oh, really," Karen stated, her annoyance and guilt getting the best of her, "you're not self-righteous. You're just a little insecure, barely non-virgin, who can't keep a guy for a moment!"

At that, Tina threw the book aside and jumped from her bed. She grabbed a very surprised Karen by the shoulders and pushed her into one of the dressers. Make-up and cologne tumbled to the floor. The glass made a sickening sound as some of the bottles broke. Tina did not hear it, though, and she began to shout.

"You'll never understand, will you?" she cried. "You're engaged to a guy who you can't even be faithful to! I get so *sick* of seeing you treat Kevin like you do, and then you get bold with me! You treat me like I'm dirt, because I don't go for what you do! You call me 'self-righteous'!"

She had Karen by the throat now, deaf to the gagging sounds that came from the girl.

"I'm not going to be your alibi anymore! I swear I'm going to tell Kevin what you do!"

At those words, Karen dug her nails into Tina's wrists. When she pulled her hands back, there were bloody marks. Tina cried out in anguish and grabbed Karen even harder. She slung her around will all of her might and pushed her into another dresser. This time when Karen stumbled, it was onto Tina's dresser. The unicorn that had meant so much a few weeks ago, rocked back and forth a couple of times before crashing onto the floor.

Karen and Tina both stared in horror as the precious unicorn broke into numerous pieces. The girls then looked at each other in utter sorrow. It was as if the shattered gift symbolized the end of their friendship. Karen held her throat and looked down at the floor. If shame was what Tina had intended for her to feel, she had succeeded.

Tina choked back tears. She stared at Karen for a few silent moments, then headed for the door.

"One day," she threatened, "I'll tell. You remember that."

Karen did not look up until the door had closed and Tina's footsteps had faded. She looked around the ransacked room and then gathered herself together. She picked up the brush and began to shakily groom her hair again. She knew that Tina had meant what she'd said, and a cold chill ran over her body.

*   *   *

Paul stood in the parking lot waiting for Hope to get the car door open. Since the episode with Christy, they had been seeing one another on a regular basis. Neither of them cared for the other in anything but sexual matters. They merely tolerated each other until better dates came along.

Allison had begged Hope to arrange a date with herself and Paul, but Hope vehemently refused. The memories of Allison's dates, mingled with the lack of her own, caused her to be selfish with Paul. Deep inside, she knew that Allison would treat him better, but she couldn't relinquish her hold on him. Instead, she gloated in the hurt look in her roommate's eyes every time she left somewhere with Paul. Her time for getting even had arrived, and she found herself adoring the moment.

As she opened the door of her car to let Paul in, she heard a car coming up from behind them. She turned around to look, and as the car passed, she recognized Karen in the passenger's seat. An evil smile passed across her face. The fellow driving the car wasn't Kevin! Was Karen *cheating* on Kevin?

"I don't believe this!" she cried in utter joy.

"What?" Paul asked, looking up at her from his seat.

"I think that girl I despise is running around on the guy that I want to date!"

She was blind to the stunned look that crossed Paul's face. He knew that Hope didn't love him, but to hear her talk about another guy hurt his pride.

"Get in the car!" he snapped.

Hope glanced down at him, surprised. She obeyed, and got in the driver's side.

"Where do you want to go?" he muttered.

Hope ignored his sarcastic tone, and smiled seductively.

"Let's see where they're going. I'm dying to see what Karen does while Kevin is at work!"

They followed the car for about forty-five minutes, until it pulled into the parking lot of a restaurant. Neither Hope nor Paul recognized the name on the sign, but they could tell from the looks of it, that it was bound to be expensive.

"I'm glad we're dressed up," Hope commented. "They'd never let us in there if we weren't!"

"Well, you can just keep looking, because we're not going in!" Paul retorted. "I'm not spending all of my money just for you to spy on some stupid girl!"

Hope whirled around in her seat and glared at Paul.

"You're going in there!" she hissed. "I've got enough credit cards to buy your soul! As a matter of fact, I've got more money than you'll ever see, so you can just relax and order what you want! I don't need to you act like a cheap coward right now, so you just do as I say!"

Paul cursed as he got out of the car. "I'll order the most expensive thing on the menu!" he growled.

"I don't care what you order!" Hope snapped. "Now let's act like we actually *like* one another and get something to eat!"

Paul reluctantly took her hand in his, and together they walked into the restaurant.

CHAPTER TWENTY-THREE

ONCE INSIDE, HOPE BREATHED A sigh of relief. They had gotten a table within sight of Karen and her date. Hope sipped happily from the glass of water the waitress had brought to her. This was like a dream come true to her, and she savored the moment! It wasn't until the waitress returned that she realized she hadn't even opened her menu.

"Are you ready to order, or shall I give you a few more minutes?" she asked Hope.

Hope turned scarlet. "Go ahead and order whatever you want, Paul."

Paul stuck to his word and ordered the most expensive thing on the menu. Had she not been so excited, Hope would have been furious.

She quickly studied the menu. It was too difficult to think about food at the moment, so she merely stated, "I'll have the same thing."

As they waited for their first course, Paul gazed at Karen.

"She's beautiful!" he exclaimed.

Hope ignored his comment as her mind churned. She'd have to think of a fool-proof plan to break Karen and Kevin up.

"I'm going to need your help," she told Paul.

"With what?"

"I've got to find a way to break them up, and you're going to help me."

"Break who up?" Paul questioned.

"Karen and her fiancé, you fool!"

"It'll cost you," Paul said firmly.

Hope glared at him. "Can't you ever do *anything* for me without my paying you back? I've slept with you several times, plus I've given you money! Now I'm paying for your dinner! What else do you want?"

"I want a wad of money for this," Paul hissed. "I'm not into breaking couples up. I've seen that girl with her boyfriend around campus. They've always looked happy. I've got to have something to 'appease' my conscious. I won't take less than five-hundred."

He looked at Hope for her reaction. Her jaw dropped and she could only stare at him for a moment. Actually he would have dated a girl like Karen for free, but he saw desperation in Hope's eyes. He knew he could name any price, and he knew that she would oblige.

When she regained her voice, she hissed. "You're crazy to think I would pay you that much to break them up!"

Paul sipped on his drink indifferently, then looked away. "It means nothing to me whether or not I help you."

"I'll find somebody else!" Hope snapped.

Paul glanced at her and snickered. "Who're you going to find now, Hope? The semester's almost over. Right now people are studying for their final exams. After that, they'll start packing to go home, then they'll be gone."

"Not everyone will leave for the summer," she challenged.

"No," he commented, "there'll be a handful of students staying for the summer courses. Good luck finding someone attractive enough to seduce *that* girl."

Hope squirmed in her seat. He was right. She couldn't bear the thought of waiting until the next semester. If they broke up soon, she was sure she'd have Kevin for the whole summer. She could forget about going home and just stay with Kevin. He would need to be comforted, and she would be the one to do it. She knew that Karen was the one person who stood in her way. As that thought entered her mind, she clutched her napkin tightly. What was five-hundred dollars compared to Kevin? Karen didn't deserve him; she did! Looking at Paul, she smiled and held out her hand.

"You've got a deal," she said.

*   *   *

Hope wanted to make sure that Karen didn't leave college before her plan was to take effect. She told Paul to make a date with Karen the day after all of the final exams. She also found out from the unsuspecting Kevin that he would be working on the designated evening.

She stood in her room and excitedly rattled off her plans to Allison. "Paul's taking Karen out to dinner! I told him to get her pretty drunk. He's supposed to bring her back to his room after dinner. While he's seducing her, I've got to go and rat on her. Kevin will see her for the slut she really is, and he'll be mine!"

Allison rolled her dark eyes. "Maybe we can have some peace and quiet around here, then!"

Hope paced the floor. "The timing has to be perfect! We've got to make sure this works!"

Allison whirled around and eyed Hope suspiciously. "What do you mean by 'we'?"

Hope threw her hands into the air. "Well, surely you're going to help me, *now*! I've come up with the perfect plan!"

"I've got plans to leave this campus," Allison answered.

Hope clutched her roommate by the shoulders. "I'll pay you," she cried.

Once again, Allison rolled her eyes. "OK, but you're going to pay dearly."

Hope was so excited, she kissed Allison on the cheek. "I'll never forget this!" she cried happily. She turned on her heels and ran out of the dorm to meet Paul. They had many things to discuss, and they had to do it quickly.

*   *   *

On the last day of the exams, students bustled around the campus. Cars and trucks were being loaded with belongings. There was much shouting and partying as students said their good-byes for the summer. Most of them would be gone by this evening—a great many more would leave in the morning.

237

Tina stood by her window and looked out as she had done many times before. With each car that left, the loneliness inside of her became greater. She turned to glance around the room. She hadn't even packed her things yet, but she'd do that later. Her ticket to leave hadn't been purchased, either. She just didn't feel like taking care of it at the moment.

The year had seen many changes for her, and she wondered if they were for the best. Innocence seemed like a foreign feeling to her. In its place were longing and sorrow. She had ruined things with practically everyone she had come into contact with. Karen wouldn't speak to her. She seldom saw Kevin. Brad and Mathew were only faded memories.

She walked back to her dresser and opened the top drawer. Inside were the pieces of the unicorn that had broken during her fight with Karen. She gingerly took them out and laid them on her desk. Opening a bottle of glue she had bought earlier, she slowly began gluing the pieces back together. When she was finished, the unicorn looked alright, except for a few missing chips.

She closed the cap on the bottle of glue and stared at her textbooks. Her last exam for the semester would be in less than two hours. Though she had studied fervently, she opened her book again for one last review.

Her studying was often interrupted with thoughts of Karen. She didn't even know when Karen would be leaving the campus. She felt as though she couldn't rest until they had made up. As strong as her pride was, Tina was willing to offer an apology. If only Karen would show up, but she had remained elusive all day! Tina pushed the thought out of her mind, and tried to study, but her ears strained for the footsteps that just wouldn't come.

*   *   *

The next day was filled with sunshine that streamed through the window and warmed Tina's face. She quickly turned in her bed to see if Karen was in hers. She was not. Tina couldn't even remember if Karen had come in at all the night before, because she had slept so hard.

Not really caring about her appearance, she pulled on a loose white T-shirt and slipped on a pair of blue warm-up pants. She sat on the edge of her bed and struggled with her sneakers, then got up and walked to the bathroom. She brushed her hair, and put on a thin layer of make-up.

Her stomach hurt for want of food, so she walked to the cafeteria. As she went through the scant line, Inez saw her and called out to her.

"Tina, Child, why haven't you left yet?" the older woman asked.

Tina smiled. "I'll probably leave sometime later today or tomorrow, Inez."

"Well, if you're not gone by this evening, come here and eat," Inez suggested. "Certain people work all year around here!"

"Yeah, you've got to feed those students who want to stay and take summer courses, huh?" Tina asked.

"Yes, Child, that's my job. I guess I'll be here 'til I die."

Tina smiled from the other side of the counter. "Well, you better wait a long time to do that."

Inez laughed. "I'll try, Child. I'll try."

After breakfast, Tina wandered back to her dorm. When she opened the door to her room, her mouth flew open. Karen's things were cleared off of the dresser. Even her pictures which had been hanging up earlier were missing.

Tina walked over to Karen's dresser and opened the top drawer. It was empty. She tried the rest and they were empty, too. Tina stood back in confusion. Hadn't Karen paid her share of this room for the following year? Of course the clothes would be gone, but why everything else?

She went to the closet and opened it. Inside were Karen's suitcases. By the weight of them, they had been packed. Karen was probably going to leave any moment now, and Tina might not get a chance to talk to her. She left the room again, deciding to stroll the campus and locate Karen.

*   *   *

239

At a nearby shopping center, Karen tried on a white dress. It was satin material, strapless, and had an inviting slit on the side. She smiled at her reflection. Everything looked good on her, and she knew it. Innocently she turned to the saleslady.

"Does it look alright?" she asked.

The woman admired Karen. If only her own daughter were that beautiful! This blonde girl in the form fitting dress looked like an angel. "I've never seen that dress look that good on anyone else!" the woman admitted truthfully.

Karen smiled modestly. She would buy the dress.

"Do you have some shoes that would go with this?" she asked.

The saleslady smiled and quickly walked away. When she returned, she presented Karen with a matching pair of strappy high-heeled sandals.

"Those are pretty!" Karen commented.

She tried them on, and they fit perfectly.

"How'd you get my size right without asking me?" Karen asked in wonder.

The woman blushed. "I've been doing this a long time. I guess it's become second nature to me."

As Karen got undressed, the saleslady commented, "Your boyfriend must be taking you out tonight!"

From behind the door, Karen answered, "Yes, he is."

"What's his name?"

Without thinking, Karen answered, "Paul."

She didn't have a chance to correct herself, because the saleslady was rambling on about how nice of a name Paul was. Karen was thankful that she didn't know the woman. In the future, she'd have to think before she spoke!

*   *   *

It was early evening and Tina sat on her bed reading. After so many months of reading in textbooks, it felt good to read a book for enjoyment. She had pretty much given up on Karen, and had decided it was too late to leave. She'd leave in the morning, but it was going to be scary spending the night alone in the silent dorm. The only people who remained were a handful of students and the campus security guards.

Suddenly, a key turned in the doorknob, and Karen entered. She was followed by a tall girl with curly dark hair. Tina opened her mouth to say something, but Karen spoke first.

"Tina, I want you to meet my new roommate, Wendy. I'm going to move into her room next semester."

Tina sat there, stunned, while Karen stared as her words sank in.

"It's nice to meet you," Wendy lied. She held out her hand and gazed coolly at Tina. "Karen's told me *so* much about you!"

Tina looked into Wendy's eyes, and she knew what she meant by that. Karen had told Wendy all kinds of bad things about her, and then had made plans to move in with her!

Tina stood up and pushed past Wendy's outstretched hand. She grabbed her keys off of her dresser and ran out of the room. She hadn't gone far, when she heard both of the girls laughing. That's when the tears came. They fell with such a violent force, that they blinded her. She was almost down the stairs, when she missed the last two. Stumbling, she cried out in pain, got up, and ran out of the building.

Running down the street, she roughly wiped the tears from her face. How could Karen have done that to her? All the confidentialities she must have betrayed—the gossip which had apparently been exchanged! How could she just drop her like that! She'd have to get used to someone all over again! Turning to look at the campus, the sun caught her eyes and burned them. She blinked until she could see clearly. It was a beautiful sunset that caught her by surprise. It was filled with the soft pink and blue that decorated the sky after a warm day. Somehow it seemed to sooth her, and she stopped crying.

"I've got to get myself together," she whispered.

Turning around, the sign to the "Fitness Center" beckoned to her. She looked down at herself.

"Well, at least I'm dressed for it," she sighed. She walked towards the building and went inside. As she handed the man at the desk her membership card, she kept her head down. If he noticed the tear-stained face, he pretended not to. Making her way to the bathroom, she didn't notice Hope and Allison. They didn't see her either. Allison was pumping iron while talking to two guys, and Hope had gone to the counter to buy a drink.

In the bathroom, Tina washed her face. Though most of her make-up was gone, she still had a healthy glow.

She walked back out to the weights, oblivious to Allison, who was working out on the opposite side of her. She picked up two dumbbells and started doing curls. As the blood began pumping through her body, she became aware of the voices around her.

"Come on, Allison, stay and do twelve more!"

"I can't guys. Hope just motioned to me, and I've got to go. I've got to help her set this girl up."

"Set a girl up?"

"Yeah, this girl's shelf date has expired on her current relationship. We're going to help finish it off."

"You're rotten to the core, aren't you, Allison?"

Allison shook her head. "Not really. It was Hope's idea. She wouldn't do something like this, normally, but she really hates that Karen girl. She's fixed her up with a friend of hers. It'll be a date to remember!"

At the mention of Karen's name, Tina froze. What were those two up to? What did they mean by "a date to remember"?"

She practically threw the dumbbells back on the rack, and then raced out of the place without picking up her membership card. As she darted out, Hope saw her, then stomped over to Allison.

"What did you say to her?" she demanded.

"To who?" Allison asked in utter confusion.

Hope jerked Allison up by her shirt. "You stupid idiot!" she cried, ignoring the glances from the other members, the blush rising in her friend's face. "You said something about what we're doing tonight, didn't you?"

Allison sputtered for a moment, then she found her voice. "I just mentioned it to the guys!" she cried.

"Well, that brat roommate of Karen's heard you!" Hope shouted.

Allison pulled away from Hope, and together they ran out of the club.

*   *   *

All the while that Tina ran to the dorm, she repeated out loud, "Please be there, Karen! Please still be there!"

She reached the dorm, and stopped to clutch her side. She had run so fast that it hurt! When the pain subsided, she ran up the stairs and threw open the door to their room.

"Karen!" she shouted. "Karen!"

She was greeted only by the silence of the room, and she clutched her head to try to think. Where could Karen be now? She didn't know where she'd go, but she'd have to find Karen to warn her! Perhaps she was in Wendy's dorm!

She whirled around to leave and bumped right into Hope!

"Where do you think you're going?" Hope hissed as she glared at Tina.

Before Hope had time to think, Tina had balled up her fist. It came crashing into Hope's face, sending the girl to the floor.

Hope sat up and cursed. She pointed at Tina. "Get her!" she ordered Allison.

Allison and Tina ran right into each other and began fighting. They appeared glued to each other, as they slammed one another into walls and dressers. Finally, Tina pushed Allison on the bed. She leapt on her and began punching. Allison screamed like a wildcat, but she couldn't get free! Tina ignored the screams and kept punching all the harder.

"You're up to no good!" She screamed.

Allison spat at her and missed. "The slut's got it coming!" she yelled.

"Leave her alone!" Tina cried.

Just then, Hope grabbed her from behind and pinned Tina's arms behind her back. She pulled Tina off the bed, and struggled with her. Tina fought, but she couldn't get loose. Instead, she kicked backwards, striking Hope in the leg.

Hope cried out in pain and cursed, "Allison, help me!" she shouted.

Allison slithered off the bed and limped over to Tina. She punched her hard in the stomach. Tina bent over in pain. She made gasping noises for breath, and began to feel light-headed. As she tried to straighten up, Allison sent another violent punch in the same place. This time, Tina's knees buckled under her. Everything was getting dim, and the voices she heard were getting softer and farther away.

"We've got to tie her up! If she gets out of here, she'll ruin everything!"

"All I can find are these mini-blind cords!"

"Well it'll have to do! Hurry!"

Tina heard a ripping sound, as Allison jerked the cords from the blinds. Then she felt her wrists and her feet being tied together. Afterwards, she was jerked up by the hair.

Hope pushed Tina to the window and made her look out. Karen and Paul were outside walking to his car.

"Everything's falling into place!" Hope exclaimed. "The Grand Finale' will be in that dorm," she said, motioning with her finger.

Tina screamed at the top of her voice for Karen, but neither Karen nor Paul heard her.

Hope laughed in a sinister way. "There's nothing you can do now, Tina. I just hope that housekeeping finds you tomorrow. It'd be terrible for you to spend several days tied up in this room!"

Before she could answer, something came crashing down over her head, and her world went black.

CHAPTER TWENTY-FOUR

O N THE WAY BACK TO the campus, Karen nestled down in the passenger's seat. She felt warm and comfortable all over. The dinner had been wonderful, the champagne magnificent! She glanced over at Paul and smiled. It would be their only night together, because she planned to leave in the morning. As she glimpsed at the clock on the dashboard, she grinned. Kevin wasn't due off work for another two hours.

Paul took one hand off of the steering wheel and started massaging the back of Karen's neck. She closed her eyes, enjoying the feeling. Her thoughts of Kevin and the time began to slowly melt away.

As they pulled into the campus parking lot, Karen didn't notice two figures by one of the buildings. Allison and Hope stood in the dark and watched as Paul helped Karen out of the car.

"That's my cue," Hope said nervously. She looked at Allison. "Wait for me in Paul's dorm."

They went their separate ways, and Hope crossed her fingers. She was going to have to put on one good act, if she planned to pull this off! As she got into her car, feelings of guilt started to creep upon her. She ignored them, started up the car, and turned the radio on loud.

*   *   *

When Tina woke up, she was frightened and disoriented. The room was dark, overpowered by an uncomfortable stillness. Her body ached all over, and she cried out loud in pain. Lying beside her head were pieces of a broken vase. They sparkled in the moonlight that shone through the window. Her mind started to sort out everything, until slowly she remembered what had happened. Drawing her body up, she balanced herself on her knees. The cords were thin, but they were so tight, that they cut into her skin. She looked around for something sharp to cut them with. There was nothing! In desperation, she glanced towards the window, and an idea came to her. She sat down, clumsily, then lay on her back, and slid towards the window. Pulling her feet back, she kicked out the window. She quickly closed her eyes as glass flew everywhere. When she opened them, again, the window was framed with jagged pieces of glass. She got on her knees and slowly stood up. Leaning into the window, she began rubbing the cords against the broken shards. Her hands were tied so tight, that she cut herself in the process. She ignored the blood that began to drip from her wrists, and kept working. Finally the string gave way, and her hands were free. She snatched a piece of glass off of the floor and began to cut at the strings around her ankles.

*   *   *

Kevin watched as Hope strolled into the grocery store. He was putting groceries into a customer's bag as she walked by. Another of the bag boys elbowed Kevin.

"Your dream girl's here!" he teased.

Kevin shook his head and threw a dirty look at the other fellow. "I don't know what she's doing here tonight," he said. "I thought she'd be gone by now."

"Maybe she wants to leave with you."

"Yeah, right," Kevin mumbled.

Hope walked up to the counter with a few sparse objects. As the cashier added up her purchases, Kevin asked, "Getting some last minute things?"

Hope smiled. "Yes," she said, "I'll be leaving tomorrow."

After she paid for her things, she waited for Kevin to carry out her bag. Instead, he walked away, and another bagger reached for it.

"Need some help with this?" he asked.

Hope snatched the bag from him and hissed, "I want Kevin to carry it out for me!"

The fellow looked embarrassed and shocked as he let go of the bag.

"Kevin!" he called out.

Kevin walked over, irritated, and stared at Hope. "You've got to be kidding," he said, his eyes focused on the bag.

"Bad back," Hope spat out.

He took the bag from her, and sighed. If he was lucky, she'd transfer to another college next year. They were both silent as they walked to her car, but when they got there, Hope summoned up her courage to ask the impossible.

"Kevin," she said, "I was wondering if you'd go out with me next semester."

Kevin slammed the bag onto the back of the car and glared at Hope.

"Don't you give up?" he cried. "You know that Karen and I are engaged! We're going to date all through college, then we're getting married! Why can't you get that through your thick head?"

Hope faked a look of intense pain. Her eyes focused on the ground, until she could muster up some tears. When they came, she looked back at Kevin and said softly, "I'm sorry. When I saw Karen with that other guy, I thought you'd broken up."

"What are you talking about," Kevin said evenly, though his eyes betrayed his voice.

"Nothing," Hope said. "This was a mistake. I'm so sorry!" She took out her car keys, and went to unlock the door, but Kevin grabbed her by the shoulders and spun her around. This time, the look in his eyes matched his demeanor, and Hope didn't have to pretend to be frightened.

"What are you talking about?" he repeated.

"Kevin . . . . please just forget it," Hope whined.

When she tried to pull away, he dug his fingers into her shoulders, causing her to gasp in pain. She stared at him, startled, never having experienced this side of him before.

"Talk," he ordered.

"I thought you were broken up!" she cried.

He squeezed again.

Hope's hand flew to her mouth. Whatever she'd started was taking a very ugly turn, and there was no way of getting out of it now. She sobbed openly, "I'm so sorry, Kevin!"

Kevin ran back into the store and jerked his uniform off. Before the other employees could ask what the problem was, he was back outside. He grabbed Hope again and snapped. "Take me to her!"

*   *   *

Back at Paul's room, Karen finished another glass of champagne. She handed her empty glass to Paul. "That was good," she said softly.

Paul took the glass from Karen, then he went to sit on the bed beside her. He brushed her hair away from her face and leaned over to kiss her. She closed her eyes and kissed him back.

"That was nice," she whispered.

Paul looked into her eyes and nodded. "It was," he agreed.

They kissed again, and each kiss that followed was more and more passionate. When her lips weren't enough to satisfy him, he began to move his mouth in the curve of her neck.

Karen tried to push Kevin out of her mind. This was her last night before summer; certainly she deserved to celebrate! After all, she *loved* Kevin, so that was what was important. She tried to justify herself, but finally had to block all thoughts of Kevin out and focus on Paul. It wasn't hard for her to do.

"It's just us right now," she whispered. "There's no one else in the world."

"No one else," he repeated.

They began undressing one another, but their lips never parted.

"Make love to me," Karen begged.

Paul kissed her even more passionately and then they began to move as one. They had barely started, when the door to the room flew open. They stopped, and Karen stared in horror. There in the doorway stood Kevin! His eyes were full of shock and hurt, his mouth open in utter disbelief at what he was witnessing.

Karen pulled the sheet over her body, and in desperation, cried out, "Oh, Kevin!"

In those few seconds, Kevin's world fell apart. Visions of the times he and Karen had made love raced through his mind. He remembered the way she used to look at him, as though he was the best person in the world, her only love. It never was real! She shared her love and her body with *other* guys!

A guttural sound of anguish rose up and escaped his lips. He tried to say something, but whatever it was, got caught between his heart and his throat. His eyes filled with tears as he grabbed at his hair with anger and denial. Overcome with rage and pain, he turned on his heels and ran out of the dorm.

Karen leapt off of the bed and began throwing her clothes on. As she raced out of the room, she almost collided with Allison and Hope. They stood there, smug, Allison laughing, and Hope smiling through her tear streaked face. Then she knew! It was them all along. Paul was nothing more than a pawn in a game to seduce her and shatter her relationship with Kevin! She had been set up! She gave them a look that could kill, then ran out of dorm after Kevin.

A few minutes later, Tina ran down the hallway of Paul's dorm. "Karen! Karen!" she shouted. She didn't know what floor Paul lived on, so she kept climbing stairs and running down hallways.

On the third floor, she saw Hope and Allison at the end of the hall. She ran past them and went into the room. "Karen!" she cried. She looked, but the only person in the room was Paul. He was sitting up in bed, the sheet partially covering his nude body. As she turned to leave, Hope laughed that same evil laugh. "You're too late!" she cried triumphantly. "Kevin's seen it all!"

"Oh no!" Tina cried. She slapped Hope hard in the face. "God help you!" she said. As she ran out of the dorm, she ignored Hope's confident laugh.

Tina ran across the dark campus. Once in a while, a lonely lamppost would shed light on her worried face. If she could have only warned Karen! If only she could have stopped Kevin from getting hurt so!

As she was running, she began to think about values. Was she not guilty, too? She knew for a long time about how unfaithful Karen was, but she had said nothing. Sure, she had blurted it out, but she had never convinced Kevin that Karen was untrue.

She reached Kevin's dorm, and ran up the stairs to his room. When she got to his room, she threw the door open, but only silence greeted her. "Karen! Kevin!" she cried.

She paced around the room. Nothing was out of place, and obviously no one had been there. Walking to the bathroom, she kept calling out, "Kevin!"

She inched her way to the shower curtain and jerked it open. Nothing! She started to leave the room, when an idea hit her. She fell to the floor and lifted Kevin's bedspread. Still nothing! Going to Alan's bed, she did the same. This time a spider darted out from under the bed, and Tina let out a blood-curling scream. She stood up, and clutched her hand to her heart. It was beating so fast that it hurt! Quickly, she left the room, barely closing the door behind her.

Once again, she ran across the campus. She'd just come across a row of tall bushes when she heard a noise. Stopping dead in her tracks, she listened. She heard it again! Knowing that it was really stupid, she moved towards the noise, anyway. It appeared to come from the end of the bushes. She walked slowly. There were only five more bushes to go before she came face to face with whatever she'd heard.

"Five-four-three-two-one!" She looked around, but there was nothing!

"I'm going crazy," she said to herself.

Suddenly, she felt a hand on her back. She screamed and turned around. Facing her was a security guard.

""Whatsh de matter?" he slurred.

Tina leaned back and held her breath. He smelled strongly of alcohol!

"What-what's the matter?" he repeated.

Tina stared in shock, as he swayed back and forth. She backed away and managed a smile. "Nothing's wrong," she lied. "I'd just taken a walk and was heading back to my dorm. You startled me."

The guard leaned right in her face. "Well, young lady, you'd better get inside. It's late! You sh-shouldn't be out by yourself in the middle of the night."

Tina looked cautiously at the guard. "Yes, I suppose you're right," she said. "Well, if you don't mind, I'd better go."

The guard grinned stupidly. "Sure," he said.

Tina turned and slowly walked to her dorm. She glanced back to make sure that the guard wasn't following her. He wasn't. She started to breath normally again. If she thought about it later, she planned to report that guard to the administration. Students didn't need drunks trying to protect them!

"With that kind of security, I'll end up getting mugged tonight," she grumbled.

She entered her dorm and glanced inside. There were more steps to climb, and she frowned.

"Why don't these places have elevators?" she fumed, but climbed hurriedly anyway. She needed to find Kevin. He might just try to kill himself over Karen! Tina couldn't bear the thought of that.

She tried the door to her room, but it was locked. Struggling, she reached into her pocket for her key, then she stopped and listened. She thought she'd heard a noise at the other end of the hall. She heard it again, and called out, "Who's there?"

When silence greeted her, she ran to the railing and looked down. There was nothing there. The shadowy stairs and vacant hallways yielded no clue as to what she had heard.

Suddenly, she realized that the drunken guard might have followed her into the building! He might be in the darkness waiting for her!

She ran back to her door and opened it. Once inside, she slammed the door behind her. She had the jitters, and her teeth were chattering! She held her hands to her mouth and breathed on them to try to warm them. She felt so clammy and cold and alone right now!

She walked around the room, but once again, she found no one. "Where the heck did everybody go?" she asked herself in frustration. She looked out of the window and saw a few cars in the parking lot. Wanting to go out there, but afraid of the guard, she searched the room for a weapon. The only thing she found was a letter opener, which she tucked into one of her socks.

She stepped back into the hallway, then locked the door behind her. It made an unusually loud 'click' as she did so, and she shuddered at the thought of going back down the stairs.

Cautiously, she made her way down, and to her relief, the guard wasn't there. This time she went out the back of the dorm. If the guard was still by the bushes, he wouldn't see her go out this way.

She walked to the parking lot and found Karen's car. There were a few other cars there. She figured they belonged to Hope, Allison, and Paul, along with a few other students.

The night air was chill, and she hugged herself. It was stupid to have forgotten her jacket! She looked up at the streetlights that pierced the darkness and tried to think about where Kevin could have gone. Her thoughts went back in time, until they suddenly stopped. In her mind she saw Kevin speaking to her, and she remembered his words, 'This is where I go when I need to get away from everything.'

Her eyes lit up. He must be in the woods! Why hadn't she thought of that before? He must have gone to his hiding place to break down and cry! He'd never break down in front of anyone!

*   *   *

While Tina reasoned Kevin's whereabouts in her mind, Hope walked to his room. Her plan would be complete when she comforted the distraught Kevin. He would see just how sweet and gentle she was, and he would fall in love with her!

The door to his room was slightly open, and Hope put her ear against it. She opened it just a little bit more, and noticed that the lamp by one of the beds was turned on.

As she stepped into the room, she noticed a large lump in the bed. "Kevin?" she called out softly.

The lump didn't move, and Hope kept tiptoeing towards the bed. She crawled on the bed, gently straddling the figure underneath.

"I'm sorry that you saw that," she lied. "I think it's horrible of your girlfriend to have hurt you that way."

No movement.

"I came by to see if you were OK," she continued. "You know you can talk to me."

There was a slight shifting underneath.

"Kevin?"

When the movement stopped again, Hope impatiently reached for the covers. "I can't talk to you when you're covered like that!" she said.

Before her hand touched the covers, they were thrown back, and the figure in the bed sat up. On the head was a pillowcase with two places cut for the eyes. At the neck, a piece of rope held the pillowcase in place. The rest of the body appeared to be dressed in black, including the gloves.

Hope screamed at the initial shock, but then she screamed again. The person sitting up held a long, shiny knife. Before she could get off of the bed, the blade was plunged into her soft stomach. Hope's eyes grew large, then she opened her mouth to scream, but no sound came out. Her hands flew to her stomach, but the blood flowed in a torrent. She looked up in disbelief and anguish at the person who had stabbed her.

"Help me!" she pleaded weakly.

The figure in the bed violently pushed Hope away, as it climbed from underneath the covers. She fell backwards, her head hitting the footboard of the bed. There was a loud crack as her head made contact with it. The attacker wiped the knife on the bedspread and ran out of the room, leaving Hope to bleed to death.

*   *   *

Tina had left the parking lot and was heading towards the woods. She kept glancing back to make sure she was going in the right direction. If she stayed lined up with the edge of the football field, she'd probably walk straight into Kevin's spot. Things appeared so different at night, and she was getting a headache from straining her eyes. If only she'd gone more than once, but she hadn't!

When she got to the edge of the woods, she stopped instinctively. She was frightened, and part of her wanted to go back to her dorm and hide. As she faced the darkness, concern for Kevin overcame her fear, and she entered into the woods. She was glad that the moon shone in spots, but it was her only light. She scolded herself for forgetting a flashlight, but it was too late to turn back.

Branches kept poking her in the face, so she had to resort to walking with her arms and hands stretched out before her. Panic almost gripped her, for she felt like she was caught in one giant wooden maze. Nearby, twigs snapped, and she tried to walk faster.

She felt as though she was nearing the place, when her foot slipped. She fell down, her foot hanging off the embankment, and she knew she'd found the place. Carefully, she clamored down the hill, straightened up, and brushed her clothes off.

She thought she heard someone breathing heavily a few feet away, and she strained her eyes to see. The moon cast an eerie glow around her, but she saw no one.

"Kevin?" she whispered.

She moved a couple of steps forward, and called louder, "Kevin!"

As the figure stepped out from behind the trees, Tina's screams pierced the night. It was someone, clad in black, with a crude pillowcase mask. Tina gaped in fear at the menacing sight.

"God help you!" she cried. "You've gone crazy!"

The person just stood there, while Tina somehow found the courage to speak. "Kevin, I'm so sorry!" she blurted out. "I tried to tell you, but you didn't believe me! I told Karen to stop, but she wouldn't listen to me!"

When she stopped talking, the other person remained still. For what seemed like an eternity, they were both overcome with silence. Finally, the figure stepped forward and held up one arm. In a black gloved hand, was a shiny knife like the one that Inez had lost!

Tina's eyes grew large. She walked backwards slowly, until she was pressed against the hill. "No, Kevin!" she screamed. "Don't do it!"

When the arm came swooping down, Tina screamed and turned to the side. The knife pierced the hill, getting embedded in the dirt. This was no longer a game! Her life was at stake! As the attacker fought to get the knife out of the dirt, Tina sent a hard, swift kick onto her assailant's stomach. The kick sent the other person reeling backwards, and onto the ground with a hard thump.

Tina pulled the knife out, placed it between her teeth, and tried to climb back up the hill, but in the darkness, her feet kept slipping. Suddenly, she felt something pull her hard, and she almost fell backwards. As she struggled to regain her balance, she dropped the knife. The attacker let go of her legs, and bent down to pick it up.

Tina screamed, and used every bit of energy to make it to the top of the hill. When she got there, she turned around to defend herself. The tears flowed down her dirt encrusted face, leaving odd lines. She bit her lip until it bled, to keep from making any noise.

Just as she had anticipated, the person wearing the pillowcase was climbing the hill. As soon as she saw the shape of the head, she kicked hard, and the attacker fell backwards to the ground. She used that opportunity to make her getaway.

On the way out of the woods, she ran, letting branches snag her clothes and scratch her face. She had to get to a phone! She had to get help! Twice she fell, but she immediately got back up and ran even harder. Her head hurt, and her lungs felt as though they could burst, but still she ran!

When she reached her dorm, she bounded up the stairs. She noticed that the door to her room was open, and she cried out, "Karen! Karen! Thank God you're here!"

She ran into the room, and stopped dead in her tracks. There was nobody in the room, but somebody *had* been there! The bedding and the mattress to Karen's bed was ripped to shreds, as though someone had repeatedly stabbed a knife into it.

As she circled the room, Tina looked for signs of blood, but there were none. Had Kevin killed Karen? If he had, where was her body? She looked around the room, then headed toward the bathroom.

*   *   *

At Paul's dorm, Allison tapped her foot impatiently. Hope sure was taking a long time to get back! She felt as though she had been standing in the hallway forever.

"Want a drink?" Paul called out to her.

Allison stuck her head into the room, and stared at Paul. He was still in the bed, a bottle of champagne in one hand, and two glasses in the other hand. He smiled at her seductively, his lips still throbbing from his prior love making session. The sheet was still draped over the lower half of his body; his chest glistened with moisture. A huge smile spread across Allison's face. She was alone with Paul, and he wanted to drink with her!

She strolled into the room, and gave him her most seductive smile. "Yes," she said, "I'd like a drink."

Paul motioned for her to sit on the bed, and she did. As he poured their drinks, her ebony eyes traced every line of his body. A black lock of her hair fell forward, and she pushed it back.

"Here you go," Paul said, as he handed her the glass. He leaned back and watched her sip on her drink. Every inch of her visible body was muscular, yet beautiful, and he still ached in his groin. He'd had to relinquish Karen, but he might have a chance with Allison.

He leaned forward, and as he'd done with Karen, began stroking the back of Allison's neck. Her muscles were still tense from her workout, and she murmured in satisfaction.

"Does that feel good?"

"Yes."

"Do you want me to stop?"

"No!"

She set her glass down, closed her eyes, and savored the moment. When she did, she immediately felt his warm lips on hers, and she opened her eyes. He leaned back, and waited to see her reaction.

"Why did you do that?" she asked, her trembling fingers touching her mouth.

"I've wanted to for a long time," Paul said, and there was some truth in it.

"What about Hope?" Allison asked.

"I'm not serious about her."

She started to say something else, but his lips were on hers again. Her body felt like a thermostat that had been tossed into a fireplace. Paul made her feel emotions that no other boy had ever made her feel. With other guys, she always seemed to be treated like 'one of the boys'. This was so different! She wanted him, and she wanted him now. Somehow she was oblivious to the fact that he'd just finished trying to make love to someone else. Her body would be his tonight, and if she was lucky, it would be his again tomorrow.

*   *   *

When they had finished making love, they lay there for a few moments in each others' arms. Paul stroked her silky hair, and kissed her alabaster skin.

As badly as she wanted to stay there, Allison knew that Hope would be back soon. Even though Hope had been notoriously rude to her, she certainly didn't want to explain this. She got out of bed and headed towards the bathroom.

"Do you mind if I take a shower here?" she asked.

"Not at all," Paul answered. He pulled the covers closer to himself, and began to drift off to sleep.

A few minutes later, he felt a movement on the bed. He smiled to himself, keeping his eyes closed. He felt hands on his shoulders, and they moved up to his neck.

All of a sudden, his eyes flew open in utter fear. Someone was strangling him! He tried to pull the cord away from his neck, but it remained there, cutting off every ounce of precious air. Fighting, he jerked his body violently, trying to throw the person off of him.

The assailant stayed on him for a while, but Paul finally succeeded in throwing the person off. The attacker tumbled to the floor, then sat up, tightening the rope on the makeshift pillowcase. As Paul sat in bed and gasped for air, his assailant stood up and ran out of the room. He cursed and leapt off the bed. Quickly, he put on his underwear and ran out of the room shouting, "I'm going to kill you! Nobody tries to strangle me!"

As he ran down the empty hallway, he searched for a sign of life, but there was nothing. "Come out!" he screamed. "Are you afraid to face me?"

His bare feet smacked against the cold linoleum of the empty hall, but he barely noticed. His anger was so intense at the moment, that he could almost taste it. He planned to put his hands on this intruder and choke the life out of him.

Just as he rounded a corner, the assailant stepped out of the shadows, holding a knife. Paul tried to stop, but he didn't have time. The knife impaled his stomach, going deep into his body. He stared down in shock at the gaping wound, trying to slow down the flow of blood with his own hands. Feeling faint, he knew he was dying, but he tried to pull the knife out, nonetheless. His fingers had barely touched the handle, though, when he dropped to the floor and died.

*   *   *

"Is Hope back?" Allison called out. She could have sworn she'd heard something, some shouting of some sort. She turned off the water and opened the shower curtain. The bathroom was filled with steam. She reached out and felt for a towel.

"Paul, is Hope back?" she called out again.

There was still no answer, so she merely shook her head. He must have passed out from all the champagne he'd drunk. She towel dried her hair, and then wrapped the damp towel around her body. Opening the door, she peeped out, and saw Paul lying in the bed.

"Hey, Paul, wake up!" she called out, again.

When he didn't move, she stepped out of the bathroom. It was then that she noticed something out of the corner of her eye. She turned, and in horror, saw a trail of blood leading up to the bed.

Too frightened to scream, she began shaking and crying violently. "Paul?" she wailed.

She went carefully to the bed, unable to shake the feeling of dread that was beginning to consume her. Weeping, she jerked the covers back and saw Paul lying in a pool of his own blood. She found her voice, and began screaming.

Suddenly, she heard a noise. She backed into the bathroom, and locked the door. With her ear against the door, she sobbed quietly, and kept whimpering, "Please be Hope! Please be Hope!"

She pressed her ear closer to the door, but she couldn't hear anything. Just then, a knife pierced the door, coming inches from her face. Allison leapt back and began screaming uncontrollably. Searching for a weapon, she rummaged through the cabinet and found a razor blade. Holding it up, she stared at the door and screamed, "Go away! I'll kill you!"

The knife was slowly pulled back, and Allison started breathing normally again. Her muscles relaxed as she stared at the door. Perhaps she'd scared whoever it was away. She was standing far enough from the door, though, so that the knife wouldn't touch her if it came through again.

For what seemed like an eternity, things were quiet. Suddenly, the door was kicked open, and it hit Allison full in the face. She fell backwards, dropping the blade, and hitting her head on the edge of the toilet.

As she started to come to, she noticed a figure in black standing over her. She looked for the razor blade, but couldn't see it. She then looked back into her assailant's eyes, for that was all that she could see.

"I won't fight you," she said meekly, trying to use psychology. "I know you're going to rape me, but please don't kill me!"

The attacker squatted down and straddled Allison. She closed her eyes, and cried quietly. She felt her hair being grabbed from behind, and her head pulled forward. She opened her eyes, but the assailant was still wearing the pillowcase, pausing to stare at her, drawing her closer. Her face almost touched the pillowcase, when the knife slit her throat. The attacker let go, as though she was an item of disgust, and watched indifferently as Allison's head hit the floor.

*   *   *

When Tina couldn't find any trace of Karen, she stepped over to her nightstand, and picked up the phone. She had to call the police! As she held the receiver to her ear, her eyes registered confusion. When she glanced down, she noticed that the cord to the phone had been slashed. Throwing down the receiver, Tina backed up. Her whole body trembled, and she bit her lip, trying to concentrate.

"The guard!" she cried out loud. She ran to the window, and looked out. If she saw someone, anyone, she could scream for help. She threw open the window and leaned out, yelling, "Help! Somebody help me!"

Tina lost track of how long she'd been screaming; her throat was raw, her face numb. Just when she was about to give up, she saw the drunken guard staggering by one of the buildings. Tina shouted, but he didn't hear her. He just swayed back and forth, trying to hold himself up.

Tina opened her mouth to shout again, but this time she saw another movement. She started smiling in relief, but her look changed to one of anguish, as the assailant stepped out of the bushes.

The guard, unaware of the enemy a few feet behind him, scratched his head, then lit a cigarette. Tina leaned as far out of the window as she could, and screamed at the top of her voice, "Look out! He's right behind you! He's got a knife!"

The guard turned around and stared at the attacker who held the knife in mid-air. His cigarette fell from his lips, while he twisted around to reach for his gun. As he struggled with his holster, the knife went through his back. The guard cried out, as the assailant pushed the knife further into his body.

"Noooooooooooo!!!!!!," Tina screamed. She clenched her fists together and laid her head in defeat on the window sill. There she cried violently. Her last bit of hope was gone! The murderer had seen her!

She tried to quickly get her thoughts together as she wiped her eyes. Staring intently out the window, a small cry escaped her lips. The assailant was nowhere to be seen!

Tina knew that a cold-blooded killer was coming for her, and she sped out of the room. If she went fast enough, she could hide in the lobby before the attacker reached the dorm.

She bounded down stairs, and fled into the darkened lobby. A couch in the middle of the floor beckoned to her. She dove behind it. Tina prayed that the assailant would do as she hoped.

When the door to the lobby creaked open, Tina bit her lip and held her breath. One movement in the silent room would bring death upon her! She listened as the footsteps ran through the lobby, then bounded up the stairs. Soon, above her, she could hear items being thrown about in frustration at her absence.

Knowing that her safety net was diminishing, Tina crept out of the room and ran to Kevin's dorm. Perhaps his phone still worked!

She arrived at Kevin's dorm, out of breath. When she reached Kevin's room, she threw open the door and ran inside. Immediately, a blood curling scream left her mouth, for there was Hope. She was on her back, her lifeless head leaning over the footboard. Her body was drenched in her own blood. The moonlight that shone through the window cast her still form in a sickly white glow.

Tina glanced down. Her tennis shoes were getting stained with Hope's blood! She grabbed her hair and pulled on it, shaking her head from side to side. This was impossible! Horrible crimes happened to *other* people! How could this be taking place here?! Now?! She dug her fingernails violently into her arms, hoping that she was caught in some terrible nightmare, but she wasn't!

Backing away, Tina stepped into the hall, trembling like a sapling in a violent storm. She heard footsteps running towards her, and she turned in horror to look down the hall.

Again she screamed, for the assailant was heading towards her! Tina dove back into the room and slammed the door shut, then locked it. She had barely stepped back, when the killer ran into the door. The knob was rattled violently. When it failed to open the door, the attacker pounded on the door furiously.

Tina's eyes, blurred from an unending flow of tears, searched the room. They rested on a dresser, and she ran to it. She pushed with all of her strength until the dresser was in front of the door.

Staring back frightfully at Hope, Tina stumbled towards the phone. Like the other one, it was cut, too, and she threw it against the wall in fear and in anger.

As soon as the phone hit the wall, the pounding on the door ceased, and the footsteps faded down the hall.

Tina collapsed in a corner, and laid her head on her knees. When would this horrible night be over? She felt as though she would go insane being in the same room with a dead person! She cut her eyes again at Hope's limp body, as if her fear would make the corpse move.

For a few minutes, all was quiet. Tina had almost stopped shaking, but she still cried silently. Never before had she felt so hopeless and alone! Her lips quivered, and for the first time in years, she muttered, "Momma!"

Without warning, a knife plunged through the door! Tina's screams pierced the night. She got up and ran to Alan's bed. "Leave me alone!" she wailed.

The knife kept stabbing at the door, splintering it, making it weak. Tina knew she'd have to get out. Her safety here was almost at an end. She'd have to go out the window.

Jerking the sheets off of Alan's bed, she quickly tied them together. As she held them, Tina knew that she needed more. She glanced frightfully at Kevin's bed. Closing her eyes, she pulled hard. Hope fell to the floor, with a loud 'thump". The blood stained sheets flew in Tina's face, causing her to cry out in disgust. She wiped her face with her shirt, then connected Kevin's sheets to Alan's.

The door was getting more and more mutilated, and Tina tried not to cry as she tied one end of her "ladder" to Kevin's headboard. She opened the window and let the sheets drop outside. Checking her knots one more time, she held her breath and hoped the sheets wouldn't tear for her three-story descent.

Just as she had climbed out of the window, she heard the door give way. Moving rapidly, she prayed she would reach the bottom, before her assailant saw her. Her hopes were dashed, though, for the killer leaned out of the window.

Tina screamed and kept going down at a steady speed. She tried to ignore the sticky part of the sheet that she was now sliding her hands and body over. She expected her assailant to run out of the dorm. If that happened, she might have time to get away. Instead, she felt a jerk, and stared up in shock. The person was cutting the sheets! She still had two floors to go!

"Please stop!" Tina begged.

The enemy kept slicing at the weak cloth, as Tina began to slide down recklessly. She had to reach the ground before the sheets were cut. She had about ten more feet to go, when the last thread snapped. Screaming, she fell to the ground, landing on her back. Her body felt a violent jolt, before the air left her lungs.

As she gasped for breath, through lungs which felt on the brink of bursting, she knew that her life was almost over. Right now the murderer would be coming down the stairs to finish her off. She rolled over on her stomach, trying to summon the strength to get up and run. Instead, she gave up, and buried her face in the ground in defeat.

In her half-conscious state, Tina heard her name. Her eyes were closed, and it was as if she were dreaming.

"Tina! Tina! Get up, Darling!"

Her mind went back to the time she'd fallen off a pony as a child. Her mother had gently urged her to get up and not give up. It was the only thing that had given her courage that day. She'd been able to get up and ride again without falling off.

Now she heard her mother's voice, *clearly*, as if she were speaking to her from Heaven, "Tina!" Tina!" she called, in a desperate attempt to save her life.

"Mom!" Tina cried out.

She opened her eyes, and came back to reality. Her body felt as though all of her bones were broken, but somehow, she got up. She wanted to live! Limping, she started off shakily in the direction of Paul's dorm. Each step was filled with intense pain, but she forced herself to run, nonetheless. With each yard of progress, she thought to herself, "I want to live! I want to live!" Ignoring the searing pain, she picked up speed. Paul's dorm was getting closer and closer. Tina wept again. She was going to make it!

In Paul's dorm, Tina raced down the hallways, screaming and pounding on doors. No one was there to hear her, and she continued blindly towards Paul's room.

"Paul! Paul!" she shouted. Never before would she have imagined herself needing his help. Now Paul seemed like a sanctuary in which she could find shelter. As the turned the corner of the hallway that led to his room, she stopped short. She was too late! A long trail of blood wound its way into his room!

Tina shook her head in denial, as she began to whimper again. She felt deathly ill, and she clutched her stomach. Surely she was about to vomit! The sick feeling was so overwhelming, she felt that she might pass out! Stepping carefully towards Paul's room, she began to sob openly. As her hand softly touched the door and pushed it open, it made a horrible, eerie screech.

Tina stepped into the room, and saw Paul and Allison lying on the bed. They were both soaked in blood, and as with Hope, the blood ran into the floor.

Tina, by this time, too shocked to notice, waded through the blood. This was it! It was about over! Not surprisingly, she heard footsteps running down the hallway. There was nowhere else to run! She was about to meet her assailant alone! In grim resignation, she found a wooden ball bat, and backed into the corner with it. She faced the door, clutching the bat tightly. As she did this, her teeth bit into her lip, until it started bleeding. She didn't even notice it.

"I'm not running from you anymore!" she swore silently, as she waited.

Just then, Kevin ran into the room. He gaped at Allison and Paul, and his eyes registered shock. Then he stared at Tina questionably.

Seeing his face without a pillowcase on it, caused Tina to drop her guard for a moment. Her hands relaxed, and her tired shoulders dropped a little.

Kevin stepped towards her, "What have you done?" he asked.

Tina held the bat back up, and screamed, "Stay away from me, Kevin! I swear I'll kill you if you come closer!"

The words had barely left her lips when she noticed the gun in his hand. Now she really didn't stand a chance against him!

Kevin started to say something, when more footsteps were heard. As the pillowcased attacker entered the room, Tina began shrieking uncontrollably. It wasn't *Kevin*! She gripped the bat tighter, and started sinking into the corner in defeat.

Kevin, several feet away from the assailant, held up his gun threateningly. "Stay away from her!" he ordered.

The killer held up the knife and stared in Tina's direction. Tina slid all the way into the floor, sitting, and crying in anguish.

"Put it down!" Kevin shouted. His arms were rigid, and sweat broke out on his face. Even in his own fear, he refused to back down.

The attacker ignored Kevin, and made a run for Tina, knife raised up, while Tina screamed again. A shot pierced the air, and the knife dropped to the floor. The murderer grabbed its stomach, the blood soaking through the black gloves. In one horrible moment, the assailant's eyes met Kevin's and stared right at him. "No," he gasped, trembling. He dropped his gun, grabbing the attacker before she fell to the floor.

Tina glanced up in confusion, as Kevin gently dropped to the floor with the other person. He struggled with the rope around the pillowcase. He untied it, and when he pulled it off, long tresses of blond hair fell about his chest. He sat on the floor, cradling Karen, weeping openly.

"Call an ambulance!" he shouted at Tina. When she didn't move immediately, he shouted louder, "Call an ambulance!"

Tina ran crying into the hall to find a working phone. When she'd placed the call, she went back into Paul's room to wait for help. She sat on the floor, near Karen and Kevin, unable to do anything, but cry.

Karen glanced up at Kevin. She managed a weak smile.

"When did you get a real gun?" she asked.

Kevin tried to answer, but he could only sob and bury his face into her soft hair.

Karen let him cry for a while, then she gently moved his head, so that she could see his face.

"I've been so bad to you," she whispered weakly. "I had you, but I was so selfish! I've dated so many other guys behind your back! I tried to be true, but I don't guess I was ready for that."

Kevin stroked her hair, while she continued talking. "The things that I'm most ashamed about are the lies. It was hell to look into your eyes and know that you believed everything about me was good."

"You are good!" Kevin insisted.

Karen motioned with her eyes to Allison and Paul. "They're not the first," she said. "The first was Clyde, then Chuck, Danny, Randy, and Hope."

"Why, Karen, *why*?" Kevin implored.

"They were out to ruin us. As bad as I treated you, I couldn't bear the thought of you finding out about me. I knew you'd leave me. I wanted you, but I wanted everybody else at the same time. Don't get me wrong, Kevin. I've never stopped loving you."

She glanced at Tina for the first time. "I guess I gave you a run for your money."

Tina nodded, wiping at her face.

"I should have listened to you," Karen said. "You tried to tell me what was right, and I hated you for it. At first, I'd thought that you had helped to set me up, but now I know you didn't."

Tina nodded in agreement.

"You remember that day when Kevin showed you that place in the woods?"

Tina's eyes grew wide in confusion.

"I'd followed you two that day. At first, I was mad, because Kevin had told you something that I didn't know about. That's when I started getting suspicious about you. It was Hope and Allison I should have worried about. Anyhow, I was looking for Kevin when you came running up. When I saw you, I got so mad, that I wanted to kill you." She paused, trying to control a coughing fit. "Well, I suppose you know the rest of the story."

Tina touched Karen's hand, and Karen smiled weakly. "You're a good fighter," she said.

Her voice had been getting softer and softer, and now she gasped for breath. As she coughed again, Kevin held her closer. She looked right up at him. "When you date again," she said softly, "find someone who'll be true to you. I know you really loved me to see no fault in me, but I never was able to be faithful to our relationship. I'm so sorry for hurting you like I have."

Kevin knew that she was almost gone, and he kissed her one last time. When his lips left hers, she whispered, "Don't let this make you afraid of relationships; they *can* be beautiful."

With that, she closed her eyes and died. Kevin cried out at the top of his voice, "Nooooo!" He gripped her tightly, his tears wetting her alabaster face.

Tina pulled her hand back from Karen's, as she sat there in shock. She could hear the ambulance and the police sirens, and then people running up the stairs, but she couldn't see them. As they bustled about the room, she stared into space. She felt a blanket being thrown about her shoulders, and then everything went black.

CHAPTER TWENTY-FIVE

THE SUN SHONE BRIGHT WHEN Tina went to visit Karen's grave. All around her, birds were singing, and squirrels ran across the grass. Life was all around her, but death's memory would not leave. A tear trickled down her face, but she didn't bother to wipe it away.

Her face seemed to have aged, her eyes to have lost their glow. Her steps, once full of energy, were now slow and heavy. The only thing youthful about her at the moment was her white cotton shirt and her denim shorts.

As the tombstone grew nearer, Tina stopped in her tracks. She was scared to go further, but she had to tell Karen "Good-bye" for the last time.

In her hand was a bright bouquet of spring flowers. She brought them to her face and inhaled their fragrance. Their sweetness tried to overcome her pain, but it was impossible. She put her hand back down and glanced to the side.

In one shocking moment, she thought she saw Karen in the trees. She gasped and almost dropped the flowers. When she looked again, there was nothing.

Breathing normally again, she stepped up to Karen's grave and gently placed the flowers there. She paused a moment, touching the letters etched in the tombstone. When she had finished tracing the letters with her finger, she bit her lip, trying not to break down.

"Good-bye, Karen," she said.

*   *   *

Back at her room, Tina slowly packed. It would be a long and lonely trip home. She wondered if she'd ever be close to anyone again.

As she pulled some clothes out of a drawer, she heard a noise behind her. Whirling around, she saw Kevin standing awkwardly in the doorway. They both just stared at each other, and then Kevin tried to speak. His voice cracked. He cleared his throat, and tried again.

"I held on so tightly!" he whispered.

Tina started to say something, but he held up his hand.

"She was like a wild bird, and I just tried to cage her all along. I'd waited for her for so long, that when I got her, I couldn't let go!"

They were both crying now, and Tina wiped her face. She didn't want Kevin to see her cry anymore, so she put her head down and continued packing.

"Where are you going?" Kevin asked her softly.

"I'm going home to Orlando," Tina said. She paused, then added, "I'm not coming back."

Kevin looked at her. The thought of Tina leaving suddenly frightened him. "Let me go with you," he said.

Tina slammed the suitcase closed and stared at Kevin. He was blinking back tears as he stood there. "There's . . . . there's just too many memories here!"

"Don't you think I know that, Kevin?" Tina pleaded. "I've got to leave, and the last thing I need is for you to go with me. I spent the whole year wanting you, and watching you get treated badly. *Now* you want to leave with me? I don't want to be somebody you want on the rebound."

Seeing the hurt look in his eyes, she softened her gaze. She went to her desk and took out a pencil and a piece of paper and wrote on it. She held it out to Kevin.

"I'm taking the two 'o clock train today. My phone number's on that paper. If, and when you decide you're ready for someone to treat you right, give me a call."

She tried to smile at him, but her eyes were sad. Picking up her suitcases, she walked past him.

"Shut the door when you leave," she said.

Kevin, his eyes focused on the paper, nodded. He didn't look up until her footsteps faded down the hall.

* * *

In a café beside the train station, Tina sipped on some coffee. She glanced out the window at the people bustling about. Her eyes rested on a couple waiting for the train. They each had suitcases, and she knew that they would be traveling together. The girl, laughing, threw her head back. When she stopped laughing, the boy planted a kiss on her lips.

Tina turned away and stared at her watch. Soon it would be time to leave. She gulped down the rest of her coffee. When she looked back out the window, the people were getting on the train. She paid for the coffee, then picked up her suitcases.

As she made her way to the train, she tried to think of happy things. She remembered the beautiful ocean, the warm sun, and her comfortable home. Aunt Beth was expecting her, and Tina knew that she would be received with open arms and understanding.

Once she boarded, she shifted both suitcases to one side, and checked her ticket for her seat number. As she glanced at the numbers above, her arm started aching, and she quickened her pace. When she was right in front of her car, she put the luggage down.

She opened the door, and her mouth flew open. Kevin was sitting there, his suitcases by his feet. Tina grabbed her things, and put them in the compartment above her. She sat in the seat across from Kevin and gazed at him questionably.

As the train pulled off, they both stared outside. When they turned back around, their eyes met, and Kevin spoke, "Before you tell me to get off at the next stop, hear me out. I'm not trying to use you for a rebound. I just can't bear the thought of being without you. During the past year, you've been some part of my life almost every day. Looking back, I realize that I took so much of what was important to me for granted."

Tina's eyes misted as she listened to him. She tried desperately not to cry, as he continued speaking.

"I guess what I'm trying to say, Tina, is that somehow, someway over the past year, you became my best friend. If nothing else ever happens between us, then I'll accept that. I just can't lose the friend I've found in you. I'm ready to be treated right, and I'll wait until you're ready for me. If you never want me again, then I've only myself to blame."

"Tina?"

"What, Kevin?"

"Please don't close the door on us."

Tina, overcome with emotion, was unable to say anything. Instead she just smiled at Kevin. She felt a warmth come over her, and her eyes sparkled. Extending her hand, she reached for Kevin. His hand met hers, and they touched for the first time in complete understanding.

Epilogue

AT ANOTHER HIGH SCHOOL, NOT too far away, students were hustling through the hallways and cleaning out lockers for the summer. One skinny girl, with straight brown hair, struggled with her items. She'd just managed to get a stack of papers out, when a rowdy boy ran past her, bumping into her. She stared in shock and embarrassment, as the papers became airborne. They scattered all about her, while students kept running past. The student who'd hit her, gave her an indifferent glance, laughed out loud, then kept running.

Embarrassed, she attempted to gather her papers, before they all got trampled. She could hear boys and girls snickering at her, and she fought not to cry. Crying only made it worse. If that happened, they'd *love* that!

As she reached for one of her things, she felt a hand. Startled, she glanced up.

"You looked like you could use some help," the boy said, as he handed her the document.

"Thank you," she said quietly, expecting him leave.

Instead he continued to help her, until everything was back in her arms.

"This is a lot of stuff for one girl," he commented. "Where are you going with it?"

"I'm parked in the third row of the student parking lot," she responded.

"I happen to be going that way, too," he said. "Give me some of that."

Awkwardly, she handed him some things, and he followed her down the hall, and out of the building.

"Don't let Russ get to you," he stated. "He's a jerk."

"Yeah, I kind of picked up on that," she answered.

When they got to her car, again she was embarrassed. Surely, he drove a nicer car than hers. Everybody did!

If it turned him off, he didn't show it. Once the items were in the car, he held out his hand.

"I forgot to introduce myself," he said. "I'm Will Stroud."

She shook his hand, and almost told him that she knew his name. How could she *not* know who he was? He was one of the best looking guys at school! His sandy blonde hair and green eyes were the things that made the girls look twice. She'd been watching him all year, longing for a fraction of the attention he gave to his pretty girlfriends. Now he was at her car, shaking her hand!

"I'm Amy Loren," she answered.

"So, Amy, where are you going to college?"

"I've been accepted at University Place by the lake," she commented.

"Me too!"

There was an awkward silence, then Will spoke up. "Well, I guess I'll see you around."

She nodded and watched as he took off in the opposite direction. When she faced her car again, she caught her reflection in the window. No wonder he'd never noticed her! She got a determined look on her face, as she ran her fingers through her hair. She had the whole summer to make changes. Glancing back at him, she felt her heart race. She didn't know when or how, but he was going to be hers . . . .